# MIXED
# DOUBLES

# MIXED DOUBLES

Ann Purser

ORION

The right of Ann Purser to be identified as the author of
this work has been asserted by her in accordance with
the Copyright, Designs and Patents Act, 1988

First published in Great Britain in 1998 by
Orion
An imprint of Orion Books Ltd
Orion House, 5 Upper St Martin's Lane,
London, WC2H 9EA

A CIP catalogue record for this book
is available from the British Library

ISBN 075280 083 3

Typeset at The Spartan Press Ltd
Lymington, Hants
Printed and bound by
Clays Ltd, St Ives plc

# I

The Hon. Susan Standing, daughter of Lord and Lady Maidford and wife of Richard Standing of Round Ringford Hall, needed a haircut.

'I suppose I could ask the Bates girl,' she said, plucking irritatedly at the dry ends of her straight, pale hair.

'Good God, surely not the village hairdresser!' said her husband.

She turned on him. 'No need for sarcasm, Richard,' she said. 'You know perfectly well that only Keith can do anything with it, but since we're not in London for a couple of weeks, I have to do something.'

Susan Standing and friends considered that only London would do for clothes, hairdresser, theatre, social lunching. The country, with its small villages, stately homes and green woods, was for family, for dogs, horses, walks, church and intrigue. Most of these women did a modicum of good works and served on a committee or two, but itchy feet took them regularly to London. When they were too old for the journey, they often ended their days in lonely Kensington mansion flats, dreaming of summer days in the shires.

'Always looks the same to me,' said Richard, risking a pat on the top of her head, and adding hastily, 'very nice, that is. But if you're serious, I should ring her soon. Mandy's pretty busy, you know, with all her ladies, and young Joey . . .'

Mandy Bates, a town girl from nearby Tresham, had

married Robert, farmer's son turned motor mechanic, borne two children, and had returned to hairdressing, setting up a lucrative, peripatetic business in Ringford and surrounding villages. She went to homes of all sorts, from Mrs Standing at the Hall to Sandra Roberts in the council houses in Macmillan Gardens. She took not only her pleasant personality and the tools of her trade, but also the latest local titbits of information. Not gossip, she told Robert defensively, just keeping my ladies up to date.

'I could fit you in tomorrow at eleven,' she said to the cool voice at the other end of the telephone. 'Though I don't see why I should put myself out,' she said later to Robert. 'She only uses me when she can't get to that poofter in London.'

Robert frowned at her. Joey, thirteen and all ears, was sitting in his wheelchair hunched over the kitchen table, homework spread out in front of him. Born prematurely, he'd never walked, and was slight and frail looking. In fact he was now tough enough, and with a fertile mind and plenty of determination, achieved a great deal.

'It's okay, Dad,' he said with a smile, 'Mum'll catch up one day. Gay's the word, Mum,' he said. 'And anyway, just because he's a hairdresser, doesn't mean—'

'Okay, okay, Mr know-all,' Mandy said good humouredly, 'spare me the sermon, and get on with your history. Poppy'll be down soon.'

Poppy was the late, last child of Susan and Richard, an afterthought, and alternately indulged and neglected. Her friendship with Joey Bates had started when Mandy and Poppy's Irish nanny had struck up a friendship in a village both found hostile and alien. Though the nanny had returned to Ireland, and Mandy was now well established in village life, Poppy and Joey remained an unlikely pair, preferring each other's company to all else, and now beginning to chafe against a community they found narrow and confining. Their closeness worried both sets of parents, the social difference being their unspoken concern, but Poppy and Joey chose to ignore hints and cautions, finding mutual affection and refuge, and, lately, something else – something only just beginning, and delightful.

'Nothing ever happens in this village,' said Poppy. 'If it wasn't for Joey, I'd probably run off with those travellers on Fletching Common.' She knew her mother wasn't listening, and turned on the old tap so hard that water splashed over the wooden draining-boards, making puddles on the quarry-tiled floor. It had certainly been an uneventful morning so far. Mum had made an appointment with Mandy Bates. Wow! And there was that letter, the one Mum was now holding as if she'd won the lottery.

Her father's old dog, smelly and comfortable in a worn armchair by the window, opened its rheumy eyes briefly and stared at her, jerked awake by the vehemence of her words. Then it settled back into its warm haven. Poppy complaining again. Nothing serious.

'Don't be silly, things happen all the time,' said her mother absently, her attention taken by the envelope in her hand. 'And do go and change, Poppy, you know the Smyths will be here any minute.' She looked at the letter again, and a broad smile crossed her face. 'Oh good,' she muttered, holding the crumpled page close to her heart. 'Darling Simon. How lovely it'll be.'

'Sod the Smyths . . . and Simon,' said Poppy loudly, well aware of what the letter contained, and scuffed off out of the kitchen into the cobbled courtyard.

Poppy was thirteen, tall and well rounded for her age. According to some of the lads on the Tresham bus, she had the makings of something quite tasty. As for Poppy, she had lately had a scratchy feeling that life was going on somewhere else, an impatience to get on with it. Round Ringford was dull, she and Joey agreed. She knew everyone, and they knew her. Most of them treated her as an irritating child, tempered with respect for her name, the daughter of the big house,

From her bedroom window in the Hall, she looked across the village that had once in its entirety belonged to her ancestors, and found the grassy parkland, the roofs of village houses, the hills beyond, without charm or interest.

Ringford had the usual mixture of old families and incomers, the latter distrusted and held at arm's length by some, welcomed and taken up by others. Elderly people found the beauty of the village, in its wooded hollow, a haven of peace and quiet. Convivial drinkers considered the pub more than adequate; churchgoers could be faithful and valued. And those who loved to shop a little and gossip a lot found Ringford Post Office and General Stores a fertile source.

The morning was unusually warm for early spring, and the village expanded in bright sunlight. The shop blind was down, shading its big window, where packets of Fairy Automatic shouldered shaky pyramids of baked bean tins, Heinz soup, Ambrosia rice pudding.

Peggy Turner, postmistress and shopkeeper, stood dreaming behind her counter in the empty shop. She looked over the Green, broad and dry in the early drought. The chestnut tree, fresh pale green leaves moving gently in the light breeze, shaded the Standing memorial seat, where a couple of old men sat with their pipes, curls of smoke ascending into the clean air.

A figure appeared in the distance: Poppy Standing on her bike, going much too fast down Bates's End, and heading for the Stores. Peggy noted her approaching customer, and patted her hair, smoothed her overall. 'Yes, Poppy?' she said, as the scruffy-looking girl, jeans torn at the knee, curly fair hair pulled back into an elastic band, slouched into the shop. Peggy leaned over the counter and straightened the pile of parish magazines, free to all, chronicles of village life.

'Packet of crisps,' said Poppy, delving into her empty pocket. Peggy looked at her enquiringly, as if she hadn't heard. Poppy frowned. 'Packet of crisps, *please*,' she said with insolent exaggeration, 'and put it on the book, can you? Left my purse at home.'

Peggy sighed, and took out the account book. She couldn't afford to quibble. Every sale counted in the village shop, and though the Hall were tardy in settling their account, they always paid up eventually. 'Just a minute, Poppy,' she said, turning to pick up a small wholemeal loaf from the shelf behind her. She put it into a large white paper bag and pushed it across the counter. 'Could you drop this into the Joneses at Barnstones for me?' she said. 'It'll save Bill . . .' Bill Turner, her second husband and village stalwart, managed the Hall estate with dedication, and also acted as delivery man for the shop.

But Poppy shook her head and, through a mouthful of crisps, mumbled that she was on her bike. She turned to go, leaving Peggy feeling foolish, but was faced by the furious entry of her mother.

'Poppy! Get out there and into the car at once. I told you the Smyths were picking us up!'

'But my bike . . '

'Out!' said Susan Standing angrily, and Poppy left, leaving a trail of crisps. Susan turned back, rearranged her face, and said apologetically, 'Could we leave the bike with you, Peggy, until later?'

Yes, Madam, thought Peggy. Three bags full, Madam. Supposing I said no? 'Of course, it will be quite safe,' she said, and smiled.

Susan Standing seemed about to leave, then hesitated, turned back. 'Oh, and Peggy,' she said, her face flushed and pleased, 'I don't know if Mr Richard has told Bill, but I'd like you to know before the rest of the village. You know how things get around . . .'

Peggy brightened. 'What's that, then, Mrs Standing?' she said.

'Simon's coming back,' said Susan, beaming. 'Quite soon, as soon as he's wound things up in Atlanta. Isn't it exciting?' She took the loaf off the counter, saying 'Is this ours?' and without waiting for an answer, swept out of the shop.

Barnstones, where the Joneses lived, had belonged to the estate, but in Richard Standing's continuing struggle to maintain the Hall and its great rooms and corridors, its crumbling roof and outbuildings, he had sold the granary and land enough to make a decent garden, and the Joneses had moved in. Greg Jones taught at the comprehensive school in Tresham, and Gabriella, his lovely and musical wife, took the reception class of children, not much more than babies, at the village school. They had one daughter, Octavia, now in her late twenties and living with them at home.

Octavia had been trouble in her teens: rebellious, shoplifting with her best friend from the village, falling desperately in love with Robert Bates, then still an eligible young farmer. She'd tried suicide for a broken heart, none too seriously, plagued her parents for years, and ventured on a number of different careers. Finally Octavia had settled in social work, choosing to deal with children and families, and had metamorphosed into a pleasant, sensible young woman, a good-looker like her mother, and with considerable strength of character inherited from her leftish schoolteacher father.

Greg Jones had needed strength and determination: he had been deaf from birth, and then decided on a career where any such handicap would guarantee him a rough ride. Octavia had always been his pride and joy – even at her worst he could see the best – but he and Gabriella were now beginning to wonder whether it wasn't time she left home, lived independently, perhaps began to think of a family of her own.

The three of them were sitting on the paved terrace, drinking coffee and admiring the garden in the evening sun, where shadows from the park trees beyond the fence sheltered knots of sheep, and birds settled to roost in the spreading branches. A ruffled pigeon sat on the garage roof, cooing softly, a sleepy, reassuring sound.

'Nothing like it, is there?' said Octavia. 'Peace, perfect peace. God, it certainly makes you appreciate all this.'

'What does?' said Greg.

'A day out on the rounds of kindly Tresham parents, who hadn't really meant to beat up the five-year-old hiding in a corner . . . I saw a skinny baby today, wouldn't eat, cried a lot. Its eyes were scared, Mum, even at that age.'

'Octavia, dear, I don't think we need to go into all that just now,' said Gabriella. 'Your father has been working hard all day, and he needs to relax.'

'Okay then,' said Octavia, shrugging. 'What's new in Round Ringford?' Her mother's job brought Octavia many an intimate story of family life. Small children confided to teacher secrets which would have horrified their parents.

Now Gabriella leaned forward in her chair. 'Big news,' she said. 'Peggy was full of it at the shop. Seems Simon Standing is coming back to this country for good.'

'Return of the prodigal,' said Greg comfortably, turning the pages of the *Guardian*. 'That'll set the old ducks a-quacking.'

'Simon?' said Octavia. 'Isn't that the bouncy one, Mummy's special darling? Oh yes, I remember him all right. God's gift, he thinks. Whizzed back from Atlanta

and pleasured all the yahs at the hunt ball last year . . .
goodness, how could we forget him?'

Her parents exchanged glances. 'I thought he was very
nice, dear,' said Gabriella.

# 2

A little swing mirror stood wobbling on the kitchen table. Susan Standing, sitting swathed in towels and gown, shifted impatiently under Mandy's expert hands. 'Must be dry now, Mandy, surely,' she said. Her neck felt hot and prickly, and she missed Keith's gentle fingers, lifting her hair, coaxing it into shape. 'It needs hardly any heat, you know. Makes it brittle.'

'Certainly, Mrs Standing,' said Mandy, switching off the drier. If Madam wanted damp rats' tails, that's what she'd get. All the same to me, Mandy thought, and picked up the hand mirror, moving it this way and that to show Susan the back view. 'Ever thought of brightening it up a bit?' she said innocently. 'Touch of colour, perhaps?'

Susan's reaction was what she expected. 'Goodness, no, thank you!' she said, as if Mandy had suggested a whorish henna red.

Most places, thought Mandy, I get the offer of a cuppa, but not here. She put her brush and drier away in the capacious box that went everywhere with her, and snapped shut the lid. 'There we are, then,' she said. 'That'll be ten pounds, please.'

'How much?' said Susan, staring at her. 'Wasn't it five, last time?'

'Inflation,' said Mandy solidly. Skinflint, she thought. Her eye roved round the scruffy kitchen and failed to see any beauty in the scrubbed table, the uneven floor, the worn stone-mullioned window over a deep, pitted sink.

9

Plenty of empty gin bottles, though, she'd seen in a bo
by the dustbin. Ah well, none of my business. The less i
have to do with this lot the better. But there, lurking in
both their minds, was the connection between them.

'How's Joey?' said Susan, counting out the last pound
in small silver coins. 'Must be difficult for him, coping at
Tresham Comprehensive?'

Mandy's eyes hardened. 'He's fine,' she said. 'Does
very well. They're talking of him goin' to college later.'

'Going away?' said Susan, brightening. 'Very best
thing, I'm sure. For him . . .' she added quickly.

Change the subject, Mandy told herself resolutely.
She'd had plenty of practice in avoiding dangerous
territory of this sort. 'And is it true Mr Simon's coming
home for good?' she said, making for the kitchen door.

Susan nodded. 'Very soon' she said, beaming now.
'We're all delighted. It'll be so nice for the village, too,
having Simon back and taking an interest in the estate.'

Blimey, thought Mandy, she really believes that.
According to Joey, there's at least one member of the
family who won't be overjoyed to see her big brother
back. 'By the way,' she said, stepping out into the
cobbled yard, 'thanks very much for the lovely flowers
Poppy brought us. Brightened up the lounge no end.'
She was perfectly well aware that Susan would know
nothing about the freesias plucked by Poppy from the
Hall greenhouse, and drove off in her little car feeling
cheerfully one up.

As she passed Bridge Cottage, empty and abandoned
now, Mandy saw Ellen Biggs waving to her from the
overgrown garden. She slowed down, winding down
her window, and yelled, 'Hi, Ellen! Just watch that
slippery path!'

Ellen, an institution in Ringford, was now retired, old
and slow moving, and lived in the tiny lodge opposite
Bridge Cottage, at the entrance to the Hall avenue.

Once she had been cook at the Hall, the hub of kitchen activity. Now, well placed to monitor comings and goings, she still occupied a central place in village life. She made no effort to control a sniping tongue, or her unerring nose for gossip, but could be kind when she saw the need.

The bright warmth of the sun had tempted her out and across the road into the garden of Bridge Cottage, where daffodils still flourished amongst the grass and weeds. She had picked a bunch, not being one to let things go to waste. Old Ted Bates owned Bridge Cottage, and since his son had moved out, had periodically put it up for sale or rent, but no one seemed interested.

Ellen waved again at Mandy's vanishing car, and turned for home, her pinny full of gold. Then she saw him, the stranger.

'Oh, my God, who's that?' she said. The gate had been stuck on its hinges for months now, and squealed loudly when pushed.

The stranger came into the garden, shielding his eyes from the bright spring sunshine with a sheet of paper in his hand. 'Good afternoon,' he said, his tone formal, correct.

'Yerse, wot can I do fer you?' said old Ellen, her expression settling into its habitual one of suspicion and distrust when confronted with the unfamiliar.

To her confusion, the stranger came swiftly down the path, turned away from the sun, and lifted his hat in greeting. 'I swear 'e did a little bow,' said Ellen later, relating the day's events to her friends. 'If not clicked 'is 'eels,' she embroidered.

Now the stranger glanced up at the cottage and back at Ellen, holding out the agent's particulars in explanation. 'This is Bridge Cottage, I presume?' he said, adding that he did hope he hadn't startled her and wasn't it the most lovely afternoon.

'Yep,' said Ellen, 'but I ain't Dr Livingstone, as you can see.' She cackled loudly at her own wit. 'You come to 'ave a look at it?' she said. 'There's not many bin lately, and the place is fallin' down with neglect. Time was when it was the best cottage in Ringford. I remember when old Grannie Bates lived 'ere, it were just like a palace. Eat off the floor, you could.'

'How interesting,' said the stranger, but there was something in his voice that told Ellen he was not the least interested in Grannie Bates, but was waiting for her to go.

'D'yer want me to show you round?' she said, noticing that he had a labelled key in his hand. 'Should've thought one of them estate agents would've brought you along.' But the stranger shook his head, and there was nothing for Ellen to do but leave. She hobbled up the path to the gate. 'If you want t'know anything else, just come and find me,' she said, turning for a last look. 'I live just over there. By the way,' she said, knowing that she would fail in her village duty if she didn't ask, 'I didn't catch yer name?'

'Chalmer,' said the man, 'George Chalmer. From Leamington Spa. And you are . . ?'

'Ellen Biggs,' said the old woman, clutching her apron close, 'Mrs Biggs, of the Lodge.'

Satisfied that she had gleaned all there was to be had for the moment, Ellen returned to her own front garden. She did not go into the house, but turned to do some completely unnecessary weeding in a bed that gave her a good view of what was going on over the road.

Ellen and her two old friends now sat comfortably in the Lodge's small, dark sitting-room for their weekly tea party. Ivy Beasley was unmarried, middle aged and stern, with grey, wiry hair and black eyes that missed nothing. Doris Ashbourne, a widow, late of the Post Office and now in an old-folks' bungalow, kept her trim appearance, dressed neatly and unobtrusively, and wore glasses that gave her an air of authority. All three drank strong tea and nibbled Ellen's offerings, turning over the gossip like old hens in the stackyard.

'A real gentleman, 'e was,' said Ellen. 'Very stiff and starchy. Name of George Chalmer. From Leamington, 'e said.'

'If you ask me,' said Ivy Beasley, 'we could do with a few gentlemen in this village. Plenty of men, but you could count the gentlemen on the fingers of one hand.' She sniffed, as if personally insulted.

'Gotta move with the times, Ivy,' said Ellen. 'T'ain't the way of folk now. They're more casual, and I fer one am all for it.'

'Well, we shall see,' said Doris. 'There's been several looking at the cottage, but none of them want it. Can't say I blame them myself. It'll need a bit spent. Anyway,' she continued, 'we shall have a real young gentleman among us soon. It's all over the village. Simon Standing's coming back to live.'

Ellen got up to refill the kettle. It was an effort, and she rested on her stick while the water boiled. She could see through to her friends and carried on the conversation, scarcely raising her cracked, harsh voice. 'Not 'ere, 'e won't be livin' 'ere. You couldn't expect him to live 'ere after 'e's bin used to America.' She put the lid on the chipped teapot and hobbled back to her seat. 'Still,' she said, pouring out with a shaky hand and refusing Ivy's offer of help, ' 'e'll want to be 'ere for a bit, seein' somethin' of his family an' that.'

'He's done well, they say,' said Doris. 'I expect he'll go to London for a job. They usually do.'

'If you ask me,' said Ivy, sitting up very straight, 'he should settle down here with a suitable wife and learn how to run the estate. That brother of his renounced his inheritance, so Simon'll be the one, in due time. It'll all be his.'

'P'raps 'e'll marry you, Ivy, and then you can keep 'im in order. Stranger things 'ave 'appened . . .' Ellen cackled heartily, relishing Ivy's outraged face. 'Now Doris,' she said, 'are you 'avin' some more of this delicious cake?'

# 3

Simon Standing couldn't have wished for a warmer homecoming. After his long flight, he'd found both Richard and Susan waiting to whisk him home in comfort. All his doubts and worries about the decision to return from a successful career in property had faded as he'd sat at the familiar dining table, eating a wonderful supper cooked by his delighted mother. The only discord had been young Poppy's sulking through the meal and slouching off to bed without saying goodnight.

That was only to be expected, he thought, looking round his bedroom, the same one that he'd had as a boy, with all his old books and model aeroplanes still on the shelves. Poppy had been an only child, virtually, for years now. Simon's brother, the eldest, had disappeared a few years ago to a commune of drop-outs in Wales and was seldom in touch, disowning his bourgeois family. The next down, another sister, came and went without much impact, a cool, vague girl, living a life that impinged on no one. So Poppy had had all the attention. No wonder she was sulking, poor old thing. He'd have to be extra nice to her.

It was dark now, but a pale sliver of moon had arisen, and the air was cool and sweet, scented by a bed of fading hyacinths below the terrace that Simon couldn't see, but knew they were there because they always had been. Ringford was the same as ever, nothing much seemed to have changed since he had left. It wasn't that long ago, of course, but it seemed like it. He'd had a few blissful years with Miss Layton at the village school, but then been sent away to board, and on to university, coming home only for holidays.

An owl hooted, calling to its mate, and was answered in a soft diminuendo from the other side of the park. Simon couldn't see much of the village beyond the black line of sheltering trees, but the squat church tower showed sharply against the sky.

From his high point above the park, looking across the village to the hills beyond, it looked much the same as it had to his ancestors a hundred years ago. His doubts surfaced again. God, I hope I've done the right thing, he thought, and reached for his mobile phone to dial an Atlanta number he knew off by heart. He'd felt sorry for the girl when they said goodbye, and had promised to ring, but he knew already he wouldn't keep it up. She'd been fun, but that was all.

Simon's return had been thoroughly chewed over by the village since the news broke, and sightings of him were eagerly awaited. Doris Ashbourne felt she had a right to be among the first, as former postmistress, and had planned to be at the shop early, but on this dismal morning she felt trapped. It was raining hard, too hard to be out with no real reason.

Since Doris had moved to the old-persons' bungalows in Macmillan Gardens, she was pleased with the light, airy sitting-room with its wide window, the back garden bordering John Barnett's home close, where he put sheep and lambs, and young calves needing shelter from the weather. In winter, she fed the birds on a bird-table bought by a grateful village on her retirement. Country-bred, she had no qualms about chasing away sparrows and starlings, which she considered the bully boys of the garden. She missed the flow of people in and out of the shop, the feeling of being at the centre of things. Above all, she missed the human voice.

The rain was heavier than ever now, and she resigned herself to a morning's baking, but chance was on Doris's side, and, with everything out on the worktop and her cake tin greased, she found the sugar tin empty. There it was, then. A very good reason for going to the shop.

She tied her headscarf tight, and, carrying her basket over her arm, opened the door and stepped out. A squall of stinging rain greeted her, and she struggled to get her umbrella unfolded. Then, without seeing anything much but the pavement under her feet, she started off down the Gardens.

'Oops!' The voice was big and jolly.

Doris tipped her brolly back to see the large, laughing woman teetering on the pavement edge. 'Jean! I'm so sorry! Can't see where I'm going in this awful weather.' Jean Jenkins lived on the other side of the Gardens, cleaned up at the Hall and in various houses in the village to eke out her farmworker husband's wages. She traded goodwill and gossip with anyone prepared to reciprocate. 'Want anything from the shop?' said Doris.

Jean held an open soggy newspaper over her head. 'There was something . . .' she said. 'Bread, that was it. Sliced white. Peggy should've put it by. Oh, and Doris,' she added, as the newspaper began to disintegrate round her ears, 'see if she knows about that character at Bridge Cottage yesterday. Old Ellen was full of it.' She turned to go, but remembered something else. 'Hey, did you know?' she said. 'Precious Simon's arrived! Ellen didn't know what to talk about first . . .'

Doris rounded the corner into the main street, avoided a deep puddle by the big drain, and approached the shop. A car drew up ahead of her and she saw a slight figure get out, a stranger. 'It's Ellen's man,' she said to herself, and with gathering excitement marched on after the promising sight of George Chalmer disappearing into the shop.

A slow-moving vehicle caused her to retreat from the

edge of the pavement to avoid being splashed, and she saw the Standings' Range Rover coasting along beside her, a young man at the wheel. Good gracious! Wasn't that Mr Richard, miraculously restored to youth, smiling at her with that knock-'em-cold smile that for years had warmed her weekly behind the Post Office counter? But of course it wasn't Mr Richard: it was Simon, who climbed out from the driver's seat with easy grace, his long legs and broad shoulders reminding Doris again of his father. He had his mother's straight, narrow nose and high forehead, she noted approvingly, and his grandfather's thick, curly hair, but cut too short for her liking. Still, all in all, a good-looking lad, Doris thought, and walked on, delighted at how the morning was turning out.

Simon was standing at the top of the shop steps, gazing into the school playground. Bet he's remembering when he splashed in puddles, just like them kids over there now, Doris guessed, and smiled at him tentatively.

'Morning!' said Simon, holding open the door for her. 'Mrs Ashbourne, isn't it?'

Doris coloured. 'Fancy you recognising me,' she said, and added quickly, 'Very nice to see you home again.'

Inside the shop, she found to her delight not only George Chalmer, but Ivy too, rooting around in the bargain basket at the back of the shop. Simon retreated politely, and Doris greeted her friend. 'Morning, Ivy,' she said, and received a grunt in reply. She looked across at George Chalmer, who moved away from the counter modestly and touched his hat.

'Nasty morning,' he said. 'Please go first. You look so wet, my dear.'

'No, it's quite all right, thank you,' she said, and thought, Oh my, Chalmer by name and charmer by nature. And just look at Ivy's face! She turned to Peggy, who was smiling amiably behind the counter, and said, 'See to this gentleman, my dear. We're all like drowned rats this morning!' Warmed by the stranger's kindly words, she put out a hand and brushed a lump of mud from his mac, saying in a motherly voice, 'Not used to the country, I expect. Old Ted Bates has always been a mucky farmer, hasn't he, Ivy?'

'If you ask me,' said Ivy, bridling, 'there's some in this village as are a bit over-forward.' Doris dropped her hand at once, and Ivy continued, 'And others, Mr Chalmer, like Ted Bates, who don't care tuppence for them as has to walk through the mess he makes. Anyway, did you find the farm?'

Well, Ivy, thought Doris, that was a long speech. She noticed Ivy's scarlet cheeks, and wondered. Definitely worth coming out for, this was, wet feet or no wet feet.

'I followed your exact directions, Miss Beasley,' said George, with a grateful tilt of his head, 'and was unlucky in finding Mr Bates had gone to market. It's clear that I shall have to talk to him on a number of matters relating to renting Bridge Cottage, and so shall be returning once more to this delightful village.'

George Chalmer's purchases were quickly made, and he made his way to the door. Ivy cleared her throat, and said in a strangulated posh voice quite unlike her own, 'If you need any more help, Mr Chalmer, do not hesitate to ask. Victoria Villa, next to the shop. You can't miss it.'

'Whitest front step in Ringford,' said Doris, not entirely without malice. 'Down on her knees scrubbing away every Monday morning, without fail. Isn't that right, Ivy?' Ivy glared at her, but undeterred, Doris continued, 'And if Ivy's out, you can find me in Macmillan Gardens. I'm always there, mostly.'

George stepped neatly out of the shop and was gone, and Ivy frowned at Doris, clearly having something sharp to add, but Simon came forward and smiled broadly at her. Ivy stopped in her tracks, stared at him and said, 'Mr Simon? Oh, my goodness, so it is . . .' She visibly collected herself, and continued, 'Well, welcome home indeed. Very nice to have you back, I'm sure.' Simon put out his hand, shook Ivy's firmly, and opened the shop door for her to depart in a fluster.

Doris adjusted her headscarf, straightened her glasses, and beamed at him. 'You in a hurry?' she said, motioning Simon forward to the counter. 'I've plenty of time.' But Simon was enjoying himself, and said that he'd forgotten half the things his mother had asked for, so would just wander around for inspiration.

The doorbell jangled again, and Simon's attention was caught by a tall, rangy-looking blonde, followed by a plump, very dark girl he thought he recognised. He studied the postcards carefully, glancing sideways at the newcomers for clues.

'Morning, Peggy,' said the blonde.

She was answered by a cheerful, 'Not much of a one, is it, Mrs Bishop?'

The name rang no bells for Simon. He looked again at the other, the dark one. She caught his eye, and smiled. My God, it was Sandra Roberts, one of the dreaded Robertses from Macmillan Gardens. 'Morning,' she said politely, and he nodded with a smile. She'd changed, though. Looked very attractive, almost foreign. It was coming back to him now. She'd been a bad lot, shoplifting as soon as Mrs Ashbourne's back was turned, sloping off behind the bushes with that building worker from the new houses. He couldn't remember what had happened about that, but knew she'd had a child.

'Now, Mr Simon,' Peggy was saying, faintly mocking, 'it must be your turn next. What can I get for you?'

In the end, Simon could remember only butter, cornflakes and the old familiar phrase, 'Put it on the book, will you, please?' He picked up the packets, and turned to look at the other shoppers, flashing them a wide, friendly smile. ' 'Bye, then, ladies,' he said. 'Nice to see you again, Mrs Ashbourne, Sandra . . .' He paused, looking enquiringly at the blonde.

Peggy helped out. 'Mrs Bishop,' she said, 'Mrs Annie Bishop, from the old vicarage. Fairly new, from London.'

That sums *her* up, thought Simon, beginning to like Peggy a lot, and ran down the steps.

Annie Bishop was the first to break the silence. 'Heavens!' she said. 'Knows how to make a good first impression, our young squire, don't you think?' She turned her pleasant smile on Peggy, who reflected that in that case Mrs Bishop and Simon already had a lot in common.

'Don't mean a thing,' said Sandra, shrugging her shoulders. 'I remember him when he was a snotty kid hanging around my brother in the holidays. Younger than Darren, and a bit older than the rest of us. Didn't fit in anywhere, poor sod. Real pest, he was.'

'Maybe so,' said Annie, managing to sound tolerant and patronising at the same time, 'but I thought he was delightful. Most attractive. Very like his father . . . like he must have been in his youth,' she added quickly, and Peggy grinned meaningly at Sandra. They all knew about Annie Bishop and Simon's father.

As Simon walked away from the shop, a shout from the playground alerted him to a football rolling across the road towards him. 'Send it back, mister!' yelled a crop-headed boy.

'Send it back *what*, David Dodwell?' The second voice belonged to a young woman, not very tall but with considerable presence, who marched across the playground and smiled apologetically at Simon. 'No manners, you know,' she said. 'We try hard at school, but some of them get no back-up from home, and, frankly, we're wasting our time.' She turned the boy around and sent him away with a pretended cuff around the ears. 'That one should know better, though,' she said confidentially. 'Good home, and all that.'

Her immediate friendliness captivated Simon. Her small brown face was lively, full of humour and confidence, and dominated by cat-green eyes that looked him up and down and seemed to like what they saw. She had a large beige mac wrapped around her, but there was a smooth swiftness in her movements that made him very aware of good things hidden from sight.

'Simon Standing,' he said, introducing himself, 'and you must be the new Head?'

'Sarah Barnett,' she said, nodding. 'Knew you were coming home. The whole village did, of course! Anyway, I must get this lot back to their grindstone . . . welcome home, Simon! See you again soon, I hope,' and she was gone, quickly disappearing into the old school building that had been built by a long-dead Standing, maintained by the family, and had suddenly become the object of special interest to its latest son and heir.

'Cooee!' Annie Bishop hovered at the Barnetts' farmhouse doorway, calling for her friend Sarah, knowing she must be home from school by now. 'Can't stop,' Annie continued, as Sarah appeared from upstairs. 'Car full of children, but just had to come up and see if you'd seen him?'

'Oh yes,' said Sarah warmly, 'I've seen him. Chatted me up over the school railings this morning.'

'What do you think, then?'

'Everything you'd expect him to be,' said Sarah, grinning at Annie, 'considering whose son he is . . .'

Annie blushed like a schoolgirl. 'That's enough of that,' she said. 'Past history. But my goodness, he had all the old tabs eating out of his hand in the shop. Looks like we're in for a treat, Sarah.'

'We can always hope,' said Sarah calmly, setting out crocks and cutlery for her husband's tea. 'Time this village brightened up a bit.'

A long horn blast from the farmyard outside sent Annie running back to her car. 'Cheers, Sarah!' she yelled. 'To be continued . . .' And she drove off at speed down the long farm drive.

'You should've heard them in the shop this morning,' said Peggy, as she relaxed with Bill in their sitting-room. It was her favourite time of day: business done, and Bill all to herself. 'What with Ivy and Doris fighting for Mr Chalmer's favours, and Annie Bishop fancying Simon on sight, not to mention Sandra's two penn'orth . . . and I could see Sarah Barnett flirting away over the school railings at playtime! Not been so lively in the General Stores for ages.'

'Randy lot, Annie Bishop and friends,' said Bill, comfortably, 'but doesn't sound like our Ivy. Nor our Doris, come to that.'

Peggy said she witnessed it with her own eyes, and added, 'There was something about that Mr Chalmer, you know, Bill. Sort of appealing, like a shy boy, and really modest and unassuming.'

'My God,' said Bill, 'you too?'

# 4

In the days that followed, an increasingly depressing round of drinks parties with his parents' friends had caused Simon to reflect that it was time to be off, to be up in London putting out job feelers, looking for somewhere to live. The village had settled down, grown used to seeing him around. His predatory, plump cousin, Alexandra Smyth was becoming a nuisance, and, to his disappointment, Sarah Barnett, who seen without the beige mac had lived up to expectations, proved to be constantly hedged about by schoolchildren and husband.

Mum and Dad were still euphoric about his home-coming, but he knew that would wear off. Everything wore off in the end, with Mum. No, it was time to move, and he announced at breakfast one morning that he'd be going up to have lunch with an old surveyor friend to make a start. He noticed the quick flash of relief in his mother's eyes, and knew he'd been right.

'Stay in the flat, darling,' she said encouragingly. 'We shan't be there for the next week or so.'

Richard looked up from his newspaper, and said in a neutral voice, 'If you're going up today, Simon, better take the train. Big hold-ups on the motorway, apparently.'

Leaving himself no time to spare, Simon sped through the narrow lanes on his way to the station, and came across the flashing lights of a level-crossing.

'Bloody hell!' he fumed, shifting impatiently in his

seat. A small red car in front belched out exhaust fumes. Stupid woman, why doesn't she switch off her engine? No sounds of a train, blast it. He opened his door and walked forward to look up and down the line. Nothing. He noticed the red car was silent now.

Then the train roared through, almost without warning, and as he hurried back he heard the ominous sound of an engine coughing, failing to start. The young woman was frowning, turning the key repeatedly. Oh no, groaned Simon. That's all I need. He glanced at his watch and saw that he'd be lucky to make it now. He hesitated, sighed, and knocked at her window. She opened it, looking furiously at him.

'I'm doing my best!' she said, and her flushed, oval face under pale hair stifled Simon's irritation.

'Sorry,' he said. 'I just wondered if you needed help?'

'It's stalled,' she said abruptly, and got out. Simon saw long legs, cold blue eyes. 'You have a go,' she said. 'Men are better at these things, aren't they?' He grinned at the challenge in her voice.

'Not always,' he said, but sat down in her warm seat, breathing in the perfumed air of the hot car. He turned the key, and the fickle engine started at once. He scrambled out and held open the door for her, looking at her speculatively.

'From round here?' he said, as she got in.

'Oh yes,' she said, 'from Ringford.' She smiled at him then, a sudden, warming smile. 'Same as you,' she said, closing the window, 'and thanks.' Before he could answer, she'd driven off.

'Must have been Octavia Jones,' said his mother speaking on the telephone to Simon. 'You remember the house they made from the granary? Well, they live there. An ordinary sort of couple, her parents. Inoffensive, you know.'

Simon, alone and feeling temporarily adrift in his

parents' London flat, turned on the television, but couldn't concentrate. Octavia Jones. Octavia . . . he remembered that name from the distant past. It was unusual, and it irritated him that he couldn't place it.

It was later, when he climbed wearily into bed after an evening in the pub with old friends, that it suddenly came to him: Miss Layton, standing at her desk in the schoolroom with a frown on her kindly face, addressing a mutinous small girl with long fair hair and a disconcerting stare. 'Octavia Jones! If I catch you and Sandra Roberts wasting time once more, I shall send for your parents.' Of course, that was her. Simon turned on his side, and with a benevolent smile fell instantly asleep.

# 5

George Chalmer had parked at the top of Bagley Hill to take an objective look at the village. There was Bridge Cottage, clearly visible through the mist, low-lying beside the Ringle. The river flowed grey and dull this morning, vanishing under the old bridge, and then on into the spinney by Home Farm. He decided to leave the car and walk into the village. He'd pick up more that way.

Unused to walking, he quickly came to a halt, glaring crossly at the wet patches on his thin shoes. He leaned tentatively against a field gate. Too late, he tried to brush the green stains off his sleeves, and his mood darkened. Then he saw Ivy Beasley. It was quite clearly Ivy, appearing on her front doorstep with a bucket of soapy water and scrubbing-brush. A nice house, Victoria Villa, solid and respectable. Ivy intrigued him. He had never met anyone quite so ramrod stiff and unyielding, so uncompromising in her critical stare and harsh voice. A challenge, George, my boy, he thought, and chuckled when he tried to visualise his very good friend's reaction back in Leamington. 'Meet Miss Beasley, my . . .' But whoa, George, not so fast.

Footsteps behind him brought George back on to the road, nervous in spite of himself. 'Did I startle you, Mr Chalmer?' said Bill Turner, rounding the corner with his gun under his arm and an old khaki kitbag over his shoulder. He'd been shooting in Bagley Woods, had seen the fiesta come to a halt and its driver set off down the hill. Bill had decided to follow at a discreet distance.

'Good morning,' said George. 'A damp one, I'm afraid.'

'Good for the gardens,' said Bill. 'Having a walk round the village?'

George nodded. He remembered now: this was the man from the shop, Mrs Turner's husband. 'I must be absolutely sure, Mr Turner, before I decide to rent Bridge Cottage. Moving house is a big step, especially when one is not so young, and alone . . .'

George's face had set in sad lines, and Bill felt obliged to sympathise. 'Wife passed on?' he said, shifting his bag to the other shoulder.

George didn't speak, but turned away as if he couldn't face the thought. 'I have been alone for some years now, Mr Turner,' he said. 'My accountancy kept me busy, and I had no time to brood, but since I retired, the empty days hang heavy, and thoughts of the past return unbidden.'

Blimey, thought Bill, sounds a bit stagey. Still, poor bugger, it must be lonely for someone in his position. 'Ringford is a very friendly village,' he said. 'They'd soon be after you for all kinds of odd jobs, you can be sure of that! And there's a good crowd in the Arms, if you like that kind of thing,' he added doubtfully.

'I'm certainly not averse to a pint of ale, Mr Turner,' said George, and gave Bill a wan smile. 'Perhaps I may accompany you down the hill into the village? I'm hoping to stroll around until I see Mr Bates at eleven. Get the feel of the place . . . I'm sure you understand.'

'Needs a lot doing to it, Bridge Cottage, before anybody could live there,' said Bill, trying to match his stride to the other's small, light steps.

'Oh yes, I'm aware of that, but I have all the time in the world, and am considering taking lodgings while the work is being done. Mr Bates and I are nearly at an amicable arrangement for renting, and I'd like to be around to keep an eye on repairs and renovations.'

Well, there's a thing, thought Bill, immediately amused at the thought of the old women vying for this eminently eligible lodger. 'I'm sure we'll find you a comfortable billet for a few weeks,' he said. 'Plenty of room in the village, and several folk only too glad of a little extra at the end of the month.'

They had reached the foot of the hill, and Bill carried on across the footpath to the shop. Friendly chap, thought George, but no fool. Not one to take for granted. He walked slowly towards the Standing Arms, wondering if he should book himself in there, or try out one of the comfortable billets Bill had suggested.

'Shall I pour, then?' said Ellen, as Ivy wandered round the Lodge sitting-room, peering at surfaces and running her hand critically along the tops of tables and shelves. 'If yer've finished inspectin' the premises, Ivy, sit down, fer God's sake. You make the place untidy. Now,' she continued, 'who's for a bit of this sponge I've been slavin' over all mornin'? Pass yer plate, Ivy.'

'Fresh, is it?' said Ivy, her plate still firmly on her lap. 'And you needn't give us that nonsense about pretending it's home-made. Anybody can see with one eye that it's Mr Kipling. Still, I'll just try a slice, if it's fresh.' She settled more firmly into the shabby sofa.

'Now then,' said Ellen, wiping her hands on her skirt, 'what's the latest?'

'Latest?' said Ivy, dabbing the corners of her mouth with a small handkerchief. 'Latest on what?'

'Don't be daft, Ivy,' said Ellen. 'You know as well as I do we're all dyin' to hear about Mr Chalmer. I saw 'im this mornin', walkin' around the cottage with old Ted. 'e didn't see me, mind. I was well behind the curtain. Reckon 'e must be decidin' to take it, else why would 'e keep comin'?' Ivy said nothing. ''e do seem a nice bloke, don't yer think, Ivy?' persisted Ellen. Still Ivy said nothing.

Ellen looked at her curiously, 'You ill, or something?' she said. 'T'ain't like you to keep quiet. What's eatin' yer, Ivy?'

Ivy brushed a few cake crumbs from her lap. 'As a matter of fact,' she said, 'I do have some news. Well, not really news, but . . .'

'Well, get on with it, then,' said Ellen, wriggling in her chair with suspense.

'Better be good, Ivy,' said Doris, 'with all this build-up.'

'Well,' said Ivy, 'I had a visit this morning from the gentleman in question, seeking my advice. Seems he can't move into Bridge Cottage for several weeks. So he needs lodgings, and he wanted my help.'

'Ivy!' gasped Ellen. 'You never . . ?'

Ivy's raised eyebrows spoke volumes. 'I've not yet decided, but why shouldn't I take a lodger?' she said. 'Plenty of room since Mother went. No gentleman could be more respectable, I'm sure. What do you say, Doris? You've got an opinion too, no doubt?'

Doris stared at her. Ivy, with a gentleman lodger? The enormity of it rendered her speechless.

# 6

'Is it right, then, Ivy's taking in that Mr Chalmer?' asked Peggy over breakfast. 'Has he decided on Bridge Cottage now, for definite?'

'Don't ask me, gel,' Bill said. 'You're the expert here in Ringford. All I know is what young Poppy tells me. Ever since Simon's been home, she's sulked about the place, getting in my way and rabbitin' on about everything under the sun.'

Peggy sniffed. 'Nose thoroughly out of joint, that one,' she said.

Bill nodded. 'Still,' he said, 'she seems to keep her ear to the ground. It was Poppy darling who told me about Ivy and George Chalmer. And her latest fantasy is that Simon's got his eye on Octavia Jones. Says he lies in wait for her in the village street, but Octavia's not interested, according to Poppy.'

'Silly child,' said Peggy, but then added, 'though she's not a child any more, is she? Half and half, poor kid. A dangerous stage, that . . .'

Ivy Beasley was not Mandy Bates's favourite client. Ivy made it quite clear that for two pins she would take the garden shears and do the job herself, if it were not for Doris getting at her. 'I've got a visitor for coffee this morning,' she said tartly, rejecting Mandy's offer of conditioner. 'Can't waste any more time than necessary. Just get it neat, Mandy, and that'll be more than adequate.'

Mandy smoothed the strong, wiry hair into its usual short bob, sighed because she knew she could make something really attractive out of it, given the chance, and shook out the towel. 'If you give me the broom, Miss Beasley,' she said, 'I'll brush up.'

'No need,' said Ivy. 'I left this floor until you'd gone. I shall do it properly,' she added, irritating Mandy with her deliberate tactlessness. 'Now, you'd best be off,' she continued. 'I have jobs to do before . . .'

'So you're expecting a visitor?' said Mandy, refusing to be pushed out. 'Not young Simon, is it? He's around the village again, sizing up the talent. Wonder who'll be the lucky girl? His cousin Alex is keen, so they say, but down in the pub there's talk of Sarah Barnett makin' eyes . . . and then again, I saw him pushing Octavia Jones's car to get it started the other morning . . .'

'That's quite enough of that, Mandy Bates,' Ivy said. 'That kind of thing is what causes trouble. Sarah Barnett's a married woman, and her John'll stand no nonsense. Take my advice, and just do your job and leave the gossip alone. Now, off you go, and let me get on.' She saw Mandy out without ceremony and banged the door behind her.

George Chalmer stood on the pavement outside Victoria Villa and looked up at the square, red-brick house with its windows and front door in perfect symmetry, and thought how like Ivy Beasley it was: stern, no frivolous decoration. The windows shone, of course, and the white step gleamed forbiddingly, daring anyone to step on it with dirty shoes. George pushed open the small wrought–iron gate and walked up the weedless path to Ivy's front door. A white enamel bell-push commanded him to 'press', and he obediently did so.

'Good morning,' said Ivy primly, as she opened the door, but before he could answer, she added in her usual critical voice, 'Not that it is a good morning, heaven knows, with all that heavy rain bashing down the flowers.' She made it sound as if God had done it on purpose. Then she remembered her new role as land-lady, and said with an attempt at a welcome, 'Come in, Mr Chalmer, the kettle is on.'

Ivy's kitchen was the one welcoming room in the house, with its comfortable, cushioned wheel-back chairs and the black range, cheerful with a pot of yellow daisies in the fire basket. Yes, thought George, the kitchen had a homely atmosphere. He noticed at once a tabby cat curled up asleep in one chair, a Burmese looking at him with suspicious blue eyes from another.

'Both cats yours, Miss Beasley?' he said. He hated cats – the smell of them, their bloody superiority and the way they jumped on his lap without invitation – but now was not the time to show his dislike. When Ivy said that the Burmese was hers and the tabby a visitor from the shop next door, he nodded, smiled, and said how very nice that they got on so well together.

A tray had been laid with an embroidered cloth and a plate of home-made shortbread. 'Shall we go through to the parlour?' said Ivy. George looked at her closely, decided that she wasn't joking, and offered to carry the tray. Ivy hesitated, then gave a gawky smile and said that was very kind of him, she would bring in the coffee pot.

God, thought George Chalmer, this room is a killer. He sat on the edge of an armchair, balanced a cup and saucer on his knee, and looked around. So the old thing was a collector. But not promising: a teaset in flowered china, nothing special; sundry silver-plate spoons and cream jugs, and an ugly pottery dog with an evil eye. Heavy, dark red curtains and figured net veiled the room from the village outside, which was all right by George.

Beside the window stood a straight-backed chair, a folded piece of knitting left on the seat. So that's where she keeps an eye on village goings-on, thought George, and smiled. He liked the idea of secret spying, of observation and gathering of information. His whole life had been based on judicious use of information.

'Shortbread, Mr Chalmer?' said Ivy, offering him the plate.

'Thank you so much,' he said. 'I hadn't expected anything so delicious! Living on one's own, you know . . .' He glanced modestly down at his shoes, then up at Ivy's face, and was gratified to see her features soften.

'How long since your wife . . . ?' she said.

'Ah,' said George, and remained quiet, allowing Ivy to think that it was a subject too painful to pursue.

Second cups were poured, and then George Chalmer decided it was time to come to the matter in hand. 'The tenancy document for Bridge Cottage seems to be going ahead smoothly now,' he said. 'No delays, and renovations et cetera agreed with Mr Bates. All of which means that the men can start almost at once, and I shall need somewhere to rest my weary head!'

Ivy pursed her lips and frowned. 'I've given the matter a lot of thought,' she said, 'and must confess I have had one or two sleepless nights considering your request,' Ivy continued.

Oh, bloody hell, thought George, don't say the dear old thing is going to back out. But no, Ivy's face cleared, and she gave him a pinched smile.

'You will be pleased to hear, Mr Chalmer,' she said, 'that I have come to a decision, and that is to allow you to rent my front bedroom, with two weeks' notice on both sides, and the possibility of meals, which we will have to discuss.'

Whew! thought George. Bless her, she's come up trumps. 'How very kind of you, Miss Beasley.' He leaned forward, extending his hand. 'Let us shake hands on a happy outcome for both of us,' he said in his gentlemanly way, and gritted his teeth as the Burmese leapt lightly on to his lap.

★

As Ivy had expected, the minute George Chalmer was out of the front door, her mother's voice entered her head, furious and castigating. *That bedroom was your father's and mine for fifty-five years, Ivy Dorothy!* There were times when Ivy welcomed the familiar tones of her long-dead mother, as when she was sitting in her kitchen on winter evenings with the wind howling in the chimney and nobody but Tiddles for company.

*It's not for long, Mother,* Ivy defended herself. *Just until the work's finished on the cottage, then he'll be moving out.*

*No doubt you'll have a taste for it by then,* said her mother nastily. *Who knows what riff-raff you'll bring in to Victoria Villa? And what do you know about this Mr Chalmer? Nothing at all. You must be mad, girl, quite mad.*

Ivy was well aware that her mother's voice was an echo of her own doubt, so she ignored it and stalked out into her rain-soaked garden. The cool, wet earth and thickening foliage consoled her. This was alive, real. Lettuces would be ready to plant out soon. Ivy reminded herself to sow a couple of rows of radishes. Nothing nicer than a dish of radishes, a small pile of salt, thin bread and butter and a good hot cup of tea. *I wonder if Mr Chalmer likes radishes? I might work out in the garden if it clears up,* she thought. Everything smelled so wonderful after the rain. Ivy sighed, not unhappily, and turned her hot face to cool in the sweet air.

# 7

In the thicket down by the Ringle river, in a thorny ring of bushes surrounding a flat, grassy space now littered with drink cans and empty crisp packets, the gang had gathered. They were not so much a formal group as an assorted bunch of Ringford's finest, held together chiefly by Poppy Standing, their acknowledged leader. Most of them were in awe of her love of roaming round the village picking up gossip and using it to blackmail those she considered her inferiors. Her most vulnerable victim was Mark Jenkins, a slow, overweight boy, son of Jean Jenkins who cleaned, and happy to be amongst other children who were younger than himself and not always better at everything, as were his peers. He was soon to leave school, and couldn't wait.

The other members of the gang were Hugo Dodwell, a tall, thin boy from the new houses in Walnut Close; Joey Bates, pushed bumpily over the meadow by Poppy, who would never have him excluded; Helen Bishop, from the old vicarage and daughter of Annie; and Georgie from Fletching, who cycled over every Sunday morning, nobody was quite sure why. He had been a friend of former member Eddie Jenkins, killed in a car accident several years ago, and Georgie had just kept coming. He said very little, but had an infectious smile.

The thicket stood on the Standing side of the Ringle, and was strictly on Hall land. This was one of the reasons Poppy was boss, but she was also well read on the important matter of sex, and had the quickest brain, the sharpest tongue. Before Poppy had taken charge, the thicket had, of course, been used by generations of village youth, a reliable place for anything that needed a bit of privacy. The grass was soft and springy, and, as Jean Jenkins once said, remembering happy days, 'That don't 'arf bounce!'

'God, I'm tired!' said Poppy, stretching herself out languidly. 'Nothing but running errands for Mum, and dodging out of Simon's way. Wish he'd stayed in London.'

'He's very nice looking,' said Helen Bishop tentatively. She was scared of Poppy, scared of saying the wrong thing.

Georgie from Fletching laughed. 'Miss Barnett seemed to think so,' he said, and his light brown eyes sparked.

'*Mrs* Barnett, stupid,' said Poppy.

Georgie was unmoved by this, and said if his mum had flirted around like Miss Barnett, his dad would have given her a good seeing-to.

'Your dad's never around, so he couldn't, could he?' said Mark Jenkins scathingly.

Joey, seeing the shadow cross Georgie's face, told Mark to shut up and pass the can of shandy to Hugo Dodwell, who drank deeply.

'Here, Doddy!' said Mark Jenkins. 'Leave us a drop . . . me dad'll notice if I take too many at a time.' Mark Jenkins was responsible for gang refreshments, and the others relied on him.

The last dregs were shared round, and Helen Bishop slung the can into the bushes.

'Pick it up!' said Poppy sharply. 'You're not in your back garden now, Helen Bishop. God knows what that must look like,' she added in her mother's voice.

Mark Jenkins, who fancied Helen Bishop though dared not declare his interest, got up and fetched the can. 'Turners say they're gettin' a new sort in at the shop,' he

said. 'Dad says their cool-drinks cabinet 'as saved the
business goin' down the drain. Long past time they
joined the twentieth century, I reckon.'

Poppy stopped chewing a piece of grass, and said,
'They could have videos. That'd be very popular in
Ringford, especially porny ones. Especially for your
Dad, Hugo Dodwell.' She sat up and grinned challen-
gingly at him.

Rising to the bait, he grabbed her and pushed her over
on to her stomach, holding her down and demanding an
apology. 'Say you're sorry!' he yelled over and over
again, and the others, fed up with Poppy, were quick to
take the opportunity and join in. Keeping up the chant,
they rolled around and on top of each other until Joey
Bates, on the sidelines in his wheelchair, shouted above
the row that they'd better shut up, it was Sunday, and
everybody'd be out of church any minute.

It was true, of course, but it was not the whole reason
for Joey's intervention. He worried that Poppy would
get really hurt, and was relieved to see her emerge from
the heap smiling. Poppy, for her part, had felt Hugo's
skinny body warm on top of hers, and cheered up.

# 8

With absolutely nothing to do between lunch and dinner, Simon suggested to Poppy they should walk through Bagley Woods with the dogs. 'Lovely afternoon,' he said. 'Do us both good.'

'Speak for yourself,' said Poppy. 'I don't need being done good to, thanks. Anyway, I'm off to see Joey.' He heard her whistling tunelessly as she went skimming out of the yard on her bike.

Richard and Susan had gone out to lunch with the Smyths at Waltonby, and although Simon had been invited, he'd once more declined. 'Can't stand the far-off sound of wedding bells,' he'd said, and Susan had been unable to persuade him. 'Just you and me, then,' he said to his father's spaniel. 'Come on, boy, walkies!'

Simon was beginning to worry. A number of interviews had resulted in nothing solid. Hopeful words, promises of calls the minute anything came up, but no actual job offer. Maybe summer was a bad time. Perhaps he should work around on the estate with Bill, and have a real push in the autumn.

In the meantime he'd have to do something to jolly up his social life, something more exciting than pat-ball tennis with cousin Alex! Maybe he'd smarten up the Hall court, invite some friends over. His mind wandered on, wondering who he could ask. Maybe get some kind of regular group together, sort of informal club. It was a possibility worth looking into, he thought, but he knew his mother would be far from keen.

The woods were cool and green, and the panting spaniel perked up gratefully. Shimmering, dappled sunlight made mirages of life on all sides. Several times Simon thought he saw somebody in the distance, but it turned out to be a swaying sapling, nothing more. Then he was sure that a figure moving through the trees was real. Female, and real. It was Sarah Barnett, in jeans and a lemon yellow T-shirt that showed off her brown arms and slender neck.

'Simon!' she said, tugging at her collie's lead. 'Don't worry, I can't let Nell off . . . she just runs home, the coward.' She ran a hand through her short, shiny brown hair and smiled broadly at him. 'So how's it going?' she said. 'Glad you came back?'

'Yes and no,' he said. 'No, when there's bugger-all to do at the Hall, and nobody wants to give me a job . . .'

'And yes?' grinned Sarah.

'And yes, when I meet a pretty girl in the woods . . .' he said, thinking it was worth the risk of a teacherly snub.

'Oh, my God,' said Sarah, laughing loudly now. 'You sound like your gentleman father! Bet you didn't talk like that to the girls in Atlanta.'

He admitted that he didn't, but said quite seriously that he'd got out of the way of chatting up English girls.

'No need, with an old married woman . . . and a schoolmarm at that,' said Sarah, but the warmth in her eyes told another story.

Nell, fed up with the delay, pulled sharply on the lead, jerking Sarah off balance. She fell forward against Simon, who put out his arm to catch her.

'Whoops!' she said, taking longer than was necessary to straighten up, giving him plenty of opportunity to feel her smooth skin, the unexpected softness of her. Her scent was fresh and sharp, and Simon felt his head swim.

'Um, well,' he muttered, when she'd steadied herself, 'shall we walk back together? Or would that compromise Ringford's head teacher?'

'Don't be silly,' Sarah answered matter-of-factly. 'You haven't exactly raped me and dragged me through the woods by my hair, now have you? Come on, you can come back to the farm and have a cup of tea. John's out. Playing cricket. A game that bores me to tears, unfortunately,' she added, ignoring Simon's horrified expression. 'Call your dog, though, we don't want to lose him, poor old thing.' And she marched off, leading the way, as was her custom.

Simon found conversation with Sarah very easy. She did most of the talking, but in a pause while she untangled Nell's lead, he said, 'If you don't like cricket, how do you feel about tennis?'

That was different, she said. Used to play all the time at home in Harrogate. 'I was pretty good, as a matter of fact,' she said, and hit an imaginary ball with an invisible racket.

Simon explained his vague plan for getting some players together on a regular basis, and Sarah was full of enthusiasm. 'Annie would love it, I know,' she said, 'and several of the others.'

They were approaching the drive up to Walnut Farm, when Simon saw John Barnett's car hovering. It stopped, and John got out. 'Thought it was you, Sarah,' he said, and looked at Simon with a faint smile.

'We met in the woods,' said Simon, and immediately regretted it. 'That is,' he stumbled, 'I was up there with my dog, and ran into . . .'

John had turned away from him and taken Sarah by the arm. 'Shove Nell in the back,' he said, 'and I'll give you a lift home.'

Not at all put out, Sarah waved a friendly hand to Simon as they drove off, shouting to him through her open window, 'See you at the fête next week, I expect!'

'Stay clear of them Standings,' said John, as they pulled into the yard. 'He looks just like his father, and no doubt behaves like him, too. Can't be too careful, Sarah, in the village. Especially in your position at the school.' He was unsmiling, and strode off to the stables without opening the car door for her. She shrugged, went off to make tea, and by the time John came in grumbling about the price of feed, she gave every appearance of having forgotten the entire incident.

Next morning's sky was cloudless again, and shafts of sunlight penetrated Ivy's hall as she flicked round with a duster in a last-minute panic before Mr Chalmer came. She smoothed her thick, bristly grey hair with a weary hand, and stared at herself in the mirror. A rough, reddened face with bright, black button eyes looked back at her. Frown lines made her look even more fierce than usual, and she tried lifting her stubby, black eyebrows to get rid of them. She yawned, and rubbed her eyes.

Ivy had had a bad night. Unable to settle to her knitting, she'd gone to bed early, and by the time she'd slid between her shiny sheets she was so tired that sleep would not come. Visions of herself making up the big double bed with lavender-scented sheets played them-selves against Ivy's eyelids, and she'd turned over restlessly, adjusting the feather pillow under her tired head.

I could just tell him I've changed my mind, she'd told herself. I don't have to give reasons, it's my house and I can do what I like. Then her mother had intruded. *Our* house, it was, my girl, she'd said. Don't forget this entire house and contents was bought by your father and me, and you had it plonked straight in your lap when we passed on. Ivy had felt too depressed to reply. It was quite true. She never felt it was really hers, and on the odd occasion when she'd thought of ditching a worn-out cushion or a rickety chair, she hadn't done it, telling herself she didn't have the right.

Very well, then, she decided, putting away her duster, I'll tell him this morning. He said he'd look in after the workmen started, then bring his things later. But Ivy knew she wouldn't tell him anything. In the sunlight coming in through the hall fanlight, she felt warmed, and remembered the soft pressure of his hand in hers when they last parted. 'Until we meet again, Miss Beasley,' he had said. She unlocked the front door in readiness, and went to tidy up.

I suppose I shall have to call her Ivy sooner or later, thought George Chalmer as he pulled up outside Victoria Villa. He switched off the engine and stared up at the house. That front window upstairs was to be his outlook on the village for the next few weeks, and as he gazed speculatively he saw Ivy Beasley place a cut-glass vase of sweet williams on the windowsill. She looked down, saw him, and an unused smile flickered across her face. Sweet williams, eh? You're going to be all right there, Georgie boy.

'Just like the ivy on the old garden wall,' he crooned to himself, opening the car door, 'clinging so tightly, whate'er may befall. . .' Very apt, dearie, he thought, and pressed the china bell button with a flourish.

If the previous night had been a bad one for Ivy Beasley, this one was torture. She lay in her narrow bed between smooth sheets, and shivered, but not from cold. Ivy had been obedient to what she saw as her duty for most of her life, and only lately had she begun to rebel. Taking in George Chalmer as a lodger was the latest and most dramatic of her rebellions, but there had been others, all in recent years. That business of the school field, for instance. They'd have no school now if Ivy hadn't donated her small plot of land for extension, to save it from closing down. It had needed courage, and a deaf ear to her mother's strictures, but she had done it.

George's first evening at Victoria Villa had been very pleasant in the end, Ivy had to admit. Ivy had made supper for them both – 'just until you decide if you want the evening meal every night' – and it had been delicious: tender roast lamb, garden peas and new potatoes, followed by one of Ivy's legendary apple pies with thick cream from Bates's Farm. She had been nervous, tongue tied, but George Chalmer handled the situation with ease, just as if repressed, inhibited spinsters came his way every day of the week. Just as if he had been through it all before.

'No, no, Miss Beasley,' he had said. 'Allow me to clear away the dishes. I am not unaccustomed to having my hands in a washing-up bowl!' And even when Ivy, horrified at the idea, had protested, he'd picked up the drying-cloth and dried everything with care and loving attention. 'Beautiful china, Miss Beasley,' he'd said, noting the Royal Worcester mark and checking that the cutlery was, in fact, good silver from Birmingham.

When all was tidy and straight in the kitchen, Ivy had had a moment of panic. Now what? Would he sit with her in the front room, and if so, what on earth would they talk about? But she need not have worried.

'If you will forgive me, Miss Beasley,' George had said, as they put out the light in the kitchen and Ivy hovered uncertainly in the hall, 'I will go upstairs now. It's been a very busy day, and I anticipate another equally busy one tomorrow. Ted Bates has more or less left the supervision to me, and the British workman can't be trusted, you know! So if you'll excuse me now, I'm sure you understand . . .' He'd smiled pleadingly at Ivy, and she had relaxed.

'Of course, Mr Chalmer,' she'd said, 'I know only too

44

well. From the school extension. A worrying time for you. Well . . .' She had hesitated, but again George took the initiative.

He'd held her hand lightly, oh, so lightly, and shaken it gently. 'Most obliged, dear lady,' he'd said, 'I know I shall sleep like the proverbial top. Until the morning, then . . . goodnight . . .'

Ivy had watched him to the top of the stairs, and then turned away, unsure herself what to do next. She couldn't settle to her knitting again, kept doing plain where it should have been purl, and spent more time unpicking than knitting. Finally she'd put the sock away in its tartan bag, and stood up.

Her eyes had been drawn to the photograph of her mother and father on the mantelshelf. Their faces were stern, as always. No words from her mother reinforced Ivy's feeling of guilt. Nothing to say, Mother? she'd thought. Silence. Ivy remembered the silences so well. They were worse than the reprimands, and equally dreaded.

So here she was, in bed at last, the dreadful deed done, her lodger moved in. A man in her parents' bed. His clothes in her father's best walnut wardrobe, and his shoes tucked under the chair with the tapestry seat worked by her mother. And, more than that, a man breathing and dreaming, and turning his body around between sheets that Ivy had ironed, his head on the pillow that Ivy had plumped up with firm hands.

I wonder if he's awake, she thought. Did I give him enough blankets, a towel for the morning? She'd better check. In the middle of the night, Ivy Dorothy? She ignored the voice, and silently opened her bedroom door, creeping out on to the landing.

She was on the threshold of the bathroom when an ear-splitting snore, followed by choking and a mur-mured curse, sent her scuttling back into her room. She was in bed with the covers pulled up around her ears in seconds, and there she stayed until dawn broke and the chorus of sparrows under the eaves gave her enough courage to fall asleep.

# 9

'Why do we have a fête, year after year, when we know it'll blow a hurricane and tip down buckets of rain?' Peggy gazed out of the shop window at a steady downpour, while Bill sat in the kitchen behind her, finishing his breakfast and trying to read the sports pages.

'Always been there, the church fête,' he said. 'We don't let a drop o' rain put us off, Peg.' He was grinning in that knowing, Round Ringford oldest-inhabitant kind of way, and it was all Peggy could do not to tip his cup of tea over his head.

Saturday, fête day, had been announced on colourful posters by the church committee, and these now flapped damply on gates and telegraph poles around the village. Noble volunteers had knocked on doors, collecting up bottles for the tombola, home-made cakes, selling draw tickets that promised 'dozens of valuable prizes', none of which were specified because they hadn't got them yet.

The Reverend Nigel Brooks never ceased to marvel at the way things came together at the last minute. Doreen Price from Home Farm, Ivy Beasley, Jean Jenkins, Gabriella Jones, Sarah Barnett from the school, and, of course, the ever-willing Annie Bishop, all got on quietly with their allotted tasks, and there, in Ringford vicarage garden, it happened with the minimum of fuss or bother.

This year they had to find a new home, and voices had been raised. The Rev. Nigel's garden was much too small, and the Bishops had recently commissioned

47

fashionable landscape gardeners for the old vicarage. They were there even now, churning up the lawns and building low stone walls, and even, to the village's amazement and disbelief, setting down squares of slate and stone to make a lifesize chess board.

'And what the buggery do they do with that?' Ted Bates had commented in the pub. There had been no answer, none needed.

'How about the churchyard for the fête?' Nigel's suggestion had met with immediate opposition from older members of the church council, although Doreen Price, always keen to encourage the vicar, had backed him up.

'We could have refreshments in the church,' she said.

Ivy Beasley had said that if anyone asked her, she would call it blasphemy. The church was the house of God. Since when had He been known to plug in a tea-urn and hand round plates of shortbread and coffee sponge?

Nigel Brooks, sighing, had refrained from suggesting that Ivy's view of God might not be generally shared. Instead, he'd smiled his matinée idol smile at her, watched her melt, and got his own way.

Now, with eyes on the heavens, the big decision was whether to carry on with the churchyard plan, or retreat to the village hall.

By lunchtime, Nigel had settled for the churchyard. The rain had eased off to a light drizzle and then faded away, leaving dampness in the air.

Stalls were set up in a spirit of optimism. A table with a white cloth had been placed amongst the gravestones for the usual fantastic array of home baking, presided over by Ivy Beasley. As a come-on centrepiece, on Ivy's best cut-glass cakestand, a strawberry and cream meringue edifice sat in splendour, and raffle tickets were to be had for twenty pence each.

Tom Price, farmer and chairman of the parish council,

had brought up straw bales, old-fashioned rectangular ones, to build a bowling alley for the skittles. A live, wriggling piglet was no longer acceptable as the prize, but it was always worth investing a pound or two in rolling the heavy balls for a side of pork for the freezer.

Gabriella Jones had offered Octavia's services, and a game for the children had been allotted to her, involving a paddling pool, plastic ducks and hoops to throw over them.

'Mum!' Octavia had exploded. 'Couldn't I do the bookstall, or something a bit more dignified?'

'We thought you'd like the children, dear,' Gabriella had said, and the fearful apprehension on her face had silenced Octavia's protests.

'I just hope it rains,' she had muttered.

'Two thirty exactly!' shouted Nigel Brooks, handsome and smiling in his tweed jacket and clean dog collar. 'Open the gates!'

'You'd think there was a jostling crowd,' said Octavia bitterly to her old friend, Sandra Goodison, who used to be Roberts until her shotgun wedding to Sam. Sandra had agreed to help with the ducks, saying she'd rather do that than sell smelly clothes on the jumble stall.

A small queue had formed, and was admitted with the usual banter about paying to come in and spend money, and there was much fumbling for change and holding up the queue. As friends and relations wandered up the church path, a weak, watery sun appeared, and Nigel Brooks could not resist popping over to Ivy's stall and pointing out that God was smiling on them, after all.

'We shall have to put in an appearance,' said Susan Standing, rinsing lunch plates and stacking them on the old wooden draining-board of the Hall kitchen. 'It is a bit of a bore, Simon, but I know everyone would love it if you came too. Just for half an hour or so?'

To her surprise, Simon agreed at once. 'Pleasure, Mother,' he said. 'Got to keep the tenants happy.'

'You are joking, I hope,' said Richard. He found he no longer knew his son at all. Here was a stranger returned from America, who seemed to bear no relation to the awkward young man he'd seen off for the first time at Heathrow five years ago. Insecure, tentative and shy, that Simon had metamorphosed into a fine, broadened-out and athletic business executive, easy in his dealings with everyone, confident of his own ability to charm and handle all comers.

''Course I am, Dad,' Simon said. 'Not a total idiot, you know.'

'It's in the churchyard this year,' said Richard, 'which might be a bit odd.'

'I suppose they could have had it up here,' said Susan, 'but we do host the horticultural lot and that's really enough, I think.' She squeezed the wet cloth and draped it over the taps. 'Right, then,' she continued, briskly drying her hands, 'you find Poppy, Simon, and we'll get going. Family solidarity, that's what's needed at these things, and then everybody's pleased.'

'Boring!' complained Poppy, as she climbed into the car next to Simon. 'Joey's not going. He said it would be boring.'

'Joey Bates is not the oracle, darling,' said Susan.

'The what?' said Poppy, though she had heard perfectly well.

'Don't argue, Poppy,' said Richard, accelerating down the avenue. Simon winced as his father swung too fast into the lane. 'And don't worry, old chap,' Richard added, looking at Simon in the driving mirror. 'I'm still quite safe at the wheel.'

The Standing family arrived at the church gates in seconds, and Simon once more wondered why they hadn't walked. Still, they were supposed to make some kind of an entrance, weren't they? But it would have been pleasant strolling down the damp, scented avenue. Ah well, things would change one day . . .

As he went through the lychgate behind the rest, he was conscious of a sudden lift of spirits, of the sun shining more warmly on the back of his neck. There was Octavia Jones. She looked very different from her tense appearances with her reluctant car. Shouting children surrounded her and Sandra, and her face was alight with laughter, her hair loose and falling forward as she bent over the dripping ducks. She was handing out hoops at five pence a go, and struggling to keep some semblance of order.

'Hello!' he said, over the heads of the shoving and pushing throng. 'Just for children? Or can anyone have a go?'

Octavia turned to him, her saleswoman smile at the ready. 'Here,' she said, handing him a fistful of hoops. 'Show us how they do it in Atlanta! Stand back, children. Let the dog see the rabbit.'

'They're ducks, not rabbits,' said Poppy Standing flatly, irritated at this warm reception from old Goody Jones for her brother. 'Go on, Simon, bet you don't get one.' But luck was with Simon, and he bagged three ducks, received the prizes of sweets and handed them out to admiring children.

'Not bad,' said Octavia, and as Simon crouched down to help her retrieve the hoops from the cold water, now full of grass and muddy stones, she caught a whiff of his aftershave. Expensive, she recognised, and took a deep breath. Might as well make the most of it, she thought, and grinned up at Sandra, who was watching with a caustic expression.

Simon straightened up, handed her the hoops, and said, 'See you, Octavia,' as his mother, missing nothing, called out to him across the churchyard.

'Wow!' said Sandra. 'Made a conquest there, Tavie.'

Octavia shook her head, and moved quickly to stop

the Jenkins terrier lifting his leg against the side of the paddling pool. She saw out of the corner of her eye that Simon had paused at Sarah Barnett's tombola stall, and heard the bright, schoolteacher voice teasing him about his lack of success.

'Fives or noughts,' yelled Sarah, as Simon moved off again, shaking his head and looking back at her with a smile. 'Try your luck, wonderful prizes,' shouted the firm tones, making it sound like an order.

'Yes, miss,' said Sandra, nudging Octavia and making her smile. 'Do what teacher says, Tavie, else she'll sting yer bum.'

'D'you reckon the lovely Sarah is first prize to the lucky winner?' Octavia said nastily, and returned to the ducks, only to see the Jenkins terrier making off with one, severely dented, in his wicked jaws.

# IO

'You are a wonder, Miss Beasley!' George Chalmer put down the heavy basket of empty plates and the cake-stand, ready for washing-up. He had been there at the fête, but had kept well in the background. Each day he sensed that Ivy Beasley was easier towards him, and he did not want to embarrass her by appearing too familiar, too proprietory in front of her friends.

Ivy, wary and suspicious, could not believe that there was so little to find fault with. Even that dreaded first breakfast had gone off without incident. There was something too intimate about breakfast, Ivy had considered in advance. I'll give it to him on his own, Mother, she had said to a silently disapproving presence. Then I'll go and make the beds while he's eating it. Make the beds! The thought of handling sheets from Mr Chalmer's bed, still warm from his manly body, had sent agonies of mixed feelings through Ivy's confused mind. No, she couldn't do that. He'd have to make his own bed. Huh! said her mother, at last breaking the silence. Some landlady you turn out to be!

George had come lightly down the stairs, waved Ivy into the chair opposite him and begged her to have a cup of tea while he ate his excellent bacon and eggs. 'Eating can be such a lonely business, don't you agree, Miss Beasley?' he had said. His smile was so warm, so friendly and unthreatening, that Ivy had poured herself a cup of good strong tea and sat down to keep him company.

When he had finished the last piece of toast and

home-made marmalade and complimented her on everything, he'd made for the stairs, saying he would never forget his mother's saying: 'A well-made bed means a well-made man.' Ivy had breathed freely again.

'Thank you, Mr Chalmer,' Ivy said now, stacking the dirty plates on the draining-board. 'I expect you'll be wanting to read the paper for a while. The parlour is quite warm still, with the sun out at last.'

She hoped he would go away and leave her to the dishes. Every conversation was a strain, with Ivy choosing her words carefully. I mustn't encourage him, she thought, squeezing washing-up liquid into the bowl. Encourage him in what, Ivy Dorothy? said her mother's voice drily, but Ivy had no answer to this.

'If you're sure?' said George. He knew that the kitchen was really a woman's province, and offers of help should be rationed with care. 'Besides,' he had said more than once to his friend in Leamington, 'start as you mean to go on, old thing. Mustn't ruin me hands doin' the dishes, must I?' His friend had smirked, and remarked that soft hands were not his cup of tea, anyway.

As Ivy stacked and dried and polished, she thought about George, and wondered nervously about next Wednesday. For the first time since George had moved in, it would be her turn to have Ellen and Doris to tea. Supposing he stayed around, looking hopeful? She'd noticed already that he loved his food, loomed about the kitchen when she was cooking, and had an especially sweet tooth. What would Ellen say, if George was sitting in her favourite chair when she arrived? And how could they possibly chew over the week's doings in the village with a man amongst them?

'Oh, dear Lord, what have I done?' Ivy said aloud, in real distress.

In the front room, with his feet up on Ellen's

footstool, George Chalmer settled back against the cushions and opened the newspaper. His eyelids drooped, and his last thought before drifting off was one of pleasurable anticipation of his supper.

Wednesday arrived, tea party day, and Ellen set off full of misgivings. She crossed the old stone bridge and from habit stopped to lean over and look down into the clear, swiftly flowing water. It was low, in spite of the recent rain, and bleached dry stones lined the bank. Ellen could see tiny fish darting about in the shadow of the bridge, where a deeper pool had been made with drifting branches left by Hugo Dodwell and Poppy Standing. Funny, that, thought Ellen, the way Poppy roams around the village with the other kids. Ellen knew Madam disapproved, but what Miss Poppy said was law up at the Hall.

'There you are, then, Doris,' said Ellen, hobbling up to Victoria Villa. 'All ready?'

'I saw you coming,' said Doris, 'so I waited.' She'd never done this before, and was conscious of a reluctance to press the bell button.

'Ah,' gasped Ellen, pausing to get her breath, 'it's that George Chalmer, i'n'it?' she said, knowing that Doris understood. 'T'ain't like usual, is it? S'posin' 'e answers the door?'

'Oh, I don't know,' said Doris, turning into Ivy's gate, 'I suppose he won't bite.' She sounded apprehensive, much the same as Ellen. It wasn't right, that man being in Victoria Villa. Everything had changed, and although Doris brought all her common sense to bear on the subject, she couldn't help feeling their stronghold had been breached. 'Anyway,' she added, gaining confidence, 'as if Ivy would let him in on our teas!'

But when they pressed the bell, saw the door open wide and a smiling George Chalmer bid them welcome, all their worst fears were confirmed.

# I I

Another fruitless day in London had hardened Simon's
tentative plan to stay in the country until the autumn,
and now, standing out on the terrace in a warm twilight,
a blackbird high on the stables clocktower rippling its
evening song over the park, he decided to break the
news to his parents.

'Always plenty to do on the farm' said Richard,
discovering that he was happy to have his son around for
a bit longer.

His mother was not so enthusiastic, though she tried
to conceal it. 'Uncle James might like an extra hand in
the business,' she said, revealing her trepidation at the
thought of coping with a dirty, exhausted farmworker
about the house. 'And you could see more of your
cousins. Alex is always inviting you over for tennis, and
you never go.'

'Can't stand her mother,' said Simon, and then
remembered the other thing he had to tell them. 'Funny
you should mention tennis,' he said, and told them of his
idea. 'The old court's not too bad,' he said quickly,
before they could disagree, 'and Bill could help me liven
it up. We could open the club to people in the village,
friends and relations, anyone who wants to join. It'd be
great fun, and something for locals to do. And me too,'
he added wrily, 'since the bright lights of Tresham don't
exactly beckon.'

'But there are already courts in the playing fields,' said
Richard, looking alarmed.

Susan began to speak, but choked, and Simon, not noticing, continued. 'Always crowded,' he said, 'and anyway, we'd have an age limit. Anybody over twenty-one, then the brats could use the village courts, and others could come up here for a civilised game.'

He turned, took both parents by the arm, and walked firmly back into the house. 'Wonderful, Mum,' he said, as if it had all been her idea, 'let's open a bottle and drink to the new Round Ringford tennis club, opening next week at the Hall, with kind permission of Mr and Mrs Richard Standing.'

With considerable hesitation, Richard poured the drinks and he and Susan tentatively raised their glasses. 'Well done, Simon,' Richard said slowly, and Susan echoed him, but her smile was strained.

'Do you really think, darling,' she said, 'that we should have just *anyone*? Could be dangerous, you know, with all kinds of people wandering about the place. Couldn't it perhaps be by invitation?'

Simon chuckled. 'Mum, really!' he said. 'This is Ringford, remember . . . No, no, let's loosen up and have some fun!'

'Morning, Octavia,' said Peggy Turner, smiling into the sun with squinting eyes. She had come out to investigate the yowling of cats in her tiny garden next to the shop, and found Gilbert and Ivy's Tiddles spitting at each other over a dead mouse, lying limp and cold on the path between them.

Octavia followed Peggy into the shop, and asked for vanilla ice-cream. 'We're too lazy to make pudding,' she said. 'It's hot today, isn't it? Mum's dozing in a deckchair saying she has no intention of moving.'

Peggy looked at Octavia, tall and slender, very brown, her long silky hair bleached even paler by the sun. Her light sundress floated loosely around her, and Peggy felt big, heavy and hot in comparison. Ah well, Octavia was in her prime, and she, Peggy, over the hill. Not that Bill thought that, she comforted herself, as he came up the steps and into the shop.

'Mornin', Tavie Jones,' he said, 'you're a sight for sore eyes this morning. Just what the working man needs on his return from slaving in the fields.'

'Tell us another,' Octavia said. 'And what's that message in the forked stick?'

Bill handed Peggy a rolled-up poster. 'Read it,' he said. 'It's Simon's latest brainwave.' He noticed Octavia's quickened expression, and grinned. Ah, he said to himself, thought as much.

'A tennis club!' said Peggy, holding up the poster. 'How lovely! Here Octavia, look at this . . . just the thing. What a good idea, Bill.'

'What's wrong with the village courts?' said Octavia flatly. 'Or are they too scruffy for Mr Simon from the Hall? I suppose membership of his club will be strictly screened by Madam?'

'Oh, no, Octavia,' said Peggy reprovingly. 'Not at all. It says here anyone over twenty-one will be welcome. A nominal subscription only. Can't say fairer than that, eh, Bill?' She looked across at him for support, willing him to encourage Octavia.

'Absolutely, gel,' said Bill. 'Whatever you say.'

Octavia said she would have to think about it. 'Depends who else is joining,' she said. 'Do you think our Sandra would be acceptable? Her being a Roberts, and living in the council houses?'

'Oh, Octavia,' said Peggy again. 'You know Simon's not like that. Now off you go and get that ice-cream home before it melts.'

'Did you see the notice, Sarah?' said Annie Bishop, sitting at the big kitchen table at Walnut Farm. The long school holidays dragged for Annie, with four children to entertain and her own independence curtailed. She couldn't go up to see her friends in London without mammoth family reorganisation, and so spent hours in Sarah's kitchen, watching her as she went about her tasks in the old house and yard.

Sarah didn't mind too much, but sometimes felt her few weeks of peace and quiet away from the schoolroom were slipping by fast. Now she finished washing eggs, and stood back to admire the rich brown shells, gleaming softly in sunlight coming through the window. She wiped her hands on a warm towel hanging over the Aga rail, and smiled at Annie. 'Go ahead,' she said, 'surprise me. No, I know . . . Luciano Pavarotti is giving a charity concert on the green in aid of church funds?' She poured another cup of coffee for Annie, and sat down.

'If only,' said Annie. 'Still, nearly as good. Simon Standing's organising a tennis club up at the Hall. Starting next week, informal and fun, it said on the poster. Anyone over twenty-one, and only a fiver to join. Shall we, Sarah? Go up there in our short shorts and give the young squire a treat?' Her mocking voice did not quite conceal a frisson of excitement.

'So he went ahead,' said Sarah, nodding agreement. 'Splendid. Be good exercise, anyway. Keep our hand in, huh?' The two of them laughed heartily, and informed John, barging in out of the sunlight, that, along with them, he'd just joined the Round Ringford tennis club.

'Why shouldn't you join, Mandy?' said Robert Bates. 'Do you good to get out of the house and away from the children for a bit. Mum'll be around, and then I can come too. I reckon we should support Simon when he's trying to get something going for the village.'

Mandy and Robert sat in the bungalow lounge, relaxed after a long day. Robert's workshop was successful and expanding, and he spent hours under a bonnet or invisible beneath all the cars in the village. Everyone came to Robert. He was so pleasant and obliging, and never overcharged. If ever he'd doubted his decision to leave his father's farm and start up his own business, he had no such qualms now.

'Poppy's furious,' said Joey, who'd been listening and watching television at the same time. 'She hates the idea.'

'No doubt,' said Mandy drily. 'Half the village playing and shouting outside her bedroom window. Not what she's used to at all.'

'The court's not that near the house,' said Joey. 'It's round by the kitchen garden, so she's not got much to grumble about.'

'Ah,' said Robert, 'but it's an invasion of privacy, Joe. Folks like the Standings aren't used to it. Still, shall we give it a go, Mandy?'

'Not sure,' said Mandy. 'Won't it be just their sort? The Bishops, and those Smyths from Waltonby, and *definitely* the Barnetts, if Sarah has anything to do with it!'

Robert looked annoyed. 'Don't be silly,' he said. 'John Barnett's a farmer, I was a farmer, you're a professional hairdresser, we've got our own business . . . blimey, what more do you need? And anyway,' he added, as an afterthought, 'I bet none of them are as good as you.'

'I haven't played for years,' said Mandy doubtfully.

'Soon come back,' he said, 'and I bet Annie snooty Bishop never coached kids like you did. Good God, woman,' he said, warming up with anger, 'you could play all of 'em off the court! Teach that lot a thing or two about tennis, that's for sure!'

Mandy smiled at him. 'Well, if you're sure,' she said. 'We could give it a try.'

'We'll need a secretary and treasurer,' said Simon, hindering Bill as he loaded sacks of fertiliser on to the long trailer. 'Got any ideas? How about Peggy?'

60

'Are you supposed to be helping, or what?' said Bill, heaving and grunting.

'Sorry,' said Simon, 'but I want to get it right. No good if it goes off half cock.'

'Quite right,' said Bill, 'but Peggy's much too busy. What about Andrew Bishop, or one of that lot? Up to their ears in computers and what have you. Should be a doddle for them.'

Simon shook his head. 'Too busy, away too much,' he said.

Bill thought for a moment. 'Ah, I've got it,' he said. 'That George Chalmer, him that's lodging with Ivy and goin' to live in Bridge Cottage. He was an accountant, he told me. Just the man: time on his hands, keen to help.' He climbed into the tractor seat and started the engine. 'There you are, Simon,' he yelled above the noise, 'problem solved. Ask him today.'

'Wonderful! Thanks, Bill,' Simon shouted. 'But who for secretary?'

Bill started off slowly, turning to call back to Simon. 'Try Octavia Jones,' he said with a grin. 'Nice girl. Just what you need . . .'

He disappeared in a cloud of powdery, dried earth, leaving Simon greatly cheered.

'Drat!' said Gabriella Jones, struggling out of the deck-chair and running into the house. She picked up the telephone and gasped into it, 'Hello? Who is it?'

The voice was pleasant, cool. 'Simon Standing here. Sorry to bother you, but I wonder if Octavia is at home?'

Gabriella frowned. 'No,' she said. 'Sorry, she's gone into Tresham. Work, you know. Some of us do.' There was a slight pause, when Gabriella briefly regretted her nasty tone. Poor chap, he'd done nothing wrong. 'Can I give her a message?' she added, distinctly more friendly.

'Thanks,' said Simon, sounding relieved. He explained about needing a secretary, that there wouldn't be much to do, and he wondered if Octavia would consider it. Especially if she was intending to join, he added.

'I'm sure she'd be delighted to help,' said Gabriella, overcompensating now. 'Greg and I will both be joining.'

It was not until after she'd put down the receiver that she remembered Octavia's words. Ask me first, Mum, Tavie had said. 'Oh dear,' groaned Gabriella, 'now I'm for it.'

# 12

Greg Jones sat in the small, rather chilly room he called his study, glad of its dark coolness on a hot day. He'd come home from a cricketing trip with a group of lads from Tresham Comprehensive, and found Gabriella biting her nails with worry. 'For goodness sake, Gabbie,' he'd said, 'if you're so bothered, I'll tell her.'

He liked to think he still had some fatherly influence over Octavia, but as he sat twiddling a pen between his fingers, he was not so sure. He'd noticed that she always seemed grateful for his advice, but seldom took it.

Gabbie would say it was time she was wed, but Greg put the thought to the back of his mind, like many a father before him. Octavia had had plenty of boyfriends, of course, but none had come up to Greg's high expectations for his only daughter. He was used to counselling youngsters and parents at school: it was his speciality. He'd come across over-fond fathers, but it wasn't like that with him and Tavie, for God's sake! He just couldn't quite erase that perky small girl who'd ridden on his shoulders across the fields . . .

'Hi! Where is everybody?' It was Octavia, and, thank God, she sounded in a good mood.

'Here, Tavie!' Greg called, through his open study door.

'Hi, Dad,' said Octavia, propping herself against the door post. 'Where's Mum?'

'In the garden,' said Greg firmly. 'But, er, just before you find her, can I have a word?'

Octavia raised her eyebrows. 'See me in the study at six o'clock . . . that sort of thing?'

Greg shifted uneasily in his chair. 'Don't be silly, Tavie,' he said. 'No, it's just that your mother's a bit nervous about—'

'Oh God,' said Octavia, 'what's she let me in for now? Teas at the horticultural show? Babysitting for the Dodwells?'

'No, no, something quite nice really,' said Greg, with too much enthusiasm. 'Seems they need a secretary for this new tennis club, and—'

'Oh no, not that,' said Octavia, backing out of the door. 'Not goings-on at the Hall . . . Where is she? This is the final straw!'

'Octavia,' said Greg, standing up. His voice was harsh. 'Your mother acted for the best. She is a very good, helpful person herself, and naturally expects her daughter to be the same. I shall not be pleased if you upset—'

But Octavia had gone, through the sitting-room and into the garden, where by the time she'd found her mother hiding amongst the runner beans, she had cooled down. 'Mum!' she said.

'Yes, dear?' said Gabriella in a choked voice.

'You've done it again, haven't you?'

'Yes, dear.'

Octavia took off her sandals and wiggled her toes in the short, thick grass by the vegetable beds. There was a pregnant silence, and then Octavia laughed. 'Oh, well,' she said, 'I was going to join, anyway. So I suppose it won't be too awful. Come on, let's go in and have tea.'

At her kitchen sink, Ivy Beasley was singing, an unusual event, signifying a great deal. Ivy sang only when she was relaxed and happy, and this wasn't often. George Chalmer, comfortable with cushions in the parlour, and unaware that the omens were so good, winced as Ivy slid from one note to another with a boisterous disregard for accuracy. He was quite glad when the whole cacophony was interrupted by the doorbell.

'Could you see who it is, Mr Chalmer!' shouted Ivy. 'My hands are wet.'

George stood up reluctantly, and went through to open the door.

It was Simon Standing. 'Sorry to bother you,' he said politely, 'but I wondered if you have a moment?'

'Me?' said George.

'Um, yes,' said Simon Standing. 'That is, if it is convenient . . . ?'

Ivy had heard and recognised Simon's voice, and came bustling through, wiping her hands on her apron. 'Come in, Mr Simon, please do,' she said, and pushed George ahead of her into the parlour. 'Please sit down,' she said. 'Would you like a cup of coffee?'

George was about to accept with alacrity, but Simon shook his head. 'Wouldn't say no to a glass of your best elderflower, though,' he said.

Ivy beamed, and George brightened. She reappeared minutes later with three glasses of sparkling, greeny-yellow wine. A sweet fragrance of the village in summer floated under Simon's nostrils, and he drank with his eyes closed.

'Good?' said Ivy.

'Perfect,' said Simon, and George nodded in agreement, glancing at the bottle and wondering if there'd be refills.

'Now,' said Simon, 'to the matter in hand.' He explained that he needed someone reliable, responsible and honest, to look after the club subscriptions and so on. They could do with a new net, he said, and it would be nice to smarten up the summerhouse for refreshments, that kind of thing.

Reliable, responsible and honest, thought George, and he swallowed hard. 'I am quite busy with the cottage, you know,' he said, hesitating. 'Mr Bates is leaving the supervision entirely to me.'

'Goodness, it's nearly finished,' said Ivy briskly. It was not her habit to say no to a Standing. 'I'll be there to help you, Mr Chalmer . . . not much work involved, is there, Mr Simon?'

Simon shook his head. Good old Ivy. He might have known he'd be on to a winner here. 'So how about it, Mr Chalmer?' he said. 'Can I count you in?'

George looked at Ivy and then back at Simon. 'Very well,' he said, his mind rapidly calculating pros and cons, 'I shall be delighted to help. Just let me know when I'm wanted.'

'Well done, Mr Chalmer,' said Ivy, when Simon had gone. She touched him lightly on the arm as she refilled his glass.

He smiled boyishly, and cleared his throat. 'A pleasure, I'm sure,' he said, 'and by the way, er, Ivy, it would be nice if you could see your way to calling me, er, George?'

Ivy, back in the kitchen, began to sing again, and this time it was an assault on even the most insensitive ear.

# 13

'It's so thick, Sandra!' said Mandy, lifting the wet, shining black hair and letting it fall like water through her fingers.

She set to work, her hands independent beings while she talked of the issue of the day. 'Robert says we should join this new tennis thing,' she said, 'but I'm not so sure. Might not feel too comfortable up at the Hall. What do you think, Sandra? You going up?'

Sandra laughed, a nice, straightforward laugh. 'Don't be daft,' she said. 'Can you see me and Sam larking about on the court with the likes of Alex Smyth? Outdoor ping-pong, Sam calls it, anyway. No, I'd never get him further than Ellen's Lodge!'

Mandy stood back and looked hard at her handiwork. 'It's going to be really good,' she said, brushing away loose hair from Sandra's neck. 'Your Sam won't be able to keep his hands to himself!'

Sandra grinned comfortably. 'Ah,' she said, 'then that'll be worth the effort, won't it?'

'Anyway,' said Mandy, moving round to get a side view of Sandra's head, 'I've said we'll go up for the first session, see what it's like. And if Annie Bishop comes her superior bit, I shan't go again.'

As Sandra watched chunks of her hair falling to the floor, she thought about Octavia, wondered if she would overcome her disapproval of the rich and idle and play tennis up at the Hall. Bet she gets asked, thought Sandra. Simon'll see to that. Lately, when Octavia had called in for coffee and a chat, Sandra had noticed his name cropped up once or twice. But then, she'd told herself, his return had been a big event in the village, his name on everyone's lips. No, Octavia was tough, always had been, and she'd see straight through Simon Standing.

'Now,' said Mandy, 'I'll just brush it into shape, and then we can relax for a couple of minutes. I wanted to show you this bit in the magazine about teenage problems . . . might help with your Alison . . .'

Sandra reflected that when she'd been a teenager, her chief problem was how to avoid her violent father's flailing fists, but she smiled kindly at Mandy, and said it was very nice of her to think of it.

This boring meeting is deadlier than usual, thought Octavia, watching a fly crashing against the dusty windowpane in her boss's office. It was hot and stuffy, and the room smelt of sweating bodies. Some of her colleagues loved meetings, enjoyed the sound of their own voices trotting out the usual jargon.

Octavia knew she should listen, gain by the experience of others who'd been in the job longer than herself, but she couldn't wait to get away, out on the road. Not that she always found magic solutions. She almost never found any kind of lasting solution. Patching up, that's what we're good at, she had concluded miserably, as time after time an apparent success reverted to the same old problem. Husbands went back to beating up their wives, single mothers failed to bring up their children, lonely old ladies were found dead in their beds, unvisited and starving.

'What do you think, Octavia?' said Harry. A medium-sized, medium-brained man, he'd spotted his opportunity. Octavia Jones always made him feel uncomfortable, with her vaguely superior air. He knew she hadn't been listening, and waited for her to wriggle out of this one.

'Well,' said Octavia, sighing, as if she'd seen it all before, 'you could look at it both ways.' She glanced at her watch and added, suddenly brisk, 'Heavens! Got an appointment in Waltonby in twenty minutes.' She gathered her papers together, saying, 'Perhaps you'd excuse me. Sorry, everyone.' With a quick smile, she left the room.

Edging slowly through the traffic in the market place, she saw a bent, shuffling figure she instantly recognised. Ellen Biggs. Octavia slowed down and leaned out of her window. 'Mrs Biggs!' she shouted. 'Do you want a lift back to Ringford?'

The old woman turned, grinned, and nodded vigorously. She pushed her way through the crowd, taking no notice of angry blasts from behind. She cackled happily. 'Let 'em wait, dear,' she said. 'All in too much of an 'urry these days.' She settled herself and her shopping bags and prepared to enjoy the trip. 'Bin at work, Octavyer?' she said.

'I'm still at work, strictly,' said Octavia. 'Off to see somebody in Waltonby.'

' 'oo's that, then?' said Ellen casually, but Octavia was not that easily caught.

'Confidential, as you very well know, Mrs Biggs!' she said, smiling sideways at the old woman. Tell Ellen Biggs, and you've told the whole village.

Ellen changed tack. 'Wot about this new tennis club thing?' she said. 'Expect you'll join, won'cha, dear?'

Here we go, thought Octavia, and nodded. 'Probably,' she said. 'Mum and Dad are going, and I've sort of agreed to be secretary.' Which is a mistake, she added to herself.

Ellen beamed. 'That'll be nice,' she said. 'Young Simon's a good-lookin' boy, ain't 'e?'

Not very subtle, Ellen, thought Octavia, but she was fond of the old woman, and patted her gnarled, spotty hand. 'Now, now,' she said, 'no matchmaking, Mrs Biggs.'

They arrived outside Ellen's Lodge, and Octavia helped her up the path, carrying her heavy shopping bags. 'I could organise someone to help you with this,' she said, 'a volunteer, you know . . .'

Ellen shook her head. 'I can manage,' she said. 'Even though I'm a bit of a poor ole thing these days. Still,' she added, grinning again at Octavia as she turned at the gate, 'play yer cards right with you-know-who, dear, and you could 'ave a chauffer yerself!'

Speechless, Octavia shook her head, climbed back into her car, and drove off with an irritated burst of speed.

# 14

The first meeting of the Round Ringford Lawn Tennis Club, in bright sunshine on a warm afternoon, had a gratifyingly large attendance. Simon Standing, greeting everyone with some surprise at the numbers, realised one court wouldn't be enough.

'We'll have to think about that, if this lot come regularly,' he said quietly to his father, who had emerged from the drawing-room windows.

'Tiddlywinks, to pass the time?' said his father flippantly, and added, 'Don't expect me to play. I'll just come along to say hello.'

And spy out the local talent, thought Simon, following his father's gaze. Sarah Barnett and Annie Bishop were like night and day, one dark and olive skinned, the other fair and golden. Mr and Mrs Jones were there, he noted with satisfaction, but not Octavia yet, though they'd said she'd be coming.

Voices were heard around the corner of the house, and a small cheer went up as Robert and Mandy Bates walked up, embarrassed in their resurrected tennis clothes, with Mandy looking distinctly apprehensive.

'Right!' said Simon. 'Welcome, everyone. Dad's come to toss the coin, so who's first to christen the court?'

Annie Bishop stepped forward.

'Of course, *she* would,' muttered Mandy to Robert.

'We don't mind starting, do we, Andrew?' Annie said, and winked at Sarah. 'Perhaps you and John—?'

Simon had noticed the wink. 'I'm sure Robert and Mandy would like to make up the four?' he interrupted firmly.

Smoothly done, thought Sarah Barnett. She went to sit with John on the grassy slope behind the court, and the others followed, stretching out and gossiping idly.

Croquet, Simon said to himself. We could get the croquet lawn going again, and then those waiting wouldn't get bored. Must see Bill about it. And ask Mum, of course, he remembered with a small qualm.

Ah, Octavia, walking with her loping stride across to the court. Longest legs in Ringford, thought Simon happily, and went forward to meet her. 'Really pleased you could make it,' he said, and took her over to sit in a canvas chair by the court. He and Bill had raided the attics and found dozens of old garden chairs in various stages of decay. They'd tacked on new canvas, mended shaky legs and brushed off years of dust and cobwebs.

'Oh, good shot!' said Simon, as Annie Bishop leapt into the air and smashed a ball right to the service line.

'Looks like she's played before,' said Octavia, unzipping her racquet. 'Still, Mandy's got a look in her eye . . . oh, good one!'

'Hey,' said Simon, surprised, 'that was terrific! Tell me about Mandy Bates and tennis.'

'She was brilliant at school, so Robert says.' Octavia flicked her hair back over her shoulder. He'd no doubt be asking her about Sarah Barnett and teaching next. Mugging up on the locals. 'Mandy was a coach, did all the training,' she added. 'But when she married Robert and had the children, she gave it up completely. Oh Lord, look at that! She's not forgotten how to play!'

Mandy had sent a cross-court forehand at speed, and Annie Bishop lunged after it with a shout. Missing it completely, she slithered along the grass and ended up in an ungainly heap. A deep chuckle reached her ears, and she glared at Richard, watching from the terrace.

Scrambling to her feet, she looked across at Mandy. 'Great shot, Mandy,' she said. 'Must be the job gives you strong wrists . . . hairdresser's advantage, we shall call it.'

Octavia, watching closely, saw Mandy's face fall, and then to her surprise Simon called out, 'Wonderful, Mandy! Just appointed you tennis club coach . . . and Annie's your first pupil!' He laughed and smiled charmingly at a scowling Annie. On the sidelines he saw Sarah Barnett giving him the thumbs-up sign, her grin wicked and conspiratorial.

'So,' he said to Octavia, putting his warm hand lightly on her arm. 'Now we know where we are, for the moment, anyway. Still, it's a good idea about Mandy, isn't it? Could encourage us all to take it a bit seriously. You know, improve our game, keep up standards. Thanks, Octavia.'

She answered that Mandy was pretty busy, but was a nice person, and would be sure to find time for anyone who needed help . . . such as Annie Bishop.

They both laughed together, and Greg Jones, glancing across at his daughter, shifted in his seat uneasily. He and Gabriella had begun to feel rather elderly in the company of younger players, but now it was their turn on court, and it was different. Greg was mustard. In compensation for being deaf and the butt of unkind jokes, he had excelled at school in all games, and tennis was his favourite. A row of silver cups in the cabinet at home stood silent witness to the swift progress he had made to Junior County Champion.

'Yours, Gabbie!' he shouted, as Sarah Barnett struck a wild shot into the edge of the tramlines.

A puff of white proved it in, and John Barnett cheered. 'Good girl!' he yelled. 'At least we got one point!' What John lacked in skill, he made up for in good humour.

Sarah glanced quickly to see if Simon was looking, and was irritated to see that he was still talking to Octavia

Jones. There were few other points for the Barnetts, and Greg and Gabriella were soon walking off court, modest victors.

'Brilliant, folks,' said Octavia.

Simon asked if she was as good as that. When she shook her head, he took her arm and said, 'Come on, let's you and me challenge the Bishops.'

Oh God, thought Octavia, it's all very jolly hockey sticks. Not sure I can take all this bonhomie. Where's Poppy, she wondered. She can usually be guaranteed to stir things up a bit.

She got her answer three games later. Simon was just poised to smash a lob from Andrew Bishop, when a high window opened in the long façade of the Hall, and Poppy leaned out. 'Si–mon!' she shouted. 'Tel–e–phone!'

'Bloody hell!' swore Simon, missing the ball completely. Ah, thought Octavia, now things are improving. 'Who is it?' he yelled.

'From America . . . that girl again.' Poppy's voice was very loud and clear.

Simon glanced quickly across at Octavia, who looked blandly back at him. 'So sorry,' he called to the Bishops, and ran off into the house.

He returned frowning, and played so badly that even Octavia's best efforts couldn't retrieve the match. 'Never mind,' she said, smiling at him, 'half an hour with Mandy will put you right.' She pulled on a cardigan and looked round for her parents.

'They've gone, Tavie,' said Robert. 'Your mum said she'd go ahead and get the kettle on.'

A heavy cloud now hung over Bagley Woods, and a few large spots of rain began to fall. 'What a shame,' said Mandy, packing away her racquet. 'It was such a lovely afternoon. Still, we got quite a few games in.'

'And there's always tomorrow, isn't there, Simon?' said Sarah Barnett, bending down to pick up her sweater. Simon had a glimpse of brown thighs and a very neat little bottom.

'Absolutely,' he said, glancing quickly at John. 'And thanks, everyone, for coming. Looks like we'll all want to go ahead?' An enthusiastic response warmed him. He'd need to have a session with Octavia and George Chalmer to get the paperwork organised, now things looked so promising.

'Could we have a get-together, do you think?' he said, as he walked with Octavia across the lawns and into the avenue. 'With George, too, of course,' he added hastily, as she looked at him sharply. Blimey, anybody'd think he'd got fangs. 'Just to go over what will be needed,' he added. 'Shouldn't take long. When are you free?'

'Can't remember,' said Octavia. 'I'll look in my diary and give George a ring, then we can fix a time, okay?'

'Fine,' said Simon, slowing down. 'Well, cheerio, then, see you soon.' He watched her stride off under the chestnuts, her single fair plait swinging from side to side, and felt oddly cheated. She didn't look back.

'Thanks a lot, Simon,' said Sarah Barnett, marching firmly along after John. 'It was great. Oops!' she added, dropping her racquet right in front of Simon's feet. John was striding on ahead. There was milking to do, and he'd already stayed longer than intended. Simon retrieved the racquet and handed it to her. Her hand brushed his, lingered. 'Thanks again.' Her eyes were warm, and she said quietly, 'Looks like we're on to something good here.'

Now just what does she mean by that? thought Simon, picking up signals. His spirits lifted again. 'Went well, didn't it?' he said. 'Nice to see you, Sarah. So glad you could come . . .'

'Time for a cuppa?' said Annie to Sarah, as they walked away together. 'I have to go and reclaim the children from Mother shortly, but there's half an hour or so yet.'

The old vicarage was quiet, dark now in the rainstorm that had moved over the village. A fresh, newly wet smell of flowers and crushed grass floated into the warm kitchen on the rising wind. Annie brought the kettle quickly to the boil, and reached for a tin of biscuits.

'No, thanks,' said Sarah. 'Got to keep an eye on the inches, you know. Specially now we're stripping off for tennis every week . . .' She smiled slyly at her friend, who rattled spoons, crockery, the lid of the biscuit tin.

'What d'you think, then?' said Annie, setting down two steaming mugs of tea on the table. She felt tired, and her legs ached from unaccustomed exercise. She looked at Sarah, and was faintly irritated that she looked so refreshed and full of vigour. She was uneasy, too. There was something determined, ruthless even, about Sarah Barnett. Their innocent, time-wasting fantasies over cups of coffee were all very well, but Annie had the feeling that some devious plan was unfurling in Sarah's mind, and that she was being left behind.

'We made a good start,' said Sarah. 'Promising, I reckon. Definitely promising . . .' She grinned at Annie, who flushed as the scalding tea went down her throat.

# 15

With Bridge Cottage almost ready for George to move in, Ivy woke every morning with a feeling of impending doom. This apprehension of change, and change for the worse, had come to a head when George dropped his bombshell. He had been lingering over his second helping of treacle sponge pudding, and blurted out, 'Bridge Cottage is nearly finished, Ivy. I can move in next week, they say.'

Ivy had stood up, pushed her chair back so violently that it tipped over, and grated out, 'Sorry, something stuck in my throat.' She'd run out of the room, and it had been five minutes before she had pulled herself together and rejoined a confused-looking George. He'd known it was time for him to go, for his plan to move forward, but Ivy's stricken look had grabbed at his heart. He'd nearly followed her with a soothing hand and words of comfort.

Now, on a windy morning with white clouds scudding across a bright blue sky, Ivy pegged out a pair of roomy underpants on her maidenly washing line and pondered her situation. It'll be lonely again if he goes . . . I've got used to him, Mother, she said. Told you so, said the acid voice, unsympathetic as always. Ivy didn't mind for once – she wanted her parent's hard replies to bring her to her senses – but then old Mrs Beasley went too far. It's no good your saying *if* he goes, because naturally he's going. Bridge Cottage is what he came to Ringford for. Probably heave a sigh of relief, anyway, to get a bit of peace and quiet.

This last cruelty was too much for Ivy. Her mother had once more disregarded the bounds of feeling. Ivy raised the prop and line to catch the wind. 'Shut up, shut up, shut up!' she yelled to her empty garden.

Peggy Turner, pulling up weeds on the other side of the fence, straightened up in alarm. She went to the knot-hole and peered through. All she could see was Ivy, grey hair blowing wildly, with a face as red as a cherry, shaking her fists at the sky.

'Morning, Poppy,' said Peggy, summoned to the shop by the jangling bell. 'What can I get for you?' she added kindly. A shopkeeper has to have a ready smile for all, and Peggy was very good at it.

'Here's a list,' said Poppy, handing over a crumpled piece of paper. 'And Mum says, can you put it on the book? Oh, and can Bill bring it up this afternoon?'

'Wouldn't you like to take the shopping with you?' said Peggy. 'I'll put the things in a carrier, and you can manage it on your bike.' Give her something useful to do, she thought, instead of snooping round the village.

Poppy shook her head. 'No, thanks,' she said. 'And by the way, Mrs Turner, what's up with old George? Saw him standing outside Bridge Cottage looking like thunder.' Peggy was reaching for the top shelf and didn't answer. 'P'raps he's wishing he'd never taken on being treasurer for Simon's boring old tennis club,' Poppy sniggered. Peggy couldn't bring herself to answer, and Poppy wandered round the shop, idly prodding packages and licking her fingers. 'Or maybe old Ivy's given him the boot . . . what d'you think, Mrs Turner?'

Peggy's palm itched, but she gritted her teeth and said as far as she knew there was nothing wrong. The cottage must be ready now, she said, and no doubt Miss Beasley would be helping Mr Chalmer to move in. Poppy shrugged and departed, pointedly leaving the shopping on the counter.

George Chalmer walked slowly back to Victoria Villa, politely doffing his straw hat to an unresponsive Poppy as she pedalled by. No Ivy around, so he went through to the back garden and wandered about, deep in thought. He walked down the weedless path, not seeing the regimented rows of beans, peas and lettuces, currants like bright beads, red and black, and carefully tied-in new growth of raspberries and loganberries.

George was thinking hard. His imminent departure seemed to have turned Ivy against him instead of spurring her on to persuade him to stay, and this would definitely not do. She was polite, still cooked wonderful meals, but the considerable inroads he'd made into her private thoughts had been firmly blocked off.

It's not that I'm particularly worried, he'd said to his friend in Leamington. But the last thing I want is an Ivy Beasley who can manage perfectly well without me. His friend had reminded him he'd worked wonders with more difficult gals than Ivy Beasley. Not much more difficult! In fact, now he could think of nobody more tricky than Ivy when she put up the barricades. It was like approaching a tightly rolled hedgehog. Or a spiny ant-eater.

He'd reached the bottom of the garden and leaned on the fence, grooved and dented where grazing horses had nibbled away the long summer days. He took off his hat, mopped his sweaty forehead, and looked over the paddock. A couple of horses were grooming each other over the far side, and a tall figure was fixing the water-trough. Young farmer Barnett, thought George, if I'm not mistaken. He had made it his business to get to know most of the people of Round Ringford.

'Morning, Mr Barnett,' he called.

John Barnett heard, and altered course for where

79

George stood. 'All ready for moving down to Bridge Cottage?' he said. 'Looks very nice now. Even Ted has to agree!'

Replying with details of delay and frustration, but remembering that everyone was related round here, George said that overall he was very pleased with the results. 'Mind you,' he said, 'I shall miss Miss Beasley's home cooking!'

'Reckon she'll miss the company,' said John, smiling.

'Well, I'm not so sure about that, Mr Barnett,' said George. He looked back at Victoria Villa, and could see Ivy moving about in the back bedroom, cleaning windows. 'I think perhaps the time has come for her to have her house to herself again. These ladies, you know, are a law unto themselves!' He gave John a brave smile.

'Ah, don't you believe it,' said John. 'They don't always mean what they say, nor what they lead you to think.' For a second, he remembered the look on Sarah's face as she talked to Simon Standing on the tennis court, and hoped he was right. He quickly shrugged off this thought, and continued, 'I reckon our Ivy'd happily keep you on as lodger indefinitely. Looks years younger these days, everybody's noticed it.'

It was true. Ivy had taken to putting curlers in at nights. She'd found her mother's old powder compact and dabbed at her face, finishing off with a touch of hardened, blood-red lipstick. She was pleased with the result, studying herself in the mirror, this way and that. Ellen Biggs had said a few caustic words, but Ivy didn't care. Instead of the usual grey and brown, she'd selected pinks and blues from her wardrobe, and liked the look of herself a great deal better.

'It's probably the thought of you leaving has made her a bit mardy,' went on John Barnett. 'Take my word for it, she'll come round, Mr Chalmer!'

George wandered down the path, and pondered. He thought back to when he'd arrived in the village, and had nearly whooped with joy on meeting Miss Ivy Beasley. Perfect, he'd thought. A doddle, he'd said to his friend. But that seemed years ago. Now he'd been privy to some of Ivy's most painful memories, and was becoming uncomfortably aware that she trusted him. Probably young Barnett was right: it was anticipating the parting that had made Ivy clam up again. But she'd soon soften up. He bent down to pick up Tiddles, and realised that he'd become quite fond of the little cat. He laughed ruefully. Seems I've taken on one tricky woman and a cat, he said to himself.

If the atmosphere in Victoria Villa had cooled, things were just as prickly down at the Lodge. It was Ellen's turn, and Doris and Ivy sat uneasily in their seats. Ellen had grumbled that her arthritis was bad, Doris worried about her, and Ivy's gloomy thoughts centred on Bridge Cottage and George.

'So, you'll be back on yer own soon, Ivy,' said Ellen, deliberately tactless. 'Them builders say they're more or less finished. And about time too, I said to 'em.'

'What business is it of yours?' said Ivy acidly. 'And as for being on my own, you know perfectly well I have lived alone for a great many years and managed very well. No doubt I shall do so again.' She sniffed.

'Got a cold, Ivy?' said Ellen. ' 'ere, 'ave one o' these lozenges. Very good they are, for sniffs and sneezes.'

Ivy waved away the paper bag, and turned to another topic. 'Them notices for the show are ripped off again,' she said to Doris. 'Disgraceful, I call it. I shall put up some more, and woe betide any of those kids if they lay a finger on them.'

Doris, aware that the subject had been firmly changed, fell in with Ivy's intentions and said she'd be happy to help.

Ellen Biggs, bored with all this, shifted in her seat and butted in. ' 'ave yer seen our Octavyer lately?' she said. If they couldn't talk about George, then Octavia and the tennis club were the next best thing.

'Saw her on Saturday, looking very nice indeed in her shorts,' said Doris, relieved that the conversation was taking an easier turn.

'Just wish I was a few years younger,' said Ellen. 'I'd join meself. Then I'd make eyes at young Simon, and 'e'd turn on the charm and sweep me orf me feet!'

'Ellen Biggs!' said Ivy, and put her cup down in the saucer with a clatter. 'What nonsense! You're going soft in the head. Don't you agree, Doris?'

Ellen was unmoved, and her eyes were misty. 'D'yer reckon I'm too old to be swep' off me feet?' she said dreamily. 'And what about you, Ivy, 'ave you ever bin tempted?'

Doris interrupted, in a last ditch attempt to save the day. 'Time for a refill,' she said, but Ellen was not to be deflected.

'Take that George Chalmer,' she said to Ivy. 'Now, 'e's unattached. Nice man, on the 'ole. Private means, Ivy? 'e don't seem to do no work, anyway. Now, 'e's goin' to want companionship, ain't 'e? 'as 'e mentioned it t'yer, Ivy? Asked yer to look out for somebody suitable? You could put in a good word fer me, should it come up!' She cackled, wickedly pleased at the expression on Ivy's face. 'Somethin' wrong, our Ivy? I reckon you must be gettin' that cold. Now, Doris,' she said, 'where did I put them lozenges?'

# 16

'It's very nice of you to come at tea-time, Mandy,' said Octavia. They were in Barnstones' kitchen, with Gabriella getting in the way, until Octavia suggested her mother might watch television and any interesting gossip could be relayed to her later. Gabriella had looked hurt, but disappeared.

'No, it's all right, Tavie,' said Mandy. 'Only takes a few minutes to tidy it up. Sure you wouldn't like me to put a few rollers in, give it a bit of body?'

Octavia shook her head, smiling. 'Sorry, Mandy,' she said, 'not much profit in me, is there? No, that's lovely, really. It's so difficult getting to a hairdresser in Bagley, and anyway, you're much better at it.'

Mandy beamed. She itched to do something a bit more creative with Octavia's long, fine hair, but knew her too well to persist. 'Nearly done,' she said. 'Mind you, I'm in no hurry tonight. Robert's home, and the kids are down at the farm with Olive. Margie's hitting a tennis ball at the barn wall, practising her backhand! Seems the club has given her ideas. Still, I think it's a good thing to have an age limit, don't you? It all went very well, didn't it?'

Octavia looked beyond her dad's shaving mirror and out of the window. She could see the willows swaying in the light breeze, already a yellowy green, and beyond them the Hall. Before she could stop herself, she wondered what Simon was doing. 'Seemed okay,' she said, 'but it's early days. I've got a meeting up there with George and Simon later.'

'Simon's lovely, isn't he?' said Mandy, watching Octavia's face closely. She'd been grateful to him for turning around Annie Bishop's snub, and had read enough romantic novels to expect something to develop from the advent of a handsome young heir up at the Hall.

Octavia smiled affectionately. 'You're incorrigible,' she said. 'If you want to know what I think of Simon Standing, the answer is very little. Too much work, too many of other people's problems, too much common sense to be taken in by charm that's turned on and off like a tap.' Unfair, she said to herself. I've never actually seen Simon turn it off.

Mandy brushed Octavia's hair until it shone, gently turning under the level ends with her cupped hand. 'Sure you're right,' she said, but her grin was knowing. 'Still, there's one or two in this village, mentioning no names, who'd not say no to a spot of fun and games extra to the tennis! There you are, then,' she added, holding up the hand mirror, 'and now I shall say no more, in case I get accused of gossiping!'

They were both laughing when Gabriella came in to say surely it was time for a cup of coffee and what on earth was so funny?

It was almost dark under the thick foliage of the chestnuts. The park beyond was still half light at eight o'clock, but Octavia felt the chill of twilight under the trees. She shivered, pulling her cotton jacket round her. 'Feels autumnal already,' she said to George, who was stepping out beside her, finding it difficult to keep up with her long stride.

Yes, thought George, and high time I was about my business. Bridge Cottage awaited him, and next Friday was moving day. 'Certainly a nip in the air,' he said, smiling up at Octavia, 'but I shall be very cosy in my little cottage, come the winter.'

They were approaching the Hall, and Octavia looked sideways at George. 'Tradesmen's entrance, Mr Chalmer?' she said, lifting her eyebrows.

'Oh, my dear, do you think so?' said George, looking uncertain. He found it hard to know what to make of Octavia Jones, was never quite certain when she was joking.

When they approached the main entrance, however, the decision was made for them. At the portico'd front door, Susan Standing stood waiting, her small yapping Yorkie in her arms.

'Good evening!' she said, with a smile. 'Mr Chalmer, isn't it? And Octavia, do come in. Simon is waiting for you in Mr Richard's study.'

Octavia followed Susan into the cool hall, with its curving staircase and huge jugs of flowers.

'George! Don't do that!' said Susan suddenly, and George Chalmer started guiltily. But Susan was talking to her Yorkshire terrier.

'Hello!' called Simon, coming swiftly through from the study. 'Very nice to see you, Octavia, and Mr Chalmer, too. Come along through.'

The business of the meeting took very little time. There was a respectable sum in the kitty, swelled by a generous donation from Mr Richard, who had had a very happy Saturday afternoon sitting at the window watching half-clad girls leaping about his tennis court. 'We'll perhaps do a spot of fundraising,' said Simon, 'and who knows, maybe afford a second court in due course.'

'But won't you be off to London soon?' said Octavia, practical as ever. 'Who's going to take charge then?'

'Ah,' said Simon, 'well, I shall be around for a while yet, and then we'll see. Depends, really, on how popular the club is. If it's a nine-day wonder, then okay, no harm done. Otherwise, well, we can see how it develops.'

You had to hand it to him, thought George, he's done

a good job here. Thought it all through. 'Just a couple of suggestions,' he said, 'if I might.' He pointed out one or two ways of making the records simpler, and said it would be child's play compared with some of the accounts he'd handled.

'Where was your office based?' Simon asked, but George hedged.

'Moved about a bit,' he said, and thought how his friend would laugh at that. 'But retirement suits me very well. This little job will be like a hobby.'

'What d'you want me to do, then?' said Octavia, looking at her watch. She was starving, and the biscuits at the Hall were disgusting. Aside from the cup of coffee with Mandy, she'd had nothing, and her mother had rightly said she'd be better eating a sandwich than wasting time in the shower. Now she could feel her stomach rumbling, and shifted in her seat. 'Is there much to it?' she asked.

Simon came round the side of his father's big desk, and leaned over her shoulder. That aftershave again, Octavia noted. 'This is the membership list,' he said, pointing to a small column of names. She knew most of them, saw that Alex Smyth had been added, and four or five unfamiliar names.

'Do you have addresses for these, Simon?' she asked.

He fumbled around under the desk and came up with the local telephone directory. 'Here,' he said, 'let's get them out of here. I know them all, old friends mostly, but we'd better make sure.'

'Um,' said George Chalmer mildly. Simon looked up enquiringly. 'Um, if you don't need me any more, Mr Standing, I would quite like to be getting along. I told Ivy I wouldn't be late. She likes to lock up as soon as the light goes, you know.'

'Right!' said Simon readily, perhaps a little too readily. 'Shan't be a minute, Octavia. I'll see Mr Chalmer out.'

So, thought Octavia. Now we'll be a cosy twosome in

Daddy's study. She began to rifle through the directory, looking for missing addresses.

'Very nice of him,' said Simon, returning to the study and shutting the door behind him. 'Always the most difficult job to fill. Nobody wants the responsibility of handling money.'

'Mm,' said Octavia, a pen held between her teeth.

'Found them?' said Simon, casually leaning over and running his finger down the list of Manninghams. 'That's it, that's old Tiger. E.J. Married now and lives at Fletcham.'

'Fine,' said Octavia, writing quickly.

For a second, Simon rested his hand on her shoulder, and then he went away to sit in his father's chair. He said nothing as she finished the list, then leaned back, smiling at her.

'Anything more?' said Octavia. 'I'll get a file, in case we have any letters. Didn't you say we needed a new net? I could do some research on that if you like.'

'Splendid,' said Simon, but his mind was not on files or nets, or anything to do with tennis, come to that.

'That all, then?' said Octavia, who knew the signs only too well.

'For the moment, thanks. Unless you can think of a reason for keeping you here a while longer,' said Simon, still smiling and looking speculatively at her.

'Get stuffed,' said Octavia, and stood up. She collected her bag, the few papers she needed, and made for the door.

Simon jumped up and followed her. 'I'll walk you down the avenue,' he said. 'You couldn't possibly object to that.'

'If you must,' said Octavia, and set off at her usual spanking pace.

# 17

'Hello?' said Annie breathlessly. She'd heard the telephone and run in from the front gate, where she had been fixing yet another horticultural show poster. 'Oh, it's you, Sarah. Just thinking about you. Wondering what we should enter for the show. How's things?'

Sarah said all was fine, she'd just given John a huge breakfast and he'd disappeared for the day. 'Cattle market in Tresham,' she said.

'What fun,' said Annie, and they both laughed.

'Haven't got much time for entries,' said Sarah, 'but I expect we'll go to the knees-up.' There was always a barn dance in the marquee the night before the show.

'Yep, I suppose so,' said Annie. 'I've promised to help behind the bar for an hour or so.'

'Me too,' said Sarah. 'Well, see you there. What are you wearing? I thought something low-cut and tempting, so I can lean over the bar and stun the farmers. What do you think . . . a treat for the young squire? Bound to be there, Annie . . .'

'I hadn't forgotten,' said Annie, with a small frown. 'See you soon, then. Pop down for a coffee, if you're free. 'Bye.' Well, it would all be a bit of fun, nothing to brood about. Sarah's a sensible person, and I'm the last person to go all moral . . .

'Octavia,' said Gabriella.

'Yes, Mum?' Octavia was reading the local paper, her long legs up on the sofa, a packet of crisps in hand. She'd seen the advertisement for the horticultural show, and knew from the tone of her mother's voice what was coming.

'Will you be free on show day, dear?'

Octavia sighed. 'What have you planned for me this time?' she said, licking salt off her lips.

'As it happens,' said Gabriella, offended, 'nothing at all . . . as yet. But Doreen Price did ask if you could help in the WI refreshment tent for an hour or so.'

'Suppose so,' said Octavia. 'Sure there's nothing for me to do at the dance? No raffle tickets to sell, no glasses of sherry at the door?'

'Don't be horrid, Tavie,' said her mother. 'No, you can just go and enjoy yourself.'

'Mum,' said Octavia, and her mother looked up hopefully. 'What do you think of a tennis tournament alongside the show, a sort of extra attraction?'

'Great idea!' said Gabriella, 'Talk to Simon about it . . . I'm sure he'd be delighted.'

'I'm sure he would,' said Octavia.

The harvest was nearly finished, and the fields of stubble shone, metallic in the evening sun. Simon Standing and his new puppy, a bouncy spaniel, walked along the edge of the wood, happy in each other's company and relieved to be away from Susan's constant carping about the coming show. And Poppy, more jealous than ever of Simon, lost no opportunity to make mischief.

'Here, boy!' he shouted, veering off through the wood. The trees were thinly spaced here, and mounds of brambles were thick with blackberries, some already ripe and others not ready, still green. Wicked deadly nightshade climbed among them, with its inviting currant-shaped berries, such a luscious red, and so evilly poisonous.

The puppy followed him, tearing through the under-growth and yelping when brambles caught his soft paws.

89

'Come on, baby,' said Simon, and picked him up. The puppy nuzzled into his chest and settled happily.

Through the trees, Simon could see the place he'd loved as a boy. It was a small, clear pond, surrounded by bracken and fed by a bubbling spring higher up the wood. He sat down on a bed of last year's dry ferns, and let the puppy wander off to the other side of the pool. It was very quiet, so quiet that when a startled moorhen squawked suddenly, Simon discovered he'd dozed off, and was now jerked awake.

'Basil!' he called, and the puppy appeared from a thicket of blackthorn. 'Time to go,' he said, and they set off again across the field. Between the cut stalks a new crop of wild flowers had appeared, vigorous, ruby pink and topaz yellow, tiny gems. No more stubble burning, thank God, thought Simon. He walked on, planting his feet down squarely, feeling the satisfying crunch beneath his shoes, and realised it was what he had done as a child.

'Haven't changed all that much,' he said thoughtfully, though his listener had now bounded out of earshot. He raised his voice. 'It's home, Basil, and that's what counts!' The little dog stopped, turned to look at Simon enquiringly, a downy ear pricked, one paw lifted up pathetically.

'Oh, all right,' said Simon. 'Come here, I'll lift you to the path.' The low sun was now full in his eyes, and he hadn't noticed a figure approaching from the opposite direction.

'Simon, good evening!'

Simon saw that it was Andrew Bishop, also with a dog, but this one was old and stiff, rescued by the Bishop family some years ago. Now it sniffed the puppy, whose tail wagged frantically, anxious at this sudden encounter.

'Wonderful evening,' said Andrew. 'Don't you love this time of year? Managed to get an early train today, thank God.' Andrew commuted to a solicitors' practice in London every day, a journey that once would have been unthinkable, but was now common practice. 'Coming to the barn dance?' continued Andrew, his ears still ringing with Annie's strictures about getting home in time on Friday.

Simon nodded. 'Yes, of course,' he said. 'Wouldn't miss it for anything. A good do, is it?'

'Great,' said Andrew. 'Lively band, plenty of beer and beautiful women. What more could we want?' He strode off laughing, pleased with life, now he had it tamed.

Could I do the commuting bit? thought Simon. Slow, smelly trains every day. I'll have to consider it. There were now several reasons why living in London didn't seem so attractive. But he couldn't live on Dad for much longer, though he'd earned his keep working with Bill. Ah well, time enough to decide when the show's over. He remembered that Octavia Jones had left a message about a possible tennis tournament. Might catch her at home around now, he thought, and quickened his pace.

# 18

'Well, I don't see why we can't go up and 'ave a look,' said Ellen Biggs. She was leaning on her gate in the sun, talking to Doris, who had just brought her a bundle of runner beans from her garden.

'Well,' said Doris patiently, 'we'll be going to the show, Ellen, like we always do, but not the barn dance. That's for young folks, not old biddies like us. And anyway, what would Ivy say?'

Ellen looked mutinous. 'Wouldn't do no 'arm,' she said. 'We could sit and 'ave a look at the dancing for a bit and then come 'ome. Used to love it, once upon a time, I did. An' I was good at it, though you might not believe it now.'

'Course I believe it,' said Doris soothingly. 'Well, I'll speak to Ivy, and if she doesn't want to go, maybe just the two of us will take a look.' The way things are going, she thought dismally, Ellen and me might spend a lot more time as a twosome. 'When does George move in across the road?' she said to Ellen.

'T'morrer,' said Ellen. 'There was a bit of an 'old-up, but now it's all fixed. T'morrer's the big day, and our Ivy'll be 'eart-broken, wotcha bet?'

'That's as may be,' said Doris, 'but I don't expect she'll want to be turning out again in the evening for the dance. Perhaps I won't ask her. P'raps you and me'd better go up there on our own, and not mention it.'

'Okay by me,' said Ellen.

Doris nodded, and then looked furtively behind her,

as if Ivy might be lurking. 'About seven, then,' she said. 'Starts early, so's the kids can join in for a while.'

'See you t'morrer, then,' said Ellen. 'And thanks for them beans.'

By twelve noon next day, George Chalmer's few belongings had been unloaded from the furniture removals van and dumped unceremoniously wherever there was space.

'Of course,' said Ivy briskly, 'you'll probably need to live here for a week or two before everything's in its right place.' Now the day had come, she had thawed, was more friendly and accommodating. After all, George had made it clear he was still going to rely on her a great deal.

'You'll always be welcome, Ivy,' he'd said, and taken her by the hand for a few seconds. 'No need to knock, my dear.'

Moving house is a rotten business, Ivy thought. Glad it's not me. George was looking peaky, and she felt protective. No, it was much too unsettling.

'Time for a cup of coffee, Ivy,' said George. 'We've certainly earned it.' They perched on chairs in the small, smartly decorated kitchen, and sipped in companionable silence.

Ivy stood up. 'Well,' she said, and her features crumpled momentarily. Taking hold of herself, she marched to the sink and washed her hands briskly under the cold tap. 'If you'll excuse me, George, I must see to Tiddles' dinner. I could come back later this afternoon, if needed.' She held her breath.

'You know perfectly well you're needed,' said George, getting up and putting his hand on her shoulder. 'I don't know what I shall do without you.'

For a second he thought she was going to cry, but she squared her shoulders, swallowed hard, and smiled at him gratefully. 'See you later, then,' she said.

Whilst George unpacked boxes and stacked books and papers, he found himself thinking about Ivy: what was she doing now? Had she remembered there was still some catfish in the fridge? He trudged upstairs for the umpteenth time, cursing the pain in his right knee. It reminded him of the frailty that comes to every man, especially one living on his own. He sat down on the edge of his bed and rubbed the offending joint. It was very quiet and strange. Although he and Ivy had been down many times to check on the workmen, now he was here for good. He felt empty, like a snail without its fleshy bits. I suppose Ivy would call it my soul, he said to himself. She doesn't know I bargained that away long ago.

He hadn't realised how long he'd been sitting there, until a voice interrupted his thoughts. 'Yoo hoo!' It was a hoarse voice, and he recognised it instantly. Ellen Biggs.

Oh God, he thought, here for a cup of sugar already? 'Coming!' he answered, and hobbled painfully downstairs.

The evening was chilly, with spots of rain in the wind. 'Gettin' dark earlier now,' said Ellen, as she and Doris set off up the avenue, macs on and umbrellas up. They could hear the music from the band, loud and cheerful. As they approached the marquee, Ellen's blood began to rise. She gave a clumsy half-skip and said, 'Come on, Doris, sounds like we're in for a good time. I tried to persuade old George to come with us, but seems Ivy's bringin' 'im after all.'

'Wait for me, you silly woman,' said Doris good-humouredly. 'If you fall, it'll be Tresham General for you again, never mind about a barn dance.' But she too felt the excitement, and as they paid their entrance money to Jean Jenkins at the door, their faces lit up at the colourful sets of dancers, the spot-lit caller on the straw-bale stage.

'Welcome, ladies!' he shouted out. 'Room for you in the next dance!'

'Silly fool,' muttered Doris, but she coloured with pleasure, and led Ellen to a seat by the bar.

# 19

'It's disgusting,' said Poppy, perched on a bale of straw next to Joey Bates.

'What is?' said Joey. It wasn't often he envied anyone, having learned young that it was a pointless exercise, but now he looked at the whirling couples and wished he could join in and sweep Poppy off her feet.

Poppy had seen that look on Joey's face, and moved in quickly to dispel it. Her trick was to make him think of something else, and it had to be something good. 'Annie Bishop's boobs, they're disgusting,' she repeated. 'And Mrs Barnett's! Never think she was the village school-mistress, would you?'

Joey laughed, despite himself, and turned his chair round to have a good look. 'Blimey,' he said. 'And look at the vicar gettin' an eyeful!'

There was a queue at the bar, and for once nobody was grumbling at the wait. Annie and Sarah, doing their hour's duty, were clumsy and unaccustomed to handling the barrels and big beer glasses, but they laughed a lot, parried witticisms, and were managing very well.

'Keep 'em sweet,' muttered Sarah, 'then they'll not notice we're giving 'em short measure.'

'It's the froth,' said Annie, giggling.

Sarah handed a pint mug to her patient husband, who'd frowned at the banter. She said reassuringly, 'Here you are, love. We'll be through in ten minutes, then we can have a dance,'

The village had turned out in good numbers, in spite of the rain. In fact, most people were pleased about it. A last-minute shower added lustre to the show entries, and there was a feeling that if it rained today, it wouldn't rain tomorrow.

Ivy and George, their arrival timed to coincide with Doris and Ellen, sat with them in a corner, and for once Ivy did not carp, criticise or put a damper on the proceedings. Even the décolletages of Annie and Sarah seemed to have escaped Ivy's notice. She's cheered up, thought Doris. It's her George, he can do anything with her. She looks quite handsome tonight, our Ivy.

Ellen was reluctantly acknowledging the same thing. 'That new?' she said, pointing at Ivy's floral blouse, tied at the neck with a frivolous bow.

Ivy simpered and nodded. 'From Adnam's,' she said. 'George helped me choose.'

My Gawd, thought Ellen, things are really coming to a pretty pass! But all she said was 'Very nice too, Ivy. Suits yer,' and with a meaningful look from Doris, she subsided.

Over by the entrance, Jean Jenkins had collared her Foxy as he went by with a pint in his hand. 'Here, Fox,' she said, 'have you seen our Ivy? My goodness, what a difference a man can make!'

'Right, gel,' said Foxy, who had noticed nothing, but was willing to agree with anything Jean said.

Resisting suggestive offers of help, Sarah and Annie were wrestling with a new barrel when Poppy Standing wheeled Joey up to the bar, and fumbled in her purse. Sarah, seeing them approach, called to the queue, 'Stand aside, lads. Let me serve this young lady first.'

'Two shandies,' said Poppy firmly, staring Sarah straight in the eye.

'Too young,' said Sarah firmly, then she saw Simon walking over towards them. She winked at Poppy. 'Two lemonades, did you say, Poppy? Coming up!' And she quickly opened two tins of shandy, poured them into glasses, and handed them to the bland-faced girl.

'Evening!' said Simon, and took his place at the end of the queue.

'He's mine,' whispered Sarah.

'Not fair,' answered Annie.

They dealt with the queue faster now, no longer dallying with the lads, and both were free when Simon reached the bar, Greg Jones following behind him. 'What will you have?' they chorused, and then all three laughed.

'How can I choose?' said Simon, enjoying himself.

'Oh, go on, Sarah,' said Annie. 'I'll serve Mr Jones.' Greg ordered two halves of Morton's and an elderflower cordial.

'Evening, Mr Jones,' said Simon, pulling out a handful of change. 'Is Octavia here? Elderflower for her, I expect. Has to keep a clear head for work, doesn't she?'

Greg looked at him, found his tone patronising where it wasn't meant to be, and answered without a smile. 'The beer's for Octavia and me,' he said, 'and the elderflower for my wife.' He turned on his heel and walked away.

Simon shrugged, looked at Annie and Sarah, and said, 'Oh dear, what did I say?'

'Take no notice of him,' said Sarah, 'he's always prickly. Something to do with his deafness, Gabriella says. She works with me in the school, you know. Well,' she added, 'our time's up, Annie, and here's Robert to take over from us.'

'Good-o,' said Simon. 'Now which of you girls is going to be the first to show me the ropes?'

'I'd love to,' said Annie quickly.

Simon took her hand, and looked consolingly at Sarah. 'Save me the next,' he said.

Don't worry, said Sarah to herself, I will.

John, standing by himself, his eyes fixed on Sarah,

walked over quickly and marched her roughly into the assembling dancers.

'Simon's lovely!' said Ellen to Doris. 'Just look at the way 'e swings 'em round. Cor, if only I was a year or two younger!'

'More than a year or two, Ellen, you daft old thing,' said Doris, quite fondly. She'd had a couple of glasses of cider and felt mellow. The marquee was warmed by a noisy heater, and the rain pattering on the canvas made her glad to be under cover.

'Look now!' said Ellen. ' 'e's holdin' that Sarah Barnett a bit close, ain't he? Look at our John's face. Not too pleased, is he, Doris?' Ellen chortled.

It was going so well, plenty to look at and Doris in a good mood. They'd already stayed longer than they had intended, and showed no signs of wanting to leave. Ivy and George had gone early, with excuses that they still had a lot to do for the show, and Ellen had spotted Ivy's hand tucking into George's arm as they crossed to the exit.

'Stoppin' for a spot of nookie at Bridge Cottage, d'yer reckon?' she said, but Doris frowned and refused to speculate.

As Simon and Sarah stood side by side, waiting for their turn to go to the centre of the circle, Sarah glanced up and said casually, 'How's the job-hunting going?'

Simon looked rueful. 'Nothing yet,' he said, 'but I'm going up on Tuesday for an interview. Hope something will come of it.' He realised his words had begun to sound as if someone else was speaking. Better watch the beer.

Now it was their turn, and they danced in, twizzling round until Sarah shrieked with delight and Simon steadied himself with difficulty. The marquee spun around him warningly.

As they paraded round more decorously, Sarah took

Simon's arm and said, 'Might see you on the train, then.' He looked at her enquiringly. 'On Tuesday,' she said. 'Going up to have lunch with my mother. She's coming down from Harrogate. We often meet at Fortnum's, catch up on the news . . .'

Ah, now there's a coincidence, thought Simon muzzily. He was hot, excited by the dancing and the delightful feel of Sarah in his arms. 'I usually catch the nine fifteen,' he said, and smiled warmly at her as the dance ended and they walked back to the others.

Over by the trailer laden with raffle prizes, John and Andrew had made a rough table from bales, and they sat drinking and talking, getting up in various permutations to dance.

'Going well,' said Simon happily, as he handed Sarah to a seat and reflected that there was a lot to be said for this tradition thing. His companions had seen him well supplied, though he kept insisting that he must buy his round.

'Nonsense,' said Andrew firmly. 'The least we can do, after all your hard work with the tennis club. Great idea. Really enjoyed it, didn't we, Annie?' They all nodded and cheered Simon on to down his glass and have a fill-up.

'My turn,' said Sarah. 'I'm a working woman, and I insist on buying my round.'

'No good arguing with her,' said John. 'She's quite likely to give you six of the best.'

'Besht of what?' said Simon, emptying his glass, and they all laughed, John the loudest of all.

'So what's it to be?' said Sarah, and took orders. In a small, sober corner of his brain, Simon knew that he'd had enough, but suspected he was on trial. With foolish bravado, he said he'd have a whisky chaser if that was okay. Sarah raised her eyebrows at Annie, and went away to the bar.

Octavia Jones was serving, not because she'd been

asked, but because she hadn't. 'I'll take a turn, Dad,' she'd said. 'You go and dance with Mum. Save her from Bill Turner's clutches. He's well away, and his Peggy's looking a big miffed.'

'Bill's not the only one who's had a few,' Greg had said. 'It's a good thing our young squire doesn't have far to go home. Look, he can hardly stand.'

Now Octavia saw Sarah coming across, and said coolly, 'Yes, Mrs Barnett?'

'Two pints, two halves and a double whisky,' said Sarah.

'Who's the whisky for?' said Octavia.

'Um, for Simon, actually,' said Sarah, looking at Octavia in surprise. 'Something wrong?'

Octavia shook her head. 'Nope,' she said. 'He's old enough, I suppose. But looks to me as if he's had enough. More than enough.'

'Oh, come on, Octavia,' said Sarah, who was well away herself. 'Don't be a spoilsport! We're only having a bit a fun. He's okay, is Simon, he can take it.'

Octavia didn't answer her smile, and said, 'Well, you'd be the best person to know what's okay, I suppose . . . being the village schoolmarm, setting an example . . .'

Sarah frowned. It was always difficult to tell if Octavia Jones meant to be rude. She carried the drinks carefully, and put Simon's down in front of him, patting him lightly on the head. 'Drink up, young man,' she said, 'and then we'll have another dance.'

The caller looked over the floor, and felt pleased. A good atmosphere, plenty of willing dancers, and all of them having a good stab at it. He was very experienced, and knew just how to encourage the faint-hearted. But hey, wait a minute. That chap wouldn't get past first base. Drunk as a lord. What were his friends doing, egging him on?

The band began to play, and after the first few seconds

there was a shout of alarm. Simon Standing stood swaying in the centre of a circle of dancers, his eyes glazed and a look of fear on his face. Then his knees buckled, and he fell flat on his face on the grass.

'Stop, stop,' shouted the caller, and the tune slowly petered out. The dancers stood silent and shocked, waiting for Simon to move.

'Fox!' shouted Jean Jenkins, with an instant mental picture of a wrathful Susan Standing. 'You're wanted!' Then everybody surged forward at once.

'Get out of my way!' The clear voice was Octavia's, and she pushed the staring bystanders aside as she forced her way to where Simon lay motionless.

'Idiot!' she said, looking down at him, and her face was white with anger. 'Here, Mr Bishop, and you, Mr Barnett. Don't just stand there, give me a hand.'

They carried Simon out of the marquee and across the wet grass towards the Hall front entrance. 'No,' said Octavia, seeing lights on in the drawing-room, 'take him round the back, to the stable yard. We can go in through the kitchen.'

'He's bloody heavy,' said Andrew Bishop.

'You should have thought of that before you filled him full of booze,' said Octavia sharply. 'Come on, up the back stairs.'

They were narrow stairs, and difficult to negotiate, but with Octavia frowning them into silence, they got to the top. There they were met by the astonished stare of Poppy Standing.

'Oh dear,' she said. 'Big brother can't hold it?' Simon was mumbling now, and his skin had an ominous greenish tinge.

'Shut up!' said Octavia. 'Just show us where his bedroom is, and then make yourself scarce. And if you breathe a word of this to your parents,' she added, grasping Poppy by the arm, 'you'll regret it.'

'Let go!' said Poppy angrily, but she walked off along

the landing, round a corner and opened a door. 'This is his,' she said, 'and don't think he'll thank you, Miss Goody Two-shoes Jones.' Before Octavia could reply, she'd vanished.

In the dry safety of Bill's car, Ellen and Doris looked out at the dark, dripping avenue, and sighed happily. 'Quite a night,' said Ellen. 'Really good, weren't it, Doris?'

'Indeed it was,' said Doris, though she was beginning to feel a little sick. 'Better for some than others, though.'

Ellen, reading her thoughts, said, 'Reckon Mr Simon'll have a thick head in the morning. My gawd, Bill, he'd put away a fair bit, hadn't he?'

Peggy, sitting beside Bill, said 'Huh!'

'Should know better,' said Bill, grandly ignoring Peggy. 'So much for travel broadening the mind. Any lad in the village would know when he was being set up. Rotten trick, if you ask me. Still, maybe he'll be wiser next time.'

There was silence as they approached Ellen's Lodge, then Ellen laughed. 'Never seen Octavyer look s'mad,' she said smugly. 'Good sign, d'yer think, Doris?'

Bill shook his head, and opened the car door. 'Come on, you wicked old thing,' he said, 'let's get you indoors.'

Greg and Gabriella were still up when Octavia walked in, slamming the front door behind her. 'In here, darling,' called Gabriella. They had decided to wait up, in case Octavia needed to talk.

'Never learn, do we?' Greg had said apologetically. 'She won't want to talk to us, but still, just in case.'

'Coffee's fresh,' said Gabriella, pouring a mug and handing it to a scowling Octavia.

'Thanks, Mum,' she said. 'I need that.' She sat down beside her father, and nothing was said for a minute or two. Then Octavia sighed, visibly relaxed, and leaned back on the sofa. 'What a bloody awful evening!' she said.

'Most people seemed to be enjoying it,' said Gabriella mildly.

'Oh, I suppose so,' said Octavia, wearily pushing her hair back. 'Is there something wrong with me?' she added jerkily. 'Am I really Miss Goody Two-shoes, just because I don't think it at all amusing to get someone completely legless to make a fool of him?'

Greg shook his head. 'No, Tavie,' he said, 'but you'll never get the likes of the Bishops and Barnetts to see that. Don't worry, girl,' he added, patting her knee. 'It'll all be forgotten in the excitement of the show tomorrow.' His tone was ironic, and the ghost of a smile crossed Octavia's tired face.

'Not tomorrow – today,' said Gabriella, looking at the clock. 'It's well after midnight, and we've got a busy day ahead.'

Octavia didn't move. 'You know,' she said hesitantly, 'when I went up to see Simon about the tournament, he was quite different. Sort of sensible and straightforward. Nice . . .'

Gabriella looked quickly at Greg, and said, 'Most people are, my love, even the Barnetts and Bishops. It'll all look different in the morning. Come on, up the wooden hill . . .'

The childish phrase comforted Octavia, and giving her mother a peck on the cheek, she went off upstairs.

# 20

The torrential rain of the previous night had left the showground muddy and treacherous, but with bright sun and a blustery wind, even the track over the field to the marquee had nearly dried out. Most of the village had turned out for the show, and there'd been the customary arguments about prizes, libellous accusations concerning the size of marrows, soothing speeches from Tom Price and Richard Standing, and a great deal of hard work for Bill Turner.

The tennis tournament got under way, with the complicated knock-out results carefully recorded by George Chalmer, and a healthy spirit of competition being kept alive by Sarah Barnett's running commentary from the sidelines. She and John were beaten easily in the first round by Mandy and Robert, and now she amused the watching crowd with what Octavia had to admit was a very funny performance.

There was still no sign of Simon, and Octavia quickly realised that everyone was carefully avoiding the subject. With their match against the Bishops coming up, she looked anxiously along the terrace. At least he could make an appearance, apologise for being unfit, or have a brave stab at it. But just vanishing like this, dumping her without a partner, made her look an idiot.

Still no Simon, but suddenly there was Poppy, running and waving at her, a look of glee on her face. 'He's coming, Octavia!' she yelled, so that everybody could hear. 'Put out the flags!'

Octavia ignored her, and went on counting money with George. 'A good total, Mr Chalmer,' she said, but her voice was strange, and George noticed her hand trembled.

'Nervous?' he said. 'You're on next, aren't you? You'll be fine, Octavia. Go out there and lick 'em!' He wasn't sure if this was the right expression, but he felt sorry for her.

Simon Standing walked slowly along towards the courts, holding his head stiffly, as if a jolt to right or left would cause him infinite pain, which indeed it would. He'd showered in icy-cold water, washed his hair, cleaned his teeth with special breath-freshening toothpaste, and chosen his best tennis gear. At least I can look the part, he'd thought miserably, even if I can't play.

Octavia stared at him as he approached. 'So sorry,' he said in a low voice. 'I don't know what you must think of me. Poppy tells me I was unbelievably horrible last night, but I don't remember a thing.' He had no smile for her, and Octavia shook her head.

'It was nothing much,' she said, amazed at how easy it was to lie.

'Well, I am in your debt, according to my charming sister,' Simon added, 'though I doubt I'll be able to repay by great play on court today. Still, if you're still willing, we could have a go.'

His politeness chilled Octavia. She would rather have had anger, or bluster. Anything rather than this withdrawn Simon. No sparkle in his eye for her, and it wasn't just his obviously sore head. I saw them make a fool of him, she thought sadly, and now he can't look me in the eye.

The game was over quickly and joylessly. Simon thanked her briefly and walked over to the Barnetts. Octavia could hear them teasing him, and he took it in good part. 'Hair of the dog, that's what you need,' she heard Sarah Barnett say. My God, thought Octavia, she's relentless. But Simon was shaking his head. 'No thanks,' she heard him reply, 'I have to help Octavia and George. They've done it all so far.'

'All right, darling?' whispered Gabriella, as she and Greg walked by for their last match. Octavia nodded.

'Could be worse,' she said.

'Good luck! Not that you'll need it, the way Dad's playing.'

It was a walkover, and the small, silver plate cup, engraved 'Round Ringford Tennis Club', was duly presented to Mr and Mrs Jones, with Susan Standing's warmest congratulations, and enthusiastic applause from the rest. As the competitors drifted away in twos and threes, Greg was reluctant to leave Octavia. He offered to stay behind and help.

'Thank you, Mr Jones,' said Simon, still pale, but looking determined, 'very kind, but we'll cope.' Gabriella pulled at Greg's sleeve, making discouraging noises, and they walked away.

'George,' said Simon, extending his hand. 'Thanks so much. You've been a wonder. It all went very smoothly. No arguments, no disputes. So grateful.'

George smiled self-effacingly and said Ivy would have his supper ready, if there was really nothing more he could do.

'Not a thing,' said Simon. 'Goodnight, George, and many thanks again.'

And me? thought Octavia. What kind of dismissal will I get? Thank you and good night? She lowered the net, and collected up a few tennis balls lurking in hidden corners. The light was soft now, as the sun disappeared behind the trees. Sounds of banging and hammering came from the marquee, where Bill Turner and friends were clearing up and dismantling. The frail, pale green flowers of Susan's nicotiana, still flowering under the long windows, gave off a warm scent. Octavia folded up the card table that had been George's admin centre, and looked at Simon. 'Where does this go?' she said.

'Don't worry,' he answered, 'I'll take it. I'm going back to the house now.' His expression was hard to read. 'Thanks a lot, Octavia,' he added, picking up his sweater. 'I know that's not adequate, but perhaps you'll . .' He hesitated, his eyes serious, and Octavia frowned.

'Please,' she said. 'I don't know what Poppy told you, but it really wasn't that bad.' And now I'll go, she thought, make it easy for him. With a quick 'Goodnight, Simon,' she picked up her racquet and cardigan and walked off towards the avenue.

Simon watched her go, and long after she had disappeared, he contemplated the shadowy space where she had been. He gave himself a little shake, winced at the pain at the back of his head, and tried to remember what it was Sarah Barnett had said to him about Tuesday.

# 21

Sarah had arrived early, driving herself to the station after John had disappeared on his huge tractor with a brief wave in her direction. She could tell he'd been trying to be nice, wished her a happy day, and said to give his love to her mother. Funny how well Mother and John got on. Nothing in common, and yet never stopped talking when they met. Still, everyone had said she and John had nothing in common when they'd first got together, and it had worked all right. Sometimes he bored her, but then she probably bored him too, talking about the school and kids he didn't know. They were still fine in bed, and since Annie Bishop had arrived in Ringford, her friendship had sufficed to fill any intellectual gaps. A bit of excitement to stir the blood, that's all I need, Sarah told herself, looking at her watch.

She scanned the platform with growing anxiety. The train was due any minute, and there was no sign of Simon. Hope I haven't wasted all that effort, she thought, and then assured herself that the trip was worth a chance to see her mother, anyway. After all, some people saw their mothers all the time. Ah, was that him? No, too porky looking. Simon was tall and lean. And dark, and charming, and his voice was so warm when he spoke softly . . . and, oh God, come on, Simon Standing . . . don't let me down.

'Morning, Sarah!' There he was, standing behind her, dressed in London clothes and grinning in the most heart-stopping way.

She collected herself rapidly, and said, 'Simon! Goodness, I'd forgotten you were going up today . . . how nice to see you.'

Her formal, light tone did not in the least deceive him, but she looked elegant and charming, and he was quite happy to play the game, said what a treat it would be to have her company on the dreary journey.

'A job interview, is it?' she said, as they settled themselves comfortably on the train.

Simon nodded. 'And your secret assignation is with your mother, am I right?' His smile took in her newly washed, smooth chestnut hair, the creamy shirt open low at the neck so that he could see the curve of her breasts, the good legs and neat ankles shown off to advantage by a short brown skirt. 'Lunch and shopping?' he said, leaning his head back on the seat, and looking at her through amused eyes. A delicious flicker brought the colour to Sarah's cheeks, and she nodded.

'Day off for me,' she said. 'Soon be back at school, and then there's no escaping.'

'Ah, then we'd better have a drink before going back to captivity tonight,' said Simon, very sure of himself.

'Um, I'm not certain . . .' said Sarah.

Oh, yes, you are, thought Simon. 'Meet you at five?' he said. 'Outside Liberty's? My appointment's in Kingly Street, just round the corner. Will that do?'

Sarah felt a moment's panic. She could stop it now, say no thanks, and get the train home straight after lunch. 'That'd be great,' she said. 'I'll be there.'

'You're looking very well, dear,' said Mrs Drinkwater, putting down her shopping bags and glancing across the table at her only daughter. 'Your father and I do worry about you sometimes, you know, stuck in that tiny village miles from any of your old friends. Still, John's a love, isn't he, and I suppose the school keeps you busy enough.'

Sarah sat through this familiar introduction to their

meetings. Let her get it out of the way, she thought, and then we can get on to the serious business of grandchildren.

Sure enough, her mother said, 'Do you remember Alice Cookham? Expecting, her mother says, in December. Isn't that exciting? I've finished one little matinée jacket, and I might knit another. You need so many, you know, Sarah, when they're very tiny. Still, you wouldn't want to hear about—'

'No, Mother, I wouldn't,' said Sarah. 'And you really could be a bit more subtle. John and I will start breeding when we feel it's the right time. He's good at judging when a cow's ready for the bull.'

'Sarah! There's no need for that sort of talk! No, I just thought that as you'd seemed so anxious we should meet, there might be some news. That's all. Now, we'd better change the subject.'

They managed to find enough safe ground for conversation after that, and both enjoyed lunch and wandering about the shops together, each encouraging the other to spend money. Sarah bought an expensive bra and pants in cream satin, and her mother thought happily that things must still be fine between her daughter and son-in-law. They parted on very good terms, with an affectionate hug.

Which door had Simon meant? thought Sarah, as she watched late customers hurrying into Liberty's. She was ten minutes early, and paced up and down between the Regent Street entrance and the two side doors. She'd be sure to see him, he was so tall. As she rounded the corner for the third time, she saw him walking across the road with someone unfamiliar. Her heart sank. What a dirty trick! But when they met, the stranger excused himself quickly, said he had a train to catch, and Simon and she were left alone.

'Good day?' he said to her, taking her arm as if it were the most natural thing in the world.

She nodded, and said, 'But what about you? Did it go well?'

He beamed. 'Yep,' he said. 'I got it. At least, it's almost certainly in the bag. Interesting job, too.'

Sarah grabbed his hand impulsively. 'Well done!' she said, with genuine pleasure.

'So it's champagne for us,' said Simon, and hailed a taxi.

'I was wondering,' he said tentatively, as they drove past the BBC and into Portland Place, 'whether you'd like to go to a bar just by the next traffic lights . . . or maybe, just relax, take your shoes off for half an hour in my folks' flat in Baker Street? It's not far,' he added, seeing a spark of interest in her eyes. Goodness, it was a relief to be with someone who knew exactly what she was doing. He reminded himself that Sarah Barnett was older, had probably had plenty of experience before she met John. He felt the afternoon's success expanding delightfully.

It was stuffy in the flat, and Simon opened windows, pointed out the loo, and disappeared into the kitchen. Sarah washed her hands, noticed that everywhere was very clean, and sniffed at the bottles of scent, exclusive creams. This is London Susan, she thought, and had a sudden picture of a different Madam, one who walked down Bond Street and felt at home. No wonder she gets fed up in Ringford, she thought.

She wandered back into the small lobby, elegant with gilt-framed looking-glass and Chinese vase. In the high-ceilinged room, her eye was caught by a watercolour of Ringford Hall, misty behind a sunlit park, with cattle grazing in the foreground. She chuckled. 'Can't get away from cows anywhere,' she muttered.

Simon had found a bottle of champagne in his father's wine rack, and, sure that Dad of all people would approve of the need on such an occasion, he opened it with a satisfactory explosion, and poured a glass for

Sarah. 'Sorry it's not chilled,' he said, 'But the effect's the same.'

Sarah sipped, said 'Mmm . . .' and lifted her glass in congratulation. 'To the new job!' she said.

They were close, glasses chinking. Sarah put down her glass, reached up to wrap her arms around Simon's neck, and kissed him slow and long on his wonderful, smiling mouth.

After that, there was no stopping them. In no time at all, the creamy shirt and brown skirt lay like a Siamese cat curled up on a chair by Susan's big bed. It had all worked out so well, with the shopping, and Mother being nice, and not having to be back at any special time; and for Simon, the excitement of the new job, no real commitments to worry about, and no tedious persuasion needed. Indeed, it was Sarah who'd taken the lead, naked in seconds, undressing him, hungrily caressing, keeping things going for such a long, long time.

They finished the champagne, now very flat, and dressed slowly. 'Time to go,' said Sarah, fishing the new wisps of satin from her bag. 'Bought these today . . . what d'you think?' And then there was another delay before they finally locked the flat door behind them and emerged into the dark, noisy London street.

Euston Station was busy, with homegoers clutching programmes from West End shows, businessmen in City suits who'd been working late, or were reluctant to go home for more intimate reasons. One of these, in his fifties, stumbled in front of Simon, and he caught a nauseating smell of stale alcohol and vomit.

Sarah seemed oblivious to this, and to everything else. She was humming happily to herself, looking into each carriage for seats as they walked down the platform. Simon glanced sideways at her. She could have been hurrying home from doing a show, he thought. A day in town with a girlfriend. I don't know her at all, he realised with mild dismay.

They were not touching now, with more than physical space between them. Their thoughts had diverged surprisingly soon. Sarah was thinking about a pile of old music she'd found in the school cupboard and sang quietly to herself; and Simon, seeing a tall girl with swinging blonde hair climbing into a carriage in front, felt a nasty, uncomfortable stab of regret.

'Come on, Si, darling,' said Sarah briskly, 'if I miss this one I shall be in real trouble.'

# 22

John Barnett said very little until the following morning, and by then he had cooled down. When Sarah had finally driven into the yard very late indeed, he was frantic with worry. He'd phoned her mother, who had said as far as she knew, Sarah had planned to return at more or less the same time as herself, and that was late afternoon. 'Perhaps she met a friend, went on some-where for a drink or a meal,' Mrs Drinkwater had said hesitantly.

Perhaps she did, thought John grimly, well aware that the day in London had been swiftly arranged by an oddly excited Sarah. Then he told himself that suspicions were pointless, and began to have mental visions of Sarah under the wheels of the train, or abducted and now lifeless in Bagley Woods. But when she'd come through the kitchen door with her usual open smile, and kissed him fondly, he'd said only that he'd been worried, and had she had a good day. He'd even accepted, on the surface at least, her explanation that a sudden impulse had taken her into a cinema to see that film they'd missed last month in Tresham. But she hadn't seemed to want to talk about it, he'd noticed.

This morning, with the sun shining into the farm kitchen, hens clucking outside, and Sarah busy with breakfast, his sleepless night seemed ridiculous. Now he said mildly, 'See anyone you knew on the train?'

Sarah did some quick thinking. There might have been a witness on the train. 'Saw Simon Standing,' she said. 'Grunted something at me about a job interview, and then read his paper all the way to London.'

'Is that so,' said John, chewing his lip. He stared at her, and slowly stood up from the table. 'If you're hiding something, Sarah,' he said, 'you'd better own up. Soonest said, soonest mended. And you know this village now as well as I do. Things get around. That's all I've got to say. For now . . .' And before she could reply that it was *least* said, soonest mended, he strode off grimly into the yard.

The evenings were dark earlier now, but the tennis players were reluctant to call an end to the season. Most had stayed loyal to the weekly meetings, and Mandy's services as coach had been in demand. She enjoyed the break from her usual round, and agreed happily when Sarah Barnett rang her with a request that maybe she should brush up her backhand before winter came and it was too late.

'I promised to have a knock-up with Octavia and Simon this evening,' Mandy said, 'so if you could come along about half past six, that would be great.' The two names linked together irritated Sarah, and she said half past six would be fine, she'd have plenty of time for clearing up the classroom and a quick cup of tea before they met.

A burst of laughter reached her as she walked up the chestnut avenue, kicking rusty leaves already fallen and shifting under her feet. She'd had a quick shower, and changed into a T-shirt and jeans before leaving a note for John and setting off. Of course she'd said nothing more to him after his outburst, and he had been taciturn for the past few days, resisting all her blandishments. She waited patiently, sure that he would come round.

Mandy and Octavia were on the court, Octavia hitting one forehand after another over the net. 'Follow through, don't forget!' called Mandy.

'I'm getting worse!' yelled Octavia, spinning a ball out of court to where Simon stood watching.

He picked it up and threw it back, and as he turned, caught sight of Sarah. She smiled broadly and joined him, reaching up to kiss him lightly on the cheek. 'Hi, Simon,' she said. 'How's it going?'

'Fine,' he said, with a quick glance at the others. 'Get home okay?'

'Yep,' she replied. 'John not too pleased, though. Still sulking.'

Oh, my God, thought Simon, this is all I need. A jealous husband, his randy wife, and Octavia Jones with antennae the size of a woodwasp's.

'Worth it, anyway,' continued Sarah. 'When shall we have Part Two?'

Oh, no . . . Simon turned his back on Mandy and Octavia, and said, 'Better lie low for a bit, don't you think? Could be big trouble if John turns nasty.'

Sarah pealed with laughter, so loud that Mandy looked across at them curiously.

Octavia studiously ignored them, asking Mandy if she could just practise a few serves and then she'd have to go.

'John turn nasty?' said Sarah. 'He'd never do that. Knows I always win the argument. No, what he doesn't see won't hurt him, dear old thing. So how about Saturday? He'll be in Birmingham for an NFU meeting, not back till late.'

Simon gulped. ' 'Fraid I'm busy all day,' he said. 'Oh, look,' he added quickly, 'Mandy's ready for us now. You first? Backhands, is it?' He walked rapidly over to the court, in time to see the back of Octavia retreating fast down the avenue.

The light was beginning to fade, and after Sarah had returned a few desultory backhands to Mandy and disagreed with her advice, she beckoned Simon over. 'Come on,' she said. 'You have a go, else it'll be dark.'

Mandy obligingly came round the net and asked Simon what help he needed.

'On all fronts,' he grinned. 'Still, forehand is the worst, so we could start there.'

Mandy watched him hit one or two, and told him where he was going wrong, then Sarah walked over and said, 'D'you mind, Mandy? I could just see from over there that he's got completely the wrong grip.' Before Mandy could say anything, she'd grasped Simon's arm. 'Like this,' she said softly, holding him close. 'No, don't tense up. Relax everything. That's it . . .'

'It was shocking!' said Mandy to Robert over supper. 'Short of stripping off, she couldn't have made it plainer! Never been so embarrassed, Robert.'

'Good heavens, calm down, love,' said Robert, but he could see Mandy was really upset, and wondered just how far all of this had gone. John Barnett's temper matched his red hair, and if the story reached his ears there could be ructions. Besides which, it was no way for the village headmistress to behave. 'Put it out of your mind, me duck,' he said, but he knew his Mandy, and was unhappily certain that there was no way of keeping it quiet.

A couple of days later, Sandra Goodison had just sat down to watch the news when the doorbell rang, twice, insistently. 'Blast,' she said. Sam had gone off to Tresham with Alison to see his mother, and she'd settled down to peace and quiet.

'Tavie! What do you want?'

Sandra stood aside as Octavia walked in, saying 'You on your own? Oh, good, I need to talk.'

Sandra sighed. 'There's this programme I was going to watch . . .'

'This is more important,' said Octavia flatly. 'Come on, Sand, make us a cup of coffee and I'll tell all.'

It was an unpleasant story, thought Sandra, relayed faithfully round the village by Mandy Bates, and some of it witnessed by Octavia herself. 'Sarah'll have to watch it,' she said, 'but I don't see why you're so upset.' She looked closely at Octavia, and saw that she was near to tears. 'Oh, God,' she said, 'you fancy him yourself! Might have known it. Smarmy bugger's got them all after him.'

'I'm not after him,' said Octavia. 'I just can't stop thinking about him. And it's so degrading for him . . .'

'Bollocks,' said Sandra. 'What you really mean is you fancy him rotten.'

Octavia glared at her, then crumpled. 'Right,' she said. 'I fancy him rotten.'

'You want his body,' said Sandra.

Octavia began to laugh, and nodded. 'Right again,' she said. 'What the hell am I going to do?'

'Go for it, gal,' said Sandra, pouring hot water into two mugs. 'You're more that a match for Teacher. Anyway,' she continued, 'he's halfway there already. Looks at you like a lovesick cow.'

Octavia drank her coffee, leaned back and regarded Sandra fondly. 'Supposing,' she said slowly, 'just supposing I did go for it, as you say . . . there's another snag, apart from Sarah. Darling Poppy hates my guts, little monster. Must be because I told her straight that night Simon was drunk. And Mummy's not much better. She's set her sights higher than a girl from the village, I reckon.'

'Wow!' said Sandra. 'You've got problems, no doubt about that, Tavie Jones. Still, you've always got your own way so far, so my money's on you. Now go away,' she laughed, showing Octavia the door, 'and leave me in peace.'

# 23

Bagley Woods slowly changed from a palette of green shades to a burning bright array of yellow, copper-orange and flame red. Blackberrying had finished, and now, as Bill and Peggy took precious time off to walk over the hill, only shrivelled husks and wrinkled sloes clung to the bushes.

Peggy took Bill's hand and looked up at him tenderly. 'You love it all, don't you?' she said. 'Even in winter, or now, when it's all fading and dying off.' She could never learn as much as Bill knew about the country. In her urban heart, she still felt uneasy, alien, if she walked in the woods alone.

This afternoon they wandered peaceably, planning for Christmas in the shop, chatting about the village and inevitably coming to the subject of Sarah Barnett and Simon Standing.

'Of course Madam knows,' said Bill, answering Peggy's tentative question. 'Not much she misses. But there's not a lot she can do about it.'

'Mr Richard's a governor of the school,' Peggy said. 'He could warn Sarah off, surely. Parents are beginning to talk in the shop.' Peggy had been unhappy about developments, aware that something very serious could be brewing. Sometimes she wished she knew less about what was going on, but in her position behind the counter she heard most things, whether she liked it or not. 'I'd had hopes of Simon and Octavia,' she said, bending down to pull a bramble away from her coat.

'That wouldn't have suited Madame, either,' said Bill. 'Village girl . . . ordinary parents . . . small house . . . no background . . .'

'Oh Bill! You sound positively feudal!'

'They are,' said Bill flatly. 'Anyway,' he added, 'the young folks'll get on with it, whatever we say. No, it's Ivy I worry about. Getting on in years, and as foolish as a young maid.'

'You've never liked him, have you?' Peggy said.

'George?' said Bill. 'No, can't say I have. Gives me the creeps. Hiding something, I reckon.'

'Then it's up to you to find out what it is,' said Peggy firmly. 'Get him in for a game of chess, and give him a grilling.' Poor sod, she thought to herself, I feel sorry for him! When Bill gets his teeth into a thing, he's like Jenkins's terrier . . .

Poppy Standing freewheeled into Barnett's farmyard and propped herself up on one foot by the stable, where she could see John inspecting his mare's hooves. 'Hello, Mr Barnett,' she said.

John twisted his head round and looked at her in surprise. 'Poppy?' he said. 'What can I do for you?' He couldn't remember seeing her at the farm before.

'Message for Mrs Barnett from Simon,' said Poppy blandly.

'Oh yes,' said John, straightening up. 'Then you'd better go over to the house. She's in the kitchen.'

Poppy shook her head. 'No, it's okay,' she said, 'you can tell her. There's no tennis on Wednesday. Simon's going to London, and Mum's having some friends over.'

Gratified by the stunned look on John's face, Poppy turned her bike around and cycled off, whistling. Well, Simon hadn't actually asked her to tell them, but he'd have to be pleased she was trying to help . . .

Sarah shook the tablecloth over the kitchen sink and folded it neatly. She looked in the programme paper, planned the evening's viewing, and went through to the sitting-room. Then the back door slammed so hard she went running back to the kitchen in alarm.

'John? You all right?' she said, seeing his face contorted by what she took to be pain.

John shook his head. 'When did you say you were meeting your mother again?' he choked.

'Wednesday,' she said innocently. 'Why? Isn't it convenient?'

'Oh yes,' said John. 'Very convenient, I imagine. That brat has just been here to tell you there's no tennis on Wednesday . . . her charming big brother is, guess what, going to London and staying overnight.'

He stepped forward and grabbed her shoulders until she cried out. 'I'm not a fool, Sarah,' he said. 'In this family we stick together. May not be fun all the time. Farming isn't. Nobody knows that better than me. But it was for better or worse, remember? You can ring your mother and tell her something's come up, and you can't meet her. And that's an order,' he added harshly.

Sarah did not flinch. 'Let go of me,' she said quietly. 'And don't give me orders. You've been overworking, John, else you wouldn't speak to me like that. Ring Mother, if you don't believe me.' She turned away, and said as she left the room, 'Poppy Standing is a brat, as you say. Her mother's daughter.'

John stared after her, feeling empty, defeated. He couldn't believe his ears when he heard her call, 'Johnnie! It's that antiques programme we like. Come on through . . . don't want to miss it . . .'

Oh dear, thought George, as he looked out of his bedroom window at threatening, slate-grey skies, forecast says this'll last the week. Tennis club won't like that. He'd enjoyed his association with young people, keeping the books and nosing along at the edge of the county set with an eye well trained for future opportunities.

And lately he'd had some really juicy snippets of gossip to relay to Ivy.

Nobody could miss the big thing between Simon and Sarah Barnett. And, he'd told a shocked Ivy, Sarah doesn't seem to care who sees her touching and flirting, and making sure he's always her partner, and disappearing off into the shrubbery with him after lost balls. And she's not all that careful when her John's there, either . . . This had offended George, a man practised in secrecy and concealment.

Ivy had been livid. 'It'll not be Mr Simon's fault,' she'd said. 'That schoolteacher has been spoiling for trouble for some time. And what an example for the children!' she'd added.

George felt tired. The wet weather had given him twinges in his legs. Well, it'd all be sorted out, no doubt, one way or another. And he had his own worries, some urgent, and some that could be shelved until a more propitious time.

Rain swept across his front garden, and he saw that once more the small gate was not shut, swung to and fro with a clang every time it hit the post. Postman must have left it open. Or the paperboy. Or the milkman. Any one of them, and all up and about hours before him. Am I turning into a slob? He thought, and pulled on his dressing-gown and slippers to go down for a cup of tea. One thing's certain sure. Nobody Ivy took under her wing would be allowed to be a slob. Soon be licked into shape. Slippers warmed in front of the fire, regular meals and church on Sundays without fail. Security, comfort, devotion. Well, George, he addressed himself as he took down a mug with a coffee stain around the rim, what more could a chap want?

As George knew exactly what he wanted, always had, ever since he escaped from that house where fecklessness and poverty reigned, he skilfully redirected his thoughts to plan for the day, and cheered up.

His post consisted of two letters. One had the familiar handwriting of his friend, and the other was clearly a bill. George frowned. He knew what it was without opening it, and he tucked it behind the clock on the mantelshelf along with several others, all unopened. Quite soon, he'd be better placed. His knack of banishing unpleasant matters from his mind came to his aid, and he continued to feel cheerful at the prospect of whist in the old reading room this afternoon. Only pennies, of course, but it was a gamble, and anything that required cunning and forethought was just up George's street.

Ivy was a dab hand at whist, too. Played all her life, she'd told him. Her father had taught her, and had been a hard taskmaster. See it as a challenge, Ivy's father had said. Everything to him had been a challenge, remembered Ivy, including bringing up a small girl who had arrived in his middle age as an intruder on his ordered life.

Poor old Ivy. No wonder she was so scratchy. Still, life with George around was working wonders, he thought to himself, smiling. He looked at his face in the shaving mirror and patted his stubbly jowls. Not a bad old sod, are you? Not really. Bring a little singing and dancing into the old girl's life, and no harm done. Quite the little Sir Lancelot, aren't we? he could hear his friend saying.

The rain increased to a steady downpour, and by the time Octavia Jones parked her car at the foot of the muddy lane leading to a pair of dilapidated farm cottages, she wished she'd remembered her wellies. Muddy water splashed over her shoes and ankles, and she could feel her hair flattening damply as the rain pelted down. She should at least have brought an umbrella. Mind on other things, she told herself crossly.

The cottages were in sight now, huddled against the dark oaks and firs of Bagley Woods. This was the other side of the woods, away from Ringford and looking towards Bagley, the farmland belonging to a cousin of Ted Bates. The cottages, no longer needed for farm-workers, were leased out to Social Services to house unfortunates who came under their care, and who for a number of reasons were homeless, and often hopeless, too.

'God knows what they make of this place,' said Octavia aloud, as she pushed her way through a jungle of weeds and perennials run riot. 'Not exactly calculated to fill you with optimism.'

She stood under the inadequate porch and waited, feeling rain dripping down the back of her neck. Nothing moved, and she knocked again, certain that there would be someone there, if only a solitary child left to fend for itself.

'It's Octavia Jones!' she shouted. 'I've not come for money. Nor to take the kids away! Just want to talk for a bit . . . come on, Elaine, open up!'

Elaine Fountain was a single mother of three small children, pale and sickly looking. They attended which-ever school was nearest their latest billet, and last time Octavia had seen them, they'd sat in sullen silence on a bench in the office, their eyes firmly fixed on the floor.

A child's face appeared briefly at the dirty window, and then vanished. 'Mum!' It was a listless voice, but it seemed to do the trick. The door opened a crack and a depressed-looking girl looked out. She's younger than I am, thought Octavia, with quick compassion.

'Can I come in?' Octavia said. 'I won't take up too much of your time.'

'Only thing I've got plenty of,' said the girl, dully. 'Mind the toys. Don't matter how often I pick them up, they spread 'em round again. Just where I fall over 'em. I reckon they do it on purpose.'

The children, all three of them, lurked in the small kitchen beyond the tiny living-room, and Octavia grinned at them. 'What are your names?' she said. No reply. 'William, isn't it? she said. 'And Melanie, and Charlie's the youngest?' She'd read the file before leaving, the sorry story of a girl from a violent home, seeking affection and finding only sex. It was touch and go whether the children, each from a different father, would be taken into care. But what would happen to their mother? She was fierce about her rights, and so far there'd been no signs of real neglect, no bruises. An elderly couple lived in the cottage next door, kept their eyes open and did what they could to help.

After a while, first one child and then the others came closer to Octavia. She knelt on the floor and tried to construct a robot from a few bits of scuffed Lego. She listened carefully to their mother, and outlined what more she could do for them.

And that was not a lot, she thought, as she squelched back down the lane, now a series of muddy lakes and streams. Octavia pictured the girl and her children, wet through and dispirited, trudging along to catch the bus which stopped at the corner, and, not for the first time, thanked God for her own comfortable home. Then she thought of Ringford Hall, and the tennis club, and all the time she'd wasted lately in monitoring Sarah Barnett's undignified campaign with Simon, and his willing complicity, and thought seriously of chucking the lot of them.

What do they know of all this? she thought, of the sorry lot who come my way, who don't stand a cat's chance in hell of making any sort of a go of their lives? I don't belong with that crowd at the club. Come to that, old George could do both jobs with one hand tied behind him. Yep, best to clear out and let them get on with it, she decided. Sandra's blunt words about challenging Sarah Barnett came back to her, but she dismissed them. She wasn't Sandra. There must be better fish in the sea, she told herself, and unlocked her car.

She took off her wet shoes and made a few urgent

notes. Driving along slowly, her windscreen wipers barely able to cope with the torrential rain, she was irritated to find herself wondering what Simon would have made of her morning. She admitted reluctantly that he'd probably have been curious, asked intelligent questions. 'But I'm not interested!' she shouted at nobody. She turned on her car radio, and tried to think of something else.

# 24

'Well, can't *you* do something about it?' said Susan. She
and Richard were driving back from London early in
the morning, the motorway clear and shining in the
wintry sun. They had been to a concert the evening
before, a new enthusiasm of Susan's which Richard
went along with, though he'd have been happier back in
Ringford and out in the fields with his gun and dog. He
looked across the flat, Bedfordshire fields, frosted and
sparkling in the sun, and pressed his foot on the
accelerator.

'I know perfectly well my things in the flat have been
moved around,' said Susan. 'I always put them in the
same place, and they were different. And there was a
new scent smell on my pillow. God!' she said explosively, suddenly very angry. 'If Simon's been having it
off with Sarah Barnett in our bed, I'll . . . I'll . . .' She
petered out in fury.

Richard sighed. He did wish Susan would not get so
steamed up about these things. She'd obviously forgotten her youth, the things they got up to when they
were in love and hungry for each other. Not that he was
happy himself about Simon's dalliance with Sarah
Barnett. Could be very awkward, what with the school,
and the Barnetts being an old village family. Why
couldn't Simon have some fun with someone else:
cousin Alex, or Octavia Jones? Much the best looker,
Octavia, and fancy free.

'Better have a word with Simon,' he said reluctantly.

'But really it's up to John to rein young Sarah in. Quite surprising, really, that he's let her have her head so far.'

Susan leaned back on the headrest and closed her eyes. 'Do it soon,' she said, 'before it's too late.'

It was quiet and warm in the kitchen behind the shop, and Peggy had warned Bill to keep the door shut while she had her hair done.

'What would we do without you?' said Peggy comfortably to Mandy. 'I hate the hairdresser's in Tresham. They turn you out looking like a boiled sausage, and never listen to a word you say.'

Mandy laughed. 'I worked there myself, you know,' she said. 'Still, the village is different. I know everybody and they know me. Like one big family, really, isn't it?' She snipped and shaped, checked the length and regarded Peggy from all sides. 'Bit more off here,' she said, and added, 'I hated it here at first, you know.'

'I remember,' said Peggy. 'And so did I, come to that. Like living in a goldfish bowl, it seemed to Frank and me.'

'Poor old Frank,' said Mandy, and they were both silent for a minute or two.

'Well, it is, really,' said Mandy. 'Nothing secret. Everything on show. Try getting away with anything, and you'd soon come unstuck . . .'

There was a small pause, and then they both spoke at once: 'Like Sarah Barnett . . .' they chorused, and stopped.

'Yes, well,' said Peggy. 'Least said about that the better, p'raps.'

'You can't keep it quiet, though, can you?' said Mandy. 'It's all round the village, and old Mrs Barnett's furious. Her John's being made a fool of, and she's threatenin' God knows what if that Sarah doesn't put a stop to it.'

Peggy sighed. She remembered only too well the tensions and censorious atmosphere in the village when she and Bill had first got together. He'd been married at the time, of course, though unhappily, and tongues had wagged viciously. Now it was the same. 'It's certainly the chief topic in the shop, Mandy,' she said sadly. 'I mean, I'm the first one to love a bit of gossip, but this is serious. The village is simmering. Half of 'em love it, and wish it was themselves up to no good with Simon Standing, and the other half, like our Ivy next door, are spitting fire and prophesying doom.'

Mandy combed through Peggy's wet curls. 'Well,' she said, 'maybe it'll just fizzle out, now winter's come. No more tennis, and that. It started up at the Hall, you know. I remember my Robert saying tennis wasn't the only game goin' on!'

John Barnett sat at his dad's old desk, frowning over bills, and writing cheques for alarmingly large amounts. 'Bloody farming,' he said to himself. 'For two pins I'd sell up and do something else.' But what could I do? he asked himself. Farming is all I know. That, and a bit about schoolteaching from Sarah. Not that she tells me much, especially these days.

He sighed deeply, and put his head in his hands. God, it was a mess. Everybody in the village was talking. Talking amongst themselves, that is. Nobody ever said anything to him, just changed the subject. He'd noticed that folks even avoided him in the pub lately, afraid they'd say the wrong thing. Sodding Simon Standing! Why couldn't he've stayed in the bloody US of A? Have all the married women he liked there, and nobody the wiser.

'Got a headache, John?' said Sarah, coming down the narrow stairs into the kitchen. She had changed after school into a clinging woollen dress not much longer than a T-shirt. 'There's some codeine in the bathroom cabinet,' she went on, when he didn't answer. 'Shall I make you a cup of tea before I go?'

'Go where?' said John, lifting his head, and looking at her with bleary eyes.

'I told you,' she said impatiently. 'It's a headteachers' meeting in Tresham. To discuss the curriculum for next year.'

'At eight o'clock at night?' said John wearily.

'Why not?' said Sarah, blandly. 'I could hardly take an afternoon off and abandon the kids, could I? It may have escaped your notice,' she said self-righteously, 'that teachers do work very hard. Farmers aren't the only ones, you know . . .'

'Very little escapes my notice,' said John, getting up and looking straight at her. 'You might remember that.' He disappeared up the stairs, and Sarah shrugged. She collected her jacket from the hook by the dresser, and left, banging the door behind her.

'Are you sure this is all right?' said Simon, looking nervously around the restaurant, a smart, intimate place, interior decor gone mad, opened up some years ago the other side of Fletching. 'Lot of the others come here, I know.'

'Relax, Si,' said Sarah. 'Look around. Total strangers! Come on, drink up and let's have another bottle. They certainly take their time with the food here, don't they? All those morning-gathered mushrooms . . .'

Simon didn't smile. Sarah looked as fanciable as ever in the soft candlelight, and her hand gently caressing its way up his thigh was hard to ignore, but he was not at ease. It was too close to home, to Ringford, to all of that. Just lately he'd found himself wishing this thing with Sarah had never started. Married women were new territory to him. Too complicated, he decided, and, exciting as Sarah could be, he was beginning to wonder if it was worth it. Dad had started to say something that was clearly going to be a rocket the other day, and only Poppy coming in like a tornado had stopped him. 'We could go somewhere else,' he said dully. 'Just get up and go.'

Sarah frowned. 'Not losing your bottle, are you, Si?' she said, and added firmly, 'No, it's me that's taking the risk. And if I'm not worried, why should you be? Oh good, here's our food. And you know what oysters are good for, don't you?' She licked her upper lip, and he felt the old quickening.

'Okay,' he said, 'you win . . . as usual.'

Sarah grinned, and blew him a kiss. 'Here's to later,' she said.

# 25

'Darling,' said Annie Bishop to Andrew, as they sat over coffee at the breakfast table. The big kitchen was the heart of the house, with Tinker stretched out with his bony back against the Aga's comforting warmth.

'Mmm?' said Andrew, deep in the financial reports.

'I was thinking, about Christmas,' said Annie. It was quite a relief to have the festivities looming. She'd become very tired lately of endless confidences from Sarah, who'd insisted on telling her much more than she wanted to know. They never talked of anything else. It had crossed Annie's mind that Sarah seemed increasingly frenetic lately. Maybe Simon was cooling off. Serve her right, Annie had thought meanly. She'd certainly lit the fire in the first place.

'Isn't it a bit soon?' said Andrew, groaning inwardly. He didn't exactly hate Christmas, but Annie always went overboard, and the whole thing took on epic proportions. These last few years she had roped in John and Sarah Barnett, and the old vicarage had come to life in a way it had never done in its history of quiet, Christian contemplation. Still, Annie was the best party-giver he knew. He lowered his paper, and smiled at her. 'What's in store for us this year?' he said.

'Well, I wondered whether we should ask some of the family to stay for a few days. Maybe Julie and Philippe?' She anticipated with dread long hours in the company of Sarah and John. They weren't much fun these days.

'That means his brother, too,' said Andrew hesitantly,

but it could be worse: Julie was one of Annie's cousins, and good value. She'd married an unbelievably handsome Frenchman, and they had kids the same ages as the Bishops'. Could be great. And Philippe's younger brother was okay, as far as Andrew remembered. 'Can't think of the brother's name,' he said.

'Guy,' said Annie. 'Sarah and John would have to come as usual, I suppose, but they'd be watered down by the others, and we could be positively Dickensian!'

Ah, thought Andrew, that's the theme for this year then. Traditional holly and ivy. Large plum pudding, set alight as carried to the table. Carols round the Christmas tree. And a goose for the poor? Annie at full steam ahead. Oh Lord, how nice it would be to go to some hotel, eat a decent Christmas dinner, sleep all Boxing Day, and then get back to work. No chance, Andrew, he told himself, and got up.

'Walkies?' he said, waving the lead at Tinker. The old dog opened his eyes and struggled to his feet, his tail waving to and fro with pleasure. 'Shan't be long,' Andrew called to Annie, but she was busy with paper and pen, making lists.

'Only a few weeks to go,' said Peggy, sorting out gift boxes of toiletries, tinsel decorations, packs of Christmas cards, bags of mixed fruit, peel, nuts, readymade almond icing. It was Bill's job to collect supplies from the wholesalers, and Peggy had taken a gamble this year, ordering more than the usual amount of Christmas stock.

The shop bell brought her out of the stockroom, and she found Poppy by the counter. 'Morning, Poppy,' she said, and waited.

The girl looked pale, and instead of fiddling with everything, she stood with her hands hanging limply at her sides. 'Do you have any aspirin?' she said. 'Mum's ill, so's Dad, and I'm feeling rotten myself.'

'Good gracious!' said Peggy, at once solicitous. 'Have you had the doctor?'

Poppy nodded. 'Yep,' she said. 'Nothing to be done but go to bed and take aspirin, he said. It's flu. All round the place, he said.'

'Dear me,' said Peggy, backing away. 'Yes, they're over there, Poppy . . . no, you stand there and I'll get them for you. How many packets?'

'Better take two,' said Poppy, 'the way Mum and Dad are looking. Put them on the book, can you?'

As Poppy opened the door, she almost collided with the next customer, Octavia Jones. 'Trust you to be in the way,' Poppy said rudely, and pushed past her.

She was off on her bicycle, taking a bumpy short cut across the green, before Octavia had recovered herself and smiled ruefully at Peggy. 'Nice girl, that one,' she said. 'So polite. That's what private education does for you. Rudeness and immorality. What a waste of money!'

Peggy raised her eyebrows. 'I get plenty of lip from the village kids too, you know,' she said. 'Rudeness is not confined to the rich.'

'Message received,' said Octavia. 'Anyway, who cares?'

You do, thought Peggy, but said nothing.

'I suppose we should feel sorry for them, struck down by illness,' continued Octavia. 'The bug's only just hit Ringford, but it's rife in Waltonby. Half the village is down with it.'

'Let's hope it's worn itself out, then,' said Peggy. 'Just what we don't need for Christmas. Are you all prepared for the festivities?'

'Well, yes and no,' said Octavia mock-wearily. 'You know Mum. Up to her ears in choir music, plans for a special midnight mass, cooking mince pies and puddens until the small hours. Dad's gone to ground in his study, and only emerges for meals.'

'Well,' said Peggy consolingly, 'it's amazing how the weeks fly by. I'm sure your mother's right to plan ahead.'

Simon, returning home on a packed train, reflected on the past days. He'd spent a week or two in London, parties and celebrations, and had grown tired of the crowded city. Thank God he'd managed to keep Sarah at bay, though she'd suggested another meeting at the flat. It occurred to him briefly that working in London was a hazard. There, there was always the flat, whereas back at home assignations would be more difficult.

Christmas Eve, and Mum had new quarters for him in the Ostler's House. It had been her idea to spruce up the old cottage across the Hall stableyard. Empty and neglected for years, it was now in good shape and would remove him from under her feet. He sighed. The train was late. Just as well he'd left London early. There had been talk of a party, and then all going on to midnight mass. Set great store by these things, did Mum, and he was already in her bad books. Of course, he knew why, but had allowed things with Sarah to drag on, though the fun had gone out of it. He hoped she'd go quietly.

He opened the *Evening Standard* and turned the pages, failing to find anything to catch his eye. Ah well, nearly at Tresham. Dad should be there to meet him, otherwise it would have to be an expensive taxi. At last, with squeaks and judders, and the awful smell of brakes, the train pulled up at the platform.

'Hi, Dad!' shouted Simon, spotting the tall figure of Richard Standing hovering by the entrance. His heart sank as he saw Poppy had come too. My God, she looks grown up, he thought. The bug had hit her hard, and she'd lost weight. He suddenly saw Poppy through new eyes. She was very like Mum, maybe even better looking. Trouble, old Ellen had said, and she was probably right.

'All ready for the fray?' said Richard, attempting to set the right tone as Simon threw his bag into the back of the Range Rover.

'Ready for the colossal bore, more like,' said Poppy, edging away.

'Not feeling festive, Poppy?' said Simon warily. It was impossible to say the right thing to her these days. Only Mum seemed to be able to get on her wavelength, and even she heaved a sigh of relief when Joey Bates invited her down to the farm.

'God, no,' said Poppy. Richard opened his mouth to reprove her, but thought twice, and shut it again. 'Wish I lived in London,' she went on. 'It's always the same in Ringford. School concert, Dad doing his Father Christmas bit, carol-singing in the freezing cold, shop full of rubbish. And now this boring old party Mum says we've all got to go to.'

'What time is the party tonight?' Simon asked Richard, as they turned into the Hall stableyard.

Richard explained that they'd been asked for late drinks with the Bishops – he choked a little over this – and then the whole party would go to mass together. 'Have to get through it somehow,' he said, turning to look at Simon. 'Owe it to the village, and all that. These things are important, you know.'

He seemed about to add something more, but Poppy, lolling in the back seat, groaned. 'Oh, my God . . .' she said, and yawned in exaggerated protest. She looked at Simon and added, 'Still, the Barnetts are sure to be there. That'll make it all worthwhile, won't it, Si?'

# 26

'I wish it wasn't so late,' said Simon, slumped in an armchair in front of a huge log fire.

'If it's midnight mass, it has to be somewhere near midnight,' said Poppy scathingly. She'd been cracking nuts just behind his chair for the last half hour, and his patience was running thin.

'Time to be off to the vicarage,' said Richard. He'd been fortifying himself with whisky for some time, and looked red and jolly. Very seasonal, thought Simon grimly.

'I'll get my coat,' said Susan. 'And Richard, please come away when I say so. Don't want to walk into church just as Octavia Jones is doing her solo bit.'

Simon's ears pricked. 'What solo?' he said.

'Have you forgotten?' said his mother. 'She always sings the first verse of "Once in Royal David's City" as the choir processes in.'

'Very moving,' said Poppy.

'Do be quiet,' said Richard, 'else we shall leave you behind.'

'Fine,' said Poppy, 'just what I want.'

'In that case, you're coming,' said her mother, and handed over her coat.

The party was in full swing, and Simon caught a glimpse of a flushed Sarah over in the corner, deep in conversation with a tall, dark young man. 'Darling Si!' she yelled recklessly above the hubbub. 'Come and meet Guy!'

Oh God, thought Simon, and looked quickly round for John Barnett. There he was, glowering at him. Nothing for it but to go and meet Guy. He was relieved to see his father engaging John in conversation.

'A pleasure to meet you,' said Guy de Rivaulx politely. He'd been nobbled by Sarah the minute they arrived, and he was grateful for a new face. 'We are off to church, I believe?' he said, with little trace of accent. 'That will be very nice. An English Christmas . . . all we need is snow!'

'You may be lucky,' said Simon, doing his best not to look at Sarah. 'It's very cold, and one or two flakes were falling as we came in.'

It was not far from the old vicarage to the church, and sounds of merriment preceded the party as they hurried down the pitch-dark lane. Ivy Beasley, settled early in a pew with George and Ellen, heard them, and whispered that if anyone asked her, she'd say it was sacrilege.

'It is Christmas, Ivy,' George hissed.

'Season o' goodwill,' cackled Ellen loudly.

In the silence that followed Bill switching off the lights, the choir shuffled in the vestry, ready to start.

'Go on, then, Tavie,' nudged Peggy.

Octavia had seen the party arrive, with Sarah clinging to Simon's arm, and wished she could go home.

'Who was that lovely girl?' said Guy, approaching Simon by the coffee and mince pies.

'Octavia Jones,' said Simon without hesitation. He'd seen Guy's face as Octavia walked up the aisle, carrying a candle that lit up her features. If only . . . But Sarah was joining them, laughing about the carol that went wrong, demanding coffee without milk.

Guy drifted away, looking over the heads of the crowd. 'Excuse me,' he said, a polite hand on Octavia's arm. 'May I introduce myself? I'm staying with Annie and Andrew, and I want so much to congratulate you on your solo. Guy de Rivaulx . . . cousin by marriage, I think you say.'

'Thanks,' said Octavia. 'Glad you enjoyed it. It's my mum, really. She does the music, gets them all together.' She liked the look of this dark Frenchman, found it easy to talk to him, and when he asked if he could walk her home – 'An old English custom?' – she glanced across at Simon, pinned against a pillar by Sarah, and said thanks, that would be very nice.

# 27

'Quick workers, the French,' said Octavia to Sandra. They stood in the shop, waiting to be served. George had a basketful of groceries, and was anxiously checking the list made for him by Ivy.

'You look a bit peaky, Mr Chalmer,' said Peggy, smiling sympathetically at him from behind the counter. George sneezed into a handkerchief, and said he had a cold threatening. 'Take care of yourself, then,' said Peggy, as she helped him with the basket. 'Looks like snow again, so wrap up warm next time you come out.'

'Wouldn't catch me going out with a Frenchman,' whispered Sandra in Octavia's ear. 'Never know where they've been. And what happened to your campaign with you know who?' The shop was all ears. Couldn't be too careful.

'Postponed,' said Octavia. 'He's gone skiing with his cousins. Anyway, I'm not sure it's worth the effort.'

'Liar,' said Sandra, and moved forward to take her turn.

Guy had called Octavia several times, and she'd enjoyed his romantic appeal, told herself it wasn't really phony, and saw Ringford and its surrounding beauties through his eyes. They drove in her little car from village to village, skidding on icy roads, calling for drinks at warm, welcoming pubs, exchanging sentimental kisses in the snowy darkness of the old vicarage garden.

Her parents looked on, pleased that she seemed happy.

Her father had reservations. What would she do when Guy went back to France? He had stayed on longer than intended, but would go eventually. And if it was serious, how would Gabriella feel about their only daughter living permanently in France? 'Good heavens,' she'd replied, 'that's jumping ahead!'

The icy weather persisted, and one bright, cold afternoon Greg answered the telephone with chilly hands. It was cold even in the house, with the central heating going full blast.

'No, she's not here, Simon,' he said shortly. He stood in the neutral silence of their sitting-room, newspaper in hand, and added, 'She's gone with that French chap.' He hesitated, and as Simon Standing said nothing, he carried on reluctantly. 'Seems they flooded a meadow near Fletching mill and now it's frozen solid. All gone skating.'

'Right,' said Simon's voice lamely. 'Thanks. I might go over.'

'What a nerve!' Greg said, going through to Gabriella in the kitchen. 'The whole village knows he's carrying on with Sarah Barnett, and he has the gall to ring up after our Tavie!'

Gabriella shrugged. 'None of our business,' she said. She was in a very difficult position, working with Sarah at the school. The whole village assumed she knew it all. So far she'd been able to say perfectly honestly that she knew nothing more than the rest, and she intended to keep it that way. She'd heard, anyway, that it had cooled off. John had taken to following Sarah wherever she went, making a fool of himself, and Simon had been in Switzerland for a couple of weeks.

Now Greg glared at her. 'None of our business?' he said. 'It bloody well would be, if Tavie got involved with Simon Standing! Good God, woman, you can't go around with your eyes shut when your own daughter's in danger!'

Gabriella coloured. 'Now who's being hysterical?' she said mildly. 'There's no question of Octavia taking any interest in Simon Standing. She's quite smitten with Guy, as you can see for yourself.'

'So you say,' said Greg, 'but allow me to think you're wrong, Gabbie. Tavie is a complicated person, and, as we know from experience, she seldom says exactly what she means.'

'Tavie's just a girl, like any other,' said Gabriella. 'She'll fall in love like they all do, and not always with the right bloke. And then we'll have to accept it, and do our best for her, as always.'

Greg exploded, yelling that even if Gabriella was determined to be blind and dumb, he was not, and would see off bloody Simon Standing if he came sniffing round after his daughter.

The frosty flooded field, surrounded by bare willows and clumps of rushes in the marshy ground, looked as if virtual reality had transferred a vivid Breughel painting to Middle England. Skates had been retrieved from dusty attics, begged and borrowed, and brightly coloured figures skimmed and crashed, and were generally cheered on by knots of spectators.

Octavia, skating insecurely with Guy, who twirled and twisted with huge confidence, was surprised to see Simon standing at the edge of the field. Guy followed her gaze and said, 'Didn't know Simon was back.'

He steered her as far away as he could from the solitary watcher, and the next time Octavia looked, Simon had gone. Then he reappeared, talking to Annie Bishop by her car, and a third person, a small, neat person, warmly wrapped in scarlet, joined them. Sarah. So it's still on, thought Octavia, and wished she was somewhere else.

'Can we go?' she said miserably. 'My hands are freezing.'

They passed by Sandra and Sam, who'd brought Alison over to fool about with her friends on the ice. 'Blimey,' Sandra said to Sam, 'what a berk that French bloke is, with his fancy skating. What's Tavie up to, for God's sake? If it was me, I'd be in there with all guns blazing. I'd not be beaten by a married schoolteacher, years older than me!'

Sam grinned at her, glad that he wasn't on the receiving end of her scorn for once.

'Ah well,' she continued crossly, 'if she's daft enough to settle for second best, that's her affair. It'd please Madam, right enough. Simon'll get fed up with Sarah, and then it'll be all clear for podgy cousin Alex.'

The sun was now low in the sky, and a chill wind arose, blowing hair and whipping colour into bare fingers and noses. Across the winter fields, beyond the water meadow, a line of winter trees stood black against the outrageous colours of the sunset.

'Off we go, my darling,' said Guy, guiding Octavia to where they left their shoes.

Wavering over Guy's offer of dinner at Fletching, Octavia took a final look at the ice, where Simon was showing off to an admiring group, including Sarah. Then John Barnett appeared, slipping and sliding over the ice, grabbed Sarah's arm and hauled her protesting away from the field.

'Oh dear,' said Guy, 'An angry man. Poor Simon!'

'Serves him right,' muttered Octavia, and blew on her fingers.

Guy helped her into the car, and said, 'Dinner tonight, then?'

'You're on,' said Octavia.

Back home, she found her parents watching television, absorbed. She flopped down on the sofa beside Gabriella.

'Had a good time, dear?'

Octavia nodded. 'Not bad. Very cold, though. Guy's

coming later, and we're going out for supper. Hope the place is well heated.'

Greg waited until she was halfway up the stairs, then, as the programme ended, said, 'Simon phoned.'

'When?' said Octavia, coming back quickly into the room.

'Just after you'd gone,' said Greg.

'What did he want?'

'No idea, didn't ask him. What time's that play, Gabbie?' he added, searching through the *Radio Times*.

'Never mind about the bloody play,' said Octavia, sounding quite unlike herself. 'You could have asked him to ring back, or something.'

'It never occurred to me,' said Greg. 'Nor did I think it would be of any interest to you. Nor should it be.' Octavia glared at him, speechless. He switched channels and turned up the sound as the titles rolled.

'Anyway,' said Gabriella placatingly, 'you could always ring the Hall.'

'No thanks,' said Octavia, 'Guy's coming for me at eight. I'm going up to have a shower, and if there's another call for me, *please* give me a shout.'

'No need for sarcasm,' said Greg to her disappearing back. She didn't answer.

Guy had borrowed Annie's car, and parked it with a screech of brakes outside Barnstones at eight o'clock exactly. Why can't he be late for once? Octavia said to herself unreasonably. It was all so perfect with Guy. Always the right things done and said: compliments for Gabriella, earnest interest in whatever Greg decided to pontificate about at that moment. Can't be faulted, thought Octavia, as she wriggled into a narrow, silky sheath. I shall freeze. I'd never dress up like this for anyone else.

'You do look nice, dear,' said Gabriella. 'Dad's gone to open the door.' She envied Octavia. There was something very attractive about the French. And about the English, come to that. Youth, she decided sadly. It's youth that's attractive.

The wine was the best Octavia had ever tasted, and she accepted her fourth glass with enthusiasm. She knew the French were experts. Guy had made a real fuss about choosing, and then tasting when it came. Touch and go before he sends it back, she'd thought, embarrassed by the waiter's expression. She knew him. He'd worked in a transport café on the Leamington road and lived over at Waltonby. His caustic glance at Octavia said it all, and she breathed a sigh of relief when Guy nodded his approval.

The food had been good, too, and now she leaned back in her chair and smiled at Guy. His dark, nearly black eyes warmed her almost as much as the wine, and she relaxed. It wasn't his fault that Simon Standing was such a shit.

When they'd finished their meal, and Guy took her hand and led her out into the garden, wrapping his coat around her as well as her own, the cold air and the rushing mill stream were like champagne. Champagne on top of red wine, she muttered, and then found herself floating blissfully inside Guy's embrace.

'Oh, Guy,' she gasped, coming up for air.

'Octavia,' he whispered, 'you are wonderful . . . I want you so much.'

Ooops, thought a small part of Octavia's reason still working, watch it, gal. 'Come with me,' breathed Guy, 'I know a place . . .'

'You do?' said Octavia weakly.

'Warm and private . . . oh, Tavie . . .'

In Victoria Villa, Ivy and George sat in the kitchen having a last cup of cocoa. 'To warm you up for walking back to Bridge Cottage,' Ivy had said. They'd been to watch the skaters, but George had shivered and sneezed and Ivy had insisted on coming home.

George warmed his feet in front of the range, where Ivy piled coal that glowed and leapt with flames radiating heat into George's bones. He began to feel very hot, hotter than was comfortable. He put his hand to his burning forehead and coughed.

Ivy turned at once to look at him. 'George?' she said accusingly, 'are you worse?'

He hesitated, wondering whether to pretend, but the thought of turning out into the freezing night was becoming more and more unattractive, so he shook his head. 'Bit groggy, I'm afraid,' he said.

Ivy peered at him, put her hand on the offending forehead, and said, 'Right, George Chalmer, it's the front bedroom for you. Bed's made up, and I'll put the kettle on for a hottie. Up you go, now.'

Tucked between Ivy's lavender-scented sheets, George burrowed down into the big feather pillows and closed his eyes. He felt rotten, but knew he was in good hands. When Ivy said he'd be fine in the morning, he had believed her, with the touching faith of a child.

# 28

A few days later, after a quick thaw had destroyed the magic of the skating field, a notice appeared in the shop, announcing a New Year's party for the village, at which Greg Jones would show his video of the choral midnight mass, for elderly people and any others who hadn't been able to get to church.

Tickets sold well, and with the heaters in the village hall going full blast, and chairs arranged around card tables in informal groups, the scene was set for Greg's big night. Supper first, Gabriella had said firmly. She'd sat through too many of Greg's videos.

Now he looked around the noisy hall, and felt gratified. So much for Octavia's snide remarks about playing to empty chairs! Pity she'd gone off to Paris with Guy . . . Most of the village had come, it seemed. The Bishops, of course, who never missed any village event, as if some divine calling required it, and Sarah and John Barnett were there at the same table. He noticed that Annie and Sarah were deep in conversation, but Andrew and John sat back, silent, and in John's case, unsmiling. Hope they're not bored, Greg thought anxiously. Still, I'll make a start with the video soon, and that'll brighten them up.

He heard a shriek from the back of the Hall, and saw that Mandy and Robert Bates had brought along Joey and Margie, and Poppy Standing too. It was Poppy who had shrieked. Greg did hope she would behave herself.

Halfway through the video, the picture juddered and

jagged lines crossed the screen. 'Blast' said Greg, and asked for the lights, so he could see to put it right.

He was still fiddling with knobs when the door at the back of the hall opened, and Simon Standing came in with a rush of cold air. He'd reluctantly agreed to collect Poppy, who'd been allowed to attend only on condition that Simon fetched her at half past nine at the latest. As he pushed his way through the tables, seeing only his sister's scowling face, he caught his foot, overbalanced, and was horrified to find himself sprawling straight into Sarah Barnett's lap.

'Simon, darling!' said Sarah, well away on several glasses of wine. 'Didn't know you cared!'

There was a dreadful silence, and for seconds it seemed no one moved a muscle. Then with a deliberation that looked like slow motion, John Barnett rose to his feet. 'Well, I bloody care!' he roared, and launched himself at Simon.

Mandy Bates was still laughing as they let themselves into the bungalow. She pushed Joey's wheelchair into the kitchen, and drew the curtains. 'What a drama!' she chortled.

'Better than that boring old video,' said Joey. He'd been grabbed by Poppy, and wheeled quickly away from the scrum that developed by their table.

'Simon Standing'll have a shiner in the morning,' grinned Robert. He'd not thought twice about joining John in his towering revenge. God, he'd not enjoyed himself so much for years. Women screaming all over the place, plates of food skidding on to the floor, glasses shattering. The high point for him had been when John had grabbed one of Ivy Beasley's best cream meringues and shoved it violently into Simon's face, massaging it in with joyful abandon.

'Yeah, well,' said Mandy, finally sobering up. 'There's going to be a reckoning, that's for sure. Squire's son'll not stand for humiliation like that . . . I mean, did you see his trousers? God, he'll never . . .' And then she was off again, clutching the Rayburn rail and gasping for breath.

Joey took himself off to his bedroom, listening to his mother's helpless laughter with a half-grin. He'd loved it, too, watching from the sidelines, and nobody could say Simon hadn't asked for it. But Poppy, clutching his hand, had not laughed. In fact, when she'd tightened her grip so that Joey could scarcely bear it, he'd turned to look at her, and seen tears cascading down her crumpled face.

# 29

In the dim farm kitchen, with only a small lamp lit next to the telephone, it was very quiet. Nell lay dozing in front of the warm stove, and an early, newborn lamb, too tiny to live without extra cosseting, stirred in the soft bed. Sarah had collapsed in the big chair that was John's, her eyes closed, hands folded in her lap.

As John came stumping in from the yard, she didn't move. Not even her eyelids fluttered. It won't work this time, Madam, thought John, as he hung his old jacket on the back of the door. He sat down opposite her, and said, 'Sarah!'

She shook her head, without opening her eyes. 'Sarah, listen to me.'

'I'm listening,' she said flatly.

John took a deep breath, rubbed his cheek where a deep red bruise was beginning to show, and began to spill out what he had kept stored up for months. 'You know I'm not good at talking,' he said. 'Farming's my job, and it doesn't need a lot of talking. But now it's got to be said. You've done badly, Sarah. I tried to warn you, but either you didn't understand or you didn't care. If you didn't care, then there's not much left between us.'

He paused, rubbed his hand across his eyes, leaving a trail of mud and dust, and continued, 'Being married, as far as I'm concerned, means being faithful, trusting one another. I know you're younger than me, different in lots of ways, but you knew that when we wed. I loved you so much – enough to make it work, I thought.

You've got the school, and everybody says you're the best teacher we ever had – or did say that. I thought you'd grown to love the farm like I do . . . you know, the hens, an' that . . .'

Sarah's eyes were open now, and a flicker of a smile crossed her face. She seemed about to speak, but John carried on relentlessly.

'No, let me finish. What you've done with that stupid sod has nearly wrecked it all, home, us, school, every-thing . . . So now it's up to you to set it straight. Barnetts've got a good name in this village. Mum is very upset indeed, and I reckon you know how I feel.' Again he rubbed his eyes. 'So that's it, really, Sarah. Finish it for good, don't disgrace us again, and let's hope folks'll forget . . . in time.'

'Finished?' said Sarah, sitting up straight. 'Well, that's good, John. Now it's my turn. If I've hurt you – and your mum – then I'm sorry. It started as a bit of fun with Annie Bishop, and got out of hand.'

'Is that it?' said John, his heart sinking. He'd expected more, but looked into Sarah's face and knew that behind her cool green eyes there was a chilly stranger he scarcely knew, nor ever would know, one who had grown up in a town, with wealthy parents and smart friends, used to having her own way, and consumed with ambition and her own interests.

'John . . .' Sarah put a tentative hand out towards him. He sighed deeply, and put out his own. She squeezed his grazed knuckles and said, 'You were great tonight, Johnnie. Terrific. And I do love you, you know.' And incredibly, unbelievably, she began to laugh. 'Wasn't it wonderful?' she said. 'You were like Attila the Hun, or an avenging angel, or something. Oh, John, let's go to bed . . .'

In the way of villages, they did not, of course, forget. Nothing more seemed to be happening, no retribution from the Hall, but rumours still flew. Someone had seen Simon and Sarah in the Bull in Tresham, another claimed they'd been spotted walking through the woods, hand in hand. Yet another had been sure it was the guilty pair sitting close together in the cinema.

Mandy, on her rounds again, had just finished Sandra's hair and was brushing up cut ends, when a small knock at the door brought Octavia tentatively into the kitchen. 'Oh, sorry, Sand,' she said. 'Sorry, Mandy, I'll come back later.'

'Just finished,' said Mandy. 'I expect you two'll have lots to talk about!' she said happily, and left.

'Suppose she means your trip to France with the naughty Frenchman,' said Sandra, looking curiously at Octavia. For one who'd had a week in Paris, thought Sandra enviously, Octavia looked curiously depressed. 'What's up with you?' she said, without preliminaries.

Octavia hung her bag over the back of a chair, groaned, and said, 'Had a terrible morning, no lunch, and half an hour before my next client. Nobody at home, so I thought of you.'

'Fine,' said Sandra, 'drop everything, shall I, to make coffee?' She brushed the top of the table and set out a couple of mugs. Sandra had had no time to clear up before Mandy came, and Octavia began to wash dirty dishes while Sandra made the coffee.

'So what's new?' Sandra said, mollified at the sight of her friend with her hands in the sink. 'Who's beaten up who, and how many kids have you taken into care today?' Sandra knew all about it, first hand, and that gave her licence.

'None,' said Octavia. 'Nothing new.' She silently continued sloshing soapy water around the bowl.

'So what's wrong?' said Sandra, getting impatient. She'd ironing to do before the school bus brought Alison home, and wished Octavia would get on with it.

'Nothing wrong,' said Octavia, turning round to look

at her, leaning her back against the sink. 'Nothing at all. Guy was charming as always, wined and dined me, lavished love and money, took me round the best sights in Paris. Even introduced me to his parents. And nothing, Sand, nothing at all. Sad, isn't it?' she added, with a feeble attempt at a smile.

'No good at it, wasn't he?' said Sandra practically.

Good old Sand, thought Octavia, straight to the point. She shook her head. 'Oh, he was good at it, all right. But . . .'

'But what?' said Sandra. 'Them Frenchmen are supposed to be the best, aren't they?'

Octavia laughed now. 'He was very good at it, Sandra. And I can't say I didn't enjoy it at the time, but afterwards . . . it was a bit like eating a really sticky cream cake and then feeling like throwing up ten minutes later'

Sandra sighed, and pushed her friend gently into a chair. 'Far be it for me,' she said, 'to say I told you so, but at least you know about him now. Won't be forever wonderin' if you should've given him a chance. Oh, come on, Tavie,' she added, seeing tears welling up, 'it's not the end of the world. And spring's here, and Simon Standing's still alive – in spite of our John – and don't look at me like that, I know you've heard all about it. Anyway, the jolly old tennis club'll be starting up again soon, won't it? Who knows what might happen?'

Simon thanked God daily that he'd been able to move into the Ostler's House, even if it was cramped and musty, to escape his mother's murderous eyes. She and his father had treated him with little more than contempt when he'd been brought home that night. Only Poppy had come anxiously into his room, giving him iced water and a piece of raw frozen beef for his eye. She'd even offered to stay with him in case he needed anything. He'd thanked her gratefully, but said he felt like being alone, probably for the rest of his life.

Since then, he'd commuted to London daily, increasingly disliking the journey. He'd kept well away from village people, and worked at weekends on the estate with Bill and Foxy Jenkins, keeping his head down.

As the warm winds brought spring to the village, he looked at the tennis court and wondered if anyone would want to get the club going again. He wasn't sure about it himself, but he'd seen Octavia Jones outside the pub, and had had an aching longing just to stop and talk to her. The club would at least give him an excuse. His all-seeing mother had faithfully relayed to him the news that Octavia had been to Paris to visit Guy de Rivaulx.

Now he looked round the dark little room, at the spring sunshine out in the yard, and felt a sudden impatience with himself. For God's sake, it was time to make some changes. The thought of spending hours on crowded trains as spring turned into summer finally decided him. He'd leave London, get a job locally, and make his life here in Ringford. Uncle James had reminded him recently he'd always be welcome in the family business that covered half the Midlands. Well, why not? He would earn his place, expecting no favours.

He flung open the windows and breathed in the warm, scented air. My God, there'd be no harm in ringing George to see if he knew how the tennis gang felt. Poppy had asked once or twice if she could play with them this year, and he should give it a try for her sake, if only to thank her for being his friend that night.

George was sitting comfortably in Ivy's parlour, and when she called him to the phone, he remembered to walk painfully slowly. Weeks had gone by, and Ivy still maintained he was not yet fit to go home. George, aware that he was letting things slide, had not disagreed.

'Yes?' He winked at Ivy. 'Tennis? Well, I've been a

bit out of circulation, but Ivy might know.' He put his hand over the receiver, and said in a stage whisper, 'Heard anybody talking about the club starting up again?'

Ivy nodded vigorously. 'Mandy Bates,' she said. 'In the shop. Said she was going to ask round.'

George relayed this to Simon, and agreed that the nights were drawing out nicely. 'Get hold of Octavia,' he said, winking again at Ivy. 'I'm sure she will understand that I am still incapacitated. Such a charming girl, and will, of course, not go ahead with her intention to resign. Just at the moment, anyway,' he added, leaning gently against Ivy's proffered shoulder.

'Any news from Mount Olympus?' said Peggy, standing back to admire her handiwork. She'd been arranging a gardening window, with packets of seeds, bags of compost, columns of plastic plant pots.

'If you mean the Hall,' said Bill, 'herself is in another spin. Couldn't help overhearing her shouting at the boss, poor bloke. Seems she's refusing to do anything for Simon: washing, ironing, shopping, none of it. Hasn't forgiven him yet.'

'Dear me,' said Peggy. 'Pity she's got nothing better to think about.'

The shop doorbell jangled, and Peggy returned from the kitchen to find Ivy Beasley, pink and springlike in a new skirt and blouse. 'Morning,' she said. 'Half a pound of ham, please. Making sandwiches.'

'How's George?' said Peggy automatically. She'd been saying it for quite some while now.

'Mr Chalmer is much better,' said Ivy. 'Dr Russell has recommended fresh air, and as it is such a beautiful day, we are off for a picnic.'

Dr Russell had summed up the Ivy and George situation with an experienced eye, taken in the rows of creams and lotions on the bathroom shelf and Ivy's dramatically improved appearance, and decided all was much better left as it was.

Ivy now hesitated, as if unsure how much she should say to Peggy. The new Ivy Beasley lingered longer, made more conversation than in the old days.

'Lovely,' said Peggy. 'It'll do him the power of good. Try that nice grassy stretch by the bend in the river. You could watch the fish.'

Ivy bridled. 'I think I know the local geography better than most,' she sniffed, and then forced a smile. 'But we'll find a nice spot, Mrs Turner,' she added, and walked out with a pleasantry about sunshine being the best medicine of all.

'She's a changed woman,' said Peggy, not for the first time.

'Not too changed, I hope,' said Bill.

# 30

One week later, George announced that it was time he
returned to his cottage. In spite of Ivy's protests that he
was not well enough, he was suddenly adamant, saying
the cottage would deteriorate if left empty.

That wasn't the reason George was leaving, of course.
He confided he was thinking of making old Ted an
offer for the place. 'Set down some roots, Ivy,' he'd
said. It would mean putting his Leamington property
on the market, raising a deposit, and all that that en-
tailed.

But that wasn't the whole story. He didn't tell her that
whilst Ivy had been round at Doris's, his friend had
telephoned. Said he'd got Ivy's number from directory
enquiries, and what the hell was George playing at?
Harsh words had been exchanged, but the upshot was
that George had agreed to get on with it. Leave it to me,
laddie, George had cautioned, and told him on no
account to telephone again.

'I'll be fine, Ivy,' George said repeatedly, and when
she'd finally left him alone in the cottage, persisting in
behaving as if he'd rejected her devotion, he sat down in
front of his own television with relief. Then when he
had to make his own cocoa, and the sheets were cold
without Ivy's hottie, he shivered, and wished things
could be different.

Next morning, listening to harshly cawing rooks in
the trees surrounding the old vicarage, he still felt cold,
and wondered whether to get up and make himself a cup

of tea. In the end, he dozed off again, only to dream that he'd left the oven on and the kitchen was ablaze.

Waking in a panic, he rushed down, half asleep, and twisted his ankle on the bottom stair. 'Sod everything!' he yelled, and hobbled into the kitchen to put the kettle on. He'd forgotten to put the milk back in the fridge, and it was sour, floating in nasty lumps on the top of his tea.

Abandoning breakfast, he heard his gate swinging and banging in the wind, and, shutting it crossly, he pinched his finger between gate and post. It was agony, and he swore loudly, sucking his finger for comfort.

Ellen Biggs, stumping along with a bundle of twigs in an old haversack, pulled up short. 'There's old George, back at last,' she said aloud. But his language! Bet our Ivy's never heard that mouthful.

'Mornin' George!' she shouted familiarly. It was a long time since she'd seen him on his own. Now's me chance, she said to herself. 'Squeezed it in the gate, 'ave yer?' she said, coming closer and seeing his finger held in the air like a smoking gun. ' 'ere, best come over to the Lodge and let me put a plaster on it,' she continued, and George was only too pleased to agree.

Reluctant to go back to his empty cottage, he stayed on, listening to tales of Ellen's days as cook at the Hall. Forgotten about the plaster, he thought, but eventually she produced a scruffy packet and demanded to see the ' 'orrible wound.'

Ivy Beasley, opening Ellen's gate and walking smartly up the narrow garden path, was puzzled by the sound of voices. She pushed open the creaking door called, 'Ellen? You there, Ellen?' She heard a voice she recognised instantly. So that was it. Already. She took a deep breath and marched into the dark little room, where she found George sitting in the most comfortable chair and Ellen bending over him with adhesive bandage and a pair of gigantic kitchen scissors.

They both turned and looked at her like guilty children. 'So kind of Ellen . . . ' began George, and ''e's 'urt 'isself, Ivy,' said Ellen, with a knowing grin.

'You'd better give that to me,' said Ivy, taking bandage and scissors out of Ellen's shaky hands. 'And let me look at it, George.' She took his hand and examined the swollen finger closely. 'Best left alone,' she said. 'The skin's not broken, so you certainly need nothing on it.'

She put Ellen's rescue kit down on the table, and turned to where the old woman was rattling cups crossly in the kitchen. 'I brought you some magazines from Tresham,' she said. 'Let's hope there's something about first aid in them. Now then, George,' she added, 'you'd better come back with me for your dinner. Can't let you out of my sight for a minute,' she added, smiling grimly.

It had been an excellent meal. George sat in Ivy's front room, his stomach gurgling contentedly and his hand supported in a sling made from one of Ivy's silk scarves. 'Now you won't try to use it,' she had said, knotting it neatly round the back of his neck.

Sounds of washing-up drifted through, and George looked out over the Green, where the big chestnut was swaying in the wind, its leaves bright and new. Two old men sat on the Standing memorial seat, gossiping and puffing at pipes. Sandra Goodison was heading for the church, a bunch of flowers in her hand, and her path was crossed briefly by the Jenkins terrier, following his nose as usual. The vicar, Nigel Brooks, pedalled along Bates's End, his feet going fast and his cassock flying out behind him; and as George watched, Foxy Jenkins narrowly missed running him down as he roared along on his tractor, an empty trailer swaying behind him. I know them all now, thought George, and they know me. Got me passport, and permission to stay.

'Ivy!' he called, and she came through to the doorway,

wiping her hands on her apron. 'Wouldn't it be nice to go for a stroll this afternoon? Sun's out,' he said. He'd come to a decision, aided by apple crumble and custard and coffee to follow. The time had come. George smothered his misgivings and made plans.

'Are you sure you're up to it?' said Ivy. 'Well, if you say so. Dr Russell did say . . . and that picnic did you good the other day. We'll go up Bagley Hill and then on to the old windmill,' she said, gathering enthusiasm.

George looked alarmed. He'd thought of flat pastures, buttercups and daisies and trilling larks, with a mossy bank and a rippling stream. 'Um, right,' he said, 'but my finger . . . ?'

Ivy laughed heartily. 'Don't worry,' she said. 'I won't forget you're a wounded soldier. And we can take it slowly.' The affection in her voice gave George an unexpected jolt.

The street was unusually busy as they left Victoria Villa, and Doreen Price greeted them cheerfully. 'Lovely day for a walk,' she said, coming down the shop steps clutching a large box of groceries. Mr and Mrs Ross nodded politely, and enquired after George's health, seeing the sling.

'Nothing much,' said George. 'My own fault, you know.' He smiled his gentlemanly smile, and touched his hat with his good hand.

He was already weary by the time they were halfway up Bagley Hill, but he kept going bravely, only stopping to examine an unfamiliar plant in the hedgerow, asking Ivy for its name. In fact, every sodding boring green weed was unfamiliar, he thought, but it gave him an excuse for a rest. His wrenched ankle was hurting again, and he realised he'd got soft in the long weeks of convalescence.

'Vetch,' said Ivy, 'purple vetch . . . I'm sure I told you that before. I'll get you a book for your birthday, and you can check them off.'

Oh God, thought George, that'll be jolly. He struggled on manfully, ignoring his protesting feet and keeping his eyes on Ivy's strong legs marching ahead of him.

At last they were at the top of the hill, and turned to look back. In the field next to the road a flock of starlings fed on something invisible in the grass under an old tree. Suddenly they were up, chattering angrily, and flying to the other end of the paddock, where a dark bay pony cropped the grass and turned up insects. Full of mysteries, the country, thought George. Secret lives going on under our noses.

'Can't beat it, can you, George?' said Ivy happily, as she surveyed the familiar panorama laid out before them. 'Here, hold the basket for a minute.' She took off her scarf, and her hair blew free in the wind. 'Not much farther,' she said, and they set off across a grassy field.

'Sure you're all right?' George nodded. It wouldn't do to weaken now.

'See over there?' said Ivy. 'That's the old windmill. There'll be shelter from the wind, and we can have our tea. Reckon we've earned it, eh?'

She set off again, and George followed, tripping on tussocks and molehills, and trying desperately not to swear. It would take a few cups of Ivy's best, he thought, to get him back in the mood.

Inside the crumbling walls, on soft grass sheltered from the strong breeze that blew over the top of the hill, Ivy set out their picnic. George lowered himself carefully on to a dry mound, and took off his hat. He wiped his brow, and accepted a cup of tea with relief. Ivy handed him a thick wedge of fruit cake, and as he got his breath back, he felt restored, invigorated, up to the task in hand.

'Ivy,' he smiled at her, 'this is such a pleasure. Being here with you, owing you such a lot. I do begin to feel at home in the country, with you as my guide.'

'. . . My comfort and my guide,' sang Ivy, a little off key. 'That's a hymn. Nice, isn't it? Nice way of thinking about someone. Not just Jesus.' She was beginning to feel nervous. There was something in George's tone, a sort of seriousness that she'd never heard before.

'Exactly,' said George. 'You know, Ivy, since I've been in Ringford I've done a lot of thinking.' He shifted his leg, and thought that the thing uppermost in his mind at present was a numb bum. Perhaps he'd better stand up. He struggled to his feet, and Ivy was immediately by his side.

'Here,' she said, 'let me help.' She held him under the elbow of his good arm and levered him upright.

Now, thought George, this is it. He put his hand to her cheek, leaned forward, and kissed her. It was a very light kiss, but it was on those thin, forbidding lips, and it was the first time they had ever felt the touch of a man. It was a very important moment for Ivy Beasley, and she never forgot it.

'Dear Ivy,' said George. He could see she was speechless, but not displeased. 'Dear, dear Ivy,' he continued, and surprised himself by the genuine emotion in his voice. 'Could you, would you . . . do you think you could possibly consider becoming my wife?'

On the top of Bagley Hill, on a mild, breezy day in spring, bells rang, thunder clapped, lightning zipped from one side of Ivy's reeling head to the other, and she had trouble keeping her balance. Then, through all the tumult, came her mother's laughter, loud and mocking, and Ivy was sober in an instant.

'Yes, George,' she said. 'Thank you very much for asking. And yes, I would consider it an honour to be your wife.' With touching dignity and grace she kissed him on the cheek.

# 3 1

Saturday afternoon was always a duff time in Ringford. 'Oh, how thrilling,' said Poppy, when her mother suggested she went into Tresham on the bus.

'It'd certainly be a change,' said Richard mildly. 'When did you last go on a bus?'

'I can make my own arrangements, thanks,' she said, and disappeared.

Mark Jenkins, still overweight in spite of his mother's best efforts, avoided any suggestions that he might join in village sports. He sensed unerringly when he was being done good to. Colin Osman, officially in charge, never failed to say, 'See you on Saturday, Mark?' but Mark Jenkins had so far sloped off as fast as his bulk would take him, muttering that Mum wanted him to do something . . .

It was Hugo Dodwell who passed the message round that he'd be in the thicket around two-ish, and that his mother was out for the day so he could bring a few consumables. His father used words like 'consumables', and Hugo was a bright lad, quick to pick up the latest and smartest in everything.

Poppy seized on the news with relief. She'd found the Simon and Sarah thing quite entertaining for a while, but when it had all come to a violent head that night in the village hall she'd suddenly realised how horrible it all was. Thank God that Barnett woman had given up, and been taken back by her stupid husband. Simon, after being nice to her for a day or two, had been foul for weeks now, though, not talking, and shutting himself up in the Ostler's House. Why couldn't he find some decent girl in London and get out of Ringford, live somewhere else?

Now he'd done the opposite: given up his London job, and gone to work for Uncle James. Still perked up when anybody mentioned Octavia's name, she'd noticed. Well, Mum was dead against that one. 'Such an ordinary family,' she'd heard her say to Dad. And if that boring little Jones man hadn't organised a party to show off his rotten video that night, the Standings wouldn't have looked such fools. I hate Greg Jones, she said to herself, as she cycled down the avenue. I hate his stupid little beard, and his ridiculous deaf-aid. And his sniffy daughter most of all. Mum's right. Who do they think they are?

She screeched into Bates's farmyard with a flurry of dust from the dry cobbles.

'Where's Adolf?' said Joey. Poppy seldom rode him these days, preferring her bike. Growing up, his gran had said. Noticed that, thought Joey, grinning to himself.

'Adolf's invading the paddock,' Poppy said smartly. 'Come on, look lively,' she added. 'We're all meeting at the thicket. D'you need to have a pee first?' It was one of the good things between them, that Poppy made no bones about his need to plan for the absence of lavatories, and was not above helping him if nobody else was around.

Conversation in the thicket was desultory. 'My dad says the hay's good this year,' ventured Mark, and was instantly squashed by Poppy.

'How hugely exciting,' she said, and sat up. 'Joey,' she added, 'D'you want to come and lie on the grass by me?'

Hugo Dodwell chuckled suggestively, and stood up. 'Come on, Joe,' he said, 'we'll give you a hand.' Joey was not heavy, and they manhandled him carefully out of his awkward chair and gently lowered him to the ground.

'Here,' said Poppy, 'put your head on my jersey,' and she settled him comfortably before collapsing again beside him. 'There,' she said, 'now you can see what we all see.'

Joey was silent. Stretched out on the spongy grass, the sun warm on his face, and his body relaxed, he realised once more than Poppy was no fool. She seemed to know, without being told. A lark began to sing a liquid, joyful song high above him, and he shielded his eyes with one hand. 'Can you see it, Poppy?' he said, and added in a quiet voice, 'Grandad used to say they go right up to heaven and back.'

'And I suppose you believed him,' snorted Hugo Dodwell.

'Yes, I did,' said Joey simply, and silence fell once more.

'How's yer brother, Poppy?' said Mark Jenkins, not at all innocently.

'Grim,' said Poppy. 'Still, at least he keeps out of my way. Been painting the place up.'

'Ready for his next girlfriend?' said Hugo, and dodged behind Joey's chair.

'Who's the latest?' said Mark foolishly.

'Shut up!' Poppy said violently. 'Mind your own business, all of you.'

'Reckon he's still after Tavie Jones,' whispered Hugo.

'I heard that,' said Poppy, 'and he's not, thank God.' Poppy snapped off a piece of long grass and leaned over to tickle Joey's face.

'Stop it, you idiot!' he said, brushing her off. But she didn't stop, and he grabbed her hand, both of them laughing as she rolled him over and over, his legs at all angles, like a grasshopper.

'Watch out, Poppy!' said Mark Jenkins, suddenly worried. He'd never seen Joey Bates out of his wheelchair before, and felt uneasy. The rest of them held back, instead of piling in for the usual affray.

Poppy sat back, laughing and straightening her clothes. 'Don't worry, our Markie,' she said. 'I'm not going to assault him. Not while you lot are around, anyway,'

Joey Bates looked at her and frowned. 'Hush, Poppy.' That was all he said, but she quietened down, and Mark Jenkins opened another can of shandy.

'My auntie's neighbour's lit'le gel over at Bagley was assaulted,' he said, throwing out the news like a challenge.

'Oh dear,' Hugo said, smirking knowingly. 'Got her bum smacked by her dad?'

Mark shook his head. 'Nope,' he said. 'Worse than that.'

'What, then?' said Poppy, chewing a biscuit and spitting it out on the grass. 'Ugh!' she said. 'Squashed flies!'

'D'yer want to know, or not?' said Mark Jenkins, gathering up the empty cans and putting them tidily in a plastic carrier.

'Put us out of our misery,' said Hugo, yawning, stretching his arms above his head.

Mark stared at them all. 'Well, it were the lodger,' he said. 'He messed about with her, my auntie said.'

'*Messed about!*' screamed Poppy, rocking with laughter. 'What on earth do you mean?'

'Shut up, Poppy,' said Joey, wriggling into a sitting position. 'You know perfectly well what he means.' He put out a hand. 'Now, come on,' he said, 'help me back in my chair.'

# 32

The afternoon sun shone through Ivy's sparkling windows into her front room, where George sat in his usual chair and Ivy officiated from the tea-tray.

'Turned out really nice now,' said Ivy, handing George a second slice of cake. 'After such a bad start. Now, my dear . . .' The endearment came out quite easily. Ivy, not used to demonstrating affection, was beginning to enjoy it. 'Now, George dear,' she repeated, 'tell me if that cake is up to scratch. A new recipe, from our Doris.'

His mouth was too full to answer, but he put out a hand and took hers. He squeezed, and she coloured. 'Mmm,' he said, biting into the light, buttery cake. 'It's just like you, Ivy, excellent,' he mumbled, and continued, with an inspiration that surprised even himself, 'Sweetness and light, with a touch of spice to make it all the more delicious.' Good God, he was really warming to his task!

'George!' said Ivy. 'You do say the nicest things.'

He smiled at her. She was not a bad old thing, really. It was probably about time. 'Now then,' he said. 'I think we should let the world, or certainly Round Ringford, know our joyful news. When do you suggest? And who shall we tell first?'

Ivy's colour rose again, and it seemed to her that although the sun had now vanished, the room was filled with a golden glow. 'Well, if you think so, George.' she said, and sat down suddenly on the upright chair by the window. For once, she had her back to the life going on outside, was absorbed in the unbelievable goodness of her own. She clasped her hands together, thinking hard. 'I think Doris should be the first to know,' she said. 'She's my best friend, I suppose. And, of course, Ellen Biggs will have to be told at the same time, else there'll be ructions.'

'This week it shall be, then,' said George, reminding himself to go through the small selection of old rings he kept in his dressing case. A ruby for Ivy, he thought. Blood red. There's more than likely a hidden fire in the old girl. Other people's lives, he thought. Getting involved was an unpredictable business. A shiver ran across his shoulders, and he drew his jacket close around him.

'Cold, George?' said Ivy, who had never felt warmer. 'I'll light the fire. Don't want you poorly again. We can spend the evening in here, making plans.'

Left alone in the parlour, George shifted uneasily in his chair. Making plans, the point of no return. He heard Ivy humming. Happier than she's ever been, dear old thing . . . Reassured, he adjusted the cushion behind his head and picked up the newspaper.

# 33

At the end of a slack day in the shop, Peggy was glad to lock the door, get out into the garden and see to her geraniums. She pushed handfuls of compost round the nobbly stems of last year's plants, and repotted the cuttings she'd done in August. Most of them had taken, and she stood back and looked at the line of pots around the yard: new, green young plants, about to burst into flower. Something for nothing, and with these, at least, she seemed to have the knack.

'Peg!' called Bill from the kitchen. 'Telephone!'

'Peggy? It's Doreen. Just wondered if you'd heard anything new. I just asked Ivy about being WI secretary again. Take it for granted, don't we, after all these years? Well, you could have knocked me down with the proverbial feather when she said she wasn't sure!'

'Eh?' said Peggy stupidly. This was so odd that she couldn't think of anything else to say.

'Yep,' continued Doreen. 'Said she'd have to give it some thought, discuss it with George . . .'

'Oh my Lord,' said Peggy. 'Are you thinking what I'm thinking?'

'Naturally,' said Doreen. 'Only thing you can think, my dear. Well, we shall see. Just thought you might have heard . . .'

Peggy turned to Bill, who was helping himself to a thick slice of new bread, spread generously with butter and strawberry jam. 'I think you'd better ask George for that chess game a bit sharpish,' she said. 'Things are hotting up in Victoria Villa.'

In Social Services reception hall, the telephone rang, and the girl, about to go home, gave it an evil look. She picked it up reluctantly, and said, 'Hello? Can I help you?' She'd tidied her desk and was almost the last to leave. Trust some berk to ring up at this hour. Well, he'd have no luck so late in the day. 'Who?' she said. She couldn't hear very well, but it was a man's voice, and he sounded very far away.

'Oh, Miss *Jones*,' she said. 'No, sorry. She's left the building. Won't be back until, hang on, let me see . . .' She cursed to herself as she smudged her nail polish. Where was that note Octavia had left? Oh yes, here it was. She sifted through a pile of papers and picked up the telephone. 'You still there? Right. Well, she'll be in after three o'clock tomorrow afternoon.' She sighed, remembered that she'd already had a warning from old Harry this week, and said quickly, 'Can I give her a message? What name shall I say?'

'Standing,' said the voice. 'Simon Standing. But don't worry, I'll catch up with her later. Goodbye and thanks.'

Nice voice, said the receptionist to herself, and switched on the answerphone.

'Octavia!' yelled Simon, leaning out of his car window. He'd been aimlessly driving around Tresham for the last ten minutes, and then there she was, waiting at the lights by the cinema. He pulled into the kerb, screwed up his courage, and beckoned her over. 'Been trying to get hold of you,' he said.

'You can't stop there,' said Octavia. 'The lights . . .'

Simon noticed that she had flushed. Might be a good sign? 'Just for a minute, it'll be okay,' he said.

'What do you want?' said Octavia. 'Something to do

171

with tennis? It'll be all right. I'll carry on till George is better.'

'Oh, right, thanks,' said Simon. He was about to say more, when he caught sight of a tall, thin young man, studious looking, with round spectacles, hovering and obviously meeting someone. Simon frowned. 'Is that chap . . . ?' he said. Octavia glanced round and nodded. 'Yep,' she said, 'he's waiting for me. 'Bye.' She walked away quickly, and was furious to find herself trembling like a leaf.

'I do love this track,' said Sarah Barnett, walking along the old railway line with Annie Bishop. They were ambling along at Tinker's pace, stopping now and then to turn over the wild strawberry leaves, finding tiny white flowers. It was early evening, with the light still good, and Sarah had called to say she needed a breath of air after a hard day in a stuffy schoolroom.

Annie, leaving a protesting Andrew to get supper for the children, had collected the dog-lead, whistled Tinker, and departed. 'He's had half a day at home,' she said to Sarah, 'so he can cope,' and they set off without a backward glance.

Now they'd come to the shaly stretch of the railway line, where great holes made by badgers peppered the ground. 'Careful here, Sarah,' said Annie. 'Watch your ankles.' Tinker was sniffing animatedly down a hole, and Annie had to pull him back.

'Too old for those larks,' Sarah said.

'What's new?' Annie said, the dangerous terrain behind them.

Sarah thought for a moment, wishing she had some real news to tell. 'Nothing much,' she said. 'Uncle James has given Simon a job over at Waltonby. The lovebirds went for a smooch up Bagley Hill.'

'Lovebirds?' said Annie quickly, her eyes suspicious.

'Oh, don't get excited,' said Sarah. 'I meant Ivy and George. They looked very pleased with themselves.'

'Ivy's walking on air,' said Annie. 'Looks years younger . . . it's love, Sarah,' she went on, 'but they're keeping it a secret. That's my guess.'

'Could be,' said Sarah, and with little real interest in the two old parties, added, 'anyway, we all need our secrets.'

'A pity you couldn't have kept yours,' said Annie bluntly. They strolled through a corridor of saplings, the greenish light filtering dimly through interlaced branches.

'Which one?' said Sarah blandly.

'Oh, come on,' said Annie. 'Let's not be coy.' Then she remembered something her daughter Helen had said, something George from Fletching had reported, about seeing Mrs Barnett with Mr Standing in Bagley last week. Annie had dismissed it as the usual muddled garbage the children brought home, but now she looked at Sarah and wondered.

'Don't preach,' said Sarah, her eyes harsh. 'Glass houses and stones and all that.'

They walked in silence for a while, then Annie said, 'Mandy's been on about tennis. Are we going?'

'Why not?' said Sarah.

'Well, for God's sake,' said Annie, out of patience, 'you know perfectly well why not!'

'All gone and forgotten,' said Sarah, smiling smugly. 'John and I will be there as usual. How about you?'

Annie struggled. 'I don't know,' she said. The atmosphere in the village had scarcely cooled, and this brazen attitude of Sarah's didn't help. 'I do know,' she said, hoping to break Sarah's shell, 'that Octavia Jones is carrying on with the secretary job after all. Seems Simon begged her,' she invented. 'Really turned on the charm. So at least we'll be well organised, and maybe tennis will be the only game we play.'

Sarah hooted. 'No wonder you fit in so well at the vicarage!' she laughed. 'Sermon over? Well, I for one hope there'll still be another game going.' She was delighted to see Annie's furious frown. 'Croquet, I mean,' she said. 'What else?'

'Simon's back early,' said Susan, seeing him across the yard, opening the door of the Ostler's House.

'Don't spy,' said Richard. 'You said often enough you wanted him to live his own life. And,' he added nastily, 'do his own washing and cooking. So don't spy. And that goes for you too, Poppy. Come away from the window.'

Richard was beginning to wonder if Simon would ever be happy again. Perhaps he should have a word with him, man to man. Give him the benefit of his own experience, tell him that these things happen. Simon's work was going well over at Waltonby, Richard knew that from his brother. Very pleased with him, he'd said. Very popular with the clients. So there was only one other thing: women. Still hankering after the schoolteacher? No, surely not. Couldn't be Alexandra. She'd jump at it. Or Octavia Jones? Ah, that was different.

He chuckled, and Poppy said irritably, 'What's funny, Dad? Share it with us, and brighten our lives.' She should have been doing homework, but no one had the strength to do battle with her, and she'd draped herself over the old armchair by the Aga.

'If something exciting doesn't happen soon,' she added, seeing her father was not rising to the challenge, 'I shall shoot myself. Or make something happen.' She unwound her legs and walked slowly over to the door. 'Think I'll go and annoy Simon,' she said. 'Maybe he's got sniffy Octavia coming for a tennis meeting, and I can hang around and make a nuisance of myself.' She seemed cheered by this prospect, and ran across the yard.

'Oh dear,' said Susan. 'What are we going to do with that one, Richard?'

'She'll be all right,' he said absently. '*Is* Octavia coming up this evening?'

'How should I know?' said Susan. 'It's a matter of very little importance to me, I'm afraid, and I intend that it shall remain so.'

Richard raised his eyebrows. 'Something bothering you, darling?' he said. 'Time for a little drinky?' he added, and without waiting for her answer, went off to fetch a couple of large gins.

# 34

Doris's heart sank when Ivy's door opened and there stood the ever-present George. Ah well, Ivy had said she wanted tea at Victoria Villa this week, and she supposed it was because old George wanted to be there, too. A sudden horrid thought struck Doris, but she suppressed it firmly. Instead, she brought up the subject of Poppy Standing and her rudeness to everyone in the village, especially Octavia Jones.

Ivy, instead of pronouncing firmly on what should be done, and throwing in some well-timed criticisms of today's youth, turned smilingly to George and said, 'What a shame, isn't it? Mind you, it's a difficult age. But she is a Standing. She'll turn out all right, if you ask me.'

Ivy's mildness was ominous. Doris had a premonition, and an urgent desire to run. She looked pleadingly at Ellen Biggs to shut up on the subject of all the girls she had known who'd gone to the bad.

A silence fell, and Ivy cleared her throat. 'Um,' she said, and Doris's heart thumped, 'um, George and I have something to tell you two.'

I knew it, thought Doris. Oh, God, let me say the right thing.

'What's that, then, our Ivy?' said Ellen, eyeing the depleted plate of shortbread.

'Will you, George . . . ?' said Ivy, coyly.

Oh, my Lord, thought Doris.

George Chalmer knew how to rise to an occasion. He'd had plenty of practice. He got to his feet and crossed the room to stand by Ivy. 'I am proud to tell you – and you two are the very first to know – that Ivy has consented to become my wife.'

Ivy beamed at him. Ellen dropped her plate. Doris choked, and searched desperately for her handkerchief. After what seemed like an age, she found her tongue. 'Congratulations, both of you,' she said. 'I am sure we are very pleased. Very pleased indeed, aren't we, Ellen?'

Ellen was bent double, retrieving her plate, and said nothing. It was only after she had straightened up and resettled herself in her chair, that Doris saw the tear, slowly falling down Ellen's creased cheeks. The old woman nodded, swallowed, and visibly collected herself. 'Well done, Ivy,' she said, 'and you too, George. I 'ope you'll be very 'appy, both of yer. And now, Doris, if you'll give me an 'and, I think it's time I was gettin' back.'

Nothing that any of them said would make her stay longer, and although Ivy agreed with George that it had been a very nice occasion, she could not suppress the feeling that Ellen Biggs had a great deal more to say.

# 35

'So when is George coming for chess?' said Peggy, stacking the last tin in a pyramid of baked beans. Summer and winter, baked beans were a staple in Ringford's diet.

'Tomorrow,' said Bill. 'He jumped at it, as a matter of fact.'

'Good,' said Peggy, 'it's WI, so he can keep you company. And don't forget to quiz him. Then we can all be happy.'

George had accepted with alacrity, chiefly because an evening without wedding talk was an attractive proposition. Ivy had the bit between her teeth, and could think of little else.

Chess had been a passion with George at one time, and he was good at it. Anticipation, dearie, he would say to his friend. Always being at least one move ahead, that's the secret of chess. And the better you know your opponent, the better you can predict the way he'll jump. This simple philosophy had stood him in good stead, in life as well as in chess.

'Evening, Peggy my dear,' he said, as he allowed Bill to help him off with his coat. 'Spitting with rain, and quite cold out there. Make sure you're well wrapped up before venturing forth. "Cooking With Butter" tonight, isn't it?' That afternoon, Ivy had huffed and puffed, saying there wasn't anything anybody could teach her about cooking, with or without butter, especially that person from Waltonby.

'I've left a few sandwiches, Bill,' said Peggy. 'And you can make a coffee when you're ready. 'Bye, then, 'bye George, have a nice evening.'

After Peggy had gone, the atmosphere cooled. Bill could not help it. There was something about this bloke that worried him. Was it his soft white hands, the slightly sweet smell of aftershave? George couldn't be more pleasant, Bill told himself. Come on, make the effort.

They began the game, and George's obvious skill sharpened Bill's wits. Before long he was enjoying the challenge. The clock ticked on, and they were on their third game when Bill realised they'd not had their coffee and sandwiches.

'Have a pause, George, shall we?' he said. 'I'll just go and put the kettle on.'

By the time he got back to the sitting room with a loaded tray, George had left the chess board and was wandering around the room. 'Nice pictures,' he said, peering closely at the Lakeland watercolours.

'Never really looked at 'em,' said Bill, clumsily pouring coffee. 'Peggy's. There wasn't much of mine left when we got married. Joyce kept most of it.'

'Ah yes,' said George, 'your former wife?'

Bill nodded. Nosy old bugger needn't think he was getting any confidences. 'And how about your former wife, George?' he said, belatedly remembering Peggy's strictures. 'Was she fond of paintings?'

George's answer was oblique. Slippery devil, thought Bill, wondering if the former Mrs Chalmer was under the floorboards somewhere in Leamington. Nobody knew anything about George Chalmer. He'd come among them with his gentlemanly ways, had charmed Ivy Beasley, the silly old trout, and still had given nothing away.

'How long since your wife passed on?' Bill persisted. His blood was up now, but George was a match for him.

He looked down at the chess board, and said, 'I'm afraid you've got me beaten here, Bill. Well done! Do we have time for another game, or is that Peggy's light footstep I hear in the hall?'

It *was* Peggy, and she burst in with a gust of cold, damp night air. 'Had a good chat?' she said, looking meaningly at Bill. 'WI was good. Ivy one-upped the butter lady, good and proper.'

'Ah,' said George, 'there is very little on which Ivy is not an expert. We are off to the vicarage tomorrow, so no doubt she'll be able to tell Reverend Brooks a thing or two about matrimony!'

There was a total silence. Finally Peggy found her voice. 'Did you say matrimony?' she croaked.

George looked surprised. 'Oh, didn't Ellen or Doris tell you?' he said. 'Well, that's a surprise. Yes, Ivy has accepted my offer, and we've decided to be married in the autumn.'

'Well,' said Bill, with false heartiness, 'I'm sure we offer you our sincere congratulations, don't we, Peg?'

'Oh, yes, of course!' said Peggy, beaming. 'How wonderful!'

After George had gone, Peggy said, 'Wow! How about that, then, Bill?' Bill didn't answer. 'Oh, come on, love,' she said. 'Why are you being so stuffy? Did he say anything wrong this evening?'

'It was what he didn't say,' Bill replied, and began to pack away his chess pieces. Then he really worried her. 'Do we know anyone in Leamington?' he asked. 'Anyone we could get to ask around a bit? There's just something, Peggy, and I can't put my finger on it. But I'd hate to see old Ivy in trouble, real trouble.'

Peggy frowned at him. 'There's my cousin,' she said. 'Haven't heard from her for years, though. But are you sure, Bill?'

'She'll do for a start,' said Bill. 'Get your address book, my lovely gel. We've got work to do.'

★

In the small sitting-room at Bridge Cottage, George Chalmer sat on a chair with the telephone to his ear, relaxed and laughing. The bell had been ringing as he unlocked the door, and he'd rushed in, getting to it just as his friend was about to hang up.

'Where've you been, you dirty old stop-out?'

George, breathing heavily, had explained that he'd been playing chess with one of the locals. 'Not much bloody good, though. Had to let him win once, of course. Good public relations. How's my doggie? Well, don't spoil him rotten. And none of those late night chocky bikkies before bedtime! No, the dog, you fool . . . still, you as well, if it applies. Any news?'

George listened to a catalogue of minor disasters and tit-bits of gossip, chuckling and clicking his tongue at regular intervals. 'Glad to know you're a busy boy,' he said. 'Oh, she's fine. Like a dog with two tails . . . What d'you mean, juggling with both balls?' He laughed delightedly, and said that that was his secret weapon, and nothing to do with his friend.

Finally he looked at the clock, and shifted in his chair. 'Well, that's enough for now,' he said. 'I hate to think of the telephone bill, should we ever have to pay it. Do I know what? . . . No, not yet. I'll let you know. Anyway, cheers for now.'

After he had replaced the receiver, George sat for some time, deep in thought. Time was certainly moving on.

# 36

'Looks like we shall be working until midnight,' said John Barnett, grabbing a quick breakfast before getting back to the fields where grass-cutting for silage was in full swing. The great trailers went through the farmyard with sweet-smelling grass every day from early morning until late at night, and Sarah was sick of the noise, the dust thrown up by giant tractor wheels. 'Soon be finished, though,' said John, seeing her face.

In a few weeks it would be harvest time, with all its tension and uncertainty, and she would see even less of her husband, be required to make endless sandwiches and flasks of tea, and run errands into Tresham with broken bits of farm machinery to be replaced or repaired.

'No chance of you playing tennis, I suppose?' she asked, watching John fork large mouthfuls of fried egg. 'First session tonight. Octavia's sent a notice round, hoping as many of us as possible will be there for the opening of the season. Jolly good, isn't she, the way she's taken it on again?' She seemed edgy, thought John, her voice sharp.

'Are you serious?' he said.

Sarah's eyes widened. 'Of course,' she said, looking straight at him with no trace of guile. 'But won't you find it a bit, well . . . embarrassing?' he said, frowning and trying hard to keep in control.

'No,' she said. 'What's done's done. And I still have to live in this village . . . no, I'll say that again: I still *want* to live in this village. All of it. Not have parts of it out of bounds.'

She'd been crossing her fingers about the school, wondering if Richard Standing would ease her out. He'd certainly have had several good reasons. Perhaps Simon had interceded on her behalf, bless him. Anyway, nothing had been said.

John looked away, defeated by the force of her will. 'Not sure I can,' he muttered.

'Don't be ridiculous, John,' she said. 'You're the hero, don't forget. Simon'll be the one everybody's watching. And me, of course. I shall need you, darling,' she added in a quite different voice. 'Please don't let me down.'

How can she say that? thought John. Time and again, since that awful night, he had tried to understand Sarah, to find a way of loving her without rancour or bitterness. He was worldly enough to know that unless he could do this, they hadn't much future. 'Maybe next week,' he said. 'See you later, love.'

Sarah blew him a kiss from across the table, and he left in a hurry.

In her shabby kitchen up at the Hall, Susan Standing stood ironing and listening to the radio. She picked up a pair of white shorts. Simon's. She supposed these were for tennis, and threw them back into the basket. She'd made it quite clear that she would not be his house-keeper. Still, she thought, picking them up again, he is my son. And he could be worse. He could be like Poppy, who is quite capable of ironing a shirt, and never does a hand's turn. She folded the shorts, and put them to one side, ready for Simon to collect.

Starting tonight, the tennis club. And Octavia Jones coming up early to have a session with Simon before everyone else arrives. So he'd said before leaving for work this morning. 'Give her some lemonade, Mum, if

I'm not back,' he'd said. 'Some of that nice stuff Jean Jenkins makes. I'll try not to keep her waiting long.'

Jean now flung open the green baize door and dropped a tin of polish with a clatter. 'Oops!' she said. 'All butterfingers this morning, Mrs Standing. Time for coffee, I reckon. Shall I make it?'

'Thank you, Jean,' said Susan, folding up the ironing board. 'I have to go out soon. Having lunch with Alexandra's mother today, and I need to round up Poppy. Have you seen her?'

Jean had seen her. She was sitting in her usual place, at the top of the back stairs, and she was reading that book again. Pity she hadn't got something better to do, like helping in the house for a start. Useless streak of nothing. And cheeky with it.

'Shall I call her?' Jean said, but Susan shook her head.

'She'll smell the coffee,' she said. 'Nothing else will bring her, except a visit from Joey Bates. It is a constant puzzle to me, what they can see . . .' She tailed off. It was not done to talk about personal matters with servants . . . servants! That was a joke! Jean twice a week, and for the rest, she was her own servant, and everyone else's as well.

'Is there any of your lemonade left?' she called to Jean, who was rattling about in the larder. Jean was a dab hand with home-made lemonade, clear and sparkling, with slivers of lemon and orange peel.

'Yep, quite a lot,' Jean replied.

'Oh good,' said Susan, 'then I shall be able to offer a glass to Miss Jones, as instructed.'

'You must be mad,' Greg said to Octavia, as she gulped down her breakfast coffee and made for the door. She'd just told him about the meeting with Simon Standing, and his reaction had been fierce. 'Head straight into the noose, Tavie!' he'd growled at her. 'Can't you see what he's up to? Your mother agrees with me. One fancy woman out of the way, and now he's set his sights on you.'

'For God's sake, Dad!' Octavia said, as she checked through her document case. 'You make me sound like the village maiden about to be deflowered by the squire's son! It's a tennis club meeting, just to check everything's okay before we start again. George'll probably be there.' She stopped, irritated that she should feel explanations were needed. 'And in any case,' she added, glaring at Greg, 'there is absolutely no reason why I should avoid Simon Standing, Robert Bates, Colin Osman, Michael Roberts, or Bill Turner, come to that!' Her voice was rising in anger, and Gabriella appeared to see what was up.

Greg turned. 'No need to look so worried,' he said. 'Octavia's prickly this morning. Wrong side of the bed, darling?' he said maddeningly, and Octavia left, slamming the door behind her.

'She gets that from you,' said Gabriella, twisting the teacloth in her hands.

'Gets what?' barked Greg.

'Door-slamming,' answered Gabriella, and went back to the kitchen.

The morning had got off to a better start in the shop. Peggy had asked Sandra to take over for an hour while Mandy gave her a quick trim, and now they were set up in the kitchen, with Sandra joining in through the open door.

'Yep, Sarah's definitely joining again,' said Mandy. 'If it was me,' she continued, 'I wouldn't have the nerve. But then, that Sarah Barnett's always gone for whatever she wanted, straight to it, without worrying about nobody else.'

'Blimey!' said Sandra. 'Almost worth joining, to see the fun.'

Peggy wiped tiny, tickling pieces of hair from her

face, and said in a sharp tone quite unlike her usual pleasant self, 'Is that all we're ever going to talk about? I'm sick of it,' she added vehemently. 'The whole village is a hotbed, and a very nasty one. All I ever hear is innuendo and sly jokes.'

Mandy shrugged and lifted her scissors, but Peggy hadn't finished. 'There was a time when people used to come into the shop and talk about good things: gardens and babies, and who was getting married, and where we planned our holidays . . .' She stared at her own distressed image in the mirror.

'Oh, well,' said Mandy, and leaned forward, but Peggy brushed her away.

'And if somebody was in trouble,' she went on, her voice rising, 'they'd come in and ask Bill to help, and we'd all do our bit. But now . . . now all we ever talk about is sex. Who's having it off with who, who knows more than they're saying. Enjoying other people's troubles, that's how it is now. Nice people, like John Barnett's old mother, worried out of her mind. School-children knowing too much, and their teacher no better than she should be. Sex, sex, sex . . . and never a word about love . . .' She was on the verge of tears.

Bill, standing quietly by the kitchen door, stared at her. He broke the silence after a few seconds. 'What's up, gel?' he said, coming over and taking her hand. She stood up from her chair and buried her wet face in his chest. He put his arms round her, towel, pins, rubbery gown and all, and held her tight. 'Plenty of love still about,' he said gently. 'Sandra here, with her Sam. Old Ivy next door, getting wed soon. You and me . . . and Mandy, she's got one of the best lovin' families in the village. Isn't that right, Mandy?' Mandy bit her lip and nodded.

Sandra's face was full of sympathy. 'You're right, though, Mrs T,' she said. 'But how the hell do you stop it? It's like Fox's bloody great tractor out of control.'

Peggy sniffed, scrubbed at her eyes, and disengaged herself from Bill's arms. 'Sorry, everyone,' she said.

Bill kissed her cheek, and said, 'Maybe it needed saying, gel.' He patted Mandy on the shoulder, smiled at Sandra, and offered to make coffee for them all.

After the girls had gone, Peggy cleared away the towels and mirror, and said gratefully, 'I'm okay now, Bill. Don't hang about, if you've got to get back to the Hall.'

'No hurry,' said Bill. 'Spent most of the day so far checking the court for Simon. He's like a broody old hen, in and out with bits o' this and that, cleaning the net, checking the croquet balls. I told him to bugger off and do some real work, and he seemed glad to go.'

The shop bell jangled. It was Sarah Barnett, grinning cheerfully. 'Just dashed over for milk,' she said. 'They left us two short at school this morning.' Her eye was caught by Octavia's poster announcing the restart of tennis. 'Ah yes,' said Sarah, 'and some shampoo please. Must look my best for the new season!' She seemed not to notice Peggy's shocked expression, and handed her a ten pound note.

'Nothing smaller?' said Peggy, taking a deep breath.

George had been on the phone for hours, defending to his friend what seemed like unnecessary delay. 'Ever been fishing?' he said. 'No? Well, you have to spend time, playing 'em in. Too fast on the reel, and you've lost your fish.'

Now he wandered down to his garden gate to chat to Ellen, who was hovering hopefully. 'Lovely day,' he said.

'Too right,' said Ellen. 'If I was a bit younger, I'd be up there tonight with them others, prancin' about the court and 'avin' dalliance with the young men . . .'

'Having *what*, Ellen?' said an amused voice behind her. She turned, and saw Octavia grinning at her.

'Ah,' said Ellen, 'just the person I wanted ter see.' She led Octavia across the road leaving George looking enviously at them as they disappeared into the Lodge.

Ellen knew that she was one of the few people Octavia talked to. She and Sandra Goodison. Now she had something to say, as well as to listen to.

'Go on, then,' said Octavia, puzzled. 'Do you need some help? You know you've only got to ask.'

Ellen shook her head. 'No, no,' she said. 'I kin manage fine. No, I wanted to know how things are with that Frenchie. Not bin round lately, 'as he?'

Octavia frowned at her. Nosy old thing. Still, she was so good, and independent, and mostly cheerful. 'Given him the heave-ho,' she said lightly, hoping to make Ellen laugh and drop the subject. 'Drove me mad, in the end.'

' 'ow's that, then?' said Ellen, unsmiling.

'Well, you wouldn't think you could have too much in the way of good manners, would you? If he'd kissed my hand just once more, I'd have clocked him.' She realised sadly that this was at least part of the truth.

'So you ain't goin' to Paris no more?' Ellen had said sympathetically.

'Doubt it,' Octavia had replied.

Now Ellen was asking about the tennis club. 'More members this year,' Octavia said. 'Mrs S has been rounding up friends' daughters from other villages. Anything to keep the son and heir happy, Ellen!'

'Anythin' to keep 'im from thinkin' about you, my dear,' said Ellen. She was serious, refusing to be deflected by Octavia's flippancy. ' 'e never really wanted that Barnett woman, you know, me dear, but no man's goin' to refuse when it's dangled in front of 'is nose. Not that I'm 'oldin' any brief for young Simon, but 'e's a good boy, deep down, an' I reckon he's learned 'is lesson. Don't 'ang about too long, Octavyer,' she said,

' 'cos there's others as won't. Now I'll get that kettle on, and we can 'ave a cuppa afore you go.'

Almost every member of the Round Ringford tennis club turned up on time, and was greeted by Simon, beaming with pleasure. Octavia, standing by his side, wished she hadn't drunk so much of Jean Jenkins's lemonade.

In the end, Simon hadn't shown up until just before the others arrived. It was too late for their meeting, and Octavia had had to make stilted conversation with Susan and a totally silent Poppy. Poppy's silence was eloquent. Nobody else could convey quite so much venom without saying anything. Foul child. Still, things seemed to be going well on court, and the atmosphere was jolly enough as they started to play. Even Poppy was smiling, as Hugo Dodwell's father paid her extravagant compliments.

'Spoilt brat,' said Greg Jones in a very audible aside to his wife.

Simon had coaxed the croquet lawn into reasonable condition, and some couples were setting off for a game before it was their turn for tennis. Greg and Gabriella said that as they were senior members, they should play croquet first.

'Not necessarily a sedate game for the oldies,' said Simon, smiling his friendly smile. 'Can get quite rough at these croquet tournament things.'

He was suddenly aware that everyone had stopped talking, and looked round. Across the grass came Sarah, already more tanned than anyone else at this start of the season, eyes shining and confident.

'Hi, everyone!' she called. 'Hope I'm not too late. John can't make it, but he'll be here next week. Hi, Simon,' she added more softly. 'Everything all right, then?' And she smiled broadly at him as she unzipped her racquet in that slow, lazy way he knew so well.

# 37

Octavia saw it all. She was standing close to Sarah and Simon, and her heart began to pound. She felt her blood rising and could do nothing to stop it. That's enough, Sarah bloody Barnett, she muttered under her breath. Now it's my turn, and to hell with everybody. The noise in her ears was deafening. It was as if she had Simon and Sarah under a microscope, huge and very close, with nothing and nobody else around, no rooks cawing in the great oaks, no barking dogs in the stableyard.

She took a step towards them, tucked her arm under Simon's, and said in a warm, friendly voice that had nothing to do with the storm inside her, 'No chance of a game for a while, Si, so why don't we have our admin session now? We could have more lemonade,' she laughed, gazing up into his amazed eyes. 'Come on,' she added, tugging at his hand, 'then we can take our turn later.'

In the shocked silence that had fallen at Sarah's appearance, she led him unprotesting past the coy, lichen-covered nymph on the terrace, through the stone arch, trailing roses already in bud, and out of sight.

Greg Jones was the first to speak. He stared at Gabriella and said, 'I'm going after them.'

'No you're not,' she said icily. 'You're staying here with me, and we're going to finish our game with Annie and Andrew, and everyone can stop staring and get on with it.'

Everyone began to talk at once, and after a few

minutes play started. Sarah Barnett, finding no one apparently willing to partner her, sat down on a frayed canvas chair that had seen better days. Her face was blank, and under her tan she was greenish white. A fool, that's what I look, she told herself. She was feeling sick with the humiliation. Right, Octavia Jones, if war is what you want, you shall have it.

Laughter and shouts of 'Brilliant, Mandy! Give us a chance!' floated through the open windows into Richard's study, where Simon had followed Octavia, dutifully carrying lemonade and glasses. Simon sat behind the desk, very straight and solemn, and looked at her without speaking. The unsmiling, indifferent face of his grandfather looked out of his heavy gilt frame, over their heads and into a grander past. 'Thanks,' Simon said, as she handed him a glass. 'For the lemonade, I mean,' he added.

'Yes,' said Octavia, 'I realise that.'

'Aren't you having any?' he said politely.

'If I drink any more lemonade,' said Octavia, 'I shall float. No, Simon, even you could see that was an excuse to get you away. Now, shall we get down to business?'

'Well, yes,' he said, his expression almost as inscrutable as his grandfather's. 'Or you could explain.'

'Do I need to?' she said, her tone as icy as his.

The silence stretched endlessly, and then Simon suddenly smiled. 'Sorry, Octavia,' he said. 'Sorry, sorry . . . for everything.' God, would he ever be able to stop saying it?

'So you should be,' she said, and though her words were severe, her voice had warmed.

'So shall we have our meeting, or shall we scarper up the fields and leave 'em to it?' Simon said, watching her closely, and crossing his fingers under the desk.

Octavia hesitated. 'We'd be missed,' she said.

'Yes,' said Simon. 'Quite right. Still, what do you think?'

'Probably best if we do the work, and then go back to the others. Shouldn't take more than ten minutes?' Octavia said, picking up a file of papers.

Simon smiled again. 'Quite agree,' he said. 'But let's not.' He retrieved the file, set it down on the desk and stood looking at her without speaking for several seconds. She returned his look without flinching. 'Right,' he said, 'follow me.'

The stableyard was empty as they crossed quickly, looking back furtively at the kitchen window, but it was shut, and no face appeared behind it. They walked up through the orchard, the thick grass and fallen blossom turning rusty brown, and reached the stile in the hedge.

'Here,' said Simon, holding out his hand, 'let me help you.'

Octavia swallowed her usual declaration of independence, allowed him to help her, and left her hand in his as they walked on. She could hear the voices from the tennis court, shrieks and laughter, gradually fading.

A footpath, beaten hard and bare by sheep and horses, led up the pasture, past Poppy's pony and Susan's mare, and under the hawthorns in new leaf. They came to a clear stream that ran down to the Ringle, and stopped on the makeshift bridge of uneven planks and swaying handrail. There was only just room for two.

'Water's very clean now,' said Simon. 'Bill swears he saw an otter upstream a couple of weeks ago.'

Octavia said nothing, and stared down into the glinting water. Simon's hand was warm and dry, and she could feel his pulse, steady and strong. Her confidence was rapidly draining away, that brave show of determination crumbling fast. I don't know anything about him. What's he like with Sarah Barnett? What was he like in America . . . in London? In a surge of panic she withdrew her hand.

He looked at her sharply. 'Everything all right?' he said. He could see from her eyes that it was not. Without fuss, he took her hand again.

At the top of the field, Bill had planted a spinney of shivering poplars, and Simon led Octavia through this, stepping high over long, tangled grass which caught at their shoes, tripping them up. Another meadow, carpeted with white daisies, cowpats to be avoided, curved in a gentle slope to the edge of the wood. As they walked, Simon chatted on to an increasingly silent Octavia, seeming not to notice her dragging footsteps.

At last he stopped by a fallen tree, moss-covered, with fleshy brown toadstools growing on its damp underside. Last year's bracken, a dry, springy bed, rustled under their feet. Simon brushed the crumbled bark with his hand, and said, 'Let's sit down.'

Octavia thought of saying that it wouldn't do her white shorts any good, but didn't. 'Can't hear the others now,' she said.

'No,' said Simon. 'And they can't hear us, nor see us. There's just us.' He put out his hand and touched her cheek with the tips of his fingers. Then he sat back and looked at her. He smiled.

'I'm not sure,' she said.

'Of me?' said Simon.

Octavia bit her lip. 'Er, yes, I suppose so. Now . . . well . . . Things are a bit complicated, aren't they?'

'Some things are,' said Simon, rubbing a scratch on his long brown legs. 'Some things always are, but other things are very simple. Like you and me, sitting here on this dead tree, wanting each other.'

'Yes,' said Octavia, straightforward as always. 'You're bleeding.' She put out a tentative hand and touched the scratch. A bead of bright, warm blood appeared on the end of her finger. 'Yes, that's quite true,' she said, as he took her hand and slowly licked the blood away. Then she smiled, and Simon was dazzled. He leaned forward and kissed her, finding her all that he knew she would be, generous and welcoming.

At the edge of Bagley Woods, with the scent of crushed ferns and the cool green shade of the trees overhead, Octavia remembered all the tricky stuff Guy had taught her, consigned it to the bin, and knew that everything would be absolutely all right. She and Simon belonged to these fields, these thickets and woods, the bramble hedges and grassy hollows. And they knew each other in the way they knew the landscape. They touched, tasted, discovered, and found everything familiar and good.

A sudden clatter in the trees parted them. 'What was that!' said Octavia.

'Only a pigeon,' said Simon, twisting her rumpled hair gently round his hand. He turned his head to look, and saw the bird, soaring away over the field, wings flapping fast in the huge effort of becoming airborne. He also saw his sister Poppy, standing a few yards away, staring at them.

'Poppy!' he said angrily, but she had turned and gone, running at full pelt across the field.

'Time to go,' said Octavia, her smile rueful. Little brat had certainly bust that up.

Simon smoothed her hair, kissed her lightly on her warm cheeks. 'Let's not go back yet,' he said. 'That's what Poppy wants, to break us up.'

The truth was that he could not bear to let her go, not even half a mile away from the Hall, to her own home. This was all such an unexpected delight. Not that the bliss of loving Octavia was unexpected. He'd known for some time that this was what he really wanted. No, it was her own part in it, and he wasn't quite sure of her. If he let her go, the delight would disappear with her, and he might never catch hold of it again.

Undeserved, all this, he admitted grimly. Down there, in the hollow, where the village waited for them, was all the baggage of his affair with Sarah Barnett, his mother's strong resistance to anything that contradicted her own intentions, Greg Jones's obvious dislike of him . . . and, of course, there was Poppy.

By the time they got back to the Hall, all the tennis players had gone, and Simon could see a light in Poppy's room.

'I'll walk you home,' he said. When a foraging owl swooped above them in a feathery rush, causing Octavia to start in alarm, Simon held her tight, as though there was real danger.

# 38

'I *saw* them!' said Poppy vehemently. She was sitting on the bed in her mother's room, while Susan put away clean shirts in Richard's drawer. 'Up by the wood . . . and they were at it.'

'Poppy!' Susan was genuinely shocked. 'What were *you* doing up there, anyway?'

Poppy's outburst was blasphemy in the lovely, gracious room, with long windows looking over the park, green and peaceful. But Poppy saw nothing of the loveliness, only her mother's bent back as she slotted the folded shirts into place. There was a silence, and Poppy thought quickly. Susan had an irritating habit of not listening, but now Poppy had her attention and intended to make use of it.

Susan said, 'Well?'

'Chasing your beloved George. He ran away,' she said.

The ancient Yorkshire terrier was certainly not capable of evading Poppy, but Susan let this pass. 'I'm sure you're exaggerating, as usual,' she said, looking worried. 'It was probably someone from the village. You know the cry-wolf story, Poppy. Well, if you persistently exaggerate—'

'Lie, you mean,' said Poppy, and to Susan's consternation, a tear slowly trickled down Poppy's cheek. 'It was Simon and Octavia! He shouted at me,' she said.

'I see,' said Susan, convinced now. 'Sorry, darling. Of course I believe you. It's just that Daddy was around, and he didn't say anything.'

'He wasn't around then,' insisted Poppy. 'He'd gone out with Bill. And there's something else,' she added, looking at her mother speculatively. 'Greg Jones said I was a spoilt brat. I heard him. He said it to Mrs Jones, and she laughed.'

'Oh, you poor darling!' said Susan. 'You did have a horrid evening. Never mind, I shall speak to your father about it. I need to have a word.' She smoothed Poppy's hair, and added, 'So much for trying to do something for the village! That's how they repay you, Poppy.'

'I promise, Mum,' said Poppy, all persistent honesty now, 'that I saw Simon and Octavia. I interrupted them.'

'I expect it was all in fun,' said Susan, desperately keeping her voice light.

'Certainly looked fun,' said Poppy, more her laconic self. 'Anyway,' she said, getting off the bed, 'I'm off to see Joey. Might stay for lunch if his Gran invites me.'

'Poppy!' said Susan, suddenly firm. 'You are not to mention Simon and Octavia to anyone. The sooner this is nipped in the bud the better.' And, handing Poppy a tissue to wipe her face, she rushed off to find Richard.

Richard was in the study, looking absently at the farming news. He'd mingled with the tennis players for a while yesterday, and felt old and tired. One game, and I'd be done for, he thought. He'd seen Annie, his little Annie, rushing about, getting impossible shots and screaming instructions at an obedient Andrew. He'd gone off with Bill feeling quite sad, and they'd met Sarah coming up the drive, looking good enough to eat. Ah, if only I was a few years younger, he'd sighed to himself. Not ready to be put out to grass, not yet.

He brightened as the door opened and Susan came in, but when she launched into a long garbled story about Simon and Octavia Jones and last night's tennis, and when he realised the whole thing had come from Poppy, he felt even more depressed.

'Hold on,' he said. 'Sit down and calm down. Now what exactly did Poppy say?' Susan repeated the details, and Richard smiled. 'Very nice too,' he said. 'Can't see what you're in such a state about.'

'Richard!' said Susan. 'Do I have to spell it out? Octavia Jones is all very well in her way. Bright and all that. But her father's that dreadful little man. Greg, isn't it? And, by the way, he upset Poppy a great deal last evening, called her a spoilt brat in front of everyone. She can't forget it.'

'He has a point,' was all Richard said, and he got up to make himself a drink before lunch.

Octavia sat at her desk and stared at a report newly arrived in her in-tray. She had read the first paragraph three times now, and realised she'd absorbed none of it. She started again, but her mind leapt away, refusing to turn the printed page into anything like sense.

Her father had turned the full force of his anger on her when she'd arrived home, long after the others. She'd not even listened. It had been extraordinary, she thought. After all that had happened, Simon and me. And he was so good and funny, and nice. And it hadn't been anything like a sticky cream cake. She must remember to tell Sandra.

She pushed the papers to one side and looked across at her fellow social worker, a middle-aged woman with grey hair and a kind face. 'What's the time, Martha?' she said.

'Nearly twelve,' said Martha. 'Having problems? Anything I can help with?'

'Oh, it's the usual,' said Octavia. 'Man trouble.'

Martha smiled. 'Not usual for you, Tavie,' she said. 'Nobody more organised, more able to keep men in their proper place.' Her smile was kind. She had known

Octavia a long time, and was fond of her. Now she looked at the shining eyes and pink face, and wondered who had finally caught her unawares.

Her next question was interrupted by Octavia's extension ringing shrilly. 'Hello?' said Octavia. 'Oh, hello. How are you? Well, I'm fine, thanks. Couldn't be better, as a matter of fact. Only problem is, I can't work. You can't either?'

Her colleague looked at her from across the room, and decided there was certainly no problem there. She had never seen Octavia quite like that before.

'Well, yes, that would be lovely,' continued Octavia. 'About one, then? That café by the river? Fine. See you there.' She put the phone down and looked across at Martha. 'All right,' she said. 'Don't ask. If you don't mind, I'll just bore you rigid for a few minutes before I go.'

Martha was a good social worker, knew when to ask a question and when to shut up and listen. She didn't often hear heart-warming stories, though, and this was certainly a winner.

'Mind you,' said Octavia, leaning her chin on her hands, 'in the cold light of day, I know I'm going to regret it.'

'Sounds perfect to me,' said Martha, raising her eyebrows.

Octavia shook her head. 'Now for the bad news,' she said. 'He's recently had a torrid affair with the village schoolmistress, and she's still pursuing, as is her irate husband. His mother and father are the biggest snobs in the world . . . no, perhaps not his father, but Susan Standing—'

'Standing, did you say?' Martha began to laugh.

'What's funny?' said Octavia.

'Richard Standing's his father?'

Octavia nodded.

'Oh my,' said Martha, 'Mr Richard had a real

199

steaming affair with my cousin. All over the county at the time.'

Octavia frowned at her. 'Well, what was wrong with that?' she said.

'He was engaged to Susan Maidford at the time, and it was only weeks from the wedding,' said Martha, sobering up and reaching into her pocket for a handkerchief.

'Ah,' said Octavia. 'Then you see what I mean.'

The river café was crowded, the lunch menu was cheap and cheerful, and on a sunny day it was a pleasant place for office workers to take a break.

Simon stood up from a small table as Octavia approached. 'Hi,' he said, and took her hand, smiling broadly. 'Hope this is okay for you. Not much privacy, I'm afraid.'

Octavia looked at him, not really listening, and was glad that he was so tall. Most men were smaller than herself, making her feel gawky, ill at ease. He's perfect, she said to herself, unabashed by such a ridiculous thought. Clear intelligent eyes, brown skin, hair full of shine and life. Yum. 'What? Oh, no, it's fine,' she said, making an effort to concentrate. 'Anything's better than the chintzy olde worlde hostelry in the marketplace.' They probably own it, she told herself, as she allowed him to take her jacket. He held her chair, and she said, 'Oh, come on, Simon, I'm not that frail! I'm not used to it, you know. Working girl, independent. All that.'

'Sorry,' he said. He felt lightheaded. This was a very different girl from the others. Maybe that's why I want her so much. Have to tread carefully, else she'll be off again, nose in the air. He couldn't believe that she was really here, after all his shitty behaviour. He realised with some alarm how much he cared, how anxious he was now to get it right.

He thought quickly of a number of topics of

conversation: tennis, her job, the political situation. In the end, he said, 'Can't stop thinking about you.' It was all right. Octavia liked plain speaking, and her face softened.

'That's nice,' she said. 'Shall we have baked potatoes?'

The potatoes went cold, only half-eaten, and neither could remember afterwards what they'd talked about. It had been nothing: families and childhood, shared memories of the village school. There'd been a second's hitch at the mention of the schoolmistress, but quickly passed over. It was all inconsequential, and very easy. When Octavia said she'd have to be getting back to work, Simon strolled hand in hand with her under the newly planted saplings by the river until they rounded a corner and came to a giant beech. They had lost the crowds, and the path was empty. Under the cool shade, he trapped her against the gnarled trunk, stroked her bare arms and kissed her gently.

'I meant it, you know,' he said.

'Mmm?' said Octavia, gazing up into the heart of the great tree. She felt an overwhelming pity for the rest of the world.

'I do love you,' he said.

They walked in silence then, to where the path became a narrow passage back into town. Octavia touched his face lightly with her lips, and he held her, reluctant to let go. At last she said, 'See you, Simon,' and walked away. He watched her in the sunlight until she was lost from sight in the crowded market place.

Years ago, Ted Bates had kept pigs in brick-built sties with yards and gates, and low walls where he could lean over and prod a pig's back with his stick. The sties had been empty for years, clean and dry now, but still smelling faintly of pig. One of these, the one with the best roof to keep out the rain, Ted had brushed out and hosed down for his grandchildren to play in. Long after

Joey had given up retiring to the den to decode messages sent to him by Poppy, the two still vanished inside when they wanted to get away, often for different reasons. Poppy's was usually an escape from her irate mother, and Joey's from an over-attentive grandmother. And lately, there had been other reasons.

'I'm fed up,' said Poppy, sitting down on the stool that Ted had filched from Olive for the den.

'Anything special?' said Joey, shifting in his chair to a more comfortable position. The roof was very low over their heads, and in the cramped space there was a nice feeling of intimacy.

'I hate those Joneses,' Poppy said.

'Octavia's nice,' said Joey. 'She takes me out sometimes. I like her.'

'I hate her,' said Poppy, and Joey was amazed to see her near to tears.

'What's happened?' he said.

'They're just horrible, all of them,' she said.

'Well,' said Joey, in his father's voice, 'if you won't tell me what's up, I can't help, can I?'

Poppy told Joey about seeing Octavia and Simon, and Joey said he couldn't see anything wrong in that. Better than Mrs Barnett, he said tactlessly. 'Mum was furious,' said Poppy.

'It's nothing to do with her,' said Joey.

'Huh, that's what you think,' said Poppy. 'Anybody who's after precious Simon'll have to be at least an Hon.'

'Still,' said Joey, 'it's nothing for you to get upset about.'

'It wasn't just that,' said Poppy. 'It was her horrible father. I heard him say to her horrible mother that I was a spoilt brat.'

Joey began to laugh, knew it was the wrong thing to do, but couldn't stop. The more he tried, the more he laughed, and then he began to choke.

Poppy looked alarmed. His gran had said to her once

202

that disabled people sometimes died from choking on an apple, and she went over to him at once. 'Joey?' she said anxiously. She patted him on the back, and the choking slowly subsided. She stroked his forehead, and smoothed his hair. 'I hate you too,' she said.

'No you don't,' said Joey, and just like the gallant Frenchman, he kissed the tips of her fingers.

George Chalmer was playing the gentleman, too, though with rather more expertise than Joey. He had arrived at Victoria Villa to find Ivy struggling with bean poles in the garden. 'My dear,' he'd said, taking the bundle from her hands, 'that's not a job for a lady. Allow me.'

She had protested, but not for long, and then said she'd go and put on the kettle while he finished the sticks. 'Should have been in weeks ago,' she'd said, 'but I've had other things on my mind.' And she positively skipped back up the garden path.

Now they sat in the front room, George well cushioned in what Ivy insisted on calling His Chair. Tea was set out on a tray, and with the sun streaming in, George reflected that you'd have to go a long way to beat this as a way of life. But things must go ahead, according to plan. He and Ivy had agreed that they would live in Victoria Villa, and he'd explained he would get on with buying Bridge Cottage, as an investment, he said, for their old age. They could let it for a regular income. He'd again mentioned the deposit needed and that had been no problem. Ivy had been transported at the thought of sharing what had for so long been the spectre of a lonely old age.

George, in spite of himself, had begun to think along the same lines, but then he remembered sadly the things that would be missing. What a pity, he thought. What a very great pity, and his expression was so gloomy that Ivy wondered if she'd said something wrong.

'No, no,' said George, 'nothing at all, my dear. A ghost walking over my grave, that's all.' He smiled sweetly at her. 'Did I tell you that tennis started again last evening?' he said.

She knew, of course, had judged it safe for him to go. It was a fiction between them that Ivy allowed him a private life of his own, for the time being, anyway.

'I think young Simon's been forgiven,' said George, happy to be the bringer of good news. 'He and Octavia vanished for most of the evening, and when I called in at the Lodge with those knitting patterns for Ellen, they were sauntering down the avenue, as one, as the saying goes. If I'm not mistaken, love was in the air.'

'Oh, good!' said Ivy, and leaned over the back of George's chair to kiss his cheek. 'Love is all around, if you ask me.'

George patted her hand, and said how right she was. Weren't they all lucky, he said. But try as he would, he couldn't keep the sadness from his eyes.

# 39

It had been a bright, blustery day, the wind rocking landlord Cutt's hanging baskets outside the pub. They were newly planted and not yet heavy with summer's trailing geraniums and petunias. He stood on tiptoe, watering liberally, aware as Ellen Biggs approached that he was a sitting target.

'Evenin', Mr Cutt,' she said, puffing painfully and leaning on her stick. 'Bin a nice day. 'Ow's yer missus?'

Don Cutt said she was fine thanks, and it was really time he thought about opening up.

'True,' said Ellen, not moving. 'Can't keep the customers waitin'. Thought I might go up and watch the tennis meself. Ivy's goin' with 'er George.'

'Ah well,' said Don Cutt. 'Can't bear to be parted from him, I expect.' He laughed coarsely, and Ellen glared at him.

'I'll thank you to show a little respect, Mr Cutt,' she said stiffly. 'Miss Beasley's bin in this village years before you came 'ere. And 'er family before 'er.' She poked at one of the hanging baskets with her stick. 'That geranium's dead,' she said, and hobbled away. When she reached her Lodge she was so out of breath that she gave up on the tennis, deciding on telly-watching instead.

By the time the tennis players gathered, the wind had dropped and all the scents of early summer filled the warm air. A good turn-out again, thought Simon gratefully. No one said anything about the strange disappearance of himself and Octavia Jones, but they smiled a lot.

'Good evening, Ivy!' he said, with real pleasure. It was like the seal of approval, having Miss Beasley there.

Ivy, faintly irritated that there was something going on in the village that she knew about only secondhand, had asked George casually whether it would be all right if she walked up to join him for a while. 'Watch the tennis, maybe have a game of croquet. Always croquet up at the Hall years ago,' she said, launching into a bout of reminiscence.

'Plenty of light this evening,' said Greg to Gabriella as they changed their shoes. 'Should get some good tennis in. I must say,' he added, 'if the membership grows at this rate, we shall have to consider ways of making another court.'

'Octavia did mention it,' said Gabriella. 'Said Simon was keen to expand. I think a lot of people like playing on grass. Those hard courts on the playing fields are not nearly so pleasant.'

'Faster though,' said Greg, his face rapidly closing up at the mention of Simon. 'Well, you're plenty fast enough!' said Gabriella, hoping to flatter him into a better mood. 'Have to give the others a chance. It's good so many have turned up.'

'Even darling Poppy over there,' said Greg drily. 'I don't see why we should bend the rules for the boss's daughter, do you?'

'No, dear,' said Gabriella, and stooped to tighten her laces.

She noticed Octavia talking to Simon, and said happily that only the truly blind would miss the change in them.

'Quite right, Gabbie,' said Greg, and Gabriella was dismayed to hear the anger in his voice. 'Our daughter has definitely been ensnared.'

She hushed him sharply, saying ensnared was a stupid word. 'Octavia's much too clever for that,' she added in an admonitory tone. 'You can be sure she knows what she's doing.'

'Huh, you've changed your tune,' said Greg, and turned his back.

Matches were played, compliments generously exchanged, and over by the summerhouse, Sarah Barnett and Annie Bishop sat out, waiting for a turn on court.

Simon and Octavia were playing Alexandra Smyth partnered by Robert Bates. Mandy had sent her apologies. She had a perm and colour to do over at Fletching, so Robert was on the loose and enjoying himself.

'Just look at that,' said Annie to Sarah, unable to resist a smile. Octavia had chased a wide ball, slid on the grass, and fallen on her back. Simon was there in seconds, lifting her to her feet, holding her for longer than was necessary.

'Charming,' said Sarah.

'Fairytale ending, do you think?' said Annie, rubbing it in.

When the game finished, Octavia walked off court with Simon and whispered in his ear, 'Ask Poppy to have a game of croquet, she's looking a bit left out.' Poppy was standing on the terrace, biting her nails and looking sulky.

'Good idea,' said Simon, squeezed her hand, and called, 'Come on, Poppy! Show us how to do it!'

She came over slowly, scowling at Octavia, and muttered, 'Might as well, I suppose.'

'Greg, Gabriella,' said Simon, seeing the Joneses wandering idly round the flowerbeds, 'can we challenge you to a match?'

'Oh, God, not them,' muttered Poppy at his side.

'Sshh, Poppy,' said Simon, and went over to choose the mallets.

Halfway round, with Greg and Gabriella in the lead, Poppy lost her temper, and hit the hard wooden ball with a swipe that sent it careering off the lawn and into the shrubbery that divided the gardens from the park beyond. It was dense, thickly grown, and formed an impenetrable screen.

Now the foursome stood looking at where the ball had disappeared, and Simon said crossly, 'Off you go, Poppy! You sent it there, you can go and look for it.'

She scuffed off, and Greg and Gabriella looked at each other. 'Not the best of sports, your sister,' said Greg tactlessly.

'She's all right,' said Simon loyally. 'Just a bit out of her depth with all these grown-ups.'

'Then why did she want to—?' Greg was silenced painfully by Gabriella kicking him sharply on the ankle. 'Oh, for goodness' sake,' he said, 'I'll go and help her find it,' and stumped off towards the shrubbery.

'Suppose I should go too,' said Simon.

'No, no,' said Gabriella, 'Greg's good at finding balls. Actually, he's good at most things,' she added, 'except being tactful. He does slip up there, sometimes.'

Her tone was apologetic, and Simon smiled at her. She looked so like Octavia. 'Don't worry,' he said. 'Poppy's used to being out of favour. Like water off a duck's back.'

They sat down on the warm grass, and looked over towards the shrubbery. No sign of the searchers, and no sounds either. It's very peaceful sitting here, thought Gabriella, feeling quite at home with Simon. No wonder Octavia . . . it's a lovely evening, beautiful garden, nice people . . .

And then, suddenly, horribly, the peace was shattered by a scream.

'Poppy!' said Simon, jumping up and dashing off towards the shrubbery. Complete silence had fallen on all the players, and Susan Standing came chasing out across the terrace. She streaked over the grass towards the shrubbery just as Simon emerged, arm round a sobbing Poppy, with an astonished-looking Greg Jones following behind.

'Darling, darling!' said Susan. 'What happened?' Poppy continued to sob, and Susan led her over to the chairs by the court. Everyone crowded round, anxious to help. 'There, there, my sweet,' said Susan, 'tell Mummy what happened.'

Poppy sniffed, rubbed her eyes and clung to her mother. 'It was him,' she said in a muffled voice.

'What did you say, darling?' said Susan.

'It was *him*,' Poppy shouted, sitting bolt upright and pointing an accusing finger at Greg Jones. 'He got hold of me out there, where nobody could see, and . . . and . . . *messed about* with me!' she blurted out, and collapsed again into frantic sobs.

# 40

The stunned silence that followed Poppy's outburst seemed to Octavia to go on for ever, then her father stepped forward angrily, and was restrained by Gabriella. Richard Standing, alerted by the scream, walked rapidly round the corner of the house and approached the crowd. 'What on earth's going on?' he said, looking at the apparently tragic figures of his wife and daughter.

It was Simon who, after a pregnant pause, answered. 'Looks like we'd better pack up for tonight,' he said. 'Mum, you take Poppy indoors, and Dad, if you could just hang on . . .'

'Here!' said Greg. 'That girl doesn't go anywhere until she takes back what she just said, and apologises! And I'm not sure that'll be enough!'

'Greg,' said Gabriella, 'Simon's right. We'd better cool down, and then I'm sure it can all be sorted out. Nothing to be gained by losing our tempers.'

'Temper!' shouted Greg. 'Hysteria would be a better word for it!' But he allowed his wife to lead him away, collect up their things and leave the court. The others followed slowly, muttering to each other, faces long and serious. Finally there was only Octavia, still shocked and motionless where she had stood, waiting with George and Ivy for sanity to be restored.

Simon, about to follow his father indoors, looked round for her. He came running back. 'Tavie, my love,' he said. 'I have to go in and sort this one out. You go home and calm down your dad, and I'll ring you later.'

She nodded, still with a shocked, puzzled expression, and turned away.

Ivy and George were waiting for her by the gates to the avenue. 'Disgraceful!' said Ivy, as she approached, and Octavia wondered fleetingly just what she meant.

George took her arm comfortingly, and said, 'Don't worry, Octavia, my dear, I'm sure it's all just a silly muddle. All blow over by morning.'

Ivy, who knew the village better than anyone, shook her head. 'Best be off home,' she said. 'Home's the place to be, at times like this.'

'Tavie, darling, it's me. Are you all right?'

'What's happening, Simon?'

'Oh God, it's deadly. Mum's stomping round threatening everything she can think of, and Dad's trying to stop her calling the police.'

'Police! You're not serious, Simon?'

There was a small silence, and then Simon said, 'Sorry. Shouldn't have said that. Well, you know Mum. Overboard, as always.'

'And Poppy?' said Octavia. Now the shock was wearing off, and her voice was strong, sharp. 'How is darling Poppy?'

Another silence. 'Well, she's gone to bed, actually. Mum tucked her up and sat with her until she stopped crying. Quite heartrending, really.' He sounded humble, as if begging for understanding. 'How's your dad?' he asked tentatively.

'Furious,' said Octavia. 'Absolutely steaming. I have never seen him so angry. I must say,' she added, 'I'm beginning to feel pretty angry myself. Not with you, Simon,' she added, desperately trying to be fair. 'Just angry at the whole bloody impossible situation. The more I think about it the worse it gets.'

'Oh, darling,' said Simon. 'Can I see you? We could meet at the pub?'

'Nope,' said Octavia at once. 'Not tonight. I'd better stay here, I think, in case Dad does anything stupid, like storming the Hall barricades and murdering your little sister.'

Another silence. 'Tomorrow, then?'

'Yes, of course. Ring me.' She hesitated, then lowered her voice. 'Love you, Simon,' she said, and put down the phone.

# 41

By the following afternoon, the dramatic events had been discussed in a dozen different kitchens, down at the Arms, and, of course, in the shop. The first person to break the news to Peggy had been Doris Ashbourne, with none of the usual pleasure at retailing a juicy bit of gossip. Doris had looked furtively round the shop, come close to the counter, and said, 'I think I should tell you, dear, before you hear some garbled version. Mind you, from what I can gather from Ivy, nobody really knows the truth, not yet.'

Peggy had been just as shocked as everyone else. 'I've seen it coming, Doris,' she said. It had been brewing up, and now here it was, with all the makings of real tragedy.

After Doris had gone, she left the empty shop to make herself a cup of tea. Others would come in with the story, and she needed to think it out, know what to say, how to react. The full horror of the situation slowly crystallised. Greg Jones was a teacher, a respected citizen, whose job took him into the company of children all the time. His wife was a teacher, his daughter a social worker. This could destroy them all. Oh, Lord, I wish Bill was here, she thought.

Bill was at work up at the Hall, and knew the minute he saw Mr Richard coming through the stableyard door to discuss the day's work with him, that something was up. Something serious, from the look on the boss's face.

'Morning, Bill,' said Richard. 'Um, perhaps you could just carry on today,' he added, without waiting for Bill to reply. 'Got things to do, and likely to take most of the day. Jolly good. See you later, then,' and he disappeared back into the house.

It was eerily quiet, Bill noticed. There was always noise, from Madam's radio in the kitchen, or loud and thudding from Poppy's bedroom. The dogs were usually out in the yard, barking their heads off. But nothing. No voices, no radio, no music. Even the dogs were shut up in the stable and, deeply offended, had gone quiet. Bill shook his head, mystified, and went off to find Foxy Jenkins. There was work to be done on the farm, and that's what he was here for, not to speculate.

When he arrived home for lunch, he found Peggy in a state of high tension, and as she stumbled and hesitated over the words, he heard a tale he could hardly believe.

'It's rubbish!' was his first reaction. He knew Poppy Standing very well. She'd tagged along behind him ever since she could walk, asking questions and being a thorough nuisance. He'd felt sorry for her, a lonely little girl in a great big house, and had answered her endless questions as best he could. He'd also experienced her deviousness. She was a great manipulator, very good at getting what she wanted, and had landed him at the edge of trouble more than once.

'It's just more of Poppy's mischief-making,' he said now. 'With a great little wife like Gabriella, what would Greg Jones want with a kid like Poppy?' He shook his head in disgust. 'No, Peg, it's not worth bothering about.'

Peggy's eyes widened. 'But Bill, it's never as simple as that,' she said. 'Doris said Mrs Standing is taking it *very* seriously. Ivy told her she was yelling at Mr Richard to ring the police, and if he wouldn't, she would.'

Bill groaned. 'Oh no,' he said. 'Trust Madam! Why couldn't she just get the truth out of that little devil, and then with luck Greg would have accepted an apology and we could all forget about it.'

'No chance,' said Peggy. 'Looks like social workers, police and the whole bit. Oh, and Bill,' she added, her lip trembling, 'just when poor Octavia had been getting together with Simon at last.' To Bill's astonishment, Peggy put her hands over her face and began to cry.

'Come on, gel!' he said. 'It's none of our business. They'll sort it out somehow, you'll see.'

But Peggy was right. Richard Standing had done his best to dissuade his raging wife from ringing the police, but nothing could stop her. Particulars had been taken, and a social worker deputed to call at the Hall.

Octavia had telephoned the office first thing, and asked to speak to Harry. He'd listened attentively, been very sympathetic, and said if she could possibly come in early, he'd got a free half hour and they should talk. He'd already had a call from the police, and realised the complications.

Now the two sat either side of Harry's big desk, and his heart was touched by the misery in her face. This was going to be one hell of a situation to unravel, and whereas in any other circumstances he would have put Octavia on to the job, it was, of course, out of the question.

'Off the record, Octavia,' he said, 'can you just tell me how it happened, what you actually saw yourself?' Her reply, that she'd seen nothing until Simon had come out of the shrubbery with a howling Poppy, added little to what he already knew, but Octavia was able to tell him exactly how her father had reacted, and he nodded gravely.

'So who's going to the Hall?' said Octavia, when he thanked her and offered all the support he could give.

'Martha,' he said. 'She's a very experienced woman, and very good with children. Oh,' he added, looking embarrassed, 'I do have to ask you not to discuss any of this with Martha, just for a while. Could be difficult, you know. In fact,' he said, thinking on his feet, 'it would probably be a good idea for you to take a few days off. I'll fix it for you right away.'

Octavia shook her head. 'Rather not,' she said. 'You can trust me, Harry, to do the honourable thing. I just want to get on with my work, if that's okay with you.'

Her face was a mask, and he felt deeply sorry for her. 'Very well,' he said, 'but don't be too proud to give up for a day or two if it all gets too much.'

Greg Jones had gone to school, as usual. He was still angry, but held it in check. This was a big test, he told himself. Always so good at handing out advice, now I could do with some myself. He forced himself to concentrate on his class, and realised that at the end of the first session he hadn't thought about Poppy Standing for one precious hour.

In the staff room at coffee time, a message came from the Head. He wanted to see Greg, straight away.

'Right,' Greg said, after they'd got explanations out of the way. 'No, I quite understand. Perhaps I'd better be off now, if you can fill in. Disappear before the tabloids arrive!' His bleak little joke fell flat, and the Head walked with him to the door, his hand on his shoulder.

'Don't worry, Greg,' he said. 'Sure you'll be back in no time.'

Greg drove away from school feeling like a criminal. It was an odd kind of limbo, leaving everyone busy in their classrooms, being around Ringford in the middle of the morning. There'd be nobody at home, so no point in going there. Perhaps he'd call in at the Arms, have a pint and a bite to eat. But when he entered the familiar bar, with its comforting warmth and smell of beer, conversations stopped and he saw faces turn away from him. Only Robert Bates came over and offered him a drink.

'No thanks, Robert,' said Greg in a strangled voice,

'I've changed my mind. Best be off home.' Robert's kind face looked at him askance, but Greg would not be persuaded.

'What a bloody mess!' said Robert, and his mates by the bar agreed with him.

# 42

Strangely enough, the last person to hear was Ellen Biggs. Usually a magnet for all the gossip around, she'd not been out for a couple of days, and so had missed out. Her hip was more painful than usual, and to her intense irritation, when Ivy and Doris arrived looking, as she said, like a couple o' wet weekends, the grim news was already two days old.

'Good 'eavens, what a load o' rubbish,' she said. 'It's just Miss Poppy up to 'er tricks agen. Nobody's goin' to believe that one, are they?'

Ivy and Doris said that Poppy's mother believed her, and had acted on it. When they told Ellen about the police and the social worker, she began to see the seriousness of it.

'Still,' she said. 'Them social workers'll get the truth out of 'er . . .' She tailed off, and added, 'Mind you, they don't come more stubborn than young Poppy.'

Finally Ivy sat up, braced herself, and said, 'Well, it's no good sitting here moping. Nothing we can do, and I always say it's no good worrying about something you can't alter.'

'Right y'are,' Ellen said, and poured second cups. 'Let's talk about somethin' more cheeful. 'ow's yer plans goin'?'

Ellen had been thinking about Ivy and her wedding before they arrived. It took some thinking about. Ivy, the blushing bride. No doubt she's busy as a bee, fillin' up 'er bottom drawer and checkin' 'er underwear.

Wonder what ole George'll think to 'er green knickers! 'e's bound to've got tantalisin' glimpses of 'em when Ivy forgets to sit with 'er knees together. Nearly down to the knee in winter, and quite right too.

The whole thing was ridiculous, Ellen concluded more than once. Whenever she allowed her thoughts to roam around the future married life of Ivy Beasley, she rumbled with laughter. It was too ridiculous by half. Women of Ivy's age didn't get married for the first time. And in church! Blimey, she reflected as she prepared tea in her tiny kitchen, taking a sniff at an elderly packet of shortbread and deciding it would do, I wonder if she's goin' the 'ole 'og and gettin' wed in white? Perhaps she'll ask me and Doris to be bridesmaids!

'It was touch and go whether I'd get down here today,' Ivy said now, sitting by the window and keeping an eye on comings and goings in the avenue. 'So much to do, and so little time to do it. We saw the vicar again this morning, so's I could put him right on one or two things. But now this business up at the Hall has upset us all.'

'You got plenty o' time yet,' said Ellen. 'It'll get done. Goin' to obey, are you, Ivy?' she added maliciously. 'Lovin' and honourin' are all very well, but I don't see you obeyin' your George.'

Unknowingly, Ellen had touched on a very raw spot. She had reminded Ivy of something that worried her in the small hours of the morning, and brought her critical mother back to taunt her with being soft in the head. George had asked her for a big favour, and she'd said yes, had obeyed even before the marriage contract. But as soon as she'd agreed, the dreadful misgivings had begun. The thought of that large sum of money haunted her. It was lent as a deposit on Bridge Cottage until the Leamington house had sold, when, George had assured her with a loving kiss, he would repay her immediately. As he reminded her, it was an investment for them both, but it niggled away in her mind, threatening to sour the whole thing.

Now she shook her head at Ellen dismissively. I won't have my lovely new life spoilt now, and I'm certainly not giving Ellen Biggs anything to chew over, she thought. For one wicked moment she was glad about Greg Jones and Poppy. At least it took the glare of Ellen's attention away from herself for a while.

Doris Ashbourne, however, Ivy's oldest friend, had seen the shadow cross her face, and wondered. All is not well, she thought. And it's not just this thing with the Joneses. 'Anything we can help you with, Ivy?' she said. 'I know you're a brilliant organiser, but Ellen and me would like to do something. Flowers in church, maybe? Or help with the refreshments?'

'Thank you, Doris,' Ivy said. 'It's very kind of you but I don't think there's anything, unless . . .' She hesitated, oddly uncertain.

'Unless wot?' said Ellen, narrowing her eyes and looking closely at Ivy.

'Well, there will be very few of George's relations and friends – in fact, so far, none have been able to accept. His friends from Leamington don't seem to . . . well, you know . . . busy that weekend, and so on.'

'Not a lot we can do about that,' said Ellen.

'So how can we help?' said Doris, frowning at Ellen.

'Well, if you two, and perhaps one or two others, could sit on George's side of the church, then it wouldn't look so one-sided,' said Ivy gratefully. 'I know it isn't usual, but it would make a difference.'

' 'Course we will,' said Ellen, seeing what this was costing Ivy. But what on earth was going on? Not a single friend or relative? Surely that wasn't possible. It was all very peculiar. Goodness, whatever would happen next? First poor little Octavyer, and now somethin' funny up with Ivy and George. She was about to question Ivy further, when Doris jumped in first.

'Have you got your wedding outfit?' she said, anxious to cheer things up.

'Yes and no,' said Ivy, and her smile was back. 'I bought a lovely piece of cloth from Tresham, and Mrs Liversidge is making it up for me. A soft blue. Heavenly blue, George says.'

Ellen gulped, and Doris put a warning hand on her shoulder. 'That'll suit you well,' she said. 'We're really looking forward to it, aren't we, Ellen?'

'Yep,' said Ellen, 'and I shall be wearin' my scarlet two-piece and the 'at with the veil.'

'No you won't, Ellen Biggs!' said Ivy, with more than a little of the old sharpness. 'That decent navy coat will be warm and suitable. It could be really chilly in October. And anyway, there'll be no scarlet two-pieces at my wedding. George has got very good taste, and I'll thank you not to let me down.'

Tactful Doris once more changed the conversation, and this time talk revolved around the reception, the honeymoon in Edinburgh. 'George says it's at its best in the autumn,' said Ivy, with a dreamy look.

Wedding details exhausted, they were quiet for a moment or two. 'It's no good,' said Ellen, after a big sigh from Doris. 'We got to talk about it. After all, it affects us all, knowing the Joneses, and bein' fond of Octavyer, an' that.'

Doris nodded. 'I wish I could think of some way to help,' she said.

'You have to be careful,' said Ivy, her mouth pursed now, in the old way. 'None of us have thought that Poppy might be telling the truth.'

Ellen cackled. 'Truth?' she said. 'That one wouldn't recognise the truth if it came up an' poked 'er in the eye.'

'Poppy's still a child, though, Ellen,' said Doris. 'There may be something in what Ivy says. Mrs Ross was going on in the shop about how she'd always thought Mr Jones was a strange one, much too protective of his daughter . . .'

There was a small silence, and Ivy said, 'And the Standings are the Standings, you know,' as if they should be given the benefit of the doubt.

'Pooh to that!' said Ellen. 'If you knew as much as I did about the Standin's, you wouldn't worry about offendin' the gentry!'

'Time to go,' said Ivy firmly, knowing she and Ellen would never agree on that one. 'I must be back for George. Been to his solicitors in Tresham, and said he'd look in on his way back. Oh, and Ellen,' she added, getting up to go, 'that shortbread is stale as old leather. You'd better chuck it out, and I'll bring you some fresh tomorrow.'

# 43

Poppy Standing was bored. She'd gone back to school for the last week of term after a weird time when Mum and Dad, and that boring social worker, had treated her as something fragile and special. They'd encouraged her to give exact details, and she'd told them that Greg had put his arms round her, and when she'd tried to get away, had laughed and tickled her under her shorts. Telling was easier than she had expected. The social worker, who'd carefully explained that she was a colleague of sniffy Octavia, as if Poppy cared, had been cool, non-committal, and had written down everything she said, made sure there was always someone else in the room. They'd actually seemed scared of her.

Sniffy Octavia . . . Poppy looked out of her bedroom window at the evening light over the park, at the empty tennis court and the shrubbery beyond, and felt pleased. At least Octavia Jones wouldn't have the nerve to come up here any more. And certainly not her horrible father.

Nothing had been said about postponing tennis, and the club had met as usual, though when Poppy appeared and asked if she could play, there was a nasty coolness in the air. No Joneses there, of course. Well, stuff them all. Mum was being very nice to her, and so were they at school, since Mum's session with the headmistress. Dad was keeping out of her way.

'Poppy? Are you there, darling?'

It was her mother, and Poppy said in a small, injured

voice that she was having a rest. A rest! If only something would *happen*! It had been great, in a way, with all that drama and everybody going on at each other, and all revolving around her. Now it was more boring than before. Not even Simon yelled at her, so she hadn't the fun of arguing and yelling back at him. And stuck up here, miles from anywhere, it was very, very boring.

'Can I come in?' Her mother had never asked permission before, and Poppy rushed to the door.

'Oh for God's sake, Mum!' she said. 'I'm not ill, or anything. What do you want?'

Susan recoiled, as if Poppy had struck her. 'Sorry, sweetie,' she said. 'It's just that Joey Bates is on the telephone for you. Do you want to speak to him?'

Poppy pushed past her mother, and rushed down the long staircase two at a time, calling back in an angry voice, 'Why didn't you say so before?' She slumped down in the chair by the telephone and said, 'Hello? Joey? Why didn't you ring sooner? What are you doing? Can I come down?'

Susan, hovering on the stairs, looked at her daughter, at the colour returning to her cheeks and the smile slowly spreading across her face, and her feelings were very mixed. The Bateses were thick with the Joneses, she knew that, and the whole thing was still simmering on, with reports being written, a court case pending. Still, Simon never mentioned the Jones family now, especially Octavia. Susan cheered up. She must ring Alex, invite her over. Then she remembered seeing Sarah Barnett laughing up at Simon outside the shop, and felt depressed again.

'Right,' said Poppy firmly. 'I'm coming, straight away. Tell your gran I'll bring her some of Bill's flowers from the greenhouse. She likes those.' And laughing gleefully in the echoing loftiness of the hall, she was the old Poppy, confident and conspiratorial.

★

The telephone call had been Robert Bates's idea. 'Get her down here, Joey,' he'd said. 'Ask her to lunch, or something, and see if you can get the truth out of her. If anybody can, you can.'

Mandy wasn't too keen. 'I don't think we should involve Joey,' she said. 'It's getting very nasty, what with them who never liked Greg Jones anyway and are making the most of it. And o' course, there's the other side, them who work for the Hall and just want to watch their jobs.'

Robert had finally persuaded her by saying they should do it for Octavia. 'She's bin a good friend to Joey, and he's very fond of her. He won't mind,' he said. Joey had not needed any encouragement. He'd missed Poppy, wondered what was going on. He had picked up most of it, of course, from the gang. Poppy had not been there, but Mark Jenkins had taken him down over the bumpy ground. The gang had been divided, like the village, and Joey himself had been silent, not knowing what to think. Much as he loved Poppy, he knew her only too well.

'I'll ask her to come to Gran's,' he'd said. 'She likes it there.'

Olive Bates, primed by Robert, put on a good spread, and Joey and Poppy downed the lot with healthy enthusiasm. 'Why don't you go and see Grandad's new pig?' Olive said. She'd been amazed when Ted had come back from market one day, saying he was getting a Vietnamese pot-bellied pig for Margie and Joey.

'Oh, I like him!' Poppy said, hanging over the low wall and grinning at the small black pig. 'He looks as if somebody's sat on him!' she said. His squashed-in face gazed up at her intelligently. 'What're you going to call him, Joey?'

'Dunno,' said Joey. 'Haven't thought yet. Margie wants to call him Butcher.'

'Oh dear,' said Poppy. 'No, I think it should sound Asian, or something. What about Hang Wang?'

'Sounds Chinese,' said Joey doubtfully.

'Same thing,' said Poppy. 'And his belly and things hang wang all over the place . . .'

They stayed in the sun, talking to the pig, until Poppy opened the sty gate. Before she could shut it again the pig had trotted out. It didn't go far, and with the yard gate shut so it couldn't escape any further, they decided to let it run for a bit.

Silence fell between them, and Poppy sat down on the warm stone of the yard, sucking a piece of straw. A pair of doves sat on the barn roof, billing and cooing, a mellow sound in the quiet farmyard.

Joey put his hand on the top of Poppy's head and stroked her hair. 'Poppy,' he said, 'what really happened?'

Her reaction was immediate. She shied away from him as if stung, and sprang up, her face furious. 'Shut up!' she shouted. 'Shut up, Joey Bates! Who d'you think you are?' And she ran swiftly to the gate, shoving the small pig aside, and disappeared.

It was some time before Joey, hurt and bewildered, wheeled himself across to the gate and called for his gran to give him a hand.

'Where's Poppy?' she said at once.

'Gone,' said Joey grimly. 'For good, probably.'

The children were coming out of school, and Poppy pushed her way through them, cycling dangerously on the pavement and circling the green before setting off for home. She couldn't think clearly, and had been aimlessly riding around, not wanting to be greeted by her anxious mother, or her taciturn father, or anybody else. Her mood was not improved when she saw ahead of her Sarah Barnett's small red car turning into the Hall avenue. What the hell did *she* want? Poppy cycled faster, her feet flying.

226

Sarah Barnett was getting out of her car as Poppy skidded into the cobbled yard. 'He's not there,' Poppy said breathlessly.

'Oh, I think he is,' said Sarah coolly, looking to where Simon's car was parked in an old barn. 'Hoped to be home early, he said.'

As Poppy glared at her, the door of the Ostler's House opened, and a worried-looking Simon emerged. Sarah said something to him that Poppy couldn't catch. He looked nervously at Poppy, and said to Sarah, 'You'd better come in, then.'

With the door shut firmly in her face, Poppy propped her bike against the old pump and slammed into the kitchen.

'I did say it wasn't a terribly good idea,' said Simon politely.

'Never mind about Poppy,' said Sarah cheerfully, 'she's had far too much attention lately.'

'It wasn't actually Poppy I was worrying about,' Simon was hesitant, not sure why Sarah had come. She had telephoned him at work, and he'd answered in monosyllables. Although her voice had been confident as usual, she had made it sound urgent.

'So aren't you pleased to see me?' she said challengingly. She reached up and kissed him lightly. 'Consolatation prize for the loser?' she grinned.

'Um, well, I've been quite busy,' he said.

'So have I, as it happens,' said Sarah, taking off her coat and throwing it on the old couch by the window. 'Are you offering me a cup of something? Or a drink . . . champagne, maybe?'

'Sarah,' began Simon, 'I really think the sooner you—'

'Spit it out and go away, the better?' Sarah looked at him, and her smile was not entirely friendly. 'Well, these things are best done delicately, I'm told. I've been busy, as I said. Busy with tests, and doctors, and all that stuff. The thing is, the tests were positive. I'm pregnant. John is over the moon, of course, but I just thought you'd like to know too. You know, being as . . .' She was enjoying watching Simon's face.

'Are you saying . . . ' he said.

'No way of knowing, short of blood tests, that kind of thing,' she answered. 'No need for that, anyway. John's mum's gone into orbit with delight, and I'm not a total monster.'

'So you don't actually want me to . . . I mean, anything I can do?'

'Oh, God, no. I'm having a wonderful time, centre of attention at Walnut Farm.' Sarah laughed now, delightedly. 'Si, dear,' she said, 'I'm not the ravished parlourmaid, you know! I'm the school headteacher, married to one of the county's most successful farmers. Why should I want . . . oh, don't look like that! I really don't know *whose* it is. I'm doing what I want to do, as usual. Come and give me a kiss, you dope.'

# 44

'Tavie? It's Simon. How are you?'

'Rotten, thanks. How are you?'

'Bloody awful. Oh, Tavie, I want you. Or at the very least, I want to see you . . . oh, love, don't cry.'

'I'm not crying,' said Octavia, and then was so overcome with tears that she had to fumble for her handkerchief. Her parents were both out, gone to the cinema in Tresham to get away from the village, and she had been blankly watching television.

'Tavie! I'm coming down. No, it's no use your saying anything. I'm coming. Five minutes. And I love you.'

Octavia put down the telephone and looked at herself in the big looking-glass over the fireplace. A wan figure gazed back at her, with a shadowy face and hollow eyes, hair pulled back anyhow. She went upstairs and sluiced her face under the cold tap. Brushing her hair loose, she went downstairs again and found Simon at the front door. She opened up, and looked at him mutely.

'Are they out?' he said. She nodded, and he walked in, shutting the door behind him. Taking her hand, he led her over to the sofa and they sat down.

Neither said anything for a moment, and then Octavia found her voice. 'I'm so sorry about it all,' she said, 'and I'll quite understand if you don't want . . .'

Simon pulled her close, and muttered into her hair, 'Don't say another word. I love you, and nothing, nothing at all, will ever change that.' He sat back from her, and shook his head. 'Don't suppose you could say the same.'

Octavia's tears began again, and she scrubbed her face. 'Oh, God,' she said. 'I'm not like this. I never cry.'

'Christ, Tavie, don't,' said Simon, then he hugged her, rocking her like a child. 'Not here,' he whispered, 'not here, in this house. Come on, let's lock up and go for a spin.'

'Where are we going?' said Octavia.

'A secret place,' said Simon, glancing sideways at her and relieved to see colour in her cheeks. 'Somewhere Dad used to take me when I was a kid. If Mum had been harrying him around, which was quite often, he'd grab some food from old Ellen and we'd sneak out in the old Land Rover, have a picnic.'

They lurched down a sandy track, the dry dust flying up behind them, and then Simon turned into a sparsely wooded spinney, and switched off the engine. 'Come on,' he said, 'let's see if it's still there.' Dappled sunshine filtered through the spindly birches, and a blackbird's alarm call sent rustles through the undergrowth.

'See if what's still there?' said Octavia.

'You'll find out,' he said, and grinned. 'Smile at me, Octavia,' he ordered. She stared at him. 'Go on,' he said, 'smile!'

'I don't feel like smiling,' she said. 'I haven't smiled for weeks.'

Simon sat down on a mossy tree stump. 'Right-o then,' he said. 'We go no further until you've managed a smile. A small one will do.' He looked up at her, and the love in his eyes was so warming that the smile came involuntarily.

'Shall we run away and never come back?' Octavia said, as they plodded on, arms linked.

'No need,' said Simon, 'here we are, look. Our own little house in the trees.'

It was really a bird-watching hide, and had been put up there by Bill Turner for Susan Standing in a sudden enthusiasm for ornithology. Her interest in birds had been supplanted by the arrival of Poppy, and the hide hadn't been used since, except illicitly by kids from the village and poachers on the roam. When they climbed the sturdy ladder and crept in, they found an empty beer bottle, and other embarrassing evidence that the secret hideaway had not been wasted.

Simon looked around, and saw a small bale of hay, broken open and strewn across the floor. 'Someone's made themselves comfortable,' he said, and added more to the soft, dry bedding. 'Sit here with me,' he instructed gently, and she took his hand.

'Don't say anything else, Simon,' she said. He'd probably brought Sarah Barnett here, she thought sadly, but what the hell, too much had been said, and now it was time to forget, forget the whole horrible nightmare, if that was any longer possible.

Richard Standing was a very unhappy man. His family had reached the stage of not talking. Every mealtime was an agony of tension, with Susan brightly addressing all her remarks to the dog, Simon gulping down his food and getting out as quickly as possible, and Poppy eating almost nothing and scowling at any attempts to coax her.

'How much longer is this going on?' he'd said angrily to Susan, when they were alone in the drawing-room.

'Oh, these things take time,' she had said vaguely.

'Well, I've had enough of it,' he'd said. 'This ridiculous nonsense is doing nobody any good. Especially Poppy. Did you see her the day she came back from the Bateses'? I've never seen the child look so shattered. No, you were out, so you didn't have to mop up. She broke down completely, you know. Real distress this time. God knows what that Joey Bates said to her.'

Now Richard walked across the hot, humid fields, his spaniel at his heels, and tried desperately to think of some way out. Deadlock, complete deadlock, as far as he could see. Susan had mentioned a prosecution, and he'd finally blown up. Not while he was master of his house, he'd said. He'd got a few friends in high places, and knew how to use them. The sooner the whole thing was settled the better. He'd go and see Greg Jones, sort the whole thing out. Probably all a mistake, a stupid misunderstanding by Poppy. That was the way to look at it. So much of this kind of thing in the papers these days, and on television. No wonder the girl had taken fright. That must be it.

He picked up a stick and threw it into a deep pool at the edge of the spinney. His spaniel splashed in and retrieved it, depositing it at his feet, trailing green, slimy pondweed. 'Good dog,' he said absently. Yes, Susan would have to accept it, call off the police and the social worker woman, and that would be that. Maybe then they could all get back to normal. They'd have to avoid all the Joneses for a while, but that shouldn't be too difficult.

It was quiet in the spinney, except for the trickling stream and clatter of pigeons. Then he heard voices, and stood still, grabbing his dog by the collar. Trespassers? As he watched, he saw his son, his very dear son, walking across an open glade hand in hand with Octavia Jones. Then he saw where they were going. It was the old hide, where Susan had watched birds once or twice, and where he and Annie Bishop had had such a lovely time.

'Oh, my God,' he muttered, and stroked the top of his dog's smooth head. Avoid the Joneses? What a disaster, a bloody awful, frightful disaster.

# 45

Summer wore on, and support for tennis gradually waned. It wasn't just the chillier evenings that thinned out the players: it was all the things they couldn't say, divided loyalties, and corrosive suspicion. Simon did his best. He organised another tournament, but not enough people entered to make it worth while. Sarah Barnett sent a message by Annie Bishop that she wouldn't be coming again for a while. For several months, actually. Then she'd be back.

Annie had been among the first to be told, and was delighted with the news of Sarah's pregnancy, but she was puzzled by the expression on Simon's face when she talked about it at the club. Andrew had been quicker, but his suggestion had been ridiculed by Annie. 'Oh no,' Annie had been shocked. 'She wouldn't be that careless.'

George Chalmer had been the next defector. He'd said confidentially that since he'd shortly be fully occupied with a new wife, perhaps Simon could think of another person to be treasurer? Simon had said yes, of course, and wished him well, but felt increasingly pessimistic.

George was fully occupied with Ivy and her wedding plans already. Only a week to go now, and the atmosphere at Victoria Villa had become feverish. George was making plans, too, not all to do with honeymoon hotels and small bands of gold.

Now it was Ivy's last day as spinster. It had been

another long night, when worry about that large sum of money, most of her savings in the bank, had threatened to take over pleasurable dreams of George waiting for her with his loving smile by the chancel steps, immaculately dressed as always, with a red carnation in his buttonhole.

All right, Mother, she said, as she washed up her single plate, bowl, cup and saucer, I know I shan't float along in a cloud of white tulle, but that's not what counts. George is my beloved, and I am his. And I trust him.

With these inspiring thoughts, Ivy's spirits rose, and she tackled the morning's housework with more than her usual zest. No doubt there'd be one or two people coming in, wanting to wish her well, bringing presents. A surprisingly large pile had already assembled in Ivy's front room, all wrapped in wedding paper with bells and ribbons. She and George planned to open them this afternoon, when he would come up from Bridge Cottage to be with her before returning to his solitary home for the last time.

Ivy gave His Chair a special dusting and plumped up the cushions with affection. She was looking forward to her honeymoon in Edinburgh, but even more to the long winter evenings when they would sit either side of the fire in companionable silence, broken occasionally by an endearment. No more lonely nights for you, Ivy Dorothy, she told herself.

Once more she took fresh, lavender-scented sheets and pillowcases and began to make up the big double bed, but this time there would be two of them in it. Ivy had managed to put bed to the back of her mind. Now, as she tucked in soft blankets and spread her mother's big white cotton bedspread over all, she had a moment's panic. Why didn't you explain it to me properly, Mother? she addressed the photograph on the mantelshelf. Because you never needed to know, came the inevitable reply in Ivy's head. Ivy reassured herself that it couldn't be much different from cats and dogs, and pigs and that, but she had vivid memories of herself and other children hanging over a pen where the great bull was doing his stuff. All that weight! And the poor old cow hadn't looked as if she was enjoying it much. Still, George was a trim figure for his age. She supposed that once things got going, it would be all right. She might even enjoy it . . .

Enjoy it? said her mother's voice. You don't expect to enjoy it, Ivy Dorothy! Just do your duty, my girl, and if you're lucky, at his age he won't want it much, if at all. Mind you, men are different from women in that respect, as you'll soon find out.

The secret truth, however, was that George's caresses and kisses had wakened something in Ivy Beasley that she'd never suspected. Desire, she thought, I suppose that's what it is. There on every page in all those Mills and Boon romances, and now to be hers.

No, Mother, she said, her face hot, I think there's a strong possibility that your only daughter, the prim Miss Ivy Beasley, might surprise you all.

'Ready, Ivy?' said Doreen, standing on the scrubbed front step. She had come to take Ivy to Waltonby to collect the wedding outfit from Mrs Liversidge, and was surprised at how pretty Ivy looked. Her black eyes were shining and her face alive, the bitterness and resentment of the lonely years all gone.

The drive to Waltonby took Doreen and Ivy through narrow country lanes and past rolling stubble fields. 'Fair waved the golden corn,' sang Ivy, in her tuneless voice. 'Very lucky we are, Doreen,' she said. 'Most of us don't know how lucky we are. All God's goodness around us, and no need for unhappiness at all.'

'Tell that to Greg Jones,' said Doreen Price. 'I saw him with Gabriella in the car, and both of them looked suicidal. He'll never get over it, you know, whatever the outcome.'

'Nothing to do with me,' said Ivy firmly. 'And as you know, Doreen, I don't believe in gossip. Does nothing but harm.' Doreen was speechless at this, and drove on until the car coasted down Waltonby street.

'The coat and skirt are all packed up in tissue, Miss Beasley,' said Mrs Liversidge, inviting them into her small cottage. 'No need for a further fitting. It'll be perfect. A bobby-dazzler, that's what you'll be for your George.'

On their way out, they passed a row of photographs, smiling brides dressed in gowns all made by Mrs Liversidge. 'Next one up there will be you, Miss Beasley,' she said. 'Don't forget, now. I want the best one of you and George, arm in arm, outside the church. That's when my brides are at their best, after the ceremony. Got their man, I suppose you might say!'

By the time Doreen had dropped Ivy off outside Victoria Villa, grey clouds had obscured the sun, and a small chilly wind caused Ivy to shiver as she opened her front door. She clutched her precious box carefully, taking it straight through to the front room. Going back to shut the door, she reflected that the change in the weather didn't matter, so long as the sun shone tomorrow. When George comes up this afternoon, she said to herself, we can open our presents and have tea.

As she drew the door curtain across, her eye was caught by a white envelope, half-hidden in the folds, and she picked it up curiously. The post had come early, and there'd been nothing but junk mail. She must have missed this one. Then she saw there was no stamp, and the handwriting was familiar. It was George's neat, copperplate hand, of which he was so proud. 'Miss Ivy Beasley. By Hand.' Ivy smiled. How sweet of him to send her a little note this morning, just when he knew she would be feeling a bit nervous. She put it down on the kitchen table, and filled the kettle. It would be nice to read while she had her lunch.

Settled with a cup of tea and Tiddles on her lap, she took a knife and opened the envelope. The single sheet of paper slid out quite easily, and Ivy unfolded it. There were two paragraphs in George's small, legible writing, and it took Ivy very little time to read them.

Her hand shaking, she put the letter down and pushed it away, out of reach. Her face was ashen and her eyes blank. 'No,' she said quietly, just once. After that, she didn't move, not even when Tiddles dug her claws into her leg in an ecstasy of affection. Ivy stared straight ahead. Her hands dropped to her sides, and she moaned softly. And then nothing. No sound, no movement, just those blank, staring eyes. The cat, sensing something dreadfully wrong, jumped down and fled in fear.

# 46

St Mary's church was cool and quiet, dimly lit now that the sun had gone, and the jewel windows were sombre, but everywhere there were flowers: on wrought-iron pedestals, in festoons along the window ledges, in a great feathery arrangement in the old stone font, and even in tiny bunches at the pew ends. Ivy had said just a couple of vases, here and there, but her fellow members of the WI had put old feuds behind them and done her proud. Annie Bishop, keen to be involved as always, had produced a ravishing altar display, and given unwanted advice to others. All morning they'd been there, gossiping and laughing and looking forward to the big day tomorrow.

Now all the stalks and leaves had been swept away, and they'd gone home. The church was full of the mingled sharp scents of autumn, and when Octavia Jones pushed open the heavy oak door, she stood in silence for a moment, amazed at the beauty of it. She'd come in during her lunch hour, between calls, to make sure the choir robes were in good order for tomorrow. It is so quiet, she thought, a special, holy kind of silence, whether you're a believer or not. It was a pool of tranquillity, insulated by the thick stone walls and hundreds of years of simple faith.

I wish I could stay here for the rest of the day, Octavia thought, walking through to the vestry. Her parents had gone in yet again to the solicitors in Tresham, and she dreaded their wounded faces when they returned. And

Mum has to sit there playing joyful music for old Ivy, when she's slowly dying inside. Something's got to happen soon, she said to herself, straightening sleeves and pulling bits of stone and twig from the smaller gown pockets, else Dad'll break down, and then we shall all have to move away and everybody will think the worst. A feeling of fury at the whole thing took hold of her so hard that she found her hands were shaking.

The gowns were sorted out, and Octavia wandered through to the chancel. The organ was open. Mum had probably forgotten to lock it last Sunday, and no wonder. Octavia sat down and fingered the keys. A well-used, dog-eared book of church voluntaries stood open, and she began to play. The music soothed her, and she carried on, slowly relaxing into the mellow sounds.

The click of the door latch didn't register at first. It was only when she heard the scuffle of feet on the tiled floor that she looked into the mirror that gave the organist a view of the church. It was Poppy Standing, and Octavia watched her slide into a side aisle pew, bending her head in a pathetic attitude of prayer.

Well, what now? thought Octavia, continuing to play quietly. Shall I pretend I haven't seen her, or go down there and beat her up with an altar candle? Then she heard the unmistakable sound of crying, and saw in the mirror that Poppy's shoulders were heaving. She came to the end of the piece and stopped, sitting quite still for a moment. Without looking round, she said matter-of-factly, 'Poppy?'

There was no answer, but the crying ceased. Still facing the old voluntary book, Octavia said straightforwardly, 'I don't suppose you came to find me, but since I'm here, perhaps you'd listen for a minute?' There was no answer, and Poppy's face remained hidden behind a screen of curly hair. 'You're too old for stories,' continued Octavia, 'but this is a cautionary tale.' She waited for the smart reply, but Poppy said nothing, so she carried on.

'I know what you call me,' said Octavia conversationally, and without accusation, 'but I am no more Goody Two-shoes than you are . . . I had a real crush on Robert Bates once, poor chap. I was fifteen, and he was going out with Mandy. I made his life a misery, but he was a good bloke and held me off kindly. I was mad at him and Mandy, and laid a trap. It was boring in Ringford, nothing to do, nowhere to go. I couldn't wait to grow up. Like you . . .'

She stopped, waiting, but there was no reaction. Now she turned round and faced Poppy, who said, 'I'm listening,' from behind her curtain of hair.

'Well, he found me wandering along Tresham road in the dark and gave me a lift. I pretended he'd had a go at me. Tried to rape me, to be blunt.'

Poppy shifted in her pew, but still did not look up. 'So?' she said in a muffled voice.

'So,' said Octavia, 'my father, who is a good and honourable man, saw that I was lying and made me own up.' The silence was thick now, but Octavia continued casually, as if talking to a neighbour in the shop. 'The point of all this, Poppy,' she said, 'is that I remember only too well how once you've told a lie, you're stuck with it. Takes a lot to admit it, but it is the only way out.'

Poppy looked up now, and her face was full of unhappiness and desperation. 'Ah well,' she said defiantly, 'maybe lying runs in your family. It doesn't in ours.' She scrubbed at her face with damp hands, and ran out of the church.

Octavia sat for several minutes in depressed silence. Well, that had been a monumental failure. So much for your well-known empathy with the young, Octavia Jones. She got up and closed the organ. Back to work and the real world, she thought, and it wasn't until she opened the church door and saw her car, that a thought struck her. Poppy must have seen it there, parked outside the gate, must have known she was inside. Perhaps, just perhaps, Poppy had been doing some thinking.

Octavia paused to admire the exquisite posies in the porch windows, and saw a prayer book on the stone bench beneath. On the flyleaf she saw Ivy Beasley's name written in a firm hand. She would want that tomorrow. 'Goin' to carry 'er old prayer book, with a spray o' freesyers,' Ellen had told her. 'Trust Ivy to be different. Why can't she 'ave a nice bookay like everybody else?'

Octavia slipped the book into her pocket. She would drop it into Victoria Villa on her way out of the village.

It was drizzling when Octavia stopped her car and walked up to Ivy's front door, pressed the strident bell, and waited. Nobody came, and she peered through the letterbox, but could see nothing. She didn't like to leave the book on the step. It was old and fragile, and the drizzle had turned into light rain. Maybe she's outside at the back, Octavia thought, and went round the house. No Ivy in the garden, and though she knocked loudly at the back door, there was still no answer. Probably down at George's, she thought, but then remembered seeing him driving off towards Tresham. He'd looked a bit strained, but she had put it down to pre-wedding nerves.

Octavia was thinking of leaving the prayer book in a wooden box by the door when she saw Ivy. At least, she saw Ivy's back, sitting in a chair at the table, motionless. 'Miss Beasley!' she called, and rapped lightly on the window. There was no reaction. Ivy sat there like a statue. Octavia felt a cat rubbing against her ankles and looked down. It was Tiddles, mewing pitifully. 'Oh, my God, what's going on?' said Octavia, panic rising.

She heard Bill Turner in the yard next door, and ran to the high fence. 'Bill!' she yelled. He answered at once, and she said to get over here as quickly as possible. Something bad had happened to Ivy Beasley.

Seconds later, Bill Turner and Peggy were round in the yard with Octavia, and they too looked in the window and yelled and banged. Finally, Bill pushed up the sash window and clambered in. He unlocked the back door and let in the others.

Peggy walked towards Ivy and touched her gently on the shoulder. 'Looks like she's had a shock,' she said, stroking Ivy's back.

'At least she's breathing,' said Bill. 'See if you can get a coat round her, Peggy. Her hands are as cold as ice.' He went over to the sink and filled the kettle, then rummaged in the drawer until he found a hot water bottle.

'What can have happened?' said Octavia. 'She was fine yesterday. I spoke to her on the Green.'

Peggy had walked round the table to look more easily into Ivy's face, and saw the folded sheet of paper, dead white against the dark, polished wood. 'What's this?' she said, picking it up.

'Might be private,' said Bill, shaking his head.

'This is an emergency,' said Peggy, glancing for approval at Octavia, who was busy telephoning the doctor. She unfolded the paper, and began to read. 'Oh, no,' she said. 'Oh, Bill, no, no.'

Octavia said into the telephone, 'Yes, as soon as possible, please,' and turned back to Peggy. 'What is it?' she said. 'Read it out, Mrs T. Go on, I don't think Ivy can hear us.'

Peggy began to read, and the others listened in silence to her choked voice. ' "Dear Ivy," ' she read, ' "I don't know how to tell you this, because over these last months I've become quite fond of you. I'm afraid, my dear, our wedding cannot take place, never could take place." '

'The bugger!' said Bill angrily.

'Go on, Mrs T,' said Octavia.

' "By the time you read this, I shall be far away. Don't try to contact me. You'll never find me, Ivy, but I'll not forget you, nor the good times we had together. I just hope I've brought a little happiness into your life, which you might not have had otherwise. Good luck! I know you'll bounce back. You're a survivor, Ivy, and if I'd ever thought of taking a wife, it would have been you. Yours, George. P.S. Chalmer's not my real name, of course, though quite apt, don't you think?" '

'If I get my hands on him . . .' said Bill explosively.

'That's a very cold letter,' said Peggy simply. 'Very cold and unfeeling. Poor Ivy. Poor, poor Ivy.'

A small movement from the still figure silenced them all, and they looked anxiously at her. 'Is that you, Doris?' Ivy said, and none of them recognised her voice.

'No,' said Peggy quickly, 'but we can get her down here in no time. Don't worry, Miss Beasley, you're among friends.'

Doris came at once, and though pale and shocked, was an instant tower of strength. She got Ivy up to bed, and tucked her in firmly. 'There,' she said. 'Now you get some sleep, Ivy, and we'll talk later.'

Peggy returned to the shop and changed the sign from Closed to Open. She stood behind the counter, trying to control herself. Almost immediately, Doreen Price arrived, and looking curiously at her, said, 'I need some shoe polish, please. We've run out, and I must be smart for tomorrow . . . you all right, Peggy?' Doreen's motherly voice was too much, and Peggy broke down. By now, Jean Jenkins and a couple of other people had come into the shop, and all stared at Peggy in dismay. Knowing the impossibility of keeping Ivy's disaster a secret, Peggy blurted out the bare bones of it.

'Oh, my God! Poor old Ivy!' said Jean Jenkins, clutching Doreen's arm. 'How could anybody be that cruel?'

Doreen, ever practical, remembered something Tom had said, something to do with sponging off old Ivy, and her heart sank even further. 'Is she talking yet?' she asked Peggy.

'Not really. She just asked for Doris, and we got her up to bed with a hot water bottle. She doesn't seem to be able to see anything. Just like a blind person. It's terrifying, Doreen, to look at her.'

'So we don't know what George Sodding Chalmer tucked away in his car boot before he left,' said Doreen harshly. 'He didn't woo our Ivy for nothing, that's for sure. No doubt it'll all come out. Is the doctor there?'

'Yes,' said Peggy. 'And Doris. Bill is still with her, too. Octavia Jones was a treasure, but she's gone off now to work. Thank God Bill was at home!'

At that moment, Bill came up the steps and into the shop. Everyone asked him questions at once, and he shook his head, waving them away like a man in a fog. He saw Mary York, who helped in the shop, and said, 'Any chance you could take over here for a bit, Mary, and let Peggy go back next door? Doris says she's fine, but I'm not so sure.'

'What did the doctor say?' Jean Jenkins asked.

'Not a lot,' said Bill. 'Said Ivy'd need watching, but was best in her own bed, with friends. He's coming back later, to take another look. Seemed a bit worried about her eyes, but said it was probably part of the shock.'

No one made a move to go home, until Jean Jenkins walked towards the door. 'The kids'll be back soon,' she said. 'I'd best be off to see to their tea, but I'll be down again, Bill. See if there's anything I can do.'

As Peggy took off her overall, she remembered something. 'Oh, by the way,' she said, 'there's a letter for you, Bill, on the kitchen table. Well, it was for me, but you'd better read it. It's from my cousin in Leamington. Remember, we wrote. Says she can't trace any George Chalmer.'

For the rest of the afternoon, Peggy, sent back to the shop with reassurances from Doris, recruited Nigel and Sophie Brooks, and they made the necessary telephone calls to as many guests, caterers, and anyone else they could think of connected with the wedding.

'Someone will just have to stand at the church gate, in case we've forgotten anybody,' said Nigel worriedly. He'd never had anything like this. Heard of it, of course, but not in his own parish. 'Not a pleasant job, I'm afraid,' he said. They were sitting in the Turners' kitchen, in front of lists of names and addresses they found in Ivy's little desk.

The shop door opened, and it was Octavia Jones, back for an update. 'Anything I can do to help?' she said.

'Not really,' said Nigel Brooks, 'unless you could stand at the church gates and explain to any guests we've not contacted?'

Peggy interrupted quickly, 'Oh no, I don't think we should ask Octavia.'

'Why not?' said Octavia firmly. 'I'll do it, Mr Brooks. It's the least I can do for Miss Beasley. There's another thing,' she said. 'Has anyone thought to tell Ellen Biggs? It'll be a shock to her, and she's not all that strong.'

'Oh, dear Lord,' groaned Nigel Brooks. 'I'd better go straight away.'

'No need,' said Octavia. 'I'll do it. She trusts me, I think. I can handle it.' She walked swiftly out of the shop, and got into her car.

Nigel watched her go, heading for the Lodge, and sighed. 'What a very brave girl,' he said quietly. 'On top of all she has to contend with at present,' and he went back to the dismal task in the kitchen.

In a small flat in Leamington Spa, an elderly man, sometimes known as George Chalmer, neatly dressed, with smooth hair and horn-rimmed spectacles, stroked his dog and sat down in a battered old armchair. 'Get us a cup of tea, then, dearie,' he said to his friend.

'Mission accomplished?' said the young man, picking up a chipped, thick china mug, and pouring water on to a teabag. 'Feeling exhausted, are we?'

'Shut up,' said the elderly man. 'Just shut up, and give me the tea.' He sipped it, and made a face. 'Ugh,' he said, 'it's lukewarm! Ivy wouldn't have had tea like this in the house.' For a moment his friend thought he was going to cry.

'Just like the Ivy,' sang the young man, thinking to cheer him up, 'on the old garden wall, Clinging so tightly, whate'er may befall . . .'

The elderly man took a deep breath, and didn't smile. 'You crafty little sod,' he said, and he tipped the pale tea into the sink. 'I suppose it's good to be back,' he said.

# 47

It was very quiet in Ellen Biggs's sitting-room. Octavia sat next to Ellen on the sofa as she sniffed, shook her head hopelessly, and fumbled in her apron pocket for a handkerchief that wasn't there. Octavia leaned across and took her hand. 'Shall I make you a cup of tea?'

Octavia had told Ellen simply and straightforwardly what had happened, and so far, the old woman had said nothing. She'd sat down heavily and stared, as if willing her to say it wasn't true. Now she squeezed her hand so hard that it hurt, and said, 'I'm not dreamin', am I? I'm not goin' to wake up and find it was a nightmare and it's Ivy's weddin' day and everythin's orlright?'

Octavia bit her lip. Bloody hell, just wait till they caught up with that disgusting old man! 'No, I'm afraid not, Mrs Biggs,' she said gently.

There was another long silence, and then Ellen spoke again, this time with a stronger voice. 'I suspected it, yer know,' she said. 'There was somethin' not quite tickety-boo about that George. Hinstinct, yer might call it, Octavyer. 'Course, when it all seemed to be goin' so well, I put it be'ind me.'

Octavia looked at her sharply. 'Did you see anything wrong?' she said, knowing that a good half of Ellen's day was spent keeping watch at the window. 'Not wrong, exactly,' said the old woman, straightening up in her chair.

Octavia was relieved to see the colour coming back into her face, and decided the very best thing for Mrs

Biggs was to keep her talking. 'But what, then?' she said encouragingly.

'It were more what I didn't see,' she said. ''e 'ad almost no furniture, yer know. A few sticks I wouldn't give you tuppence for. Ivy give 'im one or two bits. I don't s'pose she'll see them agen . . .'

'Did he ever have strange visitors?' said Octavia, more to keep the conversation going, than with any real curiosity.

Ellen thought for a moment, frowned, and then said, 'Yep. Twice. First time George was poorly up at Ivy's. But the next time 'e opened the door. I saw the light, and this young bloke went in. Then George shut the door agen, and I didn't see no more . . .'

She paused, swallowed, and then continued, now well into the swing of her story. 'Until the mornin', Octavyer. Early mornin', very early. That Jenkins dog were out on the loose, and barkin' 'is 'ead off outside my door. I got up to shoo 'im off, and 'eard this car over the road. Wouldn't start, and I could 'ear George raisin' 'is voice.'

'What did he say?' said Octavia.

'It were a bit peculiar,' said Ellen. ''e said to this young bloke, "An' don't come 'ere agen, no matter what. Yer'll ruin the 'ole thing," 'e said, then the car started, and George went back in the 'ouse and slammed the door. That's all, but it made me think. Then I forgot all about it. D'yer think it means anythin', Octavyer?'

Octavia was beginning to have grave suspicions, but thought it best to divert Ellen. 'Now,' she said, 'the most important person in Ringford for a while will be Ivy Beasley.' Except my dad, she thought bitterly, but concentrated on the job in hand. 'She's going to need all the help and support we can give her. And especially from you and Doris, Mrs Biggs. You're her oldest friends, aren't you?'

Ellen got up slowly, levering herself with her hands

clutching the arm of the sofa. 'Quite right,' she said. 'And you don't have to tell me what friends are for, Octavyer. I shall be up there t'morrer mornin' first thing, and I'll stay as long as she needs me.' She looked closely at Octavia, and said, 'Upset you, 'as this business? Don't you fret, not all men are the same. You could'a done without this, couldn't you, my dear?'

As Octavia Jones shut Ellen's gate and turned to wave, the old woman stood at her door. 'Don't worry!' she shouted. 'I ain't never let a friend down yet, an' I ain't about to start now.'

Octavia smiled, and walked slowly to her car. It was true, she could have done without Ivy's disaster. She could also have done without Sarah Barnett smirking all over her face and talking babies with Annie Bishop in the shop this morning. She knew it was for her benefit, but had tried to ignore them. Sarah's final remark resounded in her head. 'Not sure when it's due,' she'd said loudly to Annie. 'Got my dates muddled, unfortunately!' Peggy had asked them in a very sharp voice if that would be all, and they had left giggling. And then she'd spoken to John Barnett outside the pub, his pleasant face alight with pleasure as he told her about the baby. 'Put everything right, that will,' he'd said, and Octavia's heart bled for him.

In the small hours of the morning Ivy called out. Three o'clock, when Doris surfaced and looked at the little clock by her bed. It was a dreadful cry, loud and full of terror, and Doris rushed out without putting on dressing-gown or slippers, across the landing and into Ivy's room. She saw Ivy sitting bolt upright in bed, her arms clasped tight around her bosom, her hair standing on end like a wiry, brindled brush, and her mouth open in an endless scream, though now the sound had diminished to a whimper.

'Ivy!' said Doris. 'It's all right. I'm here. Tell Doris

249

what's the matter. Did you have a nightmare?' Doris went to the side of the bed, and put her arms round the shivering figure. 'Steady, now,' she said. 'You're sweating, poor thing. Just lie down and I'll make a nice cup of tea. You'll soon feel better.'

She persuaded Ivy to lie down, keeping up a comforting monologue about how she'd probably got too many covers on. It was a humid night, and perhaps they'd get a storm. It wasn't until she looked directly into Ivy's face, wondering if she should call the doctor, that she saw her eyes. The opaque blankness had gone, and Ivy was staring at her in total misery. She can see again, thought Doris, and she can see that today is going to be the unhappiest day of her life. Poor, poor Ivy.

The morning dawned bright and still. It was already warm by the time Peggy greeted the post ladies at the door. An Indian summer, said Bill. As they sorted the letters, the conversation was on one topic only. 'Everybody knows,' they said. 'News like that spreads like chicken-pox.'

The village came slowly to life. Saturday morning, and most people had a free day. No commuters roared out of Walnut Close, scattering chickens and children. Peggy stood at her shop doorway and looked at Victoria Villa, quiet and solid as ever. Wonder how she is, she thought. I shall go in later, see if Doris is coping. Saturday. Ivy Beasley's wedding day. Already the sound of the words seemed unreal. In one cruel stroke, George Chalmer, or whatever his name was, had returned Ivy to her former status. Spinster of this parish, never likely to be anything else.

Peggy turned back into the shop, and put her arms round Bill, ready for work in his rough jacket and heavy boots. 'Should be back early, gel,' he said, holding her tight.

★

Next door, Doris was wakened from a fitful sleep in Ivy's spare bedroom by the unexpected sight of Ivy standing at her door.

'What on earth are you doing?' Doris said, struggling to sit up. 'I was going to bring you a bite of breakfast in bed.'

'I am perfectly all right, Doris,' said Ivy, swaying slightly. 'You can go home now.'

It was clear to Doris that Ivy was far from all right: on the day she was to have been married to a man in whom she had placed all her pent-up affection and trust, she looked like a wraith. In less than twenty-four hours, the new Ivy had vanished, and her former sturdy figure seemed ready to give way at the slightest puff of wind. She had been up and dressed before waking Doris, but her clothes were oddly assorted. Ivy, who had lately metamorphosed into such a smart woman, had this morning pulled on the first old dress that came to hand, with a dark purple cardigan that had been her mother's. She felt cold, though the sun was shining brightly.

'Don't think I'm not very grateful,' said Ivy. 'I shall never forget your friendship at this time . . .' Her voice faltered, but she took a deep breath and carried on. 'But I have to face it on my own, Doris. I've always been on my own, since Mother died . . .' Again she hesitated, reminded of a future that had promised no more loneliness, no more fighting battles as a single, crabbed old woman. 'So I'm used to it,' she went on, with superhuman effort. 'I have a job to do today, and the sooner I get going the better.'

'Ivy!' said Doris. 'What can you possibly have to do today that we can't see to for you? There's absolutely no need . . .' But she could see from Ivy's expression that there was no arguing with her.

'Are you sure about this?' said Doris, as she took her coat from the stand in the hall. 'I really don't like leaving you, Ivy.'

'I shall be all right,' said Ivy, though her head was spinning. 'And if I need you, I know where you live.'

Doris left reluctantly, and considered going into the shop to alert Peggy, but then she saw the hobbling figure of Ellen Biggs approaching, and was in an instant dilemma. Should she put Ellen off? Tell her that Ivy was asleep and must not be disturbed? Or perhaps the old woman's company would do Ivy good? In the end, she decided not to interfere, and, waving in Ellen's direction, set off home.

Ellen Biggs lurched confidently up to Ivy's front door and knocked firmly. She shifted her basket from one arm to the other, and grasped her stick firmly. Unlike Doris, she had no qualms, no uncertainty. She waited for a minute, and, hearing nothing, leaned down, pushed open the letterbox, and yelled in a strong voice, 'Ivy! Ivy! It's me! Open up, Ivy, I ain't gonna bite yer!' A small squeak from Ivy's kitchen door set Ellen's mind at rest. Ivy was on her way.

'There was no call for you to come,' said Ivy.

Ellen did not reply for a moment, shocked in spite of herself at the ravaged appearance of her old friend. 'Wot yer mean, Ivy?' she said. 'Not come? When you've 'ad such a narsty shock? Don't be ridiculous. And let me in, for goodness' sake. It's very 'ot 'ere in the sun.'

Ivy stepped back and Ellen stumped in, through the hall into the kitchen, and sat herself down on a chair at the table. 'Right,' she said. 'Get the kettle on. I saw Doris goin' off, so I knew you must be up and about. Let's 'ave a cup of tea, and then you can tell me wot 'appened.'

Ellen's straightforward assumption that Ivy would tell her all, just as if there'd been a flood in the kitchen or a blocked lavatory, found a chink in Ivy's armour. She bridled, very much in the old way, and even snorted, just slightly. 'What makes you think I'd tell you anything, Ellen Biggs?' she said, filling the kettle nevertheless.

Ellen was not discomfited. She settled herself, and said, 'Because I'm your oldest friend, and the only one who tells you straight. I know you've 'ad a terrible blow, Ivy, but there was somethin' about that George Chalmer that I didn't like. Said so right from the beginning.' It was the first time anyone had dared to mention his name to Ivy, and Ellen had brought it out so matter-of-factly that Ivy relaxed a little.

'Don't give me the told-you-so, Ellen,' she said. 'Spare me that, at least.'

'Right,' said Ellen. 'No doubt I'd'a done the same meself. Don't get many chances at our age, do we? Still, 'e were definitely a bit fishy. 'E didn't get anythin' out of yer, Ivy, did 'e?'

Ivy's momentary hesitation told Ellen all she needed to know. She supposed it was money. What else would he have been after? Ivy realised that Ellen had guessed, but said nothing. Not even Ellen Biggs would speculate on sums as large as Ivy had handed over.

'Now then,' said Ellen, draining her cup, 'wot yer goin'a do this afternoon, Ivy? Can't stay 'ere languishin' all on yer own.'

To Ellen's disbelief, Ivy told her of her intentions, and in spite of all Ellen's protestations, would not be deflected.

'The village'll think you've gone barmy,' Ellen said flatly. And then, after several moments' thought, she added, 'Well, if you're set on it, I'd better come with you. And if I get sunstroke, it'll be your fault.'

At two o'clock, half an hour before the wedding had been due to start, Octavia Jones approached the church gates, and could scarcely believe her eyes. There, under the lychgate, stood a very odd pair. The first to catch Octavia's eye was Ellen Biggs, all but obscured by a huge, battered sunhat; next to her, ramrod straight, stood Ivy Beasley, still in the old dress and purple cardigan.

'Oh no, the poor old thing has flipped!' said Octavia aloud, and hurried on. She would have to get her back home, somehow. When she approached, Ivy gave her a very small, wintry smile, and said, 'Good afternoon, Octavia. Have you come to keep vigil with us, make sure everyone knows?' Her voice wobbled, and it was clear the effort was enormous, but Octavia could see that Ivy Beasley was as sane as ever, as stern and unrelenting, and that no amount of persuasion would change her mind.

Octavia took one look at Ellen's boiled-looking face, and reached in her handbag for a bottle of lemonade, fortified with her mother's best sloe gin, put in at the last minute for emergencies. Seems we've got one, she thought, and handed a plastic cup full of pink sparkles to Ellen, who drank it all off at one gulp.

'Very nice, my dear,' she said. 'Now Ivy.'

Ivy shook her head, but Octavia handed her the refilled cup. 'Please, Miss Beasley. I think you'll like it,' she said gently.

Ivy sipped it, and licked her lips. 'Not bad,' she said, and continued to drink.

Then it was Octavia's turn, and she looked tentatively at Ivy. 'I hope you won't take this badly, Miss Beasley,' she said, 'but I would like to propose a toast to you, for being so brave.'

Ellen waited with bated breath for Ivy's reply. Could go either way, she thought. Then Ivy brushed her cheek free of what could have been perspiration or a tear, and swallowed hard. 'Thank you,' she said, with great dignity. 'And if you don't mind my saying so, you're not doing so bad yourself, Octavia, under the circumstances.'

'Phew!' said Ellen, and it wasn't because of the heat.

When it was clear nobody was turning up in ignorance, Ellen crossed the road to her Lodge, and Octavia said she would walk back with Ivy, tactfully refusing Ivy's offer of a cup of tea.

Ivy was glad of her cool kitchen, and ran the tap for a glass of water, then she sat down and invited Tiddles on to her lap. She took up her book, but put it down again, unable to read. Stroking the little cat's soft fur, she began to weep, grieving in utter misery until she felt completely empty, drained. 'George,' she said, then put her head back on the cushion and fell into a deep sleep.

# 48

'Bliss, perfect bliss. And I don't even feel sick,' said Sarah Barnett, lounging in a deckchair on Annie Bishop's lawn.

It was shady under the great cedar tree, and Annie had given her a stool to put up her feet. 'Have to look after yourself now,' she'd said with a grin.

'Not when you're a farmer's wife,' said Sarah. 'We work extra hard until we feel the pains, you know, then like some old sheep, drop the baby and get back to the milking next day.'

'Don't be ridiculous!' said Annie, laughing.

'Well, that's how it used to be,' said Sarah.

She'd had to endure a good few old wives' tales. John had reassured her that everything would be fine from now on. 'Just what we need,' he'd said, and given her a big hug. Even his mother's icy face had melted a little, and she'd begun to talk about knitting shawls and bonnets. But it's my baby, Sarah had thought, surprising herself with warm, maternal feelings already. She needn't think she's getting her grandmotherly hands on it. And there's not much she can tell me about small children.

'I shall see you're sensible,' said Annie. 'I've got some very good books you can borrow. And my four haven't turned out so badly.'

'True,' said Sarah, though she thought otherwise. 'Anyway,' she went on, taking her feet off the stool and sitting up straight, 'enough of babies. What's new in the village? Seen anything of Simon?'

Annie ignored that. 'There's poor old Ivy Beasley,' she said, and they were both silent for a moment.

'Rotten sod,' said Sarah. 'There are some real shits about.'

After another silence, Annie said, 'But I still don't think Greg Jones is one of them, do you?'

Sarah shook her head. 'No,' she said. 'I suppose not. Trouble is, it's still his word against that Poppy's. And she's a monster. Pity I didn't have her in my school. Things might have been very different.'

Annie frowned. She'd talked it over endlessly with Andrew, who had the solicitor's practical approach, but could think of no way of helping. Annie liked to sort out problems. 'There must be something we can do,' she said, and Sarah shrugged.

'John says it'll all blow over,' she said, 'but I'm not sure Greg Jones'll survive that long. He looks terrible.' She hesitated, and her lips twitched. 'And Miss Jones and Simon meet in secret, like some hole-in-the-corner romance. Could put an end to that, you know, Annie . . .' This time she smiled openly.

'Sarah,' said Annie firmly. 'I think it's time you gave up. Especially now, with the baby and everything.' Might as well talk to myself, she thought looking at Sarah's face. She sighed, and concentrated on a positive approach to the Jones problem. 'Maybe we should get together with some of the others from the club. Hardly anybody there these days, but one of them might have seen or heard something, and not realise it's important.'

'You do it, Annie,' said Sarah, leaning back again in her chair. 'You're good at meetings.'

Gabriella sat unrelaxed in dappled sunlight under the silver birch with her eyes closed and her hands clenched on the wooden arms of her chair. She wasn't asleep. She hadn't slept properly for weeks, and even now, with the warm sun flickering over her face and the scent of late-blooming roses filling the garden, she couldn't do more than doze.

Greg was in his study, where he now spent most of the day. School had finished, and he'd had an encouraging call from his Head, wishing him well and saying he was looking forward to seeing him next term. That was, if everything had . . . well, if all was . . . Greg had thanked him gratefully, asked about one or two school matters, and returned to his papers. He was writing compulsively, over and over again, each time a clearer account, he hoped, of that awful evening. Maybe if he could get it down on paper, in a way that was irrefutably the truth, it would be enough to stop the nightmare.

'Greg?' Gabriella was calling him from the kitchen. 'Do you want a drink? Some of that sloe gin concoction Octavia makes? It's really too hot to sit in the garden.' She'd opened his study door and stood looking at him with a scared smile.

Greg had stopped talking to her, more or less. She had tried hard to keep him from retreating, but failed. Now she had no idea what he was thinking, and, isolated in her own thoughts, found herself wondering once or twice if there had been any truth in what Poppy had said. It was unthinkable, of course, and she banished the treachery immediately, but had begun to feel resentment towards him. If he wouldn't talk to her, how could she comfort him? If they didn't discuss it, how could they come up with any reasonable plan for the future?

'No, thanks,' said Greg, without looking at her.

'There's cricket on the telly,' suggested Gabriella.

'You watch it, then,' replied Greg in that now familiar flat voice.

Gabriella snapped. 'Oh, for God's sake!' she shouted at him. 'You're so bloody sorry for yourself, you can't see what it's doing to this family! Call yourself a father! We'd be better off without you, all the trouble you've brought us!' And then she burst into tears and slammed the door.

Mandy Bates was trying without much success to get one of her hens back into its run, when Annie Bishop's call came.

Robert had come down from his workshop and looked at her enquiringly. 'Annie Bishop,' she said. 'Mrs Fix-it. Wants the club to have a special meeting in the pub after tennis this week. "Exploratory", she said, "see if any of us can remember something useful about what happened that evening."'

Robert shook his head. 'It's no good,' he said, 'it's out of our hands now. Still, no harm in trying.'

He looked across the kitchen to where Joey was reading a football magazine. 'All right, then, son?' he said. Joey had worried him lately. He'd been subdued, not his usual bouncy self at all. Even his grandad hadn't been able to cheer him up. Mandy said it was since that bust-up with Poppy, and Robert agreed, though he'd seen it coming for some time. Poppy was a Standing, the squire's daughter. Feudal days were over, some thought, but there was still a gap between her and Joey Bates, motor mechanic's son, that would widen as the years went by.

'I'm okay, thanks, Dad,' said Joey. 'Bit bored, though.'

Robert felt the usual guilt smite him. 'Sorry, old son,' he said. 'I've been so busy lately with cars for folk going on holiday. What d'you fancy doing?'

'I wouldn't mind fishing, p'raps over at Flasher's Pool?' Joey could manage a rod and line well, and was never bored, down by the water. 'If you could just get me down there,' he said, his eyes brightening, 'I'll be okay. Mum can pack me a sandwich and a drink. Tomorrow, p'raps?'

★

It was cooler first thing, more seasonal, and better weather for fishing, with a hazy cloud over the sun. Robert drove Joey and his tackle down to the edge of Flasher's Pool, gave him the mobile phone in case of emergency, and left him. Poor old lad, he thought angrily, as he drove back to his workshop, none of the village kids can be bothered with him. It was a fact, he told himself, that you never got used to it, to Joey being handicapped and that. Still, if Joey could get used to it, so should he.

Settled on a firm, flat stretch of grass, Joey got on with the absorbing business of fishing. His grandad had taken him first, when he was only a small chap. He'd learnt it all from Grandad, and had never grown tired of the stories of village boys who'd caught enormous fish with a stick and a bent pin. He didn't believe old Ted, of course, but that didn't matter.

The sun was out now, and Joey began to feel uncomfortable. He reached round for the big umbrella that also acted as a sunshade, and saw something moving through the willows. It was a girl, and when she got closer, he saw that it was Poppy.

'Hello,' she said.

'Hi,' said Joey. 'You okay?'

'Yes and no,' said Poppy, and flopped down on the grass beside him, leaning against the wheel of his chair, just as she always had.

# 49

The sun rose higher in the sky, and Poppy crept under the shade of Joey's umbrella. They were both quiet, watching the line stretched out over the pool. Several times the float had bobbed up and down, but when Joey had reeled it in, nothing was there.

'D'you want a drink?' said Joey. 'Thirsty work, fishing.'

Poppy reached into Joey's haversack and brought out a couple of cans. 'Here,' she said, 'your mum's given you enough food for an army, as usual.' They'd had many picnics together, over the years.

'I've missed you,' Joey said, after a few minutes.

'Missed you too,' said Poppy, sounding choked. 'I'm sorry, Joe . . . about, well, you know . . .'

Joey nodded. 'Shouldn't have asked you,' he said. 'None of my business, really.'

'Seems it's everybody's business,' said Poppy, fiddling with her shoelaces.

'Sshh!' said Joey. 'Whisper! The fish . . .' The sun beat down on them, and they finished the Coke. 'Sandwich?' said Joey. Between them, they ate up the food and put the rubbish back tidily in the haversack.

'It's good down here,' said Joey. 'You can think your thoughts without people butting in all the time.'

'I'm sick of thinking,' said Poppy. 'Hey!' she added. 'Look! You've got something!'

Joey reeled in the small fish expertly, showed Poppy the subtle colours on its wet scales, and then threw it back.

'Joey?' said Poppy, when he'd baited the hook again and cast it into a shady part of the pool.

'Yep?' said Joey. He was feeling happy now, with the two of them back together, easy, in the old way.

'Have you ever told a lie, a really big one?' Poppy studied the grass seed head in her fingers, pulling off the little spears, one by one.

'Can't remember,' said Joey. 'I expect I did. Not lately, though. Why?' Poppy didn't answer, and Joey looked at her, concentrating, now that he felt something tricky in the air. 'Why did you say that?' he repeated, though a shiver went through him as he realised what she was about to say.

'He didn't do anything, you know,' said Poppy, in a very small voice. She turned to look at Joey, and his heart sank.

'Poppy,' he said. 'How could you? Why . . . ?'

She shook her head, close to tears. 'Don't know,' she said. 'I was just angry. Don't know why. Joey, what shall I do?'

'God, I don't know!' he answered. 'Well, yes, I do know,' he added. 'And so do you, else you wouldn't've told me.'

'Own up,' said Poppy, her voice flat and quiet.

'What else?' said Joey. 'It's not goin' away, is it? Getting worse, for poor old Mr Jones. An' Octavia and her mum. They're talking of leaving the village.'

'Simon'll kill me,' said Poppy. 'So will Dad, and Mum.'

Joey looked at her pale face and knew that he, anyway, would forgive her anything. He stroked the top of her fair head. 'Don't be daft,' he said. 'You can only die once.'

By unspoken agreement, the few tennis players finished early, and began to pack up their things. Simon didn't blame them. There was no fun in it without Octavia, but he could see it would be impossible for her to come. He hadn't seen her for a couple of weeks now. The break had been her idea, and he'd disagreed violently, but she'd insisted that their arguments and silences were destroying all that was good between them. I'll know you're not far away, she'd said. Send me messages through the ether. I'll get them. She had been serious.

Now he looked at the faces of the others, and saw something was afoot. Annie hadn't told him about the meeting, thinking his position too difficult. She privately thought he was being a bit of a wimp about the whole thing. His father would have shaken the truth out of young Poppy weeks ago, if it had been left to him. Surely Simon could have done something, if only for Octavia's sake? She hadn't seen them together lately, and wondered if all was still going well. God knows, if Octavia went ahead with it now, with the full weight of the Standings against her, and wily Sarah still determined to make mischief, it would be a truly remarkable act of love . . . or sacrifice, depending on how you looked at it.

Then Robert, dear Robert, blundered in. 'Got this meeting at the pub,' he said. 'We're all a bit sorry for old Greg, and are goin' to do a bit of what Andrew calls "brain-storming". See if we can remember anything more. Still, don't suppose you'd want to come, being Poppy's brother, and that . . .' he tailed off lamely.

'Come on, Robert,' said Mandy fiercely, 'before you dig yourself in any deeper.'

But Simon said, 'No, hang on. Perhaps I should come, if this is to be some kind of kangaroo court. I don't suppose you've invited Poppy, have you?' His tone was angry, and his face flushed. 'Maybe I should come, to represent the other side. I'll see you down there,' and he strode off.

'Well done, Robert,' said Andrew Bishop, with a

deep sigh. 'Suppose we'd better get going, though I don't see much point in it now.'

His wife was more optimistic. 'Don't be silly, Andrew,' she said, 'it might be just the thing we need to kindle a spark of truth somewhere. Don't be upset, Robert,' she said, kindly.

In the sitting-room of Barnstones, Gabriella Jones sat in the dusk, not thinking of anything much, just sitting. She hadn't put on any lights, or the television. Octavia was upstairs in her room, and Greg in his study as usual. She could hear the tap-tap of his computer, as he rehearsed that sequence of events once more. He's going mad, she thought, and wondered idly what it took to certify somebody.

She couldn't remember feeling so lonely. All her life she'd had loving companionship, from sisters, parents, then Greg and Octavia. Now Greg never addressed her directly, and Octavia spoke in monosyllables. Tavie never went out, and as far as Gabriella knew, spoke only briefly on the telephone to Simon. She'd buried herself in work, bringing it home and reading reports in her room for hours.

The telephone rang, and Gabriella got up wearily to answer it. 'Hello? Who is it? Can you speak up, I can't hear you very well. *Guy?* Oh, goodness! And how are *you?* Hold on a minute, I'll call her.' It was Guy de Rivaulx, all but forgotten by Round Ringford in the village upheaval.

Octavia thought of asking her mother to say she was out, then she thought how wonderful to talk to someone outside the compound, and came down. As she talked to him, coolly at first, and then laughing a little, in the old way, the chilly sitting-room seemed to warm up. Tactfully, Gabriella went out to the kitchen to make coffee.

'Guess what, Mum?' said Octavia, the call finished.

'Guy's coming over again. Arriving tomorrow, and staying for a couple of weeks. He wants to see Scotland, he says. Asked if I'd go with him.'

'And?' said Gabriella. She felt confused, not knowing what to think. 'Are you going?'

'Don't know,' said Octavia, 'I'll have to think about it.' Suddenly the village seemed to have shrunk to its proper size. Paris was still out there. And Scotland.

'I think it'd be a very good thing,' said Greg, coming into the room. 'You could forget about bloody Ringford and the charming Standings for a bit.'

Gabriella stared at him. Well, that was progress. Guy de Rivaulx back in favour. Any suitor is better than a Standing suitor. She felt like crying again.

Octavia began to see the escape route as increasingly attractive. She missed Simon desperately, but couldn't bear the inevitable drifting apart. She could see it happening and was powerless to do anything about it. At heart, she had finally realised, Simon did not agree with her. Just as Greg, with all his faults, was her father, that little monster was Simon's sister, his flesh and blood. Funny how basic we all are, in the end, she'd thought. It explains those poor little kids who cling on to murderous parents in spite of everything.

She wasn't sure of anything now, and any kind of future with Simon was just about equal to scaling Everest. The last time she'd seen him had been outside the shop, where they'd said a brief hello. The pain in Simon's eyes had stayed with her for days.

'You should go with Guy, Octavia,' Greg said now, and something of the old authority was back in his voice. 'Ring him back. You can get time off. Your boss said so, you know he did. Go on, do it now.'

This was the longest speech Greg had made for some time, and Gabriella felt a glimmer of hope. Maybe there'd be some solution, somehow. She decided to agree with Greg, and nodded.

Octavia hesitated. It would hurt Simon dreadfully, she knew, but maybe he would understand. She hoped he would understand, and suddenly thought of Sarah Barnett, and all those possible others Simon might not be able to resist, when understanding could be required of *her*. She dialled the number.

'Guy? Made up my mind . . . yes, didn't take long! It's a great idea, and I'd love to come.' The minute she'd said it, she knew that bringing in Sarah Barnett and those possible others was an excuse, and wished she'd given it more thought.

Gabriella cheered up, thinking that at least Octavia would have a nice holiday. She suggested to Octavia that they should have a walk up the Bagley Road, back through the playing fields and home along the High Street. 'Tavie?' she said again. 'Are you listening to me?'

Greg was left alone. He sat in the half-dark, brooding. Things were moving forward, his solicitor had said. Some kind of resolution soon, but whatever the outcome, it was extremely unlikely that he'd get a job working with kids again. And they'd probably have to move, what with half the village against him. He groaned, and closed his eyes.

He must have drifted off, because he didn't hear the doorbell the first time. The second ring was longer, and he jumped out of his chair, going through quickly to the door. Gabbie had forgotten her key, most likely. He opened the door, and stood rooted to the spot, speechless. It was Poppy Standing, and behind her, Joey Bates in his wheelchair.

The meeting in the pub had been a failure. Nobody had remembered anything new, and the conversation, with Simon glowering at them, was stilted. In the end, Annie Bishop stood up, said she had to get back to the children. Simon, deeply miserable, was on his fourth pint when

Octavia and Gabriella walked in. They'd tossed a coin in the end, to see whether they should have a drink or just go on home.

'Why shouldn't we go to the pub?' Gabriella had said defensively. 'Done nothing wrong. Come on, Tavie.' It was too late for Octavia to retreat when she saw Simon and all the others staring at her.

'Well, hello!' said Simon in a blurred voice. 'May I buy you a drink? Or would you rather I didn't?' he added challengingly.

Robert Bates went over quickly and took him by the arm. 'Simon, old chap,' he said, 'maybe we should walk back now. Nice out there, in the twilight.'

Simon looked at him, seemed about to say something, but then nodded meekly. 'Right-o,' he said. 'Night, Octavia . . . Tavie . . . Night, Mrs Jones.' Seeing tears in Octavia's eyes, he began to put out his hand to her, but then withdrew it and with dignity walked out of the bar.

'Now,' said Andrew Bishop, standing up. 'What are you two having?'

Octavia said little, but the others managed to find enough things to talk about, other than that awful thing, until it was nearly closing time.

'Light's still on,' said Octavia dully, as they walked up the garden path. 'Dad must be up.'

They walked through to the sitting-room, and stopped dead. Greg Jones had made a plate of sandwiches, a large pot of coffee, and was sitting reading a magazine, waiting for them.

'Greg?' said Gabriella anxiously. 'You all right?'

'Perfectly,' said Greg. 'Thought you might be hungry after such a long walk.'

'We went to the pub,' said Octavia apologetically. 'Didn't think you'd mind. Some of the others were there.'

'Good idea,' said Greg firmly.

He was changed, completely changed, and Gabriella felt a shiver of fear. 'What's up, Greg?' she said, and so he told them.

'It was pathetic, really,' he said. 'They seemed so young. And Poppy held Joey's hand the whole time. When she couldn't carry on for crying, he helped her out. Encouraged her. It was the most awful thing . . .' And then he broke down, and they were all crying, clinging to each other. It was some while before Greg was able to get to the end of his story.

# 50

It felt like the first day of the world to Octavia, stepping out into the garden next morning, the beginning of something completely new and fresh.

She reached the gate, now in sunlight, and lifted up her head, feeling the warm sun on her face. She had arrangements to make, ready for her holiday. For a moment, a cloud crossed the sun. She dare not think about Simon and how he would feel, not wanting to allow anything to spoil today's euphoria. Scotland, with mountains and heather, and tumbling peaty streams. How lovely! She was, though, a little dismayed to find she couldn't quite bring Guy's face into focus.

Mum and Dad had not appeared for breakfast, and Octavia hadn't disturbed them. Reprieve, she thought. No, not reprieve, vindication, and only just in time for them. It was a good thing she was going away, to leave them to each other, to settle back into their marriage. More excuses? she asked herself.

She got into her car and caught sight of Ivy Beasley, shaking a mat out of her front door. Oh lor, there's poor old Ivy, still bravely doing her housework. And here's me, thinking all's well with the world. It isn't, of course. Not just for Simon and me, but for Dad and Mum, too. There's a lot to go through yet. At least Martha would be able to smooth the path a bit at the office. Dear Martha. Octavia drove off, waving to Ivy as she passed, and felt shocked at the change in her face, the pale unhappiness.

★

It continued to be very hard for Ivy Beasley to face the village, sympathetic as most people were. In fact, the sympathy was the hardest thing to bear. If only, she said to herself, putting down the mat in the hall, if only they'd just forget it, carry on as if George had never arrived in Ringford. Still, too much to hope for. She saw with great clarity that if it had happened to someone else, the topic would have kept the tea parties going for weeks. No, she'd have to put up with it, see it out, though how she was going to manage . . .

As she returned to the kitchen and set about peeling a couple of potatoes for her solitary lunch, her mother's voice was back in her sadly confused head. Beasley's don't give in, Ivy Dorothy, it said. You're doing well, girl. The worst is over. That was all. No recriminations, no being wise after the event. Just those few words of encouragement, such as Ivy never received in her mother's lifetime, and she was grateful.

She rinsed out a couple of pairs of green knickers and an old bra, and went out into the sunny garden. It was very quiet, and she wandered down to the end of the path, to the fence where George had liked to lean. She remembered cleaning windows and seeing him, talking to John Barnett. She'd been sad that he was going off to live in his newly finished cottage. Had it all been a pretence? she wondered. Were they all lies, those things George had said? Had he ever even considered buying Bridge Cottage? The hurt was returning, and she shook herself. 'I know, Mother,' she said aloud, 'get on with some work and forget it.'

'Miss Beasley?' It was Simon Standing, walking up the path towards her, smiling enquiringly.

'Just talking to meself, Mr Simon,' she said. 'Bad habit, I always tell Ellen Biggs, and now I'm doing it.'

'How are you feeling?' he said.

'Not bad, under the circumstances,' said Ivy, managing a smile.

'Um, I wonder if I could talk to you for a few minutes?' said Simon. 'I do need your help on a couple of things.'

Ivy led the way back up the path. 'Please come in,' she said, and ushered him into her chilly, polished front room. 'If you'll excuse me,' she said, 'I'll just put the potatoes on.'

Simon had woken with a sore head and done some hard thinking. He'd drifted along lately, unable to decide where his loyalties lay. Desperately wanting to hold on to Octavia, he still couldn't ignore the fact that Poppy was his sister, and a child, in years, anyway. Tavie must think I'm pretty useless, he'd thought, torturing himself.

He was torn in half, but could not turn against Poppy, whether she was innocent or inconceivably wicked. A bleak expression he'd seen when Poppy thought she was alone tugged at his heart. He remembered his parents' joy when she was born. She had been an enchanting baby, and blossomed under the attention lavished on her. But somewhere it had gone cold. They were probably just too old, too impatient. And Mum had always got bored in the end, whatever the new enthusiasm. Awful for a child to realise she was just a new enthusiasm.

Simon sighed. He had stupidly hoped for some magic answer to this latest, and much the most serious, crisis in their lives. Not very grown up, he told himself, and groaned when he pictured Octavia's disillusioned face.

The tennis club was nearly on the rocks. He sensed it, had seen it coming last night in the pub. And now George had done a runner, and there was nobody to do the books. Better wind the whole thing up, he'd decided at breakfast, and gone over to the house. Mum and Poppy had been nowhere around and Dad looked like thunder. He hadn't asked him for a reason, but kept out of his way. Perhaps he should never have come back to Ringford . . .

He shook himself. Self-pity was the last thing needed at the moment, and here was Ivy, brave old Ivy, bustling back and asking him to sit down, offering refreshment.

'I hope you won't think it insensitive, Miss Beasley,' he said, putting his hand on her bony shoulder, 'but, well, you know George was treasurer of the club, and now I need the account books, cheque book, you know . . .' He looked at her stricken face and cursed himself. Still, it had to be done. There'd been a tidy sum in the bank account, and he'd need to refund subscriptions, that kind of thing.

It occurred to him, as Ivy went to a box in the corner of the room and starting sifting through papers, that she was probably still clinging to shreds of affection; maybe she too had a forlorn hope that there'd be some miraculous explanation. Maybe George would turn out to be not such a bad chap. Perhaps exonerating circumstances might soften the blow, make it easier to bear.

'Here we are, Mr Simon,' she said. 'George was very meticulous in his book-keeping. His profession, you know.'

Simon took the bank statements, the cheque book and the paying-in book. 'Thank you,' he said. 'He certainly did a good job while he was here.'

Ivy nodded, and for a second her face crumpled. Then she squared her shoulders and said would Simon like some elderflower wine? It was in the cellar, so cool and refreshing.

He accepted, and while she was out of the room, he leafed through the bank statements. His attention was suddenly galvanised by the very last total. Four pounds and twenty-seven pence! What was this? Oh, my God, the bugger had emptied the account before he left. And then Simon saw the whole thing, the whole crooked, scheming, cruel campaign.

'Ivy, er, Miss Beasley!' he shouted, and walked through to the kitchen, where Ivy looked round at him, alarmed at his vehemence. 'Did that charlatan take money from you?' he said bluntly.

His air was so authoritative that Ivy, determined to keep her secret, but with generations of respectful Beasleys behind her, hesitated, then she sat down heavily on a kitchen chair. 'I'm afraid he did, Mr Simon,' she said. 'He took nearly all my savings, and I was fool enough to trust him.'

'All of it?' said Simon.

'Most of it,' answered Ivy, and somehow it was a relief to tell him. 'Said he was just borrowing it, and would pay back very soon. Soon as he'd sold his Leamington house.'

'Right!' said Simon, sitting down opposite her. 'Now, this is what we do. First, the police.'

'Oh, no, Mr Simon,' Ivy said, sitting up straighter. 'Beasleys have never had any truck with the police, and I couldn't. No, no. It was my own foolishness, and I shall have to suffer for it.'

'Rubbish!' said Simon, but he could not persuade her.

She told him that George had gone with her into the bank, helped with the withdrawal and the explanations to the bank manager. 'Very good, he was, Mr Simon, with the manager. Explaining, and that.'

Simon said grimly that he was not surprised, and asked once more if she wouldn't go to the police. He would help her, see her through it, but she was adamant.

Without her permission, he knew he could do nothing official. Well, then it would have to be some other way. He left her with assurances that it would all be sorted out, and returned to the Hall, finding none of his family about. Still, it was Bill Turner he wanted, and knowing that he was down in the spinney with Foxy Jenkins, he set off to find them.

★

273

The storm broke in the quiet, dignified drawing-room of the Hall just before lunch. Richard Standing had contained himself for as long as he could, and then he yelled for Susan and Poppy and said they were to come down at once.

Poppy had been late home last night, and he'd left her to her mother, relieved that she'd finally turned up and vowing that she would never go down to those Bateses again. Then Susan had come to bed much later, and had woken him up with the ghastly news.

'For God's sake!' he'd said. 'Why did she have to go to that Jones man all by herself?'

She wasn't by herself, Susan had explained wearily. Joey Bates had been with her.

'Bloody Bates!' Richard had exploded. 'I could've smoothed Jones down, made it all right,' he'd added, but Susan shook her head.

'It was the right thing,' she said, sitting on her dressing-table stool and staring at herself in the mirror. 'Poppy had to do it herself. She said so.' She turned to look at him, and he saw that she had shut down, defying any further intrusion. 'We'd better get some sleep now, if possible,' she'd said. 'Nothing to be done until tomorrow.'

Now Susan and Poppy sat facing him, and he had no idea how to begin. Being Chairman of the Magistrates Bench was a doddle compared with this. Women. He sighed. 'All right, Poppy,' he said. 'Why did you do it?'

'Because,' said Poppy.

'Poppy, darling,' cautioned her mother.

'Have you the remotest idea of the trouble you've caused?' Richard felt his anger rising. 'Not to mention the harm you've done to our family reputation in the village.'

'Sod the family reputation,' said Poppy.

'Poppy!' said Susan, dismayed. Poppy had been so

malleable last night, but now she was different. It was like watching two cockerels squaring up to each other.

'Very well,' said Richard, his face set. 'I have given this matter a lot of thought since last night, and come to a decision. Your present attitude, Poppy, only confirms it.'

'Ten lashes at dawn?' said Poppy, raising one eyebrow.

Richard controlled himself with difficulty. 'Boarding school,' he said. 'You'll start immediately. Susan, you can see to it. I have nothing more to say to you, Poppy, except that you will tell Simon everything. At once. Now get out.'

Bill Turner and Simon walked through Bagley Woods, cool and shady as always, and talked. 'Ivy's a funny old gal,' said Bill. 'If she said no to the police, you won't shift her. But you're right, boy, we've got to do something. Rotten bugger shan't get away with it, not if I know anything.' Then he remembered Peggy's cousin, the letter that had arrived and been forgotten in the teeth of Ivy's crisis.

'Here,' Bill said, 'wait a minute. Just thought of something.' He explained to Simon that they'd had a half-hearted go at finding some clues to mystery George a while back. 'Leave it to me,' he said, 'we'll have another go.' He glanced sideways at Simon, and added, 'Everything all right? You know, with you and Tavie Jones?'

Simon shook his head. 'Not really, Bill,' he said, 'but then, you can't blame her, can you?'

When Simon got back to the Hall, he saw his mother in the yard, waiting for him. 'Ah, there you are,' she said, and he saw Poppy standing by the stable, stroking Adolf's nose, her hunched shoulders full of tension. 'Right, Simon,' Susan continued, and he noticed her clenched hands, 'Poppy has something to tell you. I suggest you walk up to the orchard. It's private there. I'll give you a call when lunch is ready.'

My God, she's making an effort! thought Simon. What on earth's going on? Half an hour later, sitting silently under an apple tree with his defiant sister, he found out.

# 51

'I don't know why I'm feeling nervous,' said Gabriella, opening a packet of biscuits and arranging them on a plate. It was a lovely day, and out of the kitchen window she looked beyond the sunlit garden, past the spreading oaks in the park and the grazing sheep, and on to where the tall chimneys of the Hall stood high above the trees.

'Don't suppose the squire's feeling so good, either,' said Greg, but try as he would to be charitable, he could not feel sorry for Richard Standing. He'd agreed to this meeting reluctantly and against his solicitor's advice, although his instinct told him it was right: parents were responsible for their children, and Poppy was still a child. Maybe he could help. He'd seen another side of Poppy, the one who'd clung to Joey Bates for strength. I hope to Christ they see she goes the right way, he thought. There's a good person in the making there, with the right handling.

'Well, I hope he's not late,' said Gabriella. 'Sooner it's over and done with the better. The child came and owned up, after all.'

'Bit more than that,' said Greg.

'Well, yes,' said Gabriella, 'so what else is there to say?'

Greg didn't reply, but he knew there could be a great deal more, with slander actions, and public court proceedings that could drag on for months. It would be up to him, and he had made his decision already.

★

The knock at the door took Gabriella by surprise. 'I didn't hear the car,' she said to Greg.

'He's walked,' he said, 'for once.'

Richard Standing looked much bigger, somehow, in their sitting-room, thought Greg. He was a tall man, but striding about the estate he looked nothing out of the ordinary. Perhaps people grow to their environment, like fish, Greg thought.

'Please sit down,' said Gabriella, and her voice cracked. For God's sake, she reminded herself, we're the injured parties!

Richard took the coffee, refused a biscuit, and cleared his throat. 'I'll come straight to the point, Jones,' he said. 'I am extremely sorry about the whole business, and apologise with my whole heart.' He realised with a start that he meant it. 'Poppy has always been a difficult child,' he continued, 'but I never thought it would come to this.' Greg saw pain in his face, and against all his expectations, felt sorry for him.

'Nor I, Mr Standing,' said Greg, and Gabriella drew closer to him, took his hand.

'I realise that you'd be perfectly within your rights to get what you can out of it,' said Richard, 'and I wouldn't blame you for one minute.' He looked at Greg, and what he saw filled him with admiration. A very dignified little bugger, he said to himself.

'But there is the other thing,' he continued. 'I'm not sure what you and Mrs Jones think about Simon and Octavia. It is, I admit, very difficult to know what to think about anything at the moment, but when the air has cleared, I just want you both to remember that I think she is a very fine girl. Very fine indeed. And, of course, I think the same of my son. He's not perfect, of course . . .' He hesitated, and they all had a quick mental re-run of Sarah Barnett dancing cheek to cheek with Simon, of John's revenge, and most clearly of all, of

Sarah's fruitful figure. 'Um,' Richard continued, 'that's all, actually, I wanted to say.'

He drank his coffee and waited. God, this was hell. All that disastrous mess for nothing. He blamed Susan as much as Poppy, but he could hardly bear to think about either of them. Of course, it was he who now had to sort it out. Then he remembered that Poppy had taken the first step, by herself. Or nearly by herself. He looked at Greg's pale face, and reflected that their fate lay in this small, quiet man's hands.

Greg took a deep breath. 'We shall not be taking the matter any further,' he said. 'Enough damage has been done already, and I've never been one for revenge. But I think I have the right to say one or two things.'

Richard Standing nodded humbly.

'Firstly, there's Poppy. She is a child, and children behave the way they do for very good reasons. She may have no idea why she did that dreadful thing. But it will be for you and Mrs Standing to work out the real reason, and, having thought about it, put it right. The only person Poppy trusts is Joey Bates. Just remember that, Mr Standing.'

Richard seemed about to say something, but subsided again.

'As for Octavia and Simon,' Greg said, 'that's more difficult for me. And Gabriella. We are too closely involved, and naturally want the best for our only daughter, but they are adults, and they'll decide what happens next. Nothing we can, or should, say will make much difference, don't you agree, Gabbie?'

Gabriella reached for his hand. 'Absolutely right,' she said. 'Though I do want to say, on my own account, that I think Simon is a very nice young man. In spite of . . .' She tailed off in embarrassment.

Richard looked up, and his face cleared. 'Thank you, Mrs Jones,' he said. 'That means a lot to me just now. Well,' he added, getting to his feet, 'I don't need to say that if there's anything I can do, Mr Jones, anything at all, then please let me know.' He was about to say that he had plenty of influence in the county, and stopped himself just in time.

# 52

Nobody was quite sure when or how Poppy's confession got round the village. Sandra had said nothing, although she had been one of the first to know. It probably started with Joey, who, for all his calm support of Poppy, had been very upset by her disgrace, and had in the end told his father the whole thing. Robert had been shocked, but tried not to show it. He could see that Joey was Poppy's only ally, a very lonely position to be in.

Robert had been so worried and confused, that when he called in for a pint at the Arms and found Bill standing there, friendly and dependable, he'd told him the bare bones of it. Bill had said a few forthright things about Poppy Standing, and then gone home to Peggy, who had listened in stunned silence.

Next morning, Doreen Price had brought the eggs to the shop as usual, and found Peggy alone. 'Morning,' she'd said, carefully putting down her fragile load. 'You all right? You look a bit middlin'.'

'No wonder,' Peggy had muttered, and then it had all spilled out, in spite of her good intentions to keep her mouth shut.

Doreen looked at her and shrugged. 'Well,' she'd said, 'we all knew it, didn't we? But what a waste. Them poor Joneses.'

Then Jean Jenkins had caught the tail end, popping in quickly for more pegs, and said that judging by the atmosphere up at the Hall yesterday, they'd be getting the vet in to put poor Poppy down.

Now a small knot of women, some still saying there was never smoke without fire, were blocking the doorway of the shop when Bill came back from the Hall. 'Excuse me, ladies,' he said good-humouredly.

Mrs Ross, a small, birdlike woman who could put in the boot as well as the rest, smiled slyly at him. 'Trouble up at t'Hall, Bill?' she said. 'Still, you never know with these things, do you?' she added, when he didn't answer. 'Never did like that Greg Jones, myself, and you're not telling me that child made it all up. Where'd she get such an idea from, tell me that?'

Bill glared at her, and was just about to answer, when Ivy Beasley cleared her throat. 'If you ask me,' she said, in her best put-down voice, 'people who know nothing about anything should keep quiet. And if the cap fits, wear it, Mrs Ross.' She banged down a block of frozen cod, paid for it, and left the shopful staring after her ramrod back.

After that, everybody drifted out, and Peggy was left alone with Bill. 'Well!' she said. 'Ivy back on form with a vengeance! Mind you, she doesn't look well. And I've never known her buy frozen food before. Very superior, she is usually, about convenience rubbish, as she calls it.'

'Poor old Ivy,' Bill said. 'Let's hope we hear from cousin Sal soon.'

Peggy said she still thought it a pretty long shot. 'I reckon we shall have to persuade Ivy to go to the police. It'd be so easy for them,' she said. 'I sometimes wonder,' she added, 'whether Ivy doesn't really want him caught. She's a funny old thing, you know. And she loved him, Bill, no doubt about that.'

'Women,' said Bill, and went upstairs.

When he came down again, Peggy was in a reverie, gazing out of the window. 'Miles away?' said Bill.

Peggy sighed. 'Yes, well . . . one thing leads to another.' She shook herself, and said, 'It's good news about the Joneses, but I do wish we could do something for old Ivy, don't you? If only I could remember something else that would help Sal.'

Bill said that George Chalmer was a slippery sod, and it was going to take all their efforts to find him, but by God, they would. And Mr Simon was just as determined. 'It'll take his mind off family troubles,' he said practically. 'I've told him to ask around in his uncle's office in Leamington. Never know when something might turn up.'

Days later, there was little improvement in the atmosphere at the Hall. Simon Standing was having a miserable time. He kept out of his mother's way, and Poppy was keeping out of his. Leaving early, coming home late, Simon threw himself into his work. Every time he passed Barnstones in his car, he stared straight ahead. Jean Jenkins had let slip in conversation that Tavie was off to Scotland with that French phoney. Simon had argued with himself, considered riding in and challenging Guy de Whatsisname to a duel, but in the end he'd decided to leave it. He had no claims on Octavia. Certainly not now. And if she wanted no more of him . . .

He decided on a walk with his pup, and now stood beside the deep pond, hidden from the world by his father's rolling acres, so absorbed in aching thoughts of Octavia that he didn't hear Richard squelching up through the wet grass behind him.

His father wasted no time on preliminaries. 'So you're going to do nothing, Simon. Just let her go? See her throw herself away on some French lightweight?'

'Dad!' said Simon, astonished at this frontal attack. 'Really, it's none of your—'

'Maybe not,' said Richard, 'but I've got eyes in my head. Can't avoid you, moping about the place, wallowing in self-pity. For God's sake, man, you're a Standing!'

283

Simon had a strong desire to laugh. This conversation was bizarre, had nothing to do with the twentieth century. Dad had no idea, no understanding of how women felt these days. 'Nice of you to worry, Dad,' he said, 'but it's not self-pity, though it might look like that. I do love Octavia, with all my heart, but I can't just bulldoze in and order her to stay away from other blokes. She doesn't belong to me.'

'Huh!' said Richard. He felt at a loss. He knew what he'd do in Simon's place. A firm hand and a bit of flattery worked wonders, never failed. He sighed. 'Well,' he said, 'you know best, old chap. Come on, now, let's go and get a drink. But anything I can do to help . . .'

Two agonising weeks while she's in Scotland, thought Simon, and nobody can help. Work is the answer, and finding that bugger George. That'll see me through. In spite of everything, he had not forgotten Ivy Beasley. He had asked around, but nobody in the Leamington office had heard of George Chalmer. Simon saw straight away that it was very unlikely they would know of a smalltime crook, whose name wasn't Chalmer anyway. A blue Fiesta was all he could describe, and a small, neat, unremarkable man, given to wearing natty trilbys and Panama hats, a man possessing a persuasive way with elderly women: pitifully little to go on.

Driving round the white crescents and streets of Leamington, Simon had kept his eyes open, and once saw a blue Fiesta, driven by a man whose back was familiar. That's him! he'd thought, but the lights had changed on a crossing, trapping him behind a learner driver. He'd watched helplessly as the Fiesta disappeared round a corner ahead.

Now Richard and Simon found the stableyard deserted, and nobody in the kitchen. It was getting late, and he could see a light in Poppy's room, poor little swine. He couldn't face the tension in the house, and said he wouldn't have a drink, thanks. In the Ostler's

House he prepared for a lonely, dismal evening, finishing off the bombshell balance sheet he had to present to the tennis club. Disaster all round, he thought, remembering sadly the fun they'd all had in the beginning.

A light tap at his door brought Poppy, chewing her nails. 'Can I come in?' she said, and he nodded.

'D'you want some lemonade? Jean Jenkins gave me a couple of bottles. Reckon she's got a production line going in Macmillan Gardens.' Not a ghost of a smile. 'Oh, come on, Poppy,' he said. 'It's not the end of the world. God, you're only thirteen. Whole life ahead of you.'

She looked at him, and said in a small voice, 'Sorry Si, I'm really sorry. I don't know what to do, how to put it right. Dad and Mum are so angry with me. And, by the way, I'm fourteen now.' He sat beside her and put his arm round her thin shoulders, but could think of nothing to say. 'Still struck on Goody Two— on Tavie Jones, I suppose,' she said, 'and I've messed it up.'

He squeezed her hand. 'Yep,' he said. ''Fraid I am. Still, things'll work out, one way or another.' He didn't sound very hopeful, and they sat in silence. Poppy began to look through a magazine, turning the pages too quickly to be reading.

Simon wrenched his thoughts away from Octavia and Guy joyfully bounding hand in hand through the heather, and concentrated hard on how he would announce the ex-treasurer's fiddle to the club members. Poor old Ivy, still struggling on. Suddenly he stared at Poppy. 'Listen,' he said. 'Do *you* remember anything special about that George Chalmer, anything he said about Leamington, about his car, anything at all?'

Poppy bit her lip again, and considered. 'His scruffy car . . . L279, um, er . . . MNH?' she said. 'Any use? We could check with Joey.'

'What!' yelled Simon, jumping up in excitement. Nobody had ever thought to ask the kids.

'That was it, I think,' she said. 'I'm good at remembering numbers. Telephone numbers, too, but Joey's better . . .'

The rest of her sentence was lost, as Simon hugged her. 'Come on,' he said, 'we're going to see Bill. Now, at once. And do stop biting your nails!'

# 53

It had been a long train journey back to Tresham, but worth it for the time spent in Scotland. Nothing like getting right away, Octavia thought. Much easier to look at things clearly.

Scotland had been beautiful, wild and foreign. The tiny cottage, way up in Sutherland and miles from anywhere, was different from anything Octavia had known. Originally a keeper's house, it had been converted for holiday letting, comfortable and nicely furnished by the laird and his wife, distant relations of Martha, who'd obligingly fixed it up.

Two weeks had gone quickly, and as the little white house had receded into the distance, the winding road across the moor vanishing finally from sight, Octavia had felt sad, as if she'd lived there for years. She could see now why people sold up everything and went off to such places for the rest of their lives. The silence and remoteness were seductive. No telephone, no fax, only the sheep wandering by.

But then, it wouldn't do, would it? She had all her life to attend to. This holiday had given her plenty of time to think it out, and she knew just where to begin. The train drew into Tresham station, and Octavia climbed out. She looked along the length of the platform, and saw Greg waving at her, grinning broadly. Good old Dad, looked a new man. She kissed him warmly, and handed over her cases.

'Had a good time?' he said. 'We got the postcard – looked a wonderful spot.'

'It was,' said Octavia, 'but it's good to be back. How's Mum?'

'Fine,' said Greg. 'She's got something to tell you.' Blimey, thought Octavia, as if we haven't had enough surprises lately.

Gabriella greeted her as if she'd been away for months, and said she wanted to know everything, all the details. 'Well,' she corrected herself, 'you know, as much as you want to tell us . . .'

'Mum,' said Octavia. 'I want your news first. Dad said.'

'Oh, that!' said Gabriella modestly. 'Well, they've asked me to be temporary acting Head in the village school while Sarah has her baby.'

'Great!' said Octavia. 'You'll do it standing on your head. They won't want Sarah back, that's for sure.'

Gabriella smiled, and said time to tell about the holiday. 'Was it really as remote as it looked?' she said.

Octavia nodded. 'It was wonderful,' she said. 'And you and Dad were quite right to make me go. It worked out well, probably better on my own. Shame about Guy, but his grandmother couldn't help dying. Poor chap never left London. Turned tail and went straight back to Paris. Let me off the hook, really,' she added, looking tentatively at Gabriella.

Her mother nodded, and gave her a quick kiss on the cheek. 'All for the best, my love,' she said.

In the Hall dining-room, under the paintings of Scottish moors and nesting grouse all innocent of their fate, Richard and Susan Standing were having an argument. This was so commonplace these days that Poppy had vanished up to her room, turned up her radio and begun to write her diary for the day.

'So what do you expect me to do?' said Susan, in her ice-cold voice. 'Crawl penitently down the avenue and humble myself before the whole village? Ask them to put Poppy and me in the stocks, so they can pelt us with—'

'Be quiet, Susan!' said Richard angrily. 'That kind of thing doesn't help at all. We have to think how to set things straight. And first you have to admit some guilt. God knows I tried hard enough to stop you getting into all that mess with police and social workers. If we hadn't driven Poppy into a corner, we might have got the truth sooner.'

Susan was quiet. She was not a stupid woman, and was reluctantly coming to see Richard's point of view. It was, however, very hard to admit any fault on her own part. Surely she'd done what any mother would have done? But she knew in her heart that her motives had been mixed. Part of her, the part that wanted Simon to marry well, take on the mantle of squire in Ringford, continue the Standing tradition in the way she and Richard had done, that part was glad of the unexpected gift that had fallen into her lap. Disgrace for Greg Jones would have made Simon's growing obsession with Octavia impossible to sustain. At least, so she'd thought.

Now, looking at Richard's stern face, and seeing so much of Simon there, she sighed. 'I suppose I'm sorry,' she sighed. 'Oh heavens, Richard, what a mess.' She hesitated, and then continued, trying to explain, 'I was worried about Poppy, of course, and yes, before you say it, it did occur to me that this was one of her tricks. But I also saw how unlikely the Simon and Octavia thing would be as a result, and I was glad.'

Richard turned and looked at her in horror.

'Yes, glad!' she went on, now with a challenge in her voice. 'No doubt despicable from your point of view, but not from mine. And don't look at me like that. We've been married long enough for you to know what I'm like, warts and all.'

'Oh, my God, Susan,' he said.

'Is that all?' she said.

'Yes,' he answered wearily. 'That's all, for the moment,' and he sat down heavily, looking miserably out of the window. He saw only Simon's wounded face, Poppy's anxious withdrawal to her room, Octavia's divided loyalties, and, most clearly of all, the dignity of Greg Jones in the face of mammoth and unjust injury. Both sat in silence, until at last Susan broke it.

'So what shall we do . . . what shall I do?' she said.

'Can't you think of anything?' said Richard. 'Plotting is your strong point.' His tone was bitter and angry.

Susan bit her lip. 'I know what you think I should do,' she countered. 'Be nice to Octavia, for Simon's sake. Then he could make up his mind about her without being lumbered by a disapproving mother. Would that do?'

'For a start,' said Richard, 'it would do.' He didn't tell her Simon had already made up his mind, and that he cared little about his mother's opinion. 'I just hope it's not too late,' he continued, 'and don't make it sound such a chore. She's a charming girl.'

Saturday morning, and Simon drove along the Tresham road, on his way to the Supashop. Bachelor shopping. What a life. He'd passed Barnstones and looked across as usual. No signs of Octavia, though he thought she should have been back by now. Well, what if she was? No chance of her rushing straight up to the Hall to find him.

He drove on through Waltonby, and noticed the trees turning quickly now. Summer's over. Nothing to look forward to except winter. Then he remembered they were one step closer to George Chalmer and felt a little more cheerful. We'll wring his stringy neck, he thought. Teach him he can't mess with Round Ringford! He laughed out loud, but then sobered up when it occurred to him that though they might soon find George and put the fear of God into him, the money could already have gone.

Tennis club meeting tonight. His mother had surprised him, coming in unexpectedly at breakfast time. Out of the blue, she had asked him about the meeting, and offered help. 'Moral support, perhaps, Simon?' Then she'd surprised him even more. 'Will your secretary be there?' she had asked. Her voice had sounded strained, but her face was in shadow, so he'd not been able to see her expression. And when he had replied that he wasn't sure that she was back, Susan had departed as oddly as she came.

Ah well, there was the car park, full up as usual. He had a moment's guilt when he thought of the village shop, but forgot it quickly in the fight for a trolley.

The evening was still and dry, though the nip in the air caused Annie and Sarah to step out smartly up the avenue, chatting about babies and wondering what Simon was going to say. 'Extra-ordinary general meeting!' said Annie. 'Sounds rather grand for our little village tennis club. Is John coming later?'

Sarah said he was going to try, but thought the darts match in the Arms might prove a greater attraction. 'He's thinking of presenting a cup in honour of our son,' she said, grinning at Annie.

Annie replied, 'Supposing it's a daughter?'

Sarah shook her head. 'I'm quite sure,' she said, and stroked her rounded stomach with an affectionate hand.

'The shade of George Chalmer might be among us, but not his person,' Annie said.

'A rotter, was George,' said Sarah, as they approached the Hall. 'An out-and-out, old-fashioned rotter. Poor Ivy. Still, she looked more cheerful when I saw her this morning.'

It had not once occurred to Sarah that she should stay away from tonight's meeting. Well, it had all been a bit of fun, seven-year-itch and all that, hadn't it? The inexorable readjustments of pregnancy, the recent flutter in her expanding belly, these had taken over from jealousy of Octavia Jones. She scarcely ever thought of Simon, and she and John had spent hours transforming a small room into a nursery. Talking idly over the paint pots, she had realised that John's love for her had subtly changed. Not lost, she'd realised gratefully, but qualified now, in a way that it had never been before. I shall be on probation, I suppose, for the rest of my life. These country folk, they never forget.

They gathered in the morning-room, and Simon greeted them unsmilingly, hardly looked at Sarah, and asked after their husbands. Robert and Mandy were already there, and Alexandra Smyth came bustling in, calling back to Susan that she'd see her later.

'Very nice of you all to turn up,' said Simon, when everyone had settled. Nobody mentioned the absent secretary, or the treasurer. 'I'll come straight to the point,' Simon said. 'I wanted to get your views on whether we should continue. But before that, I have to give you some bad news, I'm afraid.'

Mandy and Robert exchanged glances. Simon back to London to work? But no, he was talking about George.

'It's to do with our ex-treasurer,' he said. 'As you all know, George did a bunk. He dealt Miss Beasley a wicked blow, but he also helped himself to our funds before he went. I'm afraid the kitty's empty.' There was a gasp from Alexandra Smyth, and the others shifted in their seats. 'Of course,' Simon went on quickly, 'if any of you are owed money by the club, please let me know. As for what we raised in the beginning, I'm afraid that's a write-off.'

Annie was the first to speak. She said she was sure they would all like to thank Simon for his efforts on the club's behalf, and understood the difficult financial situation. 'As for the future,' she said, 'I know Andrew and I would be very happy to help. Seems a shame to let it fold up.' There were sounds of general agreement at this, and Simon smiled for the first time as they began to plan for the future.

It was while these discussions were going on that Simon heard a car, then his mother talking to someone in the big, echoing hall. The answering voice was desperately familiar, and his heart began to thud.

'Simon?' said his mother, opening the morning-room door. 'Octavia is here, just back from holiday. Isn't it nice of her to come? In you go, my dear,' she said, and disappeared.

'Ye Gods!' whispered Sarah to Annie, as Octavia came in and sat down without fuss. 'It's better than the telly.'

The morning-room faced the terraced gardens of the Hall grounds, caught the early sun, and was used by Susan for writing letters and sewing. Its proportions were perfect, graceful and soothing. The soft lamplight had warmed the meeting's sticky beginning, and now the gathering had dispersed, only Simon and Octavia were left, gazing at each other without speaking.

Finally, Simon said, 'Um, Octavia.'

'Simon,' said Octavia, and she began to smile.

'Nice holiday?' said Simon.

'Lovely, thanks.'

'Oh, shit,' said Simon, 'I don't know what to say.'

'Difficult,' agreed Octavia.

'Why are you smiling like that, then?' said Simon, shuffling papers.

'Because I'm happy. I've had a lovely holiday. Dad's in the clear, and looks years younger. Mum's got the headteacher job, and here I am . . . and here are you.'

Simon stared at her. The magic was still there. He could see it in her eyes, as he put his arms around her and held her close, not kissing, nothing, just holding her steady in his arms.

'Simon, there is just one thing.' He knew there was. He couldn't ask, though. 'In case you were wondering,' Octavia continued, 'I was alone in Scotland. Guy couldn't come, but . . .' She hesitated, and then said honestly, 'But if his grannie hadn't died, he would have come, and I'd have gone with him, and . . . oh, sod it, Simon, you would have hated it, wouldn't you?'

'Not really,' said Simon nobly.

Untrue, thought Octavia, but it didn't matter. Nothing mattered now, except Simon holding her as if he would never let her go.

# 54

Gales and rainstorms stripped the chestnut on the Green, leaving it bare and cold. The strong gusts beat down remaining Michaelmas daisies and chrysanthemums in Ringford gardens, and dispersed all the neat piles of leaves brushed up by Ringford gardeners. Autumn turned to winter, and the village drew in on itself. Ellen, Doris and Ivy hurried to each other's for tea, well wrapped up against the biting winds. Nobody loitered on the Green, and the Standing memorial seat was soggy with rotting leaves. Even the Jenkins terrier was seldom seen, preferring the fireside to following his nose around the village.

Peggy and Bill prepared for Christmas once again, and the school concert came and went with the usual acclaim. Sarah Barnett said goodbye to the children, 'but only temporarily!' and promised to bring the baby for them all to see. Greg Jones returned to school and a subdued welcome from his loyal Head, and faced bravely the curious stares of his colleagues and students.

Octavia and Simon spent all their free time together, discovering many differences between them, but determined to work hard at the difficult business of loving. Octavia had soon come to the conclusion that she would need all her father's stubborn courage, and her mother's diplomacy and understanding, if she and Simon were to succeed. She recognised the flaws in Simon's character, but was willing to acknowledge her own. And then there was his mother's well-concealed antagonism. This had been covered with a smooth gloss of politeness, but Octavia was aware of being critically observed by those cold blue eyes every time they met. She supposed the great damage done to them all would never be mended completely, but with a new maturity she saw that a compromise, a comfortable way of going on, would have to be reached. They all licked their wounds, and began to heal. As Simon said sadly to Octavia, Poppy seemed the lasting casualty.

Richard Standing was still determined she should go away to school, and Susan obediently looked around. It was very important, she said to Richard, after the trauma the child had been through, for her to be in a sympathetic environment, and so far this had not been found. So Poppy returned to her day school for the autumn term, and Richard moved the deadline to the following year. If no other suitable place had been found, he ruled, she was to go to her mother's old school in Sussex.

Poppy remained ominously quiet. Joey Bates was still her constant companion, and no one intervened, though Robert noticed the tension in Joey's face every time Poppy and her mother returned from yet another visit to some distant school.

'Why don't they just let her stay at home?' said Octavia one evening, as she helped Simon prepare supper in the Ostler's House. It seemed so obvious to her, but then, as Simon pointed out, there was no tradition of boarding school in her family.

'Standings expect it,' he said. 'And I must say I enjoyed mine. Maybe for boys it's better, though cousin Alex seemed to have a good time.'

'Huh!' said Octavia.

'Huh, what?' said Simon, grinning at her and putting his arms around her waist. Her hands were oniony, and she waved them under his nose.

'I was going to say,' she answered, 'that it didn't do much for her, did it?'

Simon released her and kissed the back of her neck. 'So where shall we send ours?'

Octavia stopped chopping, and stood quite still. 'Ours?' she said.

'Our children,' said Simon cheerfully. 'When we're married.'

Octavia turned round to face him. 'You are an upper-class twit, Simon,' she said. 'Isn't there some sort of traditional preliminary you're supposed to go through?'

'What, ask your father and all that stuff?' he said innocently. Her expression caused him to add quickly, 'Okay, okay! Now, Tavie Jones, will you marry me, and please don't say no, or muck about, because I love you more than anything else, and I shall probably emigrate . . . or throw myself at cousin Alex, or—'

'Shut up, Simon,' said Octavia, turning back to her onions. 'Of course I'll marry you. I know when I'm on to a good thing. Why else would I be cutting up these revolting things?'

'It's because of your unfailing sense of romance, Tavie darling,' Simon said, bravely ignoring the strong smell under his nose, 'that I love you so, and want us to be together always.'

'Good-o,' said Octavia. 'When shall we start?'

The wedding date was fixed for April. 'The Hall looks so wonderful at that time of the year, spring flowers and new leaves,' gushed Susan to Gabriella. She had realised at once that there was absolutely nothing she could change, and decided to let no one else see how she felt. It would be the wedding of the season, and she would mastermind it.

She pointed out the practicality of having the reception at the Hall, rather than spend enormous sums of money on a ghastly country club. 'We have so many friends and family,' she said, 'and it will be perfect. Richard can speak to, um, er . . . Greg,' she said, 'and you and I can do the fun bits: music and dresses, and so on . . .'

But Susan had reckoned without Octavia, who quickly put a stop to Susan taking over the fun bits. 'It's my wedding, and you're my mum,' she said to Gabriella. 'We'll do it, and the Standings can chip in. Don't worry about Madam,' she added, seeing her mother's face. 'I can handle her. Got to, anyway, haven't I? Best thing is to agree with her, and then do exactly what you want. She's quite good at backing down without loss of face.'

'Plenty of practice,' said Greg, *sotto voce* from behind his newspaper.

The news of the engagement and forthcoming wedding was an injection of happiness into the village. Everyone became involved, as Octavia intended. She announced firmly to Susan Standing that she couldn't see any point in wasting money outside the village, when there was so much talent ready and waiting in Ringford.

Ivy had offered to make the wedding cake, and Octavia and Simon had been immensely moved. 'Fancy Ivy doing that,' Octavia had said, tears in her eyes, 'after her own wedding came to such a sticky end. I could've kissed her.'

'Well, I shall, next time I see her,' said Simon. 'In fact, I shall probably kiss everybody, the way I'm feeling.'

'Everybody?' said Octavia, and took a deep breath.

Octavia was right about the cake. It had been a huge effort on Ivy's part to make the offer. Every time she went into the shop, conversations shut down abruptly, as if wedding talk would be tactless. It was then for her to reopen the topic, asking for the latest on the choir arrangements, flowers in church, photographers. Everyone respected her for this, and she was grateful. Her stocky figure slowly regained its energy, and her tongue sharpened again. Although Dr Russell, going up to wash his hands in Ivy's bathroom after the weekly surgery he held in her parlour, noticed that the lotions and creams had disappeared, Ivy smartened herself up, and was never quite the mannish, forbidding figure of old.

In spite of all the optimism following Poppy's recall of George's number plate, there had been no further news. Peggy spoke to her cousin from time to time, but there were no sightings. After a while, she no longer asked. Bill said privately to Simon that they'd wait until after the wedding, give Ivy time to get her breath back, and then definitely go to the police.

Snow covered the village in February, transforming it into the usual picture postcard, and the children made snowmen in the school playground, threw snowballs at the vicar, and behaved just as countless generations in Ringford had done before them. And then after the snow, daffodils began to push their way through the grass, warm winds coaxed the birds into song, and one balmy day it was plain for all to see that spring had arrived.


Bill had been up in the top field, inspecting the new growth of maize, thinking about Peggy and wondering what they'd be having for supper, when he saw Foxy Jenkins waving at him from the gateway. 'Bill!' he yelled. 'Got a call for you on the mobile!' Foxy was very taken with this new toy, given to him by Jean at Christmas. Bill made his way across, wondering what could be that important, and Fox handed him the phone. 'It's Peggy.'

'Peggy?' said Bill.

'Hello!' she said, amidst crackles. 'Sorry to bother you, Bill, but I just couldn't wait. Sal rang, and she's seen it!'

'Seen what? Eh, what did you say?'

Fox came closer. He was as anxious as Bill to know

what this was all about. Jean would never forgive him if he didn't get all the details.

'Seen George's car, of course!' said Peggy.

'My God, when?' said Bill, and Foxy moved even nearer. But the signal faded, and Bill switched off, handing it back.

'Summat happened?' said Fox, hopefully.

'Don't know yet,' said Bill. 'We shall see.'

'I just couldn't wait,' said Peggy apologetically.

'Doesn't matter,' said Bill, 'but I didn't hear it all. When did she see him?'

'She didn't exactly see him. It was the car, parked in a side street in Leamington. She drove past, but was so excited she turned round and went back.'

'Did she get the address, then?'

'Yes, of course. She stopped and got out. Walked by and wrote down the house number. Said it looked a bit scruffy, but she was sure the car belonged there. Anyway, I said you'd be really pleased, and we'd let her know what happens.'

'Not 'arf,' said Bill, going to the telephone. 'Simon should be home by now, shouldn't he? This is what we've been waiting for, gel.'

A day or two later, in the untidy sitting-room of a first-floor flat in a back street in Leamington Spa, George, formerly Chalmer, sat reading the racing paper, debating with himself whether to have a flutter. His friend would have encouraged him, he thought sadly, but his friend had gone. They always went, in the end. And now he was in a kind of limbo, between engagements, as he said to himself. Ever since leaving Round Ringford, he had been in a state of lethargy, not venturing out, not making any plans, in spite of being well aware of the need to cover his tracks. He'd banked his rewards, and hardly bothered to say good riddance when his friend had walked out.

He was astonished how often he thought of Ivy. It was not just that he missed the comfort, the cooking, the lovely feeling of being taken care of for the first time in his life. It was Ivy herself he missed. Bloody ironic, he concluded, that I should be homesick for that particular domestic set-up. He'd tried at first to shove her out of his mind, telling funny stories against her, snide, critical stories, to his friend. But then he'd felt like a traitor, even worse than he felt already. What a pity . . . but then, he knew that without question Ivy would never have allowed him his friends, his natural way of life, poor old thing. Her expectations had been something else entirely.

When the doorbell rang, he started up out of his chair, surprised at this unusual occurrence. No one had called to see him for weeks, except his landlord, and then George had pretended to be out.

At the foot of the stairs, in the dim, smelly hallway, he hesitated. Could be dangerous. Perhaps better to let whoever it was go away again. But George hadn't spoken to anyone for days, and the sound of a human voice would be very welcome. He opened the door a crack and peered out.

'Morning, George,' said Bill Turner, inserting his foot firmly into the narrow opening. 'There's a number of things we'd like to talk to you about, and most of them have to do with money.'

# 55

Down in the thicket, the gang had assembled for the first meeting of the year. The prickly hawthorns had put out new shoots, and the grassy circle seemed smaller. Mark Jenkins wasn't there, but had sent a message with Helen Bishop that he was too busy, and would probably be too busy from now on. He was helping his dad on the farm all hours that God gave, including the ones earmarked for homework.

Helen herself had almost decided not to come. Mark had tentatively asked her to meet him by the bus shelter when he'd finished work, and she had thought seriously of it, but there would be other times, she was sure of that. So now she relayed Mark's message, and looked across to where Poppy stood behind Joey's chair, one foot up on the big wheel, staring at her. It meant nothing, Helen knew that now. Poppy often stared when her mind was somewhere else entirely.

Joey was the first to speak. 'Looks like we're a bit thin on the ground,' he said.

'Time to pack it up,' said Poppy suddenly, coming out of her reverie. Her voice was firm, decisive, very like her mother's.

Several attempts were made at reviving the old jokes, but conversations faltered and came to nothing. Finally they all agreed there seemed no point in staying, and the gang dispersed. Another gang would form. There had always been gangs in Ringford.

Pushing Joey along the bumpy river path, Poppy was quiet. 'What's up?' said Joey.

'Nothing,' said Poppy.

Joey looked round at her. 'Right, nothing's up,' he said.

They moved slowly, to make the ride easier for Joey. The river was high after the rain, and long willow branches with fresh silvery leaves dipped down, touching the water.

'All set for the wedding?' said Joey, making another effort.

'Yep,' said Poppy, in a tone that told him the whole thing was a colossal bore to her.

'You still a bridesmaid?' he said, plugging on.

'Yep,' she said. She came around the front of the chair to move a large stone away from the wheel, then she straightened up and looked at him.

'Joey,' she said, 'I've got to go away in the autumn. They've decided on Mum's old school, and I've been there to look. It's not bad, actually. They do lots of sport and stuff. And there's no uniform, and you can go out and about within reason.'

Joey's face was oddly relaxed. 'So you liked it,' he said.

'Well, to tell the truth,' she answered, 'I wouldn't mind getting away from home. Never know where I am with them. Probably partly me.' She grinned at Joey. 'Will you miss me, Joe?' she said, thinking that he didn't look exactly heartbroken.

'Yes,' he said honestly, 'but you might not get rid of me that easily. They're suggestin' I go to this residential college place, down in Brighton . . .'

'Sussex!' said Poppy. 'That's where Mum's school is!'

'I know,' said Joey. 'Not far away.'

Poppy's face lit up and she cavorted round and round the wheelchair in a dance of triumph. 'So sod the lot of 'em!' she said. She grabbed the wheelchair handles and set off at an alarming pace, with Joey doing his best to hold on.

Change all around, thought Ivy, wrapping the wedding cake carefully and putting it away to mature. She'd heard about young Joey going away, but knew nothing about the locating of George Chalmer. Bill had wanted to tell her at once, but Peggy had said no, wait and see if he turned out his pockets. Didn't want to set poor old Ivy back for no reason. It was going to upset her, anyway, but if nothing came of it, then best to keep quiet.

Bill had protested that he and Simon had given the slippery bugger such a shaking, he'd be sure to cough up. It had been a strange half hour they'd spent in that scruffy little hole in Leamington. Simon had been sternly polite, not once losing his temper. Bill had been the one to threaten a punch on the nose, and worse, if George didn't put right the rotten trick he'd played on Ivy Beasley.

Calming down, he'd let Simon explain civilly that the only reason they were not accompanied by a police officer was Miss Beasley's reluctance. He made it quite clear that that could be easily overcome, and then it would be very serious indeed for George.

It had been an unpleasant duty. The thin, weedy little sod had looked grubby, pathetic, nothing like the man he'd been under Ivy's tender care, and he'd asked after her with what was undoubtedly genuine concern.

'Wouldn't have worked, though,' said Peggy, when Bill gave his account of the confrontation. 'Even if he'd gone through with the wedding. With him living a lie, and Ivy blissfully ignorant, how long would it have lasted?'

Bill agreed, and said the sooner the whole thing was wound up the better.

'How shall we know if he pays her back?' Peggy said.

'You'll know,' said Bill confidently. 'It'll be the look on her face, or some such.' Then he smiled at her, and said, 'No, seriously, I think we shall know. And if not, we'll get Simon to ask her. He'll be watching out for the tennis club funds' return, anyway.'

'And there's Ted Bates,' said Peggy.

'Him too,' said Bill. 'We didn't forget the rent George never paid.'

'What was it like, in his flat?' said Peggy, curious.

Bill frowned. 'It stank of cigarette smoke and old socks,' he said. 'Difficult not to feel sorry for him, but I managed it.'

'Don't ever tell Ivy that,' Peggy said. 'Make it sound better than it was. She'd not like to think of him living in squalor. I'm pretty sure of that.'

# 56

The day before the wedding, Mandy began work early. Robert, bless him, had offered to wash up and make the beds, so she was off in her car and up to Doreen Price's by half past eight. They were always up at the crack of dawn at Home Farm, and Doreen was ready for her. The excitement in the air was tangible.

'Busy day for you, I expect,' Doreen said, as Mandy massaged her soapy head with firm fingers.

'Certainly is,' said Mandy. 'Five blow-drys, two sets and a quick trim.'

'Blimey,' said Doreen, 'and whose is the quick trim?'

'Give you one guess,' said Mandy.

'Octavia,' said Doreen, laughing.

'Right first time. I tried hard to persuade her to let me style it. After all, you only get wed once. Leastways, we hope it'll only be once.' She smiled at Doreen in the mirror.

'I'd put money on it,' said Doreen. 'I know some folks don't give it much chance, but I never seen a couple so much in love . . .'

'Oh, my God,' said Tom, coming through the kitchen door in muddy boots. 'Shall I come back later?'

'Brilliant idea, Peggy,' Sandra had said. 'I can look after the shop while she does yours, and then she can do mine without packing all her things away.'

Now Mandy was halfway through drying Peggy's curls, and there was, of course, only one topic of conversation. 'No, I've no idea, truly,' said Mandy. They'd been talking about bridesmaids' dresses. 'Big Secret. Now hold still,' she said, wielding the scissors. 'Just need to get these stray bits. What colour's your hat?'

'Susan's wearing black,' said Annie Bishop.

'Black!' said Mandy, shocked. She brushed the thick, bouncy hair, cut into layers like shorn cornstalks.

'Well, not *all* black,' said Annie. 'White dress with black and yellow daisies, and a black jacket.'

'How do you know?' said Mandy.

'Jean Jenkins,' said Annie.

'Ah.' Mandy shook the towels and held up the hand mirror. 'All right for you?' she said. 'Should look nice with your new yellow straw hat.'

Annie stared at her. 'How did you . . . ?'

'Left the best to last,' said Mandy, flopping down on Gabriella's kitchen chair, and sipping hot tea gratefully. 'Is Octavia okay?'

'Why shouldn't I be?' said Octavia's voice from upstairs. 'I can hear you, so don't say anything I wouldn't like. Such as the vicar's gone down with chicken-pox, or Simon's done a runner, like old George.'

Mandy took a deep breath. 'She was always like that, wasn't she, Mrs Jones?' she said. 'Not a shred of romance.'

Octavia appeared in the kitchen in her petticoat, hair in wet strings over her shoulders.

'Oh, you've washed it!' said Mandy. 'I brought some special conditioner.'

'Sorry,' said Octavia. 'Thought I'd save you time. You must be on your knees by now. Anyway, you can do me quickly, and then we can have another cup of tea and you can tell me everything you've picked up round the village today.'

'Tavie!' said Gabriella. 'Honestly, Mandy,' she added,

'if I get through this couple of days without a nervous breakdown, it'll be a miracle.'

'Always like that, a wedding,' said Mandy comfortingly. 'Seen it over and over again. Now then, Tavie, sit down here and don't move until I say so.'

Mandy had plenty to tell. She reported on Bill Turner's reluctance to wear tails, praised Doris's decision to have a blue rinse, and made much of Ivy's amazing cheerfulness. She said that Sarah Barnett had bought a new dress from that maternity shop in Bagley, and then wished she'd not mentioned it. 'I didn't do Madam this time, of course,' she said quickly, to cover her embarrassment. 'She's been to London, though I must say I thought he'd made a right mess of it.'

'Good,' said Octavia absently. She'd noticed Mandy's guilty look when she mentioned Sarah. The Barnetts had been invited, 'for John's sake' Octavia had persuaded, but that affair would take a bit of forgetting.

Well, it was too late now. Boats burned, hatchets buried, problems sorted. Octavia reflected on problems. She knew perfectly well that marrying Simon, and with him the whole Standing clan, was probably the biggest challenge she would ever face. Oh, what the hell, she thought. Can't ask for guarantees. And anyway, I love him. 'I love 'im, I love 'im, Mandy Bates,' she said, 'so how's that?'

'Now you're talking,' said Mandy with relief. 'Well, I must get going. That young man of mine is getting his hair washed today, or I'll know the reason why.

# 57

'Don't you love a wedding?' said Peggy to Doreen as they walked in their best suits along the Green towards the church. There were daffodils everywhere, in clumps along the grassy verges and massed under the chestnut tree in a blaze of gold. A warm spell had hastened spring in a flurry of different shades of green, Bagley Woods sheltering butter-yellow celandines, aconites and clumps of tender primroses. The schoolchildren on nature rambles had found pink violets, and been told by Gabriella on pain of death not to pick them.

As Doreen and Peggy sauntered along, good and early, so as not to miss anything, jays chattered warningly from Prices' spinney. 'Where could you find a prettier setting?' Peggy said.

Doreen, not used to wearing a hat, tucked her hair in at the sides, and agreed. 'Just what we wanted,' she said comfortably. 'Sunshine and a little breeze. It'll lift Octavia's veil nicely for the photographs. I wonder who else is bridesmaid besides Poppy? They've all been very secretive.'

They walked on, speculating, over the bridge and sparkling water, past the lines of cars and into church. Joey, hair shining and smile broad, handed them a service sheet, and Simon's brother, finally located and recalled from his commune, ushered them to their seats. 'Bride or groom?' he had said, and Peggy thought to herself that either side would do, since they were friends of both, and this was as it should be in a village.

Olive Bates and Doreen had done the flowers as instructed by Octavia: armfuls of white daisies and tall grasses, lighting up the church's interior. Now it was filling up, and with half the village and the mighty Standing clan, together with as many Joneses as could be mustered, they had needed to bring out the uncomfortable folding slatted chairs from the village hall.

'They won't be sitting on them long,' Greg had said. 'Wedding services are soon over.' Soon over, and committed for life, he'd thought to himself, but he had finally admitted to Gabriella that Simon seemed quite a nice chap, and handled Octavia pretty well, too.

Gabriella waited in the front pew, glancing over her shoulder nervously from time to time. The Standing lot were all chattering like starlings, and their hats would have done credit to Ascot. The breeze should have fun with that lot, thought Gabriella.

Settled comfortably in a pew three rows from the back, Ivy, Ellen and Doris talked together, identifying people they knew, seeing likenesses in unfamiliar children. 'Isn't that Rebecca Smyth's fourth?' said Ellen in a loud stage whisper. 'Plain as a pikestaff, like 'er Auntie Alex.'

'Sshh!' Ivy wished she had a gag and the courage to put it on old Ellen.

'Ellen,' said Doris quietly, 'don't draw attention to us. It's not easy for Ivy, you know . . .' She hoped Ivy had not heard, but was acutely conscious of how her old friend must be feeling.

When Ivy had stepped out of the front door of Victoria Villa to join Ellen and Doris, they had both gasped. She was wearing the soft blue suit, the heavenly blue one she should have worn at her own wedding. 'Don't stare like that, you two,' she'd said firmly, shutting the iron gate behind her. 'I was brought up to waste not, want not. It's very serviceable material, and should last a good many years. And it suits me, don't you think?' There was the ghost of a brave, challenging smile round her lips, and Doris had agreed that it looked very nice indeed.

'Much too nice to waste on that no-good George,' Ellen had said, plunging in without caring. Sooner Ivy came to her senses the better. And Ellen was pleased to note that Ivy did indeed seem nearly back to her normal 'orrible self.

Outside, a crowd of people had gathered by the church wall to watch. Mr and Mrs Ross, their little dog held carefully under his mistress's arm, had arrived early, and been rewarded by a parade of guests, some familiar, others very grand and well worth coming out for.

Renata Roberts, mother of Sandra, and caretaker at the school, leaned wearily against the wall and closed her eyes. The sun was warm. She could spare an hour or so from the endless chores.

'I remember Octavia Jones when she was a snotty kid, same age as my Sandra,' she said to Mrs Ross. 'Pushed poor old Sand about something rotten. Still, they stayed friends, though goodness knows why.'

'Car should be here any minute,' said Mr Ross, but no car appeared, and Simon's brother could be seen looking anxiously down the churchyard.

'Hey!' shouted Renata suddenly. 'There she is, look, walking up the lane!'

It was, as she told her mellow husband later, the prettiest thing she'd ever seen. Greg Jones, dapper in his morning suit, walked at an even pace, with his lovely daughter on his arm. The gentle breeze stirred Octavia's long, cobwebby veil, and lifted the fine silk of her dress in flutters as she walked. As the wedding party came close, laughing and talking, Renata made a choking sound, and pulled out a grubby tissue.

'Good gracious,' said Mrs Ross, too surprised for tact, 'isn't that your Sandra and her Alison?'

Following behind, Alison Goodison and Poppy

Standing, deceptively sweet and simple in cornflower blue and white, carried Octavia's veil. And behind them, beaming quite as much as she'd done at her own wedding, came Sandra, comely and confident as matron of honour, her dark eyes shining with pleasure.

'Well I never,' said Mrs Ross to her husband, 'and her a Roberts!' Mr Ross's agonised face reminded her that Renata was still well within earshot, and she sniffed. 'Can't deny they're a rough lot,' she said sulkily.

The party moved forward up the church path, white ribbons fluttered on the flowers, cameras clicked, and the bells received them with a joyful clamour.

During the short space of time it took to join in holy matrimony a smiling Simon Standing to his beloved Octavia Jones, none of the watchers by the church wall noticed the dark blue Fiesta cruise into the village, and come to rest under the trees by Ellen's Lodge. Nobody saw the very ordinary-looking man get out and stand quite still until the wedding group emerged smiling and milling around in the sunshine. He watched as Doris, Ellen and Ivy, in her heavenly blue suit, came out of the church porch bursting with congratulations. Nobody saw as he passed his hand over his eyes. Mrs Ross's dog turned its sharp little head and barked as the car slid off again across to Victoria Villa, where it stopped. The man walked quickly up to the front door, slipped something through the letterbox, then returned to his car and vanished at speed up the Bagley Road.

The sun, dappling the Hall avenue through the over-hanging chestnuts, continued to shine, and Simon and Octavia, gazing at each other in the kind of delight that shuts out everyone else, walked slowly up the tunnel of shifting light as if it were one long triumphal arch. The guests, awkward in their spiky heels and tight skirts, followed, laughing and talking in loud voices, exchanging greetings, demanding attention. Ringford folk were the lucky ones, knowing where to avoid the potholes.

A great deal of time was spent reminiscing about other Ringford weddings, especially the last Standing one at the Hall, when Mr Richard's father had wed a lovely girl whose parents lived in India. 'Not as pretty as our Octavia, from the photos,' said Ellen Biggs loyally, hobbling along, trying to keep up with Doris. Ivy had gone back home to check on Tiddles, promising to catch them up. 'Nor s'clever,' Ellen added.

'Mind you, Madam's clever too,' said Doris. 'It'll be sparks for a bit, I reckon, between them two. Still, with the young ones living in the Ostler's House, they'll have their own privacy. It'll work out, I reckon, and I'm not often wrong, never mind what Ivy says.'

The village was quiet, empty now, with everyone up at the Hall or gone home to reflect on the day's excitement. Ivy Beasley put her key in the lock and stepped quickly into the house. She didn't want to be long, just time enough to give Tiddles her saucer of fish and a drink of milk. And she could use her own toilet. You never knew, with all those people.

She hesitated, her foot caught by a pink envelope on the mat. Not another circular, she thought, and was about to screw it up without looking, when she stopped dead. George. George's handwriting, neat and small as ever. Ivy's heart began to pound, and she hurried into the kitchen, standing on trembling legs by the window, where the sun fell brightly on the letter. 'Oh, no,' she whispered. 'Not again, George. Not again.'

It was several seconds before she reached into the drawer for a knife to slit open the envelope. Her hand shook as she pulled out a cheque, carefully made out to Ivy Beasley and signed George Glasscock, for exactly the amount that she had lent him. There was also a card, a posy of violets in an oval surround. She opened it and read the short message.

'Ivy dear,' it said, ''t'is better to have loved and lost, than never to have loved at all. Very kind regards, George.'

All thought of the wedding driven from her mind, Ivy stood in the sunlight for a long while, smoothing the card and eventually holding it close to her heart. She sniffed, and then turned to her cat, now lapping milk untidily. 'No wonder, Tiddles,' she said, 'he changed his name. Glasscock! What kind of a name is that?' And turning swiftly, she put the card in full view on the mantelshelf, the cheque behind the clock, and set off back to the Hall.

'Where you bin, then?' said Ellen, as Ivy sat down at the little table where Doris had kept her a place. 'We nearly finished our grub, and very nice it was, too. That Sheila Pearson done us proud.'

'Something came up,' said Ivy, and her smile was warm. 'And don't ask me what, Ellen Biggs,' she added, 'because I'm not telling you.'

'Huh,' said Ellen, 'don't bother, then.' She helped herself to another couple of petits fours and chewed happily. 'Still,' she said indistinctly, turning to a smiling Doris, 'whatever it was, our Ivy looks like the cat wot's got the cream, don't she?'

Ivy raised her glass to her two old friends, and her eyes were moist. 'Here's to us, then,' she said, 'and to Round Ringford, best place in the world.'

' 'ere, 'ere,' said Ellen, and drained her glass.

At last, all goodbyes were said, everyone duly thanked and kissed, the bouquet of white roses thrown and caught by Helen Bishop, who'd blushed and looked involuntarily at Mark Jenkins, and then Simon and Octavia drove rapidly away down the chestnut avenue.

314

Simon stopped as soon as they were out of the village, to remove the banging shoe tied to the car, and finally they were away. 'Okay, Mrs Standing?' he said.

Octavia nodded. 'I doubt if I'll ever come down to earth again,' she said. 'It's really very nice up here.'

'A night on the sleeper to Inverness will fix that,' said Simon. 'I do hope it won't be too awful for you. We could have flown, you know.'

'No,' said Octavia. 'I wanted to feel the miles passing, all of that left behind. And then we'll arrive at the cottage in peace and quiet, with a whole two weeks ahead of us. You'll love it. Just you and me, and the rutting stags . . .' She burst out laughing, and Simon nearly steered into the ditch as he tried to kiss her.

'Wrong time of the year,' he said, 'for rutting . . .'

'Keep your eye on the road,' said Octavia in a wifely voice.

'. . . but perfect for us,' continued Simon blithely, 'and for the rest of our lives to come. For better for worse, for richer for poorer, to love and to cherish, till death us do part . . .'

Octavia looked at his handsome profile, and said, 'I do hope so, darling Si.'

In the maternity ward of Tresham General Hospital, the bed in the corner was occupied by an exhausted Sarah Barnett, and by her side, nervously clutching a small white bundle, sat John, his grey-streaked red hair rough and tangled from anxious fingers. 'That was a waste of a new dress,' said Sarah, grinning at him. 'His timing's not up to much, but otherwise he's perfect, isn't he?'

John's heart was too full to speak. He knew that he could never be sure of Sarah keeping her promise to him as a wife, but was certain that she'd be a good and faithful mother. In some things she was solid as a rock.

'He looks like you, Sarah,' he said finally.

She beamed. 'Oh, do you think so?' she said. 'I think he's the image of his father.' She smiled fondly at John.

The baby began to grizzle, and she took him into her arms, rubbing her cheek against his downy head. 'Just like Daddy, aren't you, my precious?' she crooned. 'Ten fingers, ten toes . . . big nose . . .' Now she was laughing, and added, 'Hair's not red yet, but time will tell . . .'